A quick dazzling smile and Artorius was gone, riding along the lines and acknowledging cheers. Sarnac was left gaping after him, with barely enough time to settle back into position in line before the shrill, barbaric horns sounded again and the Visigothic cavalry broke into a charge.

Spreading his feet a little wider apart and waiting to receive heavy shock cavalry, Sarnac subvocalized (sheer habit, in this rising thunder of hooves) into his implant communicator. "Tylar, I'm sure you've got the situation well in hand. But whatever it is you're planning, now's the time."

There was no reply. He again made the motion that activated the comm link, confirming that it was already functioning.

"Tylar, this isn't funny! Talk to me!"

Dead silence inside his skull.

"Tylar? *Tylar?!*"

Then the Visigoths were on them.

LEGACY

STEVE WHITE

BAEN

LEGACY

This is a work of fiction. All the characters and events portrayed in this book are fictional, and any resemblance to real people or incidents is purely coincidental.

A Baen Books Original

Baen Publishing Enterprises
P.O. Box 1403
Riverdale, NY 10471

ISBN: 0-671-87643-0

Cover art by Larry Elmore

First printing, February 1995

Distributed by Simon & Schuster
1230 Avenue of the Americas
New York, NY 10020

Printed in the United States of America

To Sandy, again and forever.

And to Jennifer, Adrienne and Maria Tatiana, to whom the future belongs.

PROLOGUE — 469 A.D.

"It is, of course, premature to congratulate you, my dear Sidonius. We must observe the proprieties and wait until your election has become official." Bishop Faustus of Riez chuckled patronizingly. "Nevertheless, we all know that the final decision is a mere formality. I have absolutely no doubt that I will soon—perhaps before the year is out—be able to greet you as a colleague in Christ, our new Bishop of Clermont!"

Sidonius Apollinaris inclined his head graciously and wrapped his cloak more tightly around his shoulders against the unseasonably raw wind blowing in from the Bay of Biscay on this overcast spring afternoon. *Amazing that it's so chilly, given the amount of hot air Faustus pumps out!* He immediately regretted the thought—the old man had been a staunch supporter in his own maneuverings for the Bishopric of Clermont. Not that Sidonius' lack of clerical background had been any handicap—he wouldn't be the first bishop to start that way. And being the son-in-law of Avitus, who had briefly been Emperor of the West, certainly didn't hurt. Still, Faustus deserved his gratitude. And as one of the most distinguished churchmen in Gaul he certainly

1

merited courtesy, especially in light of his parentage—
the parentage that no one *ever* mentioned in his
hearing.

"Thank you, Excellency," Sidonius said in his courtier's
voice. "I have looked forward to this opportunity to
personally convey my belated best wishes upon your
birthday." Maybe that was part of the problem; Faustus
had never been one to use ten words where twenty would
do, but now that he had attained the exceptional age of
sixty he was getting positively garrulous. A man of his
years had no business out here shivering with the rest of
the welcoming committee. But of course it was incumbent
upon him to be here. And he was hardly in a position to
be fulfilling his duties in Riez just now.

Sidonius, on the other hand, had more or less invited
himself. No one had really tried to discourage him. As a
distinguished landowner of the Auvergne, litterateur of
some note, city prefect of Rome until recently, and the
likely Bishop of Clermont, he carried too much weight
for anyone to openly object to his presence. And, despite
the hazards and hardships of travelling, he was not about
to miss this chance to meet the man who, he suspected,
was the most remarkable of the many with whom he had
corresponded. The man who had set in motion the scene
before them here in the Loire estuary.

The fleet of ships had sailed as far inland as the Loire
was navigable, anchoring here near Nantes. That the island
of Britain had produced such a swarm of seagoing craft
had generated unspoken amazement. But they all knew
that the High King Riothamus had revived the old Saxon
Shore Fleet, as he was trying to revive so much else.
Before long, a procession of boats had started bringing
ashore the carefully bred warhorses that had carried
Riothamus' famous cavalry galloping over Saxon and
Pict, fetlock-deep in barbarian blood.

Now, now, let's not wax poetic, Sidonius chided himself.

*I've written so many congratulatory poems—to poor
old Avitus, and then to Majorian a few months later,
and now to Anthemius—that it's in danger of becoming
a joke. Besides, unlike them, Riothamus isn't Emperor
of the West. Yet.*

Or is he something more?

Now, wherever did such a strange thought come from?

He grew aware of Faustus' drone. "Yes, my dear
Sidonius, I am certainly not getting any younger. My
health, by God's mercy, continues to be good, though
my eyesight has deserted me to such an extent that writing
has become quite impossible. And I fear my joints will
not soon let me forget this damp chill today. I know full
well that I cannot expect to weather many more winters."

"Come, Excellency! You'll bury us all."

"No, I do not complain—especially if I depart leaving
you as Bishop of Clermont. For I know that you will be
a voice for the *true* Catholic faith in the councils of the
Church in Gaul! Otherwise, I fear my soul would depart
burdened by the sin of despair. Everywhere, all around
us, the Arian heresy rises like a tide, threatening to drown
us all in damnation with its horrid, perverse doctrine that
the Father and the Son are of *like* substance, rather than
the *same* substance, as every true Christian must
affirm. . . ." Color mounted in Faustus' cheeks, and
Sidonius knew there was no stopping him now.

Faustus was bound to be a fire-eater on the subject
of heretics, having only last year been driven from his
bishopric and sent scurrying to Soissons by the Arian
Visigoths. *Earnest theologians all*, Sidonius reflected drily.
*No doubt they debated the nature of the Trinity while
stealing the candelabra*. But Faustus' obsession dated
back much further than that—back to his youth on the
misty island that had put forth the fleet now filling the
Loire estuary.

Old as Faustus was, it still came as a shock to realize

that he had been born just a couple of years after the day—the last day of 406, to be exact—when the Suevi and Vandals and their rabble of allies had crossed the frozen Rhine into a Gaul that had been stripped of troops by Stilicho to defend Italy, and the world had begun to go horribly wrong.

No hope had existed for the provincials of Gaul save the legions of Britain, which had landed under the usurped command of a lowborn lout whose only recommendation was the auspicious name of Constantine. The barbarians had continued their looting undisturbed while the Empire had put down his clownish bid for the purple, and Alaric the Visigoth had raped inviolate Rome herself, shattering the spell of centuries. Afterwards, the Empire had hired the Visigoths to slaughter their fellow barbarians, paying them with the lands of southwestern Gaul—which they were now finding too narrow—and people told each other that all was restored. But the restoration was a patchwork thing—and it did not include Britain, which the Emperor Honorius had graciously permitted to arm itself while awaiting succor from an Empire that had none to give.

So the Britons, left without the troops who had followed Constantine to the continent and to their deaths, just as their fathers had followed Magnus Maximus to theirs in 383—no question about it, that island was almost as notable for usurpers as it was for inedible cooking—had placed themselves under the protection of powerful landowners. Some were half-pagan brutes, like Ceredig and Cunedda on the frontiers. But others had had larger ideas, like Vortigern of the Gewessei. As a youth he had married the considerably older Sevira, daughter of Magnus Maximus, the larger than life Spanish adventurer whose name was still one to conjure with among the Britons. The matrilineal ideas of the native Celtic people had never altogether died out, and the *mana* of Maximus had descended through Sevira, whose mother had been British.

Vortigern's primacy among the British lords had been one fruit of that marriage; Faustus had been another.

Looking at the self-satisfied old man before him, Sidonius tried—and failed—to imagine Faustus as a rebellious youth. What had touched the son of the newly installed High King of Britain? Had it been Vortigern's second marriage? The story was that Faustus never referred to Vortigern's second wife as anything other than "the pagan sow." Sidonius had always felt that Vortigern had been blamed too harshly for his solution to the Pictish threat, in the early days of his High Kingship. He had merely been following a time-honored Roman precedent by using barbarian *foederatii*, even as the Empire had used the Visigoths. But if the Visigoths were barbarians, then the Saxons were howling savages, untouched even by heretical forms of Christianity. They reeked of the old death cults from Europe's foggy, sinister North— the same breed of two-legged beasts who had established themselves here on the lower Loire. And Vortigern, lacking the Empire's ability to overawe them, had married the daughter of their chieftain, replacing Sevira who had died giving birth to a second son at an age beyond that at which most women bore children . . . or, for that matter, lived.

Or was the official reason the true one? Vortigern, while seeking a popular base for his artificial High Kingship, had sponsored the Pelagian heresy that had won the hearts of many of the islanders. Sidonius lacked Faustus' fervor on the subject of heresy in general; had he not visited the Visigothic court at Toulouse during the reign of the late lamented Theoderic II and found it almost disturbingly refreshing in its simplicity? But the British-born Pelagius had gone beyond metaphysical hairsplitting—he had actually denied original sin, and asserted the freedom of the *individual*—even individuals of the lower orders— to make autonomous moral choices! It had all died down, but Sidonius still shuddered at the thought of such madness. Did the man really have no conception of the chaos he could have loosed on the world?

At any rate, the young Faustus' two wellsprings of discontent had flowed together in his twentieth year. Vortigern had married Renwein the Saxon, and Bishop Germanus of Auxerre had landed in Britain to combat heresy, furiously anathematizing the High King. Faustus had publicly broken with his heretic father and joined the church in protest, departing for the continent with Germanus. Vortigern had never been the same again. Renwein had failed to produce a male heir, and as the years passed, the Saxons had changed from watchdogs to wolves, tearing at the throat of Britain. In his last years, Vortigern had been a shadowy, almost pathetic figure. He became more and more detached from the epic of resistance, whose hero, Ambrosius Aurelianus, had refused to seek the High Kingship even while Vortigern was letting it slip away. Instead Ambrosius, a Roman of the old school, had entered the service of the new High King, who had caught the scepter before it could slip into nothingness, and consigned Vortigern to a twilight so obscure that his very death had gone unremarked.

Apparently, Faustus was talking even more than usual to calm his apprehension at meeting the man who had held the British High Kingship to which Faustus—son of Vortigern and grandson of Maximus—arguably had a better right. The old bishop had long ago relinquished all political ambitions . . . but would Riothamus know that?

Faustus paused for breath in mid-tirade and Sidonius, hearing Tertullian's diffident cough behind him, turned gratefully.

"A thousand pardons, Prefect," his secretary said, giving him as a courtesy the title he had only recently relinquished. "The High King is coming ashore, and

the other distinguished lords request your presence—
and yours, Excellency—on the beach."

"Thank you, Tertullian. Shall we go, Excellency?" They
started down the path from the bluff, Tertullian following
at a discreet distance.

"Where *did* you find him?" Faustus asked in a voice
touched with the sin of envy.

"He came from nowhere and joined my staff in
Rome," Sidonius replied. "His references were a bit
obscure, but I'm glad I took him on in spite of all the
mystery. He's made himself absolutely indispensable
to me, as you know."

Faustus did know. He shot a surreptitious look
backwards at Sidonius' secretary. "But where is he
originally from? He's not a Gaul, obviously."

"I couldn't help being curious about that myself.
He told me that his family originally came from India,
in the time of the late Republic when there were still
Greek-ruled states there. He says they moved west,
living in Mesopotamia until the Sassanids took over,
later moving to Italy and becoming completely
Romanized. Of course," he added emphatically, "he's
a Christian of unimpeachable orthodoxy, as all his family
have been for some time."

Privately, Sidonius was still a bit curious. Tertullian
didn't look much like an Indian—at least as he visualized
the inhabitants of that far off subcontinent. He might
have a lot of Persian and Syrian blood, but still. . . .

They rounded a bend in the trail, and the delegation
stood before them on the beach. It was a fair-sized group,
as it must be to represent all the factions involved. *Caesar,
Caesar! How many parts would you say Gaul is divided
into now?* At least five, Sidonius thought: the Visigoths
of the southwest; the British colonies of Armorica (or
Little Britain as it was being called), whose allegiance
was to Riothamus; the Burgundians of the southeast,

barbarians but fairly reliable Roman allies; and the two
whose representatives stepped forward now.

"Greetings Excellency, Prefect," said Syagrius, King
of the Romans, as he had styled himself since succeeding
to the Kingdom of Soissons, which his father Aegidius
had set up twelve years ago while loudly proclaiming
his continued loyalty to the Empire whose general he
had been. Sidonius suppressed a smile, for it was a title
no one had held since Tarquin the Proud, of whom
Syagrius had probably never heard. Contrary to the general
rule that successful usurpers' heirs were cultivated idlers,
Syagrius was neither. He was, however, capable of a
dignified courtesy.

"We are all delighted that you could be here, Sidonius,"
he continued, "even though it represents a considerable
detour in your journey home from Rome."

"So it does, your Majesty," Sidonius acknowledged.
"But I could not resist the chance to meet the High King
of the Britons, with whom I have corresponded. . . ."

"As you have with so many!" Arvandus, outgoing
Praetorian Prefect of Gaul cut in, skirting the edge of
rudeness. "Sidonius, you are almost as eminent a letter-
writer as you are a poet. We all look forward to the
panegyric you will undoubtedly compose for our British
ally."

Sidonius sighed. Yes, perhaps he *had* overdone it with
his verses. Some felt that he might have waited just a
little longer after his father-in-law had been murdered
before dedicating a poem to his successor Majorian. *All
right, maybe it* was *a bit unseemly. But I am* not *just a
shallow flatterer, whatever some may claim! Let's be
honest. I probably would not have supported Avitus if
he had not been Papianilla's father. On the other hand,
Majorian had real potential. He could have become the
new Restorer, the new Aurelian or Diocletian or
Constantine. Majorian could have set the Empire back*

*on course. It has always been restored after the storms
of the past, with a strong new hand on the steering-
sweep. It must happen again!*

Syagrius addressed Arvandus with a frown. "Doubtless,
Sidonius is waiting for the coming triumphs which will
inform his muse, Prefect. As all Romans" —he pointedly
included himself— "await our joint victories over the
barbarians. . . ."

"Which we shall win for the Greek Emperor!"
Arvandus grinned recklessly amid the frigid shock that
followed. The grin almost banished the now habitual
bitterness from his face, and made him as handsome
as he had been thought to be when he had become
Prefect five years earlier. His charm had enabled him
at first to make a success of an increasingly meaningless
post. But his second term was shadowed by a rash
accumulation of debts, and the exactions which he had
been accused of by certain prominent Gauls. He was
now in a kind of limbo: officially out of office, called
to Rome to answer charges, but still publicly treated
as Prefect in the absence of a successor. So his presence
embarrassed everyone, and he clearly relished the
opportunity to embarrass them even more by giving
vent to his well-known feelings about Anthemius, the
"Greek Emperor" of the West.

"I also wrote Anthemius a panegyric, Prefect," Sidonius
said mildly. "It may be cause for regret that our own
failure to set our house in order has forced the Eastern
Emperor to appoint an Augustus for the West. But we
may at least be thankful that Emperor Leo chose a man
of character and ability." *The Restorer? Possibly. At least
he had the initiative to try a departure from policy when
King Euric's aggressions became so blatant as to exceed
even our capacity for self-deception. Instead of playing
yet another horde of barbarians off against the Visigoths,
he turned to our British former provincials, who are only*

keeping civilization precariously alive in the face of their own barbarians.

The British alliance *had* been handled well. Anthemius' masterstroke had been his proposal that an attack on the Saxons of the lower Loire be the first order of business. Riothamus had had to agree. Those sea raiders had been preying on his subjects in Armorica for many years. Now that he and Ambrosius had drubbed the British Saxons into a semblance of good behavior, they constituted his chief military problem. He could not pass up an opportunity to solve that problem at its root. Afterwards, the allies would advance inland, keeping north of the Rhone until reaching Berry, where they would turn south and threaten Euric, while shielding the Auvergne.

Yes, Sidonius thought, *Anthemius is clever. But can he muster the support he needs in the West? Or are there too many like Arvandus?*

The damnable thing was, he couldn't help liking Arvandus, who was an old friend—as were a couple of his accusers. *Maybe it's true that I'm too easy to get along with. Too accommodating, as Papianilla says. And says. And says.* Sidonius sighed. He was glad he was no longer City Prefect, for he would have been forced to become involved in Arvandus' prosecution. This delegation was the outgoing Praetorian Prefect's last semiofficial act before departing for Rome. *I shall advise him to deny everything.*

"Sidonius is right," said Syagrius, on whom Arvandus' charm had always been lost. "This alliance is long overdue. My father and I have always found the High King to be reliable in keeping his commitments."

"High King! This British self-styled royalty of usurpers and barbarians has so little trace of legitimacy that he must claim it through Magnus Maximus, another usurper, although admittedly one with a certain style. . . ." Belatedly, Arvandus noticed the look in Syagrius' eyes and realized what he had been saying. He trailed to a halt with as good grace as he could manage. Even in a mood of embittered recklessness, one did not speak of usurpers in the presence of the King of the Romans.

Syagrius glared for a long moment of what was not really silence—the seabirds and the disembarking army saw to that—but seemed to be. Finally, he spoke in a voice chillier than the late afternoon wind. "The fact remains, Prefect" —he stressed the title, emphasizing that Arvandus was still receiving it only by courtesy— "that this alliance has been entered into by the Augustus of the West, and we must all strive to effectuate his policy. And," he continued, indicating the beach to the west with a sweeping gesture, "we will never be in a better military position."

No one argued with him. The throng on the beach was growing steadily as the boats continued to ply back and forth across the shallows. The crowd was sorting itself out with the unforced orderliness of an army of veterans. The bulk of it was composed of the trained and disciplined infantry so rarely seen anymore—unarmored archers and javelin men, and the heavy shock troops that were Ambrosius' creation, with their ring-mail *lorica hamata*, large round shield, and visorless helmet with moveable cheek-pieces. But what made this army special was the heavy cavalry that was coming ashore now—Riothamus' unique contribution—and his birthright. And he was arriving with them.

An honor guard of dismounted cavalry was forming up, fully turned out in scarlet cloaks. The men carried shields smaller than the infantrymen's, and these were painted with garish kinship symbols. They wore standard helmets, but did not bear the long lances that were their chief weapon. Their scale hauberks and the long *spatha* hanging at each man's side, like the dark hawklike look in some of their faces, reflected the origins of the core around which Riothamus had built a cavalry that might, at anything close to even odds, have given the *cataphractii* of the Eastern Empire pause.

Arvandus seemed to read his thoughts. "Ironic, isn't it, Sidonius? A descendant of barbarian auxiliaries that we Romans posted to Britain almost three centuries ago now comes as our savior from *admitted* barbarians!"

Syagrius overheard him. He visibly controlled his fury, and spoke in a tight voice. "As you point out, Prefect, it has been centuries since the auxiliary cavalry arrived in Britain—centuries in which they have served Rome loyally. And by now, their descendants, including the High King, are less Sarmatian than they are British and Roman in blood."

"And," Faustus put in, "most importantly, his Christian orthodoxy is unquestioned."

"And," Sidonius added diplomatically, "he is now approaching."

The High King's boat was inconspicuous, like all the fleet, with sails of the same light blue-grey as the sailors' tunics. *What an extraordinary idea*, Sidonius thought. *A color scheme designed to make it harder for your enemy to see you! Who ever heard of the like?* But there was no mistaking the man it carried, for the blood-red dragon that accompanied him everywhere soared and swooped above him as the wind filled the sleeve-like cloth device that was yet another vestige of the steppes. That banner had filled the Saxons with superstitious terror when they had first encountered it. Now it filled them with entirely rational terror.

As the boat drew ashore, two sailors jumped into the surf with lines to draw it up on the beach. The delegation advanced to meet the man who stepped onto the wet sand. And as he did, the clouds parted for the first time in hours, and the westering sun blazed behind him, making him momentarily invisible and dazzling Sidonius' eyes. When he could see again, Riothamus stood before him.

An omen? So our pagan ancestors, who worshipped Mithras the Unconquered Sun, would have thought. But not enlightened Christian men, of course.

So why does the skin at the nape of my neck prickle?

It was strangely hard to concentrate on anyone else in the High King's presence. Not because of any outward display of magnificence; he was unarmored, bareheaded, and dressed in the same red and white tunic, with horseman's leggings, as his *cataphractii*. But Sidonius never felt the slightest uncertainty as to who this man was. Neither, apparently, had Syagrius, who had stepped forward and was exchanging stately courtesies with him. No, it was some indefinable quality of the man himself, so compelling that the beach, the fleet, the town of Nantes to the east, the soldiers, and the dignitaries all seemed mere background in a painting of which he was the subject—a drab background.

Riothamus was strongly built but only moderately tall. And yet it did not seem strange to Sidonius that people always described the High King as towering. His thick dark hair and beard were trimmed with a neatness that he could never hope to maintain in the field, and were barely touched with grey in his forty-second year. His features were strongly marked, his eyes an intensely dark brown under thick black brows. He moved with a smoothly controlled leonine strength.

Sidonius grew aware that the introductions had reached him. "*Ave*, Riothamus," he said, using the honorific with the smoothness of the trained rhetorician. "Welcome to Gaul."

"Sidonius! What a pleasure to meet you face-to-face at last." Riothamus' resonant baritone added unaffected enthusiasm to everything he said. His Latin held an odd variation of the Britons' usual accent. "I can't tell you how much I've enjoyed your letters. Almost as much, in fact, as Ambrosius has." He smiled with a boyishness that somehow did not seem incongruous. "He regards you as an inspiration, you know—a torchbearer of classical culture."

"I am overwhelmed, Riothamus," Sidonius replied, and meant it.

Again came the smile that seemed to reveal some tiny fraction of a vitality that, Sidonius suddenly knew, needed a larger setting than Britain. *This*, he thought with simple certainty, *is the Restorer*.

"You know, Sidonius, I still can't get used to that honorific, although I know it's how I'm always referred to in Gaul. But, except on formal occasions, hardly anybody uses it in Britain. It's a little grander than we like things. 'Supremely Royal' indeed! Grant me a favor as a friend, and be the one man over here who calls me by my *name*."

Sidonius was mildly scandalized at the informality, but he could not refuse. "Very well . . . Artorius."

There were, he told himself firmly, limits. At least he wouldn't use the worn-down form of the fine old Latin name favored by uneducated British rustics, which sounded like "Arthur."

CHAPTER ONE

The canals of Mars stretched toward the nearby desert horizon beneath the shrunken sun, their waters flowing slowly toward the Phoenix Sea.

And, reflected Lieutenant Robert Sarnac, Solar Union Space Fleet, *wouldn't that have made a classic pulp science fiction line in the days before there really* were *canals on Mars?*

It was hard to avoid thinking in such terms in this year of 2261, on this planet that was celebrating the bicentennial (Earth-style) of the human-engineered asteroid strike that had initiated its Terraforming. Whenever the war news ran dry, every pundit with time to fill trotted out the well-worn irony that the hard necessities of water distribution had dovetailed with an old fantasy, born of optical illusion and wishful thinking among the pioneering astronomers who had peered through their primitive telescopes at then lifeless Mars.

Of course, Sarnac thought, getting into the spirit of the thing, *there were differences*. The view from the parapet of the roof landing pad lacked something. Granted, the flat desert of reddish dust beyond the canal's fringe of cultivation was right. But no wild green raiders galloped in from it on thoats and zitadars, and the distant pumping station could not possibly be mistaken for a palace of the dying aristocracy of Leigh Brackett's dying world, or for one of Robert Heinlein's slender Towers of Truth. And there were no hurtling moons overhead—even if Deimos and Phobos *did* hurtle, you wouldn't have been able to see them do it from beneath Barsoom's . . . er, Mars' thick new atmosphere. Sarnac leaned on the parapet and mourned for romance, for he had not quite outgrown youth's self-conscious and self-congratulatory flourishes of melancholy.

But while romance might be dead, mystery was not. It just didn't get talked about as much, even by the most desperate members of the chattering classes. It was, he thought, too uncomfortable—the mind shied from it. And too big, as though the *Titanic*, instead of decently sinking, had ended as a *Mary Celeste* with passengers and crew numbered in the thousands. So even as people recalled the ice asteroid called Phoenix that had smashed into this world two centuries ago, obliterating the old Mars as it birthed the new one, they left unspoken the most haunting of all history's enigmas: the fate of the people who had lit the fusion fires that had launched that asteroid on its sunward course. Or, at least, the nine-tenths of them who had *not* awakened aboard the lifecraft with no physical marks—but also with no recollection of what had happened since the inexplicable moment when everyone in their habitat-asteroid, Phoenix Prime, had collapsed unconscious.

Coming in a time of endemic mass hysteria, it had perhaps hastened the socio-political collapse that followed. Which in turn, according to certain revisionist historians, might have shortened the interval before the recovery. The decay that had already begun was cut off, however brutally, before it could permeate Western culture to the core of its cells. The collapse would have come anyway;

as it was, the rubble of the past could still make sound building material for the future.

Sarnac shivered slightly, not just because the sun was travelling west. No doubt about it, romance was far more comfortable. Hell, practically anything was more comfortable! Like speculating about the limitless commercial possibilities here. Amazing that nobody had thought of opening a theme bar by the banks of the canal, decorated to suggest Mars as it was in the good old days before the early space probes had ruined the Solar System. Graceful towers and gallant red warriors. . . .

He heard a rustle behind him. Dejah Thoris? No, Winsome Rogers. He turned and smiled, for she was a friend and a fellow citizen of the Gulf States/Antilles Confederacy. They had known each other in college, in her native Jamaica, where they had had a brief affair. That had been in the golden prewar years, before the universe that had seemed a limitless starry playground had turned out to contain the Realm of Tarzhgul. Their lives, like those of the rest of humanity, had been bent to a sustained war effort like none since the near-mythical Second World War. They had gone their separate ways, lost touch—and then collided one day in a corridor of the Survey Command Advanced School here at Tharsis.

"Hi, Winnie," he called out, turning his smile up a notch. But she was having none of it.

"Bob, do you have any idea how late it is?" she began with as much sternness as her lilting voice could generate. (The Confederacy's English-speakers hadn't altogether lost their various regional accents, and her origin was obvious to anyone who knew what to listen for. So, too, with Sarnac, due to his birth in what had once been called the Florida panhandle.) "You're going to be late for commencement. That would be all you'd need just now!"

Sarnac made practiced finger movements, as if with

an imaginary keyboard, and the time seemed to appear in red digits floating about two feet in front of his eyes. "Oh, God!" he groaned, pushing himself up from the parapet. "I lost track. Pretty late hours last night, you know."

"You might say that! Do you plan to make a career of determining just how much Survey hotshots can *really* get away with? You should have heard Commander Takashima and Captain Eszenyi in the officers' mess earlier! When I passed their table, I caught something about a fight in the bar."

"I swear I don't remember that!" Sarnac protested, standing fully upright and then thinking better of it and leaning on the parapet again. "Or Carlos falling into the canal. I admit the part about mooning the Patrol," he allowed, managing a grin.

Her face, the color of Blue Mountain coffee with a moderate dose of cream, lost its primness and dissolved into a grin of her own. It was, she decided, more than just the leeway all Survey types were supposed to be allowed. It was simply impossible to stay angry with Bob, as she knew all too well. They hadn't resumed their liaison; that was long ago and far away—or what seems so in one's mid-twenties—and she now had a fiance standing guard on the frontier, at a star the astronomy boffins guessed was probably somewhere in Sagittarius. But they could still be friends, for they both cherished the sunny memories. And while there were other North Americans in their class here, from the various successor states that had reacquired civilization and obtained full Solar Union membership, the two of them were the only Confederates.

She gripped his upper arm and hauled him up from the parapet. "Let's go," she ordered, ignoring his low moan. "This is a command performance. You know how Captain Suslov feels about formal ceremonies, and this one's too formal for any shared virtual reality hookup.

At least you remembered to get into your shit-hots."
Sarnac's blue, white and gold dress uniform was all
regulation, without a flaw that even a Marine drill
instructor could have put a finger on—but somehow he
contrived to make it look raffish.

"Mercy!" he groaned, then collected himself and stood
under his own power. "Yeah, you're right. Can't miss
an in-the-flesh formation." He squared his shoulders, took
a deep breath, and after a shaky start, walked a straight
line toward the access hatch.

"... And now Admiral Entallador would like to say
a few words." Captain Suslov, CO of the school,
relinquished the podium to the living legend.

Vice Admiral Jaime Entallador y Kruger ran his dark
eyes over the new graduates filling the small auditorium.
His face, with its harsh Aztec cheekbones and wide slit
of a mouth, was as immobile as ever—a mask of elemental
strength, with all else worn away by years of unrelenting
war. He stood silent for a moment, giving them time to
recall his history: the first contact with the Realm of
Tarzhgul by the Survey squadron (of which he had brought
one half-wrecked ship back to warn Earth) and the Battle
of Amaterasu, where he had won the Solar Union time
to prepare for the war it had thought it would never
have to fight.

"You've all completed your first tour of duty with
Survey Command," he finally said, "or you wouldn't be
here. And now you've completed advanced training, so
you're ready for independent field assignments in
exploratory work. Which means you're ready to perform
the most important task humans have ever undertaken.
We're sending you out into the great dark on a quest for
far more than the Holy Grail. What you're looking for
is our species' survival.

"In the early days of interstellar exploration, your kind

of work was seen as pure glamor. Those were the days when the scientific establishment was firmly convinced that we were the only tool users in the entire history of the galaxy." He smiled slightly. "They had watertight logical arguments for that proposition, believe it or not. The universe was ours for the taking—an endless, risk-free frontier full of readily Terraformable, prebiotic planets, and shirtsleeve-environment worlds with young biospheres. Even when we discovered some evolved biospheres, they merely seemed to add a little variety to the cosmos—color without danger. After all, any sentient life forms must be too primitive to constitute a threat. No vast civilizations can exist, because if they did, they would have colonized the whole galaxy by now. And the chance of there being another race at our particular stage of development at this particular time, is so remote as to be ignorable.

"Or so we thought until we encountered it."

The stillness in the auditorium was disturbed only by Sarnac's whispered "Whatever happened to upbeat commencement addresses?" and subsequent grunt of pain as Winnie punched him in the thigh. Entallador heard neither, and let the silence stretch a little before resuming.

"We've learned very little about the Realm of Tarzhgul except that their technological capabilities are comparable to ours, and that they have absolutely no interest in making peace. In their view, no other intelligent life form has any right to exist, save in a subordinate capacity to their race. They regard themselves as standing in a perpetual state of total war with the rest of the universe."

He didn't flash a projection of one of humanity's enemies on the holo dais, for which Sarnac was thankful. There were weirder-looking life forms around, but none that aroused the queasy sense of *wrongness* induced in humans by the Realm of Tarzhgul's dominant race, who called themselves—Entallador had forgotten to include it among the facts that had been learned about them—the Korvaasha.

"We don't know the full extent of the Realm," the Admiral continued, "but it's clear that their resources dwarf ours. Their willingness to expend an enormous tonnage of ships, with the personnel losses that must entail, in frontal displacement point assaults has allowed them to press us slowly but inexorably back, in spite of the stolid and unimaginative quality of their tactics. We can't fight them head-to-head on such uneven terms.

"Instead—and this is where you come in, ladies and gentlemen—we've had to push forward our exploration program, not from the scientific curiosity and sheer adventurousness that originally motivated it, but as part of the war effort. We need to discover new displacement chains leading into the Realm. We need to turn this into a war of movement, rather than a slugging match in which they have all the advantages."

He paused. "You're all in Survey Command because you want to explore new frontiers, to look on sights no one else has seen. Someday, perhaps, we humans will once again be able to indulge that need to see what is beyond the next hill, which is one of the qualities that makes us human. But for now your efforts, like everyone else's, must be focused on one overriding imperative: survival. The war has forced a narrowing of all our lives and aspirations, and you are not exempt.

"That's all. May our God, by whatever names you know Him, go with you." He returned to his chair, moving with a natural ease that belied the percentage of him that was bionic replacement parts.

That man has made grimness an art form, Sarnac thought—silently, as one bruise was enough.

Suslov reclaimed the podium. "Thank you, Admiral. And now, ladies and gentlemen, before we conclude, I have an announcement. On the basis of your final class standings and prior service records, the three Scout billets for Commodore Shannon's expedition have been filled." He produced a sheet of hardcopy, smiling at his suddenly electrified audience.

Dierdre Shannon, fast becoming as much a legend as Entallador, was taking a Survey squadron beyond the outermost limits of the Capella Chain, and it was an open secret that she was waiting for this class to graduate before filling her roster of Scouts—the self-admitted *corps d'elite* who made the initial landings on life-bearing planets. It had lent an added edge to the competition, even among the natural competitors who specialized in Scout work.

Suslov spent a moment fumbling with the hard copy before clearing his throat. *He's got a sadistic streak almost as wide as his butt*, Sarnac thought.

"The names of the graduates in question are. . . ." Suslov trailed to a halt, did a double take at the hard copy, then resumed in a tone of disapproving skepticism. "Sarnac, Robert . . ."

Sarnac stifled a whoop and slapped himself on the thigh, not noticing that it was the one Winnie had already injured. Nor did he notice Winnie herself, who wasn't a Scout candidate and was now looking at him with an expression that couldn't quite be defined, least of all by her, but which held an inarguable element of sadness. Nevertheless, she smiled; at this moment, his eyes seemed an even more startling blue in a face that was darker than average in his part of the Confederacy. His curly black hair had begun to recede, ever so slightly, from the temples, and his mustache skirted the edge of regulations. Yes, she reflected, there was no disputing that he had a kind of Gypsy attractiveness. If only he hadn't been quite so well aware of it!

". . . Liu, Natalya . . ."

Lieutenant Liu Natalya sighed resignedly, for the comma had been audible. Her family, emigrating from the

war-ravaged lands of Manchuria and the Russian Far
East to join the first wave of settlers who had resumed
Mars' interrupted Terraforming, had been part Chinese
and part Russian from the beginning, but they had held
to the Chinese custom of putting the surname first.
That style of nomenclature was unusual on Mars, and
she knew she should probably be used to people getting
it wrong by now, but still . . .

". . . and Kowalski-O'Hara, Francis Nicholas Mario."

The chestnut-haired lieutenant junior grade drew
himself up in the full dress uniform that seemed made
for him (as, in fact, it *was* made for him, by an expensive
tailor), face flushed with pride. Sarnac caught his eye
and they exchanged thumbs-up signs. They had become
friends at Tharsis after an inauspicious start, for they
hailed from two North American nations that wasted
little love on each other. The Great Lakes People's
Domain had maintained more continuity with the old
United States as it had become by the end of the
twentieth century under the rule of political careerists.
Kowalski-O'Hara, a scion of the Incumbent class of
the People's Domain, had arrived at Tharsis with a
valet. He assumed that everyone would be properly
impressed by the fact that none of his ancestors had
sullied the bloodline with even one day of private sector
employment since three generations before the East
Asian War. He expected deference from the common
herd—he called them "Voters," a term that he knew
didn't carry an implication of social inferiority
everywhere. Regulations had forced him to give up
the valet, and his classmates had disabused him of
his other assumptions and expectations. And in the
end, everyone at Tharsis had reluctantly acknowledged
the husky young man's abilities. Family influence might
smooth the path to a commission, but it didn't get
anybody through this school with top marks! Sarnac

was glad to have him, as well as the utterly reliable if frightfully earnest Liu, for the team of which he would be the senior.

Still, some imp made him wonder what had the most to do with Frank's transcendently pleased look: being chosen for one of the coveted billets in Shannon's expedition, or winning his point with the school's authorities and having his name announced in its full form.

At once, he became guiltily aware of the woman sitting beside him, and put on a roguish face. "I'll bring you back a souvenir, Winnie. Of course, they may not have dirty postcards on the planet where I end up. . . ."

". . . And if they do, the models will have green scales and tentacles," she finished for him. "No problem, mon," she continued, slipping from Standard International English into dialect. "Jus' watch you'self."

"One minute to transit."

The ritual announcement didn't even interrupt conversations in the officers' lounge. After all, there was no need for people not directly involved with astrogation or engineering to take any particular action. The ship wasn't under acceleration, and as it coasted toward the displacement point the artificial gravity maintained a steady one gee. And whatever effect the transit would have on them was immaterial, and would have the same impact wherever they were or whatever they were doing. And none of them belonged to the small minority of the human race that could not tolerate displacement transit; if they had, they wouldn't have been here. So the only reaction from the lounge's few occupants was a scattering of involuntary glances toward the viewscreen.

Of course there was nothing to see yet, if one didn't count the innumerable points of unwinking light that were the stars, in the great dark out here beyond the outermost worthless planet of this red dwarf star, which would have only been visible as a zero-magnitude star had it been in the right part of the sky for them to see it at all.

Also outside the screen's pickup were the squadron's other ships. The frigates *Ramilles* and *Sekigahara* had already transited, and the tenders and specialist ships were following along, aft of the flagship on which they rode. Commodore Shannon had rated one of the new Sword-class battlecruisers, and *Durendal* was a never-ending source of awe to those among them who had pulled their deep-space time in the old Survey cruisers. It wasn't that she was opulent. She was unmistakably wartime construction, and the legend-illustrating mural, customary in the officers' lounges of this class of ship, was the only ornamentation in view. (In this one, Roland sounded his horn on the stricken field of Roncesvalles, while colorful Saracen hordes closed in, unmindful of the tedious history buffs who kept insisting that they had really been ragged-assed Basque tribesmen.) But all her systems were on the cutting edge of a technology that had resumed a rate of advancement unknown since the twentieth century, when R&D had also been driven by total war. And the accommodations, however Spartan, were unprecedentedly spacious—including this lounge, where Liu and Kowalski-O'Hara sat across the table from him arguing politics as they waited for the third displacement transit since the squadron had passed beyond the limits of the known.

"But Natasha," Frank was asking, "how can you have true Equality if you let just *anybody* run for office?" His puzzlement was genuine. So was Liu's incomprehension of how governments unlike the Martian Republic's computer-moderated participatory democracy could function. She had even more trouble with the Confederacy's happy-go-lucky laissez-faire federalism than she did with the system into which Frank had been born.

Nevertheless, she had a ready-made crushing retort for Frank. "All well and good, but it was the twenty-first century United States—the system from which yours is descended—that brought the collapse on the world."

"That wasn't the _real_ American system," Frank argued. "That was after it had gone wrong, fallen under a dictatorship—"

"But the system, as it had become by then, contained the seeds of that dictatorship!" She looked primly triumphant, and Frank couldn't find the rebuttal he so obviously wanted. The understandable self-loathing of the late twentieth century's bankrupt intellectual establishment—its uncomprehending hatred of technology and its simpleminded faith in long-discredited collectivist economic theories—had, with the addition of a nasty strain of anti-Semitism, hardened into the ideology of a new totalitarianism and, by 2060, had put an end to the American experiment in constitutional self-government. Seeking to distract popular attention from the economic collapse it had brought about, the regime had turned to the time-honored expedient of a foreign scapegoat. The Sino-Japanese alliance had been this policy's natural target, the Far Eastern War its inevitable result.

Orbital defensive systems had kept the devastation within the self-repairing capacity of Earth's biosphere, but the intricately interlocked global economy was another matter. Eventually the world had recovered. Even some areas of the old United States and its North American neighbors had won their way back to the heights they had once scaled, and joined with the other polities that had grown up on Earth and elsewhere to form the Solar Union. They had written into the Union's fundamental law the lesson they had learned at such awful cost: societies must be allowed to work out their own destinies in their own way, in defiance of the temptation to universally impose a single set of ideals. The Solar Union was intolerant only of intolerance. A member state could rule itself in any way it chose, as long as it did not seek to force that way on others, and as long as it guaranteed certain elementary human rights, including the uniquely human rights of property and emigration.

It had worked. The totalitarian state had followed slavery and human sacrifice into history's museum of arcane horrors. It had worked so well that Frank and Natalya could sit here and argue their homelands' differences without dreaming that one might try to impose its pattern on the other, while Sarnac—as apolitical as a human being could be and still have a detectable pulse—silently wondered how well the Union would have held together if it hadn't encountered the Korvaasha of Tarzhgul.

"Ten seconds to transit," the computer-generated voice said, and Sarnac shushed the other two. All other conversations in the lounge also ceased as *Durendal* coasted up to the invisible point in space where this particular star interrupted the gravitational pattern created by the distribution of stellar masses. A faint thrumming and a vibration felt through the soles of the feet were the only signs that the ship's power plant was preparing to momentarily distort space with a pulse of artificial gravity.

All at once, the stars in the screen seemed to clench like a hand forming a fist, and everyone aboard felt an undefinable wrongness as familiar physical reality was violated. Then the stars rearranged themselves into a new pattern—as seen from a point some unknown number of light years from where *Durendal* had been an immeasurably small fraction of a second before.

The existence of displacement points had been deduced in the last century, but the knowledge had been useful only for winning its originator a Nobel prize. The invention of artificial gravity had changed that. Displacement points only occurred in association with a tiny percentage of stars—including, fortuitously, Sol—and it was only possible to transit from any one such point to one other. But no one felt inclined to nitpick the universe on these minor annoyances. All that mattered was that it was finally possible to cheat Einstein.

"I was reading," Natalya said absently, "a paper theorizing that it may eventually be possible to create artificial displacement points, given an enormously powerful gravity generator that can run continuously, simulating a stellar gravity well—"

Frank snorted derisively. "Crazy science fiction stuff! What would it use for fuel, out in interstellar space? And even if it would work, it wouldn't do us any good. You'd have to send the thing to where you wanted it by ramscoop—the war would be over before it got there!"

"We're only talking long-range theoretical possibilities, Frank," she replied with ostentatious patience. The tone suited her face. Her Russian genes had molded basically Oriental features into a nearly universal standard of severe regularity—too immobile for beauty, despite her long blue-black hair. "Obviously the concept is irrelevant to the war effort—"

"Wait a minute!" Sarnac's voice was so much more serious than usual that it got their instant attention. He pointed at the viewscreen. "Am I going nuts, or is that . . . ?"

"Ursa Minor," Natalya stated flatly.

"And Cassiopeia," Frank added. "Although it looks a little funny."

Constellations were hard to recognize without an atmosphere to filter out all but the brightest of the stellar multitudes. But others were beginning to notice that their new sky was almost, if not quite, the familiar one of home. Lieutenant Rostova, a junior astrogator, was already out of her seat and halfway out the door at a run.

The answer came shortly in a voice that belonged to no computer.

"This is the Captain speaking. As some of you are

aware, we have emerged at a displacement point surprisingly close in realspace to Sol. In fact, astronomy has identified the local star as Sirius. This displacement point is very remote from it, as is typically the case with massive stars, so Sirius A appears as an extremely bright star. Sirius B cannot be distinguished visually. If you'll look in the direction of Cygnus, you may note a star that shouldn't be there. That, ladies and gentlemen, is Sol, distance, eight-point-six light-years.

"Standard survey procedures to locate other displacement points are being implemented. Stand by for further announcements. That is all."

The lounge was quiet, as eyes swung toward Cygnus. One of the peculiarities of interstellar travel was that the displacement network brought the stars into a proximity that had nothing to do with realspace distances. The squadron's previous transits had taken it hundreds of light years from Sol, and subsequent ones would do the same. But here they were, in Sol's backyard, with the home sun visible to the unaided eye—and utterly inaccessible. A ramscoop was perennially in the design stage, ever since space-based instruments had detected a life-bearing planet at Alpha Centauri. But none of Commodore Shannon's ships had such equipment, nor did any other operational spacecraft. All their fusion drives had to do was get them from one displacement point, across a planetary system, to another displacement point at which they would instantaneously transit to yet another star.

The odd though by no means unprecedented doubling back of the displacement lines was a conversational staple for a few days. Then the discovery of another displacement point on the far side of Sirius made it old news. The ships followed a flat hyperbola across the planetless skies and transited to another new sky, this time a properly unfamiliar one.

They did it two more times. Then they hit the jackpot.

CHAPTER TWO

Standing in the tropic breeze, looking northward out to sea, and east and west along the curving beach of white sand, Sarnac took a deep breath of salt air and imagined himself home.

Granted, the swaying trees behind the beach were not palms, nor even related to them. Any resemblance was merely the superficial one of life forms filling similar ecological niches. And the low-tide smell of decaying aquatic animal life was not the same as it would have been had he been standing on Santa Rosa Island, looking south at the Gulf of Mexico. But all such differences paled beside the single tremendous fact that there *were* animal species to decay, and plant life that had evolved into a multitude of specialized forms. For Danu was one of the few priceless worlds where life had had time to not merely arise but proliferate.

Soon after emerging from a displacement point of this G3v sun that Shannon had dubbed Lugh, they had become aware that the second planet had free oxygen and, therefore, life. But their jubilation had held a restraint born of experience. Few stars were as old as Sol, and while many stars—perhaps a majority of the main-sequence K, G and late F ones, exclusive of unsuitably close binaries—had worlds with the right conditions for life, most had not yet given birth to it. And of the biospheres that existed, few had developed beyond simple aquatic plants that produced a breathable atmosphere but left the world a bleak place, with continents of naked rock and sand lapped by scummy seas. Such a young planet was a great find, of course, and a prime colonization site. But nothing could match the wonder of a world permeated by life, blossoming with the almost infinite diversity of Earth's own. When this had proved to be such a world, Shannon had again exercised her prerogative and named it after ancient Ireland's goddess of fertility.

It was time to return to camp, for the slightly too yellow sun was setting behind the western headland. Stars were winking to life near the zenith, the constellation which, remembering Winnie, he'd dubbed Dolphin and the Jolly Mon.

As he hitched up his satchel of specimens and turned inland, he saw a thin crescent of moon rise swiftly over the sea. Contrary to various Terracentric theories of the early space age, a large natural satellite had not proved to be essential for a planet to bring forth life. But it helped, if only by providing the tidal pools that made ideal nurseries for primordial microorganisms. Maybe that was one reason why Danu's biosphere had had a chance to develop so far—even reaching the rare pinnacle of sentience.

"I still can't believe it," Frank said, not for the first time. His bluntly handsome face flushed with more than the heat of the campfire. "A toolmaking race! The odds against it . . ."

"Well," Sarnac drawled, "*somebody's* got to get lucky. And who more deserving than us? Right, 'Tasha?"

Natalya nodded seriously. "Let's not get too carried away," she added. "Remember, the most advanced Danuan cultures we've observed from orbit are only high-grade Neolithic. Making contact with those cultures will be a full-time job for the specialists, armed with our data."

"Oh, I know," Frank waved the point aside. "That's why we're on this island—so any cultural shock waves we cause will be limited to the local Mesolithic food-gatherers. Still . . . !"

Not even Natalya argued with him. They sat in silence for a moment on the analogue of grass that covered this clearing. Their shuttle rested just outside the circle of firelight, beyond the tents that housed their lab and living quarters.

To some observers it might have seemed incongruous, these three children of a civilization that burned fusing deuterium atoms and sailed between the stars, setting aside that civilization's tools and warming themselves with a wood fire. But scouts were like that. Their bodies had, at the taxpayers' expense, been artificially maximized for the primitive environments where they were the first to set foot. Gene-tailored retroviruses protected them against a broad spectrum of possible infections and diseases. Muscle tissue grafts increased their strength. Implanted monitors paid fussy attention to their physiological state, and in response to certain warning signs, unceremoniously administered injections. Calculators in their heads provided information from their own limited resources, or called it up from nearby big cousins like the shuttle's computer. Tiny interlopers among their optic nerves could make video recordings of whatever their eyes saw. All of which enabled them—and, somehow, made them wish—to live as naturally as possible on worlds innocent of Man.

"Let's also remember," Natalya resumed after a few moments, "that this isn't really what the expedition is about. It's a great find, but it's almost a distraction . . . an irrelevance. We won't be able to stay here long."

"Yeah," Sarnac agreed moodily. Picking up a pine cone's

functional equivalent, he pitched it onto the fire, where it flared and crackled like a living world in the flames of modern space war. "Piss on this world. Piss on a race that's begun to look up at night and wonder what the little lights are! Piss on all that. Gotta move on to more important things."

"Hey, Bob," Frank said, frowning, "I know how you feel. But it's as Admiral Entallador said. Our first priority has got to be the war, at least for now. If we're to make any use of worlds like this, or do anything for races like the Danuans, we have to survive."

"Oh, yeah, I understand all that." Sarnac flashed his piratical smile. "Hey, I come from a long line of people who understood their duty. Did I ever tell you that my family used to have a tradition of supplying naval aviators for the old United States? They even kept doing it in the twenty-first century, when the United States had stopped being worth doing it for."

Frank's frown intensified, but as usual his good nature triumphed—with the help of the flask Sarnac passed across to him. (Strictly non-regulation, of course; Sarnac was legendary for his ability to get booze aboard ship, and for his generosity with it.) Frank passed it back and he took another swig of the rum that tasted of the islands. Thank God Jamaica had missed all the fallout!

Natalya, who didn't drink, wore a puzzled look. "Naval aviators?"

"Right. Wet navy, flying hydrocarbon-burning aircraft off the decks of surface ships—and even coming back and landing there. God, the guts they must have had back then!" He remembered being taken, as a child, to tour the ruins at Pensacola. "Later they went into the Space Force. One of them was slated to go to the asteroids on the Mars Project, before . . ."

He trailed off, and for a time the silence was broken only by the nocturnal fauna of Danu. None of them spoke aloud the enigma that haunted their era. The fire began to die, but that couldn't account for the sudden chill.

Finally, Natalya got lithely to her feet. She could have done it under Danu's 0.87 G pull even without her enhancements. A few generations under Martian gravity hadn't robbed the human body of as much of Earth's evolutionary heritage as had once been thought. "Well, if we're to take advantage of whatever time we have here, we'd better get an early start tomorrow. I'm going to turn in."

Danu's almost Earth- and Mars-like rotation period of 22.9 hours was another of its sterling qualities. They hadn't had to make the wrenching adjustments in sleeping patterns for which their training had prepared them. The two men responded with drowsy good-nights, and soon followed her to the sleeping tents.

The obnoxious siren-like wail inside his head brought Sarnac instantly awake.

The dystopian fiction of the Totalitarian Era had been full of the nightmare potentialities of implant communicators—utter loss of personal privacy, and absolute control by the threat of unendurable, inescapable ultrasonic whistles at the touch of Big Brother's finger to a button. The image had been taken to heart, and now that such devices were actually possible, a rigid code of written and unwritten laws mandated that they be designed to be completely under the control of the individual in whom they were implanted—who alone could activate them. The military was an exception. But even Fleet's special override was used only in the most dire of emergencies. Sarnac hadn't heard the siren since training.

He sprang from his bunk, his fingers almost unconsciously making the movements that caused his nervous system to summon up the current time from his implanted chronometer. Predawn awakening always induced depression and Sarnac had a feeling that it was going to get worse. He stumbled from his tent and ran for the shuttle (whose communicator had activated the emergency signal). Frank and Natalya joined him there just as he raised *Durendal's* communications officer.

"Emergency!" Lieutenant Papandreou wasn't given to panic, but he seemed close to it now. "Get off the planet and rendezvous with the squadron immediately. Our orbital elements are being downloaded to the shuttle's computer now."

"Wait a minute, Theo! Talk to me! What the hell's going on?"

"A Korvaash force is approaching this planet. We need to pick you up before we can leave orbit."

"*Korvaash!*" Frank exploded. "You mean they've emerged from one of Lugh's other displacement points?" Sarnac knew what Frank was thinking; the odds against themselves and the Korvaasha stumbling onto this system at the same time were—well, "astronomical" was too small a word.

"Negative. There's been no displacement point emergence. They were *already here!*" Papandreou's effort at self-control was nearly visible. "They've been here all along. They're approaching from somewhere in the outer system, maybe one of the gas giants."

Papandreou stopped and looked to the side, as if he was being addressed from beyond the visual pickup. Then his image dissolved momentarily into snow, and was replaced with the Black Irish features of Commodore Shannon. Sarnac felt his spine move involuntarily into a seated position of attention.

"My order is not subject to discussion, Lieutenant Sarnac," she clipped. "Get your team off that planet and rendezvous with *Durendal*."

Sarnac drew a deep breath. "Sir, with all respect, we'd just be passengers in a space battle. You don't need to wait for us before breaking out of orbit to engage them. If you win, you can come back and pick us up later. Otherwise . . . well, when the Korvaasha land here, they can't kill us any deader than we'd be aboard *Durendal*."

He could almost smell his companions' desire to be somewhere else—anywhere else—as Shannon's glare began to build. Then, incredibly, she smiled slightly. "Your reputation as an insubordinate smart-mouth is not exaggerated, Lieutenant. The fact is, we're not going to engage them if we can avoid it. That force is too strong for us to do so with any realistic hope of success. We're going to head straight for our displacement point of entry. Unfortunately, they've clearly anticipated that, and their course will probably enable them to intercept us before we can get there. But we're going to make every effort to escape. And," she continued, glare back at full force, "I will *not* abandon any of my people. Raise ship *now*, Mister!"

"Aye aye, sir." Even Sarnac knew the subject was closed. "Signing off." He cut the connection and turned to the others. "All right, boys and girls. You heard the lady. Suit up and strap in."

"But the lab equipment . . ." Natalya wailed.

"Forget it!" Sarnac was already commencing the prelaunch checklist. "Likewise any personal stuff. We lift off in exactly one minute." He turned the process over to the computer and then sought his own light-duty vac suit in the locker just aft of the cramped passenger compartment.

Little more than the stipulated minute passed before the shuttle rose into the alien night on grav repulsion, landing gear retracting into her belly. Sarnac swung her out past the beach and over the darkened sea on gravs, not wanting to ignite the fusion drive before getting well away from the Danuans he had met. *What*, he wondered, *will they make of our unannounced departure?* And this overpowered little military craft could make it to a fairly respectable altitude before being too high above the surface to maintain stability while reacting against the local gravity.

"Bob!" Natalya suddenly cut into his thoughts from the sensor station. Her voice got his full attention, for it was controlled in the same way Papandreou's had been. Too controlled. "Bogies—two bogies—at four o'clock high. Range about two hundred klicks, and closing fast."

Sarnac whipped his acceleration couch around to face her, feeling the bottom fall out of the universe of common sense. "Natasha," he said slowly, "did I understand you to say 'bogies'?" Unbidden came a lunatic image of Neolithic Danuans rigging a glider of vegetable-fiber fabric stretched over a wood frame, and rising in pursuit.

"Affirmative, sir," she replied, armoring herself in formality. "Performance parameters are consistent with the Korvaash Talon-6 fighter-configured shuttle."

Sarnac was saved from blithering only because Frank found his tongue and started doing it first. "But . . . but the Korvaasha are still coming in from the outer system . . . God knows how far out they are . . . they can't be."

"It looks like they are!" Sarnac snapped. "Prepare for acceleration! Frank, get all weapon systems on-line." His hands swept over the controls, going to lift-only with the gravs and bringing the shuttle around into an eastward course. He also dropped to a lower altitude; to continue to try to make orbit would be to invite interception. Then he activated the fusion drive. The shuttle sprang ahead, pressing them into their deeply padded couches, leaving a roar of sonic boom and a wake of boiling seawater behind.

" 'Tasha, raise *Durendal* and report our status." The orbiting battlecruiser was now below the horizon, but Shannon, applying standard procedure, had deployed a necklace of relay comsats around the planet.

As the sun broke over the eastern horizon—Lugh of the Shining Spear, sun god of a small island on a world that suddenly seemed very far away—the continental coastline seemed to Sarnac to zoom insanely toward him. In an instant, they were feet-dry, fleeing eastward over forest rather than sea.

"I'm unable to raise *Durendal*," Natalya reported. Sarnac was not surprised—if fighters could be down here, so could other things able to take out a comsat. "And," she added, "bogies still closing."

"I see they are," Sarnac muttered, most of his attention on flying the shuttle. Natalya had the details, but the gross tactical situation appeared on a small simulation for the pilot. They were indeed closing; those were high-performance combat craft. And it was too much to hope that the Korvaasha would approach from six o'clock, allowing him to use the fusion drive as a short-range plasma cannon. However, like every Fleet craft in wartime, they carried some defensive armament. And the fact that the opposition was approaching gave them a range advantage.

"Launch at will, Frank."

"Roger," Frank called out from the weapons station. He waited until the hostiles had crept up within range of the aft-facing launchers, taking finicky care with his targeting solution. He called out "Missiles away!" and they felt a slight lurch as a brace of deadly little rockets dropped away and howled toward the approaching fighters—only to vanish in sunlike fireballs, detonated by the bogies' antimissile lasers. The Talon-6s— identification was now positive, according to the computer—flashed through the afterglow of the blasts, wobbling slightly from the turbulence. It gave Sarnac an idea.

"Frank," he called, breaking the other's string of curses. "On my command, launch two more missiles. And both of you stand by for a rough ride." They knew what *that* could mean with Sarnac at the controls. Then he yelled "Launch!" and cut the grav-repulsors that were providing their lift.

The shuttle's stubby wings and horizontal stabilizers were never intended to serve alone as lifting surfaces at low altitude. But nobody—not even Sarnac—was crazy enough to try what he had in mind on gravs. As the hostiles were momentarily blinded by the flare of exploding missiles, he went to full throttle with the fusion drive and, relying on sheer forward velocity to keep them in the air, he turned the shuttle over in a quick barrel roll.

In the forward viewport the universe seemed to rotate, the forest horizon swinging up and displacing the sky. Fighting the G-forces for consciousness, he heard a strangled "Holy shit!" from Frank and a stream of Russian—better for both praying and cursing than either Mandarin or Standard International English—from Natalya.

Then they were level again, at little more than treetop altitude, and he engaged the gravs. The terrain below was getting more hilly as they roared further inland, and he didn't want to rely on the airfoils as he brought the shuttle around onto the new course he hoped would lose their pursuers, who hopefully wouldn't realize what had happened until it was too late.

"Bob," Natalya began.

"Yeah, I see them." Two silvery gleams high in the royal blue sky, sweeping around onto an intercept vector. The Talon-6 was large for a single-seat fighter—anything designed for Korvaasha had to be large—and not too maneuverable. But it was overpowered—even by military standards—and it carried a large weapon load, including the missiles that were beginning to appear on his tactical readout.

Their one antimissile laser lashed out under computer control—human reflexes were far too slow—and missiles flowered in blossoms of flame as Sarnac tried evasive action. But there were too many missiles.

He felt a slender hand squeeze his left shoulder. "It was a good try, Bob," Natalya said calmly.

"Damn' straight," Frank added, as a missile slid through their defenses. Sarnac flung the shuttle sideways with a lateral manipulation of Danu's gravity, just as the proximity fuse activated. That last split-second maneuver probably saved their lives.

The deep-blue sky turned sun-colored, and only automatic viewport polarization preserved their eyesight. *Good thing our antirad shots are up to date*, Sarnac thought, in a small, calm corner of his mind, knowing that they wouldn't live long enough to worry about radiation sickness. Then an ogre's fist of superheated air smote the shuttle, sending it staggering across the sky.

Their enclosing couches kept them from being flung about the cabin to their deaths. But Sarnac was half-stunned as he fought to right the shuttle and restore grav repulsion to halt the sickening dropping sensation. A glance at the board told him that the fusion drive was a lost cause. The severed fuel feeds were the least of it.

"Natasha's hurt!" Frank called out through clouds of acrid smoke and the crackle of savaged electronics.

"I am not . . . not seriously," the Martian snapped. And, as if needing to prove it, she reported in a ragged voice. "Communications are dead. So are some of the sensors, but we've still got basic radar."

Sarnac wasn't paying attention. As he struggled to keep them aloft with the dying gravs, he saw out of the corner of his right eye the bogies swooping in. *Yeah, finish us off with lasers. It's a nice clear day, and why waste more depletable munitions?*

What followed happened almost too quickly to register on the mind.

With a thunderous roar, one of the bogies exploded in a gout of flame and smoke, raining wreckage on the forest below. Then, like a streak of silver, a new craft screamed in from the west. Once past the bogies, it began to shed velocity, and started a 180 degree turn. It couldn't be doing it on gravs, which wouldn't have maintained stability—yet there was no sign of any kind of reaction drive at the tail of that sleek shape.

The remaining bogie tried to maneuver, seeming as slow and clumsy as Sarnac suddenly felt his own craft—or any craft he had ever flown—to be. But the stranger came around and, while Sarnac was still wondering whether to admire the pilot or the technology the pilot commanded, launched a missile that flashed home with preposterous speed, and sent the Talon-6 to join its fellow in fiery death.

But the stranger cut it a little too close, unable to kill all of his velocity, before he swept through the flying chunks of debris that had been a Talon-6. He flashed on, but now a trail of smoke appeared behind him as he began to lose control.

Sarnac snapped out of his trancelike concentration on the impossible dogfight, when he suddenly saw that the damaged grav-repulsors were failing. But the fate of their inexplicable savior could not concern him as he sought to nurse the shuttle to an emergency landing.

As the forest's green roof—Danuan plants used a pigment very similar to Earth's chlorophyll—drew closer, he remembered that he hadn't heard any sound from the other two for a while. And he discovered that he needed some human noise . . . badly.

"Did I just see what I think I just saw?" he asked the shuttle at large.

"You did." Natalya's voice sounded frayed from

more than merely pain. "We all did. But the radar didn't."

It was all Sarnac could do to concentrate on the gravs. The development of sensors had advanced to keep pace with stealth technology. What they still called radar was a far more broad-spectrum affair than the twentieth century original. State of the art stealth hulls could fool sensors— but not at this close a range.

Then a wicked-looking tangle of tree limbs was whipping upward at them with vicious speed, and all he could think about was getting the shuttle down.

CHAPTER THREE

Sarnac brushed what he decided he might as well call an insect—there were no pedantic biologists around—from his face. It wasn't the exercise in futility it would have been on Earth, for *these* insects hadn't acquired a tormentingly persistent taste for homo sapiens. Sarnac's visitor instinctively recognized a life form it couldn't live on, and took the hint.

Of course, it cut both ways. If the local life forms couldn't live on them, the reverse also held true. It wasn't that Danuan food would poison them. Some of the plants would—but even without the notes and specimens they had left behind at their base camp, they could recognize the safe ones. But it also wouldn't sustain them. Certain essential vitamins were missing. Luckily, they had salvaged some vitamin supplements from the shuttle. What would happen when those ran out was something Sarnac had resolved not to let himself think about just yet.

He had brought the crippled shuttle down to a near-miraculous landing, *sans* gravs, in the dense forest. At first, the shuttle had been suspended in a tangled canopy, formed by gigantic ancient trees, and it had taken some ingenuity to lower themselves and the gear they could carry to the ground. After which they had gotten as far as possible from the alarmingly swaying shuttle and the creaking, groaning trees that supported it. The support soon gave way and the shuttle smashed to the ground, breaking its back and bursting into flames.

And now they were doing the only thing they could think of: continuing to get as far as possible from the wreckage, which the Korvaasha should have no trouble finding. In fact, they evidently *had* found it, for the trio— the sole humans on this planet—had already dodged one patrol. The three decided to head for the river they had noted during their descent, and to follow it westward to the sea. There, on the coast opposite the island they had explored, maybe they could find natives who spoke a dialect close enough to that of the islanders, which would allow Natalya to communicate, using the language disc in the pocket computer she had salvaged.

What they would do then—besides wait for some miraculous rescuers and try to think of a way of signalling them—was something else Sarnac decided to defer for future consideration. For now, they had a goal. Analysis might prove the goal irrational, but it was better than hopelessness.

"Bob!"

Frank's voice, vibrating inside Sarnac's skull, interrupted his brown study. "I'm blocked by a tributary. Come ahead. I'll stay out of sight."

"Roger," Sarnac spoke softly into his implant communicator. It wasn't necessary to subvocalize; if the Korvaasha were *that* close, the humans would be dead or prisoners. But they didn't dare shout at each other, any more than they could venture into the open area near the riverbank. To avoid Korvaash orbital surveillance they were keeping under the forest canopy, with the river visible as an occasional flash of reflected sunlight on the water through the trees to their left.

"Come on, 'Tasha."

Natalya nodded wearily and trudged a little faster. The exploding instrument panel had showered her left shoulder and upper arm with shards of metal and plastic, and their first aid supplies were minimal. It wouldn't get infected—and drugs kept the pain at bay—but her body cried out for healing rest. So far, she had kept up without complaint.

Soon the trees began to thin out ahead, and Frank motioned to them through the undergrowth. They settled in beside him on the edge of a bluff and joined him in staring morosely through the trees at the confluence of the river they were following and the tributary that blocked their further progress.

"Well, Fearless Leader, what now?" Frank inquired. "Do we try to swim it?"

Sarnac chewed his lower lip. It was the obvious course—or would have been if Natalya had had two good arms. Still, they could probably get her across. Sarnac was a good swimmer, Frank a competent one.

"Yeah," he decided. "But we can't risk it now. We'll wait till dark." He stole a look at Natalya's haggard face and decided it was just as well that they were being forced to take the break she would never have asked for.

Swinging their satchels to the ground, they settled down on the pseudo-turf, and tried to relax in the heat. They were still wearing their light-duty vac suits, having had nothing else on but underwear. The suits weren't really heavy, but they weren't intended as tropical wear. At least they provided some protection from the undergrowth.

"Hey," Sarnac spoke with a crooked grin, "have you considered that we're doing what Scouts are *supposed* to do? Haven't you ever noticed that in the VR adventures Scouts always seem to be trekking through jungles?"

"Yeah, right," Frank replied sourly. "Those bullshit artists ought to show the kind of places we usually end up. Deserts, or landscapes where the vegetation is so sparse and primitive . . ."

". . . that it isn't very picturesque," Natalya finished for him. Even in her haze of exhaustion she disagreed out of habit. "You know perfectly well that those programs are all made in Brazil, Frank. Shouldn't we be making some kind of raft for our gear? These satchels aren't waterproof."

Sarnac decided to put his foot down. "Frank and I will make one. Your job is to get some rest so you'll be able to keep up tomorrow." She subsided with minimal protests, and the two men got busy with monomolecular-edged knives and carbon-fiber rope carefully doled out from a line they might need later for climbing.

"Why don't we make a full-sized raft and float down this river?" Frank wondered out loud as he cut off another limb. "We could cover ourselves with branches and leaves during the day."

"Don't even think about it. We might be able to fool surveillance satellites, but the first time a Korvaash patrol on the riverbank eyeballed us we'd be dead meat."

"Aw, come on, how many patrols can there be in this area? I think . . ."

Sarnac never learned what Frank thought, for a loud *crack!* shattered the stillness. At the same instant, the woodpile they had been accumulating seemed to explode into flying splinters. They were instantly flat on the ground, for they knew the sound of a bullet-sized projectile breaking mach. When Sarnac stole a look upward he saw a Korvaasha gesturing silently with his heavy railgun for them to rise. Even in his shock, he couldn't help but reflect that his captor looked as wrong on Danu as he would have on Earth—or anywhere in a universe ordered according to human standards of rightness.

Many people had tried unsuccessfully to analyze the stomach-churning effect that the Korvaasha had on humans. Some of them lacked the crude bionic parts attached, with such obscene obviousness, to the

anatomies of the specialized lower castes—but they were
equally hideous.

Part of their eight-foot height was accounted for
by long thick necks, with gill-like slits that opened and
closed in a sucking action, as they performed respiration
and produced inaudible speech. The thick, wrinkled
greyish hide was not really what made the Korvaasha
repulsive—nobody finds elephants nightmarish. There
was something indefinably odd about the angles and
proportions of the torso and limbs, but compared to
some extraterrestrials, the bilaterally symmetric, two-
armed, bipedal shape should have seemed positively
homey. Maybe, Sarnac thought as he got to his feet,
that was it: the Korvaasha weren't quite different
enough. Except, of course, for the head.

The thinness of the skin over the roughly serrated skull,
the slowly pulsating tympani that served as ears, and
the wide lipless mouth that ingested food in a way that
he couldn't bear thinking about . . . all were bad enough.
But the single umber eye—large and faceted in a pattern
that allowed depth perception—was truly disturbing.

Their Korvaasha captor made another jabbing motion
with his long, heavy railgun. Among human infantry it
would have been a tripod mounted squad support
weapon. High technology didn't always act as an
equalizer. The heaviest gauss weapons that humans could
use as small arms accelerated mere steel slivers—like
the weapons they had left with Natalya. Unarmed, they
felt no inclination to argue with a being aiming a weapon
at them. They shuffled together through the forest in
the direction the Korvaasha had indicated.

They soon emerged in a small clearing where Natalya
crouched beside their satchels, under the eye of a second
Korvaasha. This one had more obvious enhancements
than the first one, including a metallic forearm which
was probably some kind of weapon housing. He was

talking silently into a portable communicator, just as the pair of them could have been communicating in their subsonic speech for some time, for all the humans knew.

The alien put his communicator away, leaned down, and grasped Natalya's arm in a massive hand of four, mutually opposable digits. Her self-control broke in a strangled scream of pain as he jerked her to her feet. Sarnac saw Frank's jaw muscles clench and his eyes narrow, clearly estimating the distance to the satchel holding their needlers. *Don't do it, Frank*, he silently pleaded. Then the men's captor jabbed them in the backs with the muzzle of his railgun, pushing them forward as the other Korvaasha shoved Natalya ahead and scooped up the satchels, and the moment was past.

Sarnac thought he saw something off to the side. He could hear a rustling sound. And there it was again—or was it? It wasn't an object, it was more a flickering . . . no, a *wavering*, in the shape of a swiftly moving human form in the woods. Wait a minute, now there was an object—a knife blade, floating in mid-air where it would be if the phantom were real, and holding it. What the hell . . . ?

With the eerie silence that, it seemed to humans, accompanied everything the Korvaasha did, the one with the railgun convulsed, his neck-slits palpitating madly with what must have been a horrifying subsonic scream as the seemingly magical blade swept in from the side and slashed him across the base of the neck. Blood—thick, pale red Korvaash blood, that unpleasantly suggested human blood mixed with white syrup—fountained.

The other Korvaasha could hear his comrade's cry. He whirled around with a speed that Sarnac doubted his bionic enhancements could entirely account for. With a sharp *snick!* a long blade extruded itself from his artificial forearm. He shoved Natalya to the ground, and dropped the satchels as he moved toward his fellow, writhing weakly on the ground.

Before Sarnac could move, Frank sprang forward in a desperate dive for the satchels. As the Korvaasha swung back toward him, he snatched out one of the needlers—about the size and shape of an old-time machine pistol—and fumbled with the safety.

Then the Korvaasha was on him and he instinctively lifted his left hand with a repelling gesture. The Korvaasha's implanted blade flashed, and Frank's hand flew off from the blood-spurting stump of his left wrist.

"Frank!"

At Natalya's scream, Sarnac snapped out of his paralysis. He sprang forward, unmindful of futility—and then, with a flash of reflected sunlight, that magical-seeming knife flew past him, as if thrown in a flat trajectory, and embedded itself in the Korvaasha's side.

The alien arched his back in surprise and pain as Frank rolled over on his left side, face contorted with agony, and brought the needler practically into contact with his enemy. There was a rapid-fire, crackling noise, and a row of tiny, closely spaced holes appeared on the Korvaasha's back. For an instant, the tableau held. Then blood gushed from the Korvaasha's neck-slits and he crashed to the ground.

It was over. It had only taken a few seconds. The first Korvaasha's convulsions had ceased, and Natalya was applying a tourniquet to Frank with material snatched from the first aid kit. Sarnac was also on the ground beside Frank, whose pain was ebbing thanks to his biomonitor implant, but whose eyes were glazing over with shock and drugs. It was then that they heard, coming from midair, a sentence in a liquid, altogether unfamiliar language . . . and a slender, apparently female human figure suddenly stood there, dressed in a grey coverall with a face-concealing hood.

Sarnac felt an odd calm. Too much had happened too fast and he was beyond worry. But then he noticed that Natalya was also staring at the impossible new arrival, her mouth hanging open like his own. The stranger touched something at the base of her throat, and the hood spread apart. Pulling it back, she revealed a face, as human as her form, although the features and coppery complexion were exotic. Then she spoke in an English that was oddly accented but clearly her language from birth.

"Quickly! Let's carry him this way to the cache where I left my first aid kit. Oh, don't forget the hand! We need to get as far away from here as possible. These two" — she kept talking as she reclaimed her knife from the body of the Korvaasha, and slid it into a pocket of her coverall — "had reported in, so they'll be expected. And . . . and what are you staring at?"

Sarnac opened his mouth several times, but there were so many questions that he couldn't frame any one of them. All that finally came out was, "You . . . you look human."

The most out-of-place sound imaginable, there and then, was laughter. But the stranger laughed. "I'm sorry," she said when she'd caught her breath, "but you just unwittingly repeated one of history's most famous lines— a line spoken by my great-grandfather. And the reply I'm supposed to make is: 'Thank you. So do you.' "

"But . . . but . . ." Sarnac forced himself not to start dithering. "But . . . who *are* you?" he exploded. Then something clicked. "Who, that is, besides the pilot of that fighter that saved our bacon?"

The woman regarded him with very dark eyes. "Very astute, Lieutenant Sarnac. Oh, yes, I know your name; we've been monitoring your communications." She took a deep breath. "Again, I'm sorry. In answer to your question, my name is Tiraena zho'Daeriel DiFalco." She raised a forestalling hand. "And, for now, that must suffice. I know I've got a lot of explaining to do, but it will have to wait. It's more urgent—wouldn't you agree—to tend to your friend's wound. Move!"

Sarnac moved.

Frank was asleep, after being treated with a pen-sized device that Tiraena assured them would stimulate cells to regenerate themselves.

"I suppose," Natalya said, "you can grow the hand back." Her sarcastic tone didn't quite last to the end of the sentence; the change in Frank's stump was too obvious to allow much scoffing.

"Oh, no," Tiraena replied, deadpan. "Regeneration on that level of complexity hasn't been made workable yet. And when it is, I'm sure it will require much more complex equipment than this. As it is, I'm afraid he won't be able to use his hand until the nerves are reconnected."

It was late afternoon, and they were in a glade near the riverbank, sheltered from satellite surveillance by an overhanging bluff. Tiraena had assured them that she had devices emplaced nearby that would warn of any foot patrols.

"And now," Sarnac said firmly, "I seem to recall we were promised an explanation."

"You were." Tiraena sat on the ground, and the two Scouts lowered themselves down, facing her, with their backs to the bluff. "I hardly know where to begin. I suppose the beginning is as good a place as any." She paused thoughtfully. "I assume your world still remembers that two of your centuries ago there was a project to terraform a planet in your home system."

"Mars," Natalya supplied. "And of course we remember it. I'm a native of that world."

"Ah, so the terraforming was finally completed!" Tiraena looked strangely pleased by the news.

"Yes . . . after the disappearance of almost all the project's personnel from their asteroid base," Sarnac put in. "It's considered the greatest mystery in centuries. And why do I have a feeling you're about to solve it for us?"

Tiraena smiled. "It's a rather long story, and I'll have to ask you to forego questions until I'm done. You see, during that same period, the inhabitants of Raehan, a world about a thousand light-years from the Solar System, had discovered displacement point travel. They began an expansion that brought them into contact with an aggressive, expansionist alien empire."

"Sounds familiar," Sarnac commented.

"Ah, but these people—the Raehaniv—had been at peace for five hundred years. In fact, they had been socially almost static for all that time. You see, they'd been through an era of war and social disintegration that almost destroyed them, and they had deliberately halted change in the name of stability. Their technological prohibitions had begun to break down, but not their attitude toward war, which was to simply deny that it could happen any more. When it *did* happen, they were philosophically paralyzed.

"Oh, one other thing about the Raehaniv: they were human. Yes," she added as her listeners' mouths began to open, "I know, that's impossible. Well, you're right. It is. It's one of the things I'll have to ask you to just accept for now."

"All right," Sarnac said, gritting his teeth. "We'll just accept that—and the fact that you know English, and have the technology you do, and are here on this planet where you don't seem to have any business. For now we'll accept all that. So go on with your story of these philosophically paralyzed Raehaniv."

"Actually, one of them wasn't: my great-great-grandfather, Varien hle'Morna. He had invented the technique of utilizing displacement points, among other things, and used his discoveries to grow rich beyond the dreams of avarice. Before the war, he had discovered—and kept secret—a displacement chain connecting the sun of Raehan with the star you call Alpha Centauri." She smiled at their expressions. "And he wanted so badly to investigate the high-energy civilization that he knew existed at the yellow star four-and-a-third light-years from there, that he also invented an application of gravitics that allowed faster-than-light travel without recourse to displacement points."

Sarnac was halfway to his feet when Tiraena gave her forestalling gesture. With an effort, he subsided.

"Varien saw very clearly that the Raehaniv were doomed," she went on. "So he decided not to give the secret of the new drive to his government. Instead, he went to your system with the idea of offering Earth's governments Raehaniv technology, including the secrets of interstellar travel in exchange for help for Raehan. He first made contact with the people working on what I think was called the Russian-American Mars Project in the asteroid belt. His offer placed those people in a quandary for two reasons. First, the empire the Raehaniv were fighting had a fixed policy of planetary extermination for any world that attacked it; the prize of a technological quantum leap was tempting, but the penalty for failure was too terrifying. Second, they knew that their homelands on Earth were falling under the control of antitechnology fanatics who were rabidly opposed to any presence in space whatsoever."

"That's true," Sarnac admitted. "Our civilization was falling apart—had been for some time. From what I've read, those people in space had grown pretty alienated from the nut-house Earth had become."

"As it turned out," Tiraena stated, "that very alienation held the solution to the dilemma. The Mars Project people accepted Varien's offer on their own, without informing their governments. With Varien's help, they outfitted a small fleet with Raehaniv-level technology, and departed the Solar system under the leadership of the military commander of the asteroid base . . ."

"Wait a minute! I *knew* there was something vaguely familiar about your last name! That commander, one of those who vanished . . ."

Tiraena nodded. "Yes. Colonel Eric DiFalco, United States Space Force, my great-grandfather. My great-grandmother was Varien's daughter, Aelanni. They led the exodus from the solar system, going to great lengths to keep Earth in ignorance, and to obliterate all evidence of the expedition's star of origin. You see, Colonel DiFalco—I never knew him, but my parents and grandparents used to tell me about him—was resolved to protect Earth from the consequences of possible failure on his part. However little he thought of his country's political leaders, he continued, to the end of his life, to love the *idea* of the 'United States,' even though he knew it had become unworthy of the loyalty he and the rest of its soldiers still lavished on it. The mysterious disappearance was part of the wall of secrecy he erected around Earth."

Sarnac squirmed uncomfortably. Could it be that the ghost of the nation his ancestors had defended still had the power to haunt him? He was glad Frank was asleep . . . but no, Frank needed to hear this.

"The upshot," Tiraena continued, "was a colossal irony. The war was won, and Raehan was liberated from its occupiers. And then DiFalco and the other Terrans found that they couldn't go home. They couldn't even *find* home. You see, the displacement chain to Alpha Centauri wasn't there any more."

For a long moment the two Scouts sat in silence, awaiting Tiraena's explanation of the patently nonsensical statement she had just made. Finally, when the silence had stretched on, Sarnac spoke hesitantly. "Ah, Ms. DiFalco . . ."

" 'Tiraena' is sufficient, Lieutenant."

"All right, Tiraena. We obviously have a linguistic problem here, despite your admittedly impressive command of English. I thought I understood you to say . . ."

"I meant precisely what I said, Lieutenant. Not only that displacement chain, but all previously charted chains had ceased to exist, and new ones had come into being." She sighed. "After the fact, our ancestors were able to deduce what had happened. Displacement points, as you must know, given your apparent level of technology, owe their existence to the gravitational relationships of the stars. But the stars are not stationary with respect to each other. The 'shape of space,' to employ a fallacious but widely used term, had changed at a very inopportune moment."

"But that's *ridiculous*!" Sarnac blurted. "The stars are in continuous relative motion! So this 'shape of space' is in a constant state of flux. Displacement points shouldn't be able to remain stable—even momentarily!"

"You overlook the staggering number of factors involved, and the complexity of the pattern," Tiraena retorted in her rather patronizing way. "That pattern has a tremendous . . . 'inertia' is as good a term as any. But when the stellar distribution has altered enough to overcome that inertia, the effect is instantaneous throughout its range, which seems to encompass much of the galactic spiral arm."

Sarnac started to protest further, but Natalya cut in. "No, Bob, this has been theorized before, but the theories have been ignored. Wishful thinking, I suppose." She turned to Tiraena. "So you're saying that the existing displacement network, on which all our interstellar contacts depend, is just a temporary phenomenon?"

"Precisely," Tiraena nodded.

"But . . . but that means that any day now our links with all our colonies, all our bases, could just go blooey!" Sarnac shook his head like a punch-drunk prizefighter. "How often does this happen?"

"We have no idea. That one time, two of your centuries ago, is the only recorded occurrence. But you're right about the unreliability of the displacement network. We now probe through displacement points very cautiously, pausing to determine the realspace location of each new system. As I mentioned, we have a means—called the continuous-displacement drive—for effectively exceeding lightspeed. But it's relatively slow; a ship built for speed and little else can cover almost fifteen light-years a day, but most ships are lucky to make a fifth of that. We want to make sure we can maintain contact that way, for we've learned the danger of overdependence on displacement chains. So, of course," she added with a smile, "did our enemies. Their empire ceased to exist as an empire."

"But bits and pieces of it must have survived," Natalya opined.

"True, and that's another reason we've been very cautious about displacement point exploration. We're always alert to the possibility of meeting one of those bits and pieces. We never have, though. Until now. In this system."

She paused and let it sink in.

Sarnac shook his head again. *Too much.* He needed sleep. "Do you mean that this alien enemy of yours was the Realm of Tarzhgul?"

"No," Tiraena denied, and her voice suddenly acquired a hard edge. "The Realm of Tarzhgul is merely a kind of free-living polyp of the monster we faced—an entity which the Korvaasha called the Unity. It expanded for more centuries, and incorporated more of this spiral arm, than we can know. It was a centralized state, distended far beyond the sane limits of such a structure, and still expanding under the drive of an ideology that had become institutionalized monomania. It demanded the enslavement of all accessible sentient life—including the Korvaasha themselves." She paused moodily. "I'm named after a granddaughter of Varien, a child who was murdered during the Korvaash occupation of Raehan. Someone in every generation of my family has been named after her. It's been a way of keeping alive our memory of what the Korvaasha did to our world, and of what renewed contact with their survivors could mean if we ever relax our vigilance.

"But we've never met such survivors. We once found a dead world that had been part of the Unity. The Korvaasha there must have been unable to function in the absence of rigid centralized control. They didn't—*couldn't*—do what they needed to survive, because the proper authorities weren't telling them to!"

"Then," Sarnac challenged, "how do you account for the Realm of Tarzhgul?"

"Like all surviving Korvaasha everywhere, it must be descended from the ones who were able to adapt to new conditions—the dangerous ones. So the Unity didn't really die. It was like a cancer, metastasizing through the galaxy."

The sun was setting behind her, forming an appropriate, blood-red backdrop.

Sarnac finally prompted, "But you mentioned that you had finally encountered the Korvaasha in this system."

Tiraena's head bobbed up and she blinked. "Oh, yes. Although, strictly speaking, there has been no encounter because we've been concealing our presence from them ever since they entered the system. We had been here for some time, you see. As I said, we explore very cautiously, and as a matter of routine precaution, we built a *very* heavily stealthed underground base after we determined there was no Korvaash presence. But we didn't keep any space-combat capability here. Maybe the fact that this planet is so homelike—nearly identical to Raehan, in fact—made us grow lax. All we had were pickets stationed in the outer system, which immediately departed under continuous-displacement drive. The rest of us remained in hiding in our base, spending our time fantasizing about what the relief fleet would do to the Korvaasha once it got here.

"Then *you* came! We've never entirely given up trying to locate Sol, or stopped wondering what became of the Terran branch of humanity. You can't imagine how frustrating it was! We couldn't contact you without revealing our own presence. All we could do was watch while the Korvaasha withdrew to the outer system—except for a few light units they left concealed on this planet—as soon as they detected your arrival."

"You mean," Sarnac demanded, "that there've been *two* cat-and-mouse games going on in this system the whole time we've been here?"

"Surely you could have done *something* to warn us!" Natalya said accusingly.

"We tried to think of something, but we were in a quandary. Especially because we knew that they were only letting you get settled in before attacking. Finally, we decided to risk dispatching an armed courier aircraft to make contact with you three at your camp."

"Piloted by you," Sarnac stated, while assimilating the fact that what they had seen was considered an armed courier, not a full-fledged fighter.

Tiraena nodded. "As bad luck would have it, their attack commenced while I was en route. By the time I was approaching your island, you were headed east, pursued by those two fighters."

"From which you proceeded to save us. I haven't gotten around to thanking you for that."

"Well, I couldn't just do *nothing*," she snapped.

Why so defensive? Sarnac wondered. Then it hit him: she had acted against orders, running the risk of compromising the Raehaniv base's secrecy, to save them. Sarnac looked at Tiraena with new eyes, seeing a kindred spirit. As if to cover her embarrassment, Tiraena put on her light-gathering goggles. It was getting dark, and a fire was of course out of the question. The other two followed suit, with their bulkier but still effective models.

"At any rate," Tiraena hurried on, "I had to make a very rough landing, and a lot of things were damaged beyond repair—including my sidearm. I had to make do with this." She patted the pouch which held her knife. "At least my suit's chameleon surface was still functioning."

"We wondered about that," Natalya interjected.

"It's useful, but it's only completely effective when you're standing still. There's a finite time gap between the sensors picking up the background and the microcircuits reproducing it." With a slightly playful expression, she spoke a few syllables of what Sarnac assumed was Raehaniv. Suddenly her head and hands floated in midair with no seated body beneath. Then the hands fumbled with the hood behind her neck, and the head vanished as well.

I will not *gape like a yokel!* Sarnac told himself firmly. He stole a glance at Natalya. She was wearing an expression of grimly determined nonchalance.

Natalya and Sarnac heard more Raehaniv, and Tiraena reappeared, pulling back the hood. "My suit was very expensive," she continued. "It was issued to me in case I found myself in a situation like this one."

"Well, now that you're in it, what do you plan to do?" Sarnac asked.

"Continue down the river to the coast and make contact with the Raehanvoihiv in that area. I can—"

"With the what?" Natalya asked.

"Oh . . . the native sentients. We call this planet Raehanvoi—New Raehan. The culture around the estuary carries on a limited coasting trade with other high-neolithic groups to the south. We can travel concealed on one of their large sailing rafts, and once we reach the southerners' region it will be only a short trip to the base. Even if we don't get all the way there, we'll be in concealment while we await the arrival of the relief fleet."

"Maybe we won't have to wait that long," Sarnac said truculently. "Ever consider the possibility that our squadron may whip the Korvaasha and come back for us?"

"It would be unwise to invest much hope in that. The Korvaash force in this system has a prohibitive advantage in tonnage, and we've seen nothing to indicate that you possess any significant technological advantage." She seemed to realize that she might have been just a mite tactless, and continued in what Sarnac thought probably represented her best effort at a conciliatory tone. "But don't worry. Our fleet will be arriving eventually. In the meantime you are welcome to accompany me to the base. You'll be a sensation: people from the lost homeworld we've been searching for for two centuries!"

"But for now," she continued, rising to her feet, "we'd better get some sleep. Your friend will be able to travel in the morning, and we'll want to cover as much ground as possible."

"Wait a minute!" Natalya was almost plaintive. "You can't stop now! You still haven't said anything about the fact—which you asked us to accept, even though it's patently absurd—that homo sapiens could have evolved independently on another planet, this Raehan."

"I never said anything about independent evolution, Lieutenant Liu. The human race did, in fact, evolve on Earth. Its presence on Raehan dates back about thirty thousand of your years."

I really wish she'd stop saying things like that, Sarnac thought, too numb to feel more than mild irritation with this impossible woman for continuously kicking the foundations out from under his intellectual universe. Aloud: "Uh, Tiraena, do you mean . . ."

"I do. And to answer your next question, we have no idea how our original Raehaniv ancestors—Palaeolithic savages like their Terran contemporaries—got to Raehan." Her face wore an odd little smile. "We're completely in the dark about it, Lieutenant Sarnac. And now your people will join us in that darkness."

Tiraena had a skullcap-like device which granted its wearer electromagnetically induced sleep for any preset period. Sarnac envied her, for sleep would not come to him under the alien stars.

CHAPTER FOUR

They were following what was clearly a well-used trail when they met the Danuans.

"Let me handle this," Tiraena said. "We've had dealings with this culture before. My translator is programmed with the trade language. I'm afraid the language of the islanders you met isn't even related." She stepped forward, taking a small device from one of her coverall's pockets and putting what resembled an old-style hearing aid in one ear. Then she made a stately gesture to the small group.

The Danuans—Tiraena had adopted the name, admitting that it was shorter than what her people had inflicted on the locals and had a fairly civilized, meaning Raehaniv-like, sound to it—stood their ground calmly, as the handheld voder began translating Tiraena's greeting into their own fluting language. They must have met humans before, or at least heard of them. The latter was not unlikely; this culture might not have metallurgy, or writing, but it was surprisingly cosmopolitan.

Sarnac, with nothing to do except look unthreatening, contented himself with watching the Danuans. It was always eerie looking at a nonhuman

life form you knew housed sentience. But compared
with the Korvaasha it was easy to meet a Danuan's
eyes. For one thing, they *had* eyes, plural—two of
them, like they were supposed to. Binocular vision
seemed to be the most common pattern, though
evolution had produced trinocular arrangements on
at least two known planets. The overall form was
not unattractive: a slender centauroid, covered with
a short cream-colored coat of what was not really
fur, not really felt. The head, which tapered to a
mouth that performed all the functions of its human
equivalent, sat atop a long neck that was flexible
enough to point the large dark eyes in any direction.
Sarnac wondered how different the Danuans'
worldview must be from that of a being like himself,
for whom the universe was a hemisphere in front
of whatever direction his body was facing.

The conversation concluded, and Tiraena turned back
to the other humans. "It's all right. Her name is . . .
Cheel'kathu is close enough. She's the leader of a caravan
that's proceeding in the direction we want to go. Her
clan is organizing a trading voyage south, and the raft
will be departing when she arrives. She learned about
us from her relatives, and she's eager to help us in
exchange for the trade goods I've promised her once
we reach the base." She looked grim. "Also, she's heard
about the Korvaasha. I told her we're their enemies,
and I think she believes me. That's almost enough to
make her help us for free."

"Does that mean there are Korvaasha around here?"
Frank's voice was almost back to normal now. Only
drugs—and Tiraena's promise of a prosthetic hand that
would make the Solar Union's state-of-the-art products
look like an iron hook—had enabled him to keep pace
at first. That, and Natalya's constant attention.

"No, she's just heard stories. They're enough," said

Tiraena with a grim look. "Which is to be expected, as even you must know." She instantly looked annoyed with herself. "What I mean, of course, is. . . ."

"Yeah, I know," Sarnac cut her off. He couldn't help thinking of what had been found when Nueva Patagonia had been retaken from the Korvaasha, and the tales the survivors had told.

She must have read his expression. "No, really, I apologize." Wryly: "I remember, as an adolescent, hearing my grandparents wonder out loud if I had been cloned from original cells of my great-great-grandfather Varien hle'Morna."

"Sounds like a compliment," Sarnac ventured. "Wasn't he a great historical figure?"

"Yes. He was also, by all accounts, an insufferable, condescending old *grolofv*." She smiled crookedly. "He didn't suffer fools gladly—and his definition of 'fools' was a bit more inclusive than most people's!" She hefted her pack and motioned the others to follow her, and they set out after the Danuans.

Sarnac and Tiraena walked side by side in a silence which he finally broke. "I suppose we really can't compare our experience of the Korvaasha to yours. I mean, Earth's never been occupied by them."

"No, and you should be thankful. Remember what I told you about why my name is a traditional one in our family? Well, there's another reason: it's a way of reminding ourselves what we still owe the Korvaasha!"

Sarnac glanced sideways at her. She didn't return the look. Her profile was set and hard, eyes focused inward on remembered horrors that he could only guess at. And he decided he was very glad Tiraena DiFalco was on their side, for reasons that had nothing to do with her people's technology.

They continued along the sun-dappled forest trail, and soon the river's mouth appeared through the trees ahead.

✧   ✧   ✧

The raft had passed beyond the forest zone in its southward progress, and the shoreline to the left was clothed in the Danuan equivalent of mangrove. Sarnac, relaxing under the awning in the breeze that filled the sail, watched the shore slide by and wondered at the sophistication of the trading network established by Cheel'kathu's people—for "people" was how he had come to think of them.

The raft followed a course that took advantage of the prevailing currents, using the sail—invented only a few generations ago—as auxiliary propulsion. They carried a cargo of obsidian, which the southerners lacked. The return voyage, laden with jewelry, spices and other southern specialties, would be more difficult, despite the countercurrents that made it possible at all for craft such as these. But by then the humans would be gone, proceeding inland toward the Raehaniv base.

When they had passed a certain latitude, Tiraena had risked a short tight-beam message to the base with her pocket communicator. There had been no question of carrying on a conversation; it had been a mere "squeal," letting her fellows know her location and plans. For most of their overland trek, the Raehaniv would be able to keep track of their progress by means of an implanted homing beacon whose signal, Tiraena assured them, the Korvaasha could not detect. Sarnac could only take her word and marvel at the thing's range.

Now, with nothing to do except keep out of sight of any orbital spy-eyes which might by chance focus on this raft, he gazed around him. Frank was resting after the drug-induced overextension that had allowed him to complete the overland journey. Natalya, as usual, was nearby.

It occurred to Sarnac that, of all the surprises he had had lately, what had developed between those two habitual bickerers was not the least. And he found it bothered him a little, inexplicably and almost perversely, as he had never had the slightest sexual interest in Natalya and still didn't. Annoyed with himself, he looked elsewhere. The Danuans were either resting or performing obscure tasks around the piled cargo or with the lines—you couldn't really speak of "rigging"—except for Cheel'kathu, who was deep in conversation with Tiraena.

Again, he found himself wondering how old Tiraena was. She seemed to be in her late twenties, but if she was the great-granddaughter of a couple who had married two hundred years ago, simple arithmetic showed that the Raehaniv must have longer lifespáns. Her hair, militarily short when they had met, had grown and now she kept it pulled back and gathered behind her head with brightly colored Danuan string. It was a very dark auburn, as though the reddish tint of her skin had seeped into it. With wide, high cheekbones and a rather prominent, straight nose, her features were not conventionally beautiful, but they were striking in their exoticism and strength.

She finished her talk with Cheel'kathu and strolled in Sarnac's direction. He caught her eye.

"What's the word from the skipper? Are we on schedule?"

"Approximately. But of course a culture on this level has no concept of fixed schedules. That may be even more true of Danuans than it would be of neolithic humans."

"You like them, don't you?"

"Yes. They're fascinating in many ways. There's the sexual pattern, of course." Danuans had three sets of chromosomes; impregnation by both of the two kinds of males was necessary for a female to conceive. "And the fact that they're evolved from hexapods. That's another point of similarity with Raehan, you know. All the higher

animals there, except those of Terran origin, have six
limbs. That's unusual for oceanic planets, most of which
have quadrupeds. Greater numbers of limbs are generally
retained on dry planets, where life leaves the sea earlier."

"We haven't explored enough planets with highly
developed land animals to generalize," Sarnac admitted.
"But Earth itself fits the pattern."

"Yes, I remember hearing that Earth is a water planet.
I've never seen an accurate map of it, though. They all
went into the fire along with the star charts." Her dark
brown eyes took on a faraway look, then blinked back
into the here and now. "Another interesting thing about
the Danuans . . ."

"No, it goes beyond interesting," Sarnac interjected.
"You *like* them."

"Yes, I do. It's not just for our own sakes that we
Raehaniv hope our fleet gets here soon. The thought of
the Danuans being subjected to a Korvaash occupation . . .
troubles us."

"You keep saying 'we Raehaniv,' but you're partly of
Terran ancestry. And you speak English like you were
born to it."

"Strictly speaking, I'm *entirely* of Terran ancestry,"
she said with a slight smile. "But I know what you mean.
There's one planet, called Terranova, where descendants
of the Terran exiles make up most of the population, for
reasons that go back to the war against the Unity. But
elsewhere, including Raehan, where I was born, we're a
tiny minority—though one that's overrepresented in the
military." Another ironic little smile. "Varien went to the
Solar System looking for military expertise, and we've
tended to follow that calling over the generations. And
we've tried to retain as much of our heritage as possible,
including English as a second language. Some people
on Terranova have tried to preserve Russian as well. But
English was the common language of the Mars Project,

so all the Russians could speak it. For their descendants as well, it's become the link with lost Earth."

"Not lost any longer," Sarnac smiled. "After your fleet gets here and wipes out the Korvaasha, our peoples will be reunited. Sol is just a medium-length displacement chain away—remember, it has a couple of displacement points now. Once we join forces, the war'll be over in no time; the Realm of Tarzhgul won't stand a dog's chance in hell!" Tiraena blinked, but caught the sense. "You'll be able to see Earth for yourself!"

"Yes, I'd like that." Her face broke into a rare, dazzling smile. "It's become almost a place of legend for us. I remember, as a child, being told the old hero tales—like Francis Drake sinking the Japanese Armada, and Davy Crockett defending Masada against the Mexicans!"

"Er, they may have gotten a few of the details mixed up."

Tiraena waved the point aside. "But what's Earth like today? Tell me about it."

"Well . . . where to begin?"

He began talking, and the time flowed past like the shore.

The attack came as they were nearing their landfall.

They had entered the shallows, and the Danuans were preparing to pole the raft in closer, when Natalya pointed to the north and cried out, "Look there!"

Sarnac squinted in the indicated direction. A flash of reflected sunlight. And he could hear a humming sound that didn't belong in this scene.

Tiraena already had her compact electronic binoculars out. "Yes. They're approaching rapidly. Two air-cushion vehicles—quaint but serviceable."

"The quaintness doesn't exactly help us much," Sarnac snapped. Now was *not* the time! The Korvaash ACVs were drawing closer, and he saw the smoke trail from some kind of missile arch out from one of them. "Abandon ship!" he yelled. "Everybody try for the shore. Tiraena, tell the Danuans they've got to . . ."

Then the missile exploded in midair, not with a roar and flash, but with a popping sound, and a spreading cloud of mist. Sarnac snapped his jaws shut, for if that was what he thought it was, the water was the last place they wanted to be.

With frantic haste, Tiraena started stripping off her coverall. After an instant's incomprehension, Sarnac understood. She, too, had a good idea of what the mist was, and she wanted to throw her telltale technology overboard, weighted down, while she was still capable of doing so.

But then the unmistakable odor of capture gas entered Sarnac's nostrils, and he remembered to fall flat, so he at least wouldn't topple over when the paralysis took him. The Danuans didn't know what they were in for. One of them, keening in bewilderment like the others, was too near the edge of the raft. He fell off and sank like a stone.

Sarnac, lying on his side, conscious, but with muscles paralyzed, found he could, with great slowness and difficulty, move his eyes. He did so, and brought Tiraena into his field of vision. She had only gotten the coverall half peeled off, and looked peculiarly undignified in underwear from the waist up. He couldn't think why he found that so worrisome at this of all moments. Beyond her, the first of the hovercraft pulled alongside. And the Korvaasha came for them.

Some of them were beginning to move, tentatively and with an unpleasant tingling numbness in the limbs, when the drop shuttle arrived.

It appeared in the sky at dusk, falling rapidly from orbit until it reached a low enough altitude for grav repulsion to take hold. Then it swept around and settled down on the beach amid a flurry of disturbed sand. One Korvaasha—apparently the boss of their captors—emerged from its hatch and was greeted with unmistakable signs of respect, bordering on obsequiousness.

After a short colloquy, the new arrival stalked toward the beachside clearing where the captives huddled under the guns of the silent guards. He was obviously an upper-caste Korvaasha, for he had none of the crudely obvious bionic enhancements that made the lower classes seem an obscene hybrid of organics and machinery. And he wore a pendant which, with a small mechanism attached by suction to the side of his head, performed the same functions as Tiraena's translation device.

He ran his eye over the four humans who sat together amid the larger group of Danuans. The latter had been strangely quiet as they emerged from the effects of the capture gas, fatalistic in the face of the incomprehensible and the irresistible.

Tiraena, whose translator had been taken along with the rest of her gear, and who now sat hugging her underwear-clad body against the growing chill, would have been unable to talk to them even if they had not withdrawn into a place of their own philosophy, beyond communication with the Strange Ones.

The Korvaasha held up Tiraena's coverall and examined it for a moment. Then he spoke, and all at once he seemed even more machinelike than his blatantly cyborgian guards, for the translator pendant emitted a computer-generated Standard International English that was flat, tinny, and devoid of inflection.

"I am the Interrogator. The voder would only produce a meaningless sound in your aural range to represent my personal name, which, in any event, is not to be revealed to inferior beings." Nor, Sarnac knew, to his subordinates in the Korvaash caste structure; it was a characteristic of the culture of the Realm of Tarzhgul.

He addressed Tiraena. "This coverall, and the rest of your equipment, is different from the standard issue of the Solar Union, and far more advanced. How do you account for this?"

Tiraena hugged her knees more tightly and launched into her prepared cover story. "I am from a human-settled world, independent of the Solar Union but allied to it, which has made a specialty of highly refined technology. I am here with this expedition as an observer . . ."

The Interrogator gestured to one of the guards, who extended an artificial forearm. With a whirring hum, a device extruded itself and touched Tiraena's bare upper arm. Instantly she shrieked in agony, her back arching. The Interrogator immediately made another gesture, and the guard withdrew the device. Tiraena collapsed, shuddering convulsively. Sarnac grasped her hand, unable to do more and despising himself for his inability.

"You lie," said the mechanical voice. "There is no such world. We know from prisoner interrogations that the Solar Union holds jurisdiction over all worlds Sol has colonized." And after a pause, "But not necessarily over all *human* worlds. Just prior to the Great Realignment of the displacement network that caused the downfall of the old Unity, we received reports in our sector of the conquest of a race of inferior beings called the Raehaniv, identical with yours. The report was followed by loss of contact with the Unity's forces in that race's system. I believe that there is a connection—just as there is a connection between you and the loss of two of our fighter craft that were assigned to prevent the departure of the exploration team that were landed on this world."

Tiraena raised herself, panting with effort. "You are wrong. I swear that my ancestors came from Sol. Use truth drugs, or whatever methods you employ, to confirm this."

It was impossible to read expressions from the Korvaash eye, but the Interrogator looked long and hard at her. "It is true that evolution cannot repeat itself on two different worlds. And yet we know that the humans of the Solar Union did not attain interstellar travel until some time after the Great Realignment. This contradiction must be explored further.

"I have other business in this region, in connection with the inferior beings native to this planet, that we will begin to incorporate now that we have annihilated your pathetic forces." Sarnac heard a shuddery intake of breath from Natalya and a low growl from Frank. "Afterwards, you will be taken to an orbiting ship where facilities are available to properly interrogate you. I am aware of your implanted communications devices. They will be surgically removed. The effectiveness of the anesthesia will be in direct proportion to your cooperativeness."

Tiraena spoke haltingly. "Let these Danuans . . . these natives go. They are primitives, and know nothing."

"I see, then, that their welfare concerns you." The Interrogator's translator-voder continued to emit ghastly mechanical English as its owner addressed one of the guards. "Kill this one" —he indicated Cheel'kathu— "so that the female inferior being will take me seriously when I say that I will make her watch me kill them all if she does not speak the truth."

Tiraena staggered to her feet as the guard's weapon swung around and the red dot of a laser designator appeared over Cheel'kathu's uncomprehending eyes. "No! I'll tell you everything. There's no need—"

"Good. But since there is an ample supply of them with which to assure your continued obedience, there is also no need to countermand my order." He gestured, the guard's railgun emitted a single sharp crack on single-shot mode, and Cheel'kathu's head exploded in a wet, pink and grey shower.

As the echoes died away, the Danuans broke into a low moaning—all but two males, of the two different sorts, who edged forward to touch what had been their mate. And Tiraena—all reason gone from her eyes—began to step forward. Sarnac half-rose and caught her around the waist, holding her motionless, until sanity returned.

The Interrogator's face was as unreadable as the dead tones of his voder. But his massive frame stiffened in a way that Sarnac would have sworn revealed some powerful emotion under tight control. "It is as our founder, Tarzhgul, who organized the Realm after the Great Realignment, said. This concept of pity for others is one of the hallmarks of inferior beings, who ape the true sentience of which only our species is capable. He explained it to us clearly. Even if the Great Realignment had never occurred, the Unity would eventually have fallen anyway because of its own rigidity and inner weakness. Our ancestors sought to treat inferior beings in a way that they could never comprehend or appreciate, allowing them a place—subordinate to our race, of course—in the great scheme of the Unity, and resorting to extermination only when recalcitrance left them no alternative."

"Yeah," Sarnac drawled. "Ingrates everywhere you look! Ain't life a bitch?"

The Interrogator gestured abruptly, and the guard with the artificial forearm thrust it forward and jabbed Sarnac in the neck. Instantly, his nervous system became nothing more than a carrier of pain—more pain than he would have believed the cosmos could hold. He didn't even hear his own screams, for he was in a universe where sound did not exist, where nothing existed but agony.

Then the neurolash was withdrawn, and it was like going into free fall, for the sudden absence of pain was disorienting. He lay shuddering spasmodically, growing aware that Tiraena was holding him and that Frank and Natalya were by his side.

"You will find," the Interrogator continued as though there had been no interruption, "that we of the Realm of Tarzhgul have outgrown this folly. Tarzhgul taught us that the Unity's fair-mindedness was futile and self-defeating when applied to inferior beings, who are inherently incapable of responding appropriately to it. The interests and convenience of our own race are the only relevant considerations in dealing with vermin like yourselves.

"Keep them under close guard tonight," he continued to the chief guard. "I will deal with them further in the morning."

He turned and walked toward his drop shuttle as the guards began to herd them toward an enclosure, and Sarnac recalled Tiraena's earlier remark that the Korvaasha that had survived to the present must be the truly dangerous ones.

CHAPTER FIVE

Dawn had not yet broken when Sarnac was awakened from a fitful sleep by the low whine of gravs. A second drop shuttle descended in a blaze of running lights and settled down on the beach alongside the Interrogator's. The activity that followed was carried on in Korvaash silence, and he drifted off again.

A vicious jab from a guard's weapon was the next thing of which he was conscious. As the Korvaasha moved on, rousing the others, he got slowly to his feet and looked around. The sun had risen and the new drop shuttle was still where he dimly remembered it landing in the night. The camp was alive with activity, and Sarnac thought he detected a difference from the leaden stolidity with which the Korvaasha seemed to do everything. They actually looked mildly agitated to human eyes, and he wondered what that implied.

The other humans and the listless-seeming Danuans were up and moving about, carefully avoiding the wire enclosure—one of the Danuans had brushed against it and discovered that it carried a mild neurolash effect. The Interrogator approached with a brace of guards in tow, and spoke with the emotionlessness of his voder.

"Plans have been changed. I must depart immediately.

You will travel into orbit aboard the second shuttle."
His eye rested on Tiraena. "We will take the local inferior
beings along to assure your cooperation. Also, they will
add variety to our personnel's rations. We discovered this
in the course of extracting, from their community in the
north, the secret of your presence on their raft." Without
further explanation he turned and strode off, and
disappeared into his shuttle.

Sarnac glanced sideways at Tiraena's face, and decided
no useful purpose would be served by mentioning that
he hadn't seen any sign of Cheel'kathu's remains in the
morning light.

"I've brought nothing but death to these people," she
said dully. "I should never have made contact with
them. . . ."

"Don't say that!" Sarnac surprised himself with his
anger. But he came from a culture born of revulsion against
the ethical idiocy that had permeated the Western
civilization from which Tiraena's ancestors had fled. "The
Korvaasha have brought death to them—not you—and
eventually they'll pay!"

They watched in silence as the Korvaasha began to
dismantle the camp and load the hovercraft aboard the
second shuttle. Soon a guard deactivated the fencing wire,
then swung a gate open and motioned them out. As they
shuffled toward the second shuttle's ramp, the
Interrogator's shuttle drifted upward and swept around
into a westward course, dwindling rapidly. Soon the tiny
sun of its fusion drive awoke over the ocean and began
to climb.

"So much for the Interrogator's 'business' among the
local Danuans," Frank muttered. "I wonder what's got
them in such an uproar?"

"No telling," Sarnac replied in an equally low tone,
as the guard stepped onto the ramp, stood near its halfway
point, and gestured at them to proceed into the shuttle.

Sarnac led the way up the ramp, past him, and toward the maw of the hatch. "It's almost as if . . ."

Something arrived with a shriek of cloven air. A Korvaash weapon emplacement on the strand vanished in flame and smoke, followed by a thunderclap that arrived with the first of the aircraft—grav propelled, obviously, but dead silent and impossibly small and fleet—that swept across the camp, raking the Korvaasha with barely visible lasers.

For a split second, everyone on the ramp stood stunned. Then Tiraena yelled, "They're from the base!"

At the same instant, without pausing for analytical thought, Sarnac flung himself back down the ramp, diving under the guard's weapon and sliding into his columnar legs. The guard was thrown off balance on the ramp's edge, and they both toppled off and crashed into the sand, with the guard breaking Sarnac's fall.

Sarnac rolled off the momentarily stunned Korvaasha and looked frantically around for something to use as a weapon. The guard, recovering, surged to his feet and began to bring up his railgun . . . when Tiraena jumped off the ramp above him and landed on his back, locking her arms around his throat.

The Korvaasha dropped the railgun, freeing his hands to grasp at Tiraena. With a convulsive motion, he hauled her off his back and flung her several yards. The wind whooshed out of her as she landed on her back in the sand.

But the Danuans had used the seconds she had gained to rush the guard, and one of Cheel'kathu's mates reared up and lashed out with its forelegs. A Danuan's four walking limbs ended in hard surfaces resembling hooves; two of them caught the guard in the side as he turned to try to retrieve his weapon. The guard went down, and the Danuan reared again, bringing his forehooves down. One of them punched through the Korvaasha's eye with

a sickening, wet, crunching sound. Then the rest of the
Danuans were all around, trampling the Korvaasha into
bloody ruin.

Frank and Natalya had jumped off the ramp just as it
started to retract into the shuttle. All three Scouts sprinted
for the railgun as the shuttle lifted in a swirl of sand.
Sarnac hefted the weapon—he couldn't have carried it
very far, but he could lift it. Intelligence briefings came
back to him, and he recognized a firing stud.

"Bob!"

Natalya pointed inland, where a firefight was developing
between the Korvaasha and the human troops who were
bounding from the open sides of some kind of grav
personnel carrier. A trio of the aliens were moving toward
them. One of them opened up with a railgun, blasting a
Danuan open and sending the rest of the locals scattering.
Then the Korvaasha spotted Tiraena, who had recovered
and was running toward the Scouts with a flash of long
bare limbs. Their railguns swung toward her.

Sarnac clumsily aimed from the hip a railgun designed
for Korvaash hands. With a silent prayer that the safety
was off, he squeezed the firing stud. He immediately
discovered that the weapon was on full automatic setting.

Gauss weapons didn't have much recoil compared with
chemical-explosive ones, but nothing could hurl large
caliber slugs at such velocities without producing some
kick—and this one was designed to be held on target by
a Korvaasha. With desperate effort, Sarnac managed to
halt the muzzle's climb, frantically applying downward
pressure that caused the weapon to slew sideways, and
sent the stream of hypervelocity missiles through two
of the oncoming Korvaasha, ripping their torsos apart
in showers of gore. Then, unable to maintain his balance,
he dropped the heavy weapon as the third Korvaasha
drew a bead on him.

Then one of the mysterious flyers swooped in along

the beach, and they heard the unmistakable snapping sound of air rushing in to fill the tube of vacuum drilled in atmosphere by a weapon-grade laser. A sparkling of ionization marked the beam's path, spearing the Korvaasha and hurling him backward with the knockback effect of energy transfer. With a puff of steam from vaporized body fluids and a stench of overcooked meat, he fell. At that moment, the shuttle, under attack from other flyers, exploded over the water, generating a shock wave that flung them all to the sand.

Raising his head and spitting out grit, Sarnac saw Tiraena spring to her feet and run to a dead Korvaasha's railgun. Hoisting it off the ground—she was, Sarnac knew, a lot stronger than she looked—she set it down on a hummock and lay on her stomach behind it. *Yeah, give the thing some support for accuracy, like I should have*, Sarnac thought, annoyed with himself. Picking up his railgun, he staggered forward to join her.

Natalya tried unsuccessfully to lift another of the weapons unaided, then got it off the ground with Frank's one-handed help, and the two of them fell prone beside Sarnac. All three railguns proceeded to pour fire into the Korvaash positions from the rear.

They ceased fire as they saw the rescuers, clad in some kind of light body armor, advancing toward them past the now silent Korvaash weapon emplacements.

Tiraena sprang to her feet and trotted forward to meet their leader. Joining them, the Scouts arrived in the middle of an animated conversation in rapid-fire Raehaniv. Catching Tiraena's eye, Sarnac gave her what he hoped was a universal gesture of incomprehension.

"Sorry," she said. "This is Dorleann hle'Soru, our security chief."

Dorleann doffed his combat helmet, revealing a face that seemed to accentuate all the features that made Tiraena exotic—a pure-blooded Raehaniv, Sarnac supposed. He gave a small bow and called to one of his men, who produced a device like the one Tiraena had used to communicate with the Danuans. Sarnac and Dorleann affixed earpieces, and the latter spoke.

"I thought we might need a translator," the earpiece said to Sarnac. "Welcome! You'll be glad to know that our fleet has arrived—"

"But hasn't engaged the Korvaasha yet," Tiraena cut in, speaking English for the benefit of Frank and Natalya. "They got as close to this system as the displacement network allowed, then proceeded the rest of the way under continuous-displacement drive, approaching from nowhere near any of this star's displacement points. But now the Korvaasha have detected them and are scrambling out of orbit to fight." She turned to Dorleann. "Unfortunately, the one who questioned us—obviously a high-ranking intelligence officer—has already departed and rejoined their fleet. If you had struck just a little earlier, you might have gotten his shuttle!"

Dorleann's coppery complexion grew a little redder.

"We were cutting it very fine, Tiraena. We couldn't mount this rescue operation until the Korvaasha had spotted our fleet and were too busy to strike at us from orbit. At the same time, if we'd delayed any longer, it would have been too late: you would have been taken aboard one of their ships—and died with it." His expression grew harsh. "Don't worry about this Korvaash officer getting away. They're about to learn a lesson in state-of-the-art space combat! And our fleet's approach vector was planned to foreclose any possibility of them getting away through the displacement point by which they entered this system."

"But they have courier boats stationed at that displacement point—" Tiraena began.

"Had," Dorleann corrected. "A special task group cut

their continuous-displacement drives well outside grav-scan range, then proceeded to the displacement point in free fall. The couriers never knew what hit them!" Sarnac marvelled at the Raehaniv translator programs' capacity for idiomatic speech.

Tiraena began to be mollified—and aware of her own grimy seminakedness—as combat reaction wore off. "Well, I suppose we don't have to worry about the Realm of Tarzhgul learning about us, then."

"No," Sarnac offered. "Not until we're ready to let them know!" He turned to Dorleann, remembering that handshaking was not a Raehaniv custom. "For now, we just want to thank you, even though it adds to the debt we owe. You see, Tiraena has already saved our lives . . ."

"Twice," Tiraena interjected primly.

"All right, twice! Anyway, on behalf of the Solar Union . . ."

"Please don't mention it," Dorleann interrupted, smiling. "We needed this action as much as you—well, almost as much. We were about to go insane with frustration, you know. Not being able to strike at the Korvaasha was bad enough, but then our distant cousins from Sol appeared and we couldn't even signal them!" He shook his head in wonderment. "I still can't quite credit the reality of it! We've dreamed of reestablishing contact with you for centuries. As soon as we're finished here" —he gestured at the smoking wreckage of the Korvaash camp, which his men had patrolled in search of survivors, while the deadly little grav flyers settled onto the sand— "we'll take you to the base. Everyone's mad with curiosity to meet you. I think I can promise you everything but rest!"

Thrufarn Taraen Sergeyevich Murchison was from Terranova and, despite his first name, entirely of American and Russian ancestry. It clearly hadn't hindered his rise in the Raehaniv Federation's space navy—the rank "thrufarn" being more or less comparable to vice admiral. But it had made him especially eager to meet the Scouts when his fleet had arrived at Danu after smashing the Korvaasha. For their parts, Sarnac and his companions had been relieved to share the burden of celebrity with the new arrivals, especially at this reception.

"Yes," the _thrufarn_ was telling his circle of listeners, "our losses were minimal. Korvaasha military technology doesn't seem significantly better than what their ancestors had two centuries ago. The Realm of Tarzhgul may have rejected the ideological constraints of the old Unity, but as a race they still don't seem to be very inventive. We, on the other hand, have advanced quite a lot since then." He turned to the Scouts. "Of course, your squadron made it easier for us. Comparing the Korvaash forces that originally entered this system with the ones we faced, it's clear that your people didn't go alone. In fact, they must have given far better than they got."

"Thank you, _Thrufarn_ Taraen," Sarnac said gravely. He could have said "Admiral Murchison"; the _thrufarn_ would have understood, and the non-English-speakers' translator programs could have handled it. But this man rated his proper mode of address. "Knowing Commodore Shannon, I was pretty sure of that. Naturally, the Interrogator implied otherwise."

"Naturally," Murchison nodded. He was stocky and of average Terran height, in contrast to the generally tall, slender Raehaniv—a heritage of his homeworld's high gravity. His black uniform showed the influence of the old United States Space Force, though with Russian-style shoulder boards and an unfamiliar system of rank insignia. He and his officers made an austere contrast to the multicolored civilian garb and the turquoise and white uniforms of the Raehaniv survey service.

We can hold our own, Sarnac told himself, though he was still adjusting to the notion of attending a formal reception in his underwear while tiny holo projectors in his belt, linked with the computer to which the Scouts had meticulously described their service's uniforms, wrapped the illusion of the Solar Union Space Fleet's mess dress around his body. Knowing what a glare he would get from Natalya, he had resisted the temptation to award himself a few of the medals that any fair-minded person would surely agree he deserved after this . . . this . . . the centuries-old expression "charlie foxtrot" came to mind.

Of course, I'm not in too much pain right now, he admitted, twirling his oddly shaped wineglass and glancing around.

Three walls of the base's social hall were flat-screen holo projectors, and the room seemed a roofed terrace jutting out over water beneath Raehan's two moons. Across the water, Brobdignagian towers blocked off half the night sky like a shimmering wall of faceted light, as their reflections seemed to fill half the wide bay. Beyond them, inconceivable cityscape climbed up a low range of hills. Overhead, unending swarms of brightly lit grav craft drifted by to the intricate music that he could barely hear over the jubilant hubbub.

Loruin hle'Saelarn, the base's CO, was addressing Murchison. "Has there been any word on that *Torafv*-class frigate that was listed as missing?"

"No," Murchison admitted. "All our other ship losses have been accounted for, but that one hasn't turned up. We'll find some wreckage eventually—probably in the course of hunting down the Korvaash survivors."

"Survivors?" Loruin looked worried. He was pudgy for a Raehaniv, and stretched his survey uniform—an altogether unlikely figure in a paramilitary service.

"Oh, yes. A couple of ships, including one big one. They may be hiding in the outer system, maybe among the gas-giant moons. But they can't threaten us here.

And they can't hope to escape via the displacement point that connects with Korvaash space." Murchison smiled unpleasantly. "That one is *very* heavily guarded. Any ships that enter this system through it are going to be turned into rarefied gas before they can even think about going back to report anything amiss here."

"I'll bet!" Frank's enthusiasm was as unfeigned as his delight in the bionic left hand that only a medical sensor could have recognized as such. He had followed the battle in space raptly, growing more openmouthed with each offhand mention of rapid-repeating plasma guns, grav deflectors, tractor beams, X-ray lasers that didn't require the detonation of a nuclear bomb, and all the rest.

Natalya read his thoughts—as she did more and more of late. "And yet, as impressive as your weaponry is, the truly decisive innovation is your continuous-displacement drive. It changes the entire strategic picture. In fact, it *abolishes* the strategic picture, in the traditional sense!"

"Not quite," Murchison smiled. "Remember, paired displacement points tend to be very far apart in realspace, typically hundreds of light-years. So the Solar Union and the Realm of Tarzhgul—and the Raehaniv Federation—extend over enormous reaches of space, within which they've only visited a tiny percentage of the stars. For really long-distance movement within a reasonable length of time, we still need to make use of the displacement network. The Raehaniv Federation resembles a series of bubbles in space, connected by displacement lines. We emerge from a new displacement point, stop to determine where we are in realspace— we've learned *that* lesson—and then probe outward on continuous-displacement drive. Sometimes two of the bubbles grow into each other. Remind me to show you a holoprojection of it." He snagged a fresh wineglass from one of the serving robots that floated about on the silent Raehaniv grav repulsion, from which all the annoying side effects had been banished. "Of course, the biggest of the bubbles is the one centered on Raehan itself. That one includes Terranova, which used to have a displacement point, but no longer does."

"Every Terranovan I've ever known takes a perverse pride in their isolation," Loruin put in. "They claim it builds character!"

Everyone laughed, but Sarnac found himself wondering if that isolation had preserved the descendants of a few thousand Americans and Russians from traceless submergence into the Raehaniv billions, and allowed them to retain a distinct cultural identity with which even the non-Terranovans of Earth descent like Tiraena could identify.

"But, Lieutenant Liu," Murchison resumed, "you're right in the sense that continuous-displacement drive will place us in an unbeatable strategic position. Once we have access to your astronomical data on the known Korvaash-held systems, we'll be able to use the displacement network to get as close as possible to them in realspace, then attack from completely unexpected directions."

"So the whole sky becomes one big displacement point, from the standpoint of the defender!" Frank grinned, shooting his right cuff . . . the illusion was so perfect that even the person "wearing" it could easily forget, and the holoprojectors made the appropriate adjustment. He was constantly exercising the bionic hand, and Sarnac wondered if he'd be able to part with it when the cloned replacement had finished being force-grown and was ready to be attached.

"And," Natalya added, "such an attack could be made in conjunction with a frontal displacement point assault. Tiraena, wasn't that what your ancestors did to the Korvaash occupiers of the Raehan system?"

Tiraena nodded. Her hair was in the short Raehaniv

military style again, and she wore survey turquoise and white. (Actual fabric—she had explained that expense, and the possibility of cold weather, plus sheer conservatism, had restricted the holo belts to special uses.) She looked stunning, and Sarnac was still trying to square the Tiraena he knew—or thought he knew—with this elegant lady.

"Yes," Murchison confirmed. "After the Liberation, we were planning to launch a sustained counteroffensive against the Unity using these tactics. That was before the disruption of the displacement network, which left us as thoroughly out of contact with the Korvaasha as with Earth." He paused and shook his head slowly. "I knew we were going to find Korvaasha—the first we've faced in two centuries—in this system. But to arrive and find that we've also reestablished contact with Earth . . . !"

He shook his head again and ran a hand over his bald scalp. The *thrufarn*'s lack of hair had distressed Sarnac, who worried about the very slight, thinning out at his temples—surely the Raehaniv had a cure for baldness! (He'd later learned, to his chagrin, that they did, and that Murchison hadn't thought it worth bothering with.)

Loruin lacked the *thrufarn*'s ethnic interest in the scouts, but had his own enthusiasms. "Aside from the military considerations—although I agree that dealing with the Realm of Tarzhgul has to have the first priority—we'll now be able to explore the problem of Raehaniv origins from a whole new perspective."

"Yes," Natalya said earnestly, maintaining concentration with obvious effort. The Raehaniv were justifiably fanatical about their wines, and she had perhaps overdone the social obligations to which she was unaccustomed. "We've more or less taken that whole subject on faith until now—too much else to occupy us. But it has to be faced. It goes without saying that

homo sapiens couldn't have evolved independently on
Earth and on Raehan. But it's equally impossible that
a spacefaring culture could have existed on Earth thirty
thousand years ago. In the first place. . . ."

"Oh, yes," Loruin cut in. "All the arguments are very
familiar, and beyond dispute. And yet it is certain that
humans, and various other species now known to be of
Earth origin, appeared on Raehan at that time. A classic
paradox. Especially given the indisputable evidence of
a spacefaring culture at that period of time."

"Tiraena mentioned that," Sarnac said. "I understand
this evidence all came to light at the time of the liberation
of Raehan."

"Yes," Loruin affirmed. "And we've had so much else
to talk about that you've never seen it. Would you like
to view the records?"

There was a basic technological incompatibility
between virtual reality as known to the Solar Union
and to the Raehaniv. The former required the wearing
of special helmets and other sensory-input gear, to
replicate the product of a computer program which
had only become practical in the last couple of
generations. The Raehaniv used none of this, for they
had achieved a practical application of direct neural
interfacing. Tiraena, like most other specialized
Raehaniv personnel, had a tiny socket behind her left
ear, by which she could link interactively with a
computer for full sensory input. Sarnac and his
companions had no such sockets, and therefore could
not use Raehaniv equipment.

Thus it was that they all sat in front of a holo dais,
passively viewing a scene two centuries old.

"My great-grandfather," Tiraena said quietly, and
Sarnac gazed at the image of Colonel Eric DiFalco,
wearing a light-duty vac suit that must have been far

beyond what his own twenty-first century Earth could produce.

"This," the image was saying in an English that held an unmistakable period flavor, "is a chamber in the heart of the base." He had already led the viewer into the long-abandoned installation that he and his companions had discovered on a gas-giant satellite when they had first entered the Terranova system. Now he proceeded into the chamber, his audience travelling with him.

"My great-grandmother," Tiraena said as the tall Raehaniv woman came into the pickup's scope. Sarnac looked on Aelanni zho'Morna and found himself approving of Colonel DiFalco's taste.

But then the image centered on the relief sculpture on the wall . . . and Sarnac forgot everything else.

After some passage of time he heard Frank's shaken voice. "The Bering Strait is a land bridge. . . ."

"And so is the English Channel," Natalya finished for him. "But this is unquestionably a map of Earth during the last ice age." It was anticlimactic when the image of Colonel DiFalco confirmed the conclusion, and then moved on to what he declared to be a map of Raehan.

"Since then, we've discovered two of the other planets whose maps decorate the walls of that chamber," Loruin murmured from the shadows behind them.

Abruptly, the scene shifted to a similar chamber, full of Raehaniv whose speech Sarnac's translator rendered into English. They, too, were indicating a sculpture carved into a rock wall—but this one was a face.

Sarnac gazed for a long moment into that face, so entirely human, despite the exotic features—equally exotic to a Raehaniv, he had been assured—before turning to Tiraena.

"You say this second base was discovered in the asteroids of Raehan's sun at the same time as Colonel DiFalco's people blundered onto the one at Terranova?"

"Yes. The Free Raehaniv Fleet that operated in that asteroid belt during the occupation 'blundered onto' it, as you put it."

"Doesn't that strike you as just a little . . . unlikely?"

"Indubitably," Loruin answered for her. "The observation is far from new, I assure you. But we must face facts. The dating of both bases is beyond question; there is no possibility of some elaborate hoax. There was a space-travelling culture thirty thousand of your years ago, apparently human. And it is, of course, established that humanity evolved on Earth." He had received Natalya's full-bore lecture on the manifest scientific illiteracy of anyone who believed otherwise on today's Earth, which had outgrown the dogma that all viewpoints, however uninformed, were of fundamentally equal worth.

"So the ancestral Raehaniv must have been transferred from Earth," Sarnac said slowly. "And we have to assume that it was done by these people, rather than bringing some unknown *other* space-travelling civilization into the argument. You've got to shave with Occam's Razor." Loruin's translator couldn't cope, but Tiraena explained that Sarnac was referring to Hlaeronn's Fourth Fundamental Principle of Logic.

"Yes," Loruin gave his professorial nod. "And as to the obvious question of where that civilization came from, and where it has gone since, the answer is that we don't know. After the simultaneous discoveries of the two deserted bases, we thought it was only a matter of time until we'd find other sites, providing more clues. But none have come to light. We know no more than our ancestors did then. The paradox still stands." He turned to the holo dais, where long-dead Raehaniv were explaining other, less interesting finds, and ordered the computer to terminate the display. The lights came back on, and they looked at each other, awkward in the face of their inexplicable common humanity.

CHAPTER SIX

"The problem," Loruin addressed the meeting, "is that *Thrufarn* Taraen didn't bring any accredited diplomatic representatives with his fleet. There was no reason for it; we sent for help before we knew, or imagined, that they'd be needed."

"But," Murchison picked up the thread, "we want to proceed with as little delay as possible to finalize an alliance with the Solar Union. The sooner we commence joint operations against the Realm of Tarzhgul, the better."

"I'm sure our government will agree, *Thrufarn*," Sarnac nodded, carefully not letting himself contemplate the humor in such sonorities coming from a lieutenant senior grade.

"Therefore," Murchison resumed, "we suggest that both governments be informed simultaneously, by those most intimately connected with the reunion. The news will have all the more impact for being delivered by people who, by their very existence, underline its reality." He paused. "Clearly, I can't give you orders. And if you feel that your duty demands that all three of you return to the Solar Union as quickly as possible, I'll provide transportation. But if you're agreeable, I suggest that

Lieutenants Liu and Kowalski-O'Hara go to Raehan aboard one of my fastest frigates, to propose, in the name of your government, that a diplomatic mission be sent to this system to meet with representatives of the Solar Union."

"Agreeable?" Frank blurted. " 'Agreeable' is hardly the word, *Thrufarn*! My God, what a chance!"

"Yes!" Natalya's eyes flashed. "To see a world that we never imagined could exist. . . ." She trailed off, suddenly looking troubled. "But, *Thrufarn*, we are . . . well, we're only . . ."

Murchison smiled. "I know. You're being asked to speak for your government in matters of tremendous importance while still very young, and very junior. But I assure you that no one on Raehan will be worried about it. They'll only be interested in the news you bring." He turned to Sarnac and spoke formally. "Lieutenant Sarnac, you are the senior Solar Union officer in this system, so I must ask your concurrence."

"Of course, *Thrufarn*. But . . . what about me?"

"Ah, yes," Loruin reentered the conversation. "We feel that you, as senior surviving member of the Solar Union's expedition to this system, should represent the facts to your government. We propose that you return in company with my chief alien-contact officer, Rael zho'Vorlann." He smiled ruefully. "Not terribly appropriate, is it? This is hardly an 'alien contact,' but it's the best I can do. I don't have a 'reunion officer.' " He chuckled at his own wit, then continued.

"We also feel that Tiraena should accompany you. It is fortuitous that she is here, for her ancestry gives her a unique status—a living link between our people and yours, as it were. And her role in rescuing the three of you should enhance that status."

"No question about it," Sarnac agreed. "She'll be a sensation. The media will see to that." He exchanged a glance with her across the table, and knew that he was glad—very glad—that she was coming.

"As to your travel arrangements," Murchison continued, "you've told us that Sol is eight displacement transitions from here, but that the fifth will bring one to the outermost fortified system of the Solar Union."

"Yes, New Laurentia," Sarnac supplied. "I see where you're headed, *Thrufarn*. Our ship won't be broadcasting the right recognition code when we enter that system. But I can start transmitting on Fleet frequencies as soon as we come out of the displacement point, identifying myself and telling them not to shoot."

"Still, I think it would be best to appear as unthreatening as possible." Murchison turned to Loruin. "Don't you have a *Taelarn*-class courier boat here?"

"Yes, the *Norlaev*," Loruin confirmed, then turned to Sarnac. "The *Taelarn*-class is a small vessel with no armament except an antimissile laser, but capable of long hauls without refueling stops, and with comfortable accommodations for up to four passengers. It should cause less alarm at New Laurentia than one of the *thrufarn*'s warships."

"Yes, I would imagine so," Sarnac acknowledged, adjusting to the thought of spending the trip with Tiraena in the close quarters of some little VIP transport instead of having a frigate or something similar to rattle around in. Of course, Rael would be along, and so would the crew. . . .

"Well, that's settled," Loruin beamed. "You can depart as soon as your personal arrangements are complete."

"Some people have all the luck," Frank groused. " 'Tasha and I will be lucky to get junior officer staterooms aboard that frigate. You're going to be travelling like a goddamned ambassador aboard *that*." He waved at the *Taelarn*-class craft.

"That seems only fair," Sarnac said judiciously. Frank snorted and Natalya muttered something in what sounded like Russian.

They were standing in a flat clearing outside what seemed to sensors (including the Mark One Eyeball) to be a hillside but was in fact the entrance to the base's hangar. In the distance, Tiraena was saying her goodbyes to the Danuans, who would soon be transported by the magic of the Strange Ones back to the North, to rejoin what was left of their people. The three Scouts were saying their own goodbyes, and gazing at the bluish-silver shape that gleamed in the sunlight.

More remarkable than the sybaritic comfort of the transport's passenger accommodations, was the fact that it was sitting here, on the ground. In Sarnac's experience, interstellar vessels were, of necessity, orbit-to-orbit craft serviced by shuttles that could actually land on a planet. But the Raehaniv were able to cram the gravitic machinery that allowed displacement point transit, and even their continuous-displacement drive, into a streamlined hull able to operate in atmosphere under grav repulsion.

Even harder to accept was the fact that this ship could make it to New Laurentia without stopping to scoop reaction mass from some gas giant's atmosphere. The efficiency of the Raehaniv torch drive, plus the ability to store hydrogen as a hyper-dense plasma inside a containment field, explained it—or so he had been assured. But it still seemed to him that *Norlaev*, though it filled most of the clearing, was nevertheless impossibly small for its capabilities.

Tiraena approached, as Rael and *Norlaev*'s two-member crew joined them.

"Well," Natalya asked, "is the grav raft ready to take them back?"

"Yes," Tiraena replied. "Them, and a large load of trade

goods. It can't bring Cheel'kathu back, but it should help them rebuild their lives, and those of their people."

"It's the least we can do," Rael said. The alien-contact specialist was tall, slender and sharp-featured even by Raehaniv standards. She was also visibly middle-aged— which meant she was probably pushing an Earth century.

"Well," Command Pilot Saefal hle'Tordonn said, "we're ready for departure any time."

Sarnac felt an unaccustomed sensation of awkwardness. He clasped hands with Frank, then gave Natalya a quick hug. "Hey, you two shouldn't be complaining about your travel accommodations. Just don't tell the skipper that one stateroom is all you *really* need!"

Frank aimed a light punch at Sarnac's stomach, which he dodged, and they grappled for an instant of playful shoving.

"Boys will be boys," Natalya commented to Tiraena drily. "Bob, we'll see you again—on this planet."

"Right, 'Tasha. We'll all come back with the diplomatic missions. In the meantime, don't let Frank screw things up on Raehan too badly. We've already got *one* war!"

"Yeah," Frank retorted. "And remember to mention us once or twice while you're lying your ass off about your daring exploits! Tiraena, try and keep this crazy Creole honest, will you?"

She looked demure. "Oh, I think you can count on it."

The Raehaniv had come no closer than the Solar Union to achieving true artificial sentience. But their computers could do incredible things, including almost all aspects of astrogation. So Saefal was not overworked, and most of his piloting chores were performed by direct neural input to the ship. Similarly, his subordinate Taeronn hle'Sheina was able to spend more time as a purser than as an engineer.

With time on his hands, Saefal had no objection to

visits to the small bridge by passengers. Sarnac and Tiraena availed themselves of it when Saefal began lining up on the displacement point that would take them from the Lugh system. Rael, as usual, was absorbing Standard International English via neural induction. They stood behind the command chair where Saefal sat silhouetted against the star-blazing blackness, which featured a gas-giant planet close enough to show a visible disc.

"So we're all alone out here?" Sarnac asked.

"Not quite," Saefal said absently. "There's a small picket ship watching this displacement point. Pure routine, certainly. No danger from the Capella Chain, as you call it. But other than that, there's no one in this part of the outer system. Our heavy forces are concentrated at the displacement point connecting with Korvaash space. So basically you're right—we're all alone. . . ."

An alarm sounded, and Sarnac thought that he had never heard so obnoxious a noise.

Frowning, Saefal inserted the cable that linked him to the ship's brain. His expression went rapidly from annoyance to alarm, and his eyes lost focus as he concentrated on imagery being displayed via his optic nerve. After a moment, he turned to the two passengers.

"No point in concealing it." He spoke rapidly. "This is too small a ship for secrets. There's a large Korvaash vessel outbound from a satellite of that gas giant. Like us, he's headed for the displacement point. Projections indicate he won't intercept us before we transit—but he may get within missile range."

"Could you display your data on this Korvaash ship in a form I can access?" Sarnac requested with unusual calm.

Saefal gave the ship a wordless command, and a holographically projected display screen awoke.

"Tiraena, could you interpret this?"

His translator wasn't much help with the written

Raehaniv floating in midair. She complied, with a
calmness that equalled his own, but which surprised him
not at all. He listened, studied the visual imagery, then
turned to Saefal.

"That," he stated, "is what our intelligence types have
dubbed a *Gorgon*-class battlecruiser. A big mother, as
Korvaash ships generally are. We've encountered it often
enough to have learned something about its capabilities.
It carries some long-range missiles, but it's mostly armed
with energy weapons—lots of lasers, and some plasma
guns for really close-in work. It's not maneuverable,
but it's faster than you'd expect, and has tremendous
endurance."

"The ship that escaped into the outer system," Tiraena
breathed. "It must have been hiding among that gas giant's
moons."

"Yeah. And that planet currently happens to be on the
same side of the sun as the displacement point. Shit,"
he added dispassionately.

"The planet might have been so close that they could
have intercepted us before we were able to reach it," she
offered.

"Why am I not feeling grateful?" He turned back to
Saefal. "Can I also see our tactical situation?"

The holo tank that was part of *Norlaev*'s backup nav
system suddenly showed the gas giant, the displacement
point and the two ships. The baleful red dot of the *Gorgon*
was clearly maneuvering to approach the displacement
point at the correct bearing for transit. The Korvaasha
must have reached the same conclusions about the
impossibility of intercepting *Norlaev* before she could
transit, and were preparing for the possibility of a long
stern chase. Sarnac consulted his implanted calculator.

"I think you're right about them coming into missile
range before we can transit," he told Saefal.

"We have the antimissile laser," the pilot said hopefully.

"Yeah. But unless they shot away most of their missiles in the battle they should be able to overload our targeting capability. Oh well, at least we're not dealing with a primarily missile-armed ship."

"Look!" Tiraena pointed at the tactical display. "Our picket ship is accelerating away from the displacement point, toward us."

"He must want to give whatever help he can—precious little, against what's pursuing us." Saefal paused. "The *thrufarn's* fleet has received the distress signal this ship sent out when we heard the alarm." Neutrino-pulse communication was effectively faster than light within interplanetary ranges, and the message would have had time to cross the system. "He'll be dispatching his fastest units on a pursuit vector." He didn't need to add that there was no way those units, just now getting up speed on the other side of the system, could possibly catch up to the Korvaash battlecruiser this side of New Laurentia, or Sol.

"I'd better tell Rael," Tiraena said, and left the bridge.

Sarnac and Saefal watched the crawling points of light in the holo tank in silence. Presently Tiraena and Rael joined the silent vigil. The Raehaniv tendency toward emotional reserve—Sarnac understood that it had been much more extreme in the old days—could be annoying, but at least they weren't given to panic. Shortly, Taeronn arrived and manned the communications station.

The picket, accelerating sunward, was closing at a tremendous relative velocity. Taeronn raised its skipper, who calculated that he would approach *Norlaev* at about the time that the latter came under missile attack and offered to contribute his antimissile firepower. It was all he could do.

Then the small blips of missiles began to appear in the tank, moving ahead of the *Gorgon*, slightly sooner than Sarnac had expected to see them. Then another wave of them, and another. He counted them and whistled silently through his teeth.

"He's launching at his missiles' extreme range. And he's launching *all* of them—that's a *Gorgon*'s full complement! It must be an all-out effort to saturate our antimissile defenses before we can transit."

"One which may very well succeed," Saefal added grimly. "We'll have to engage the first wave, at least, without the help of the picket."

The missiles came on, seemingly at a crawl in the tank, actually adding with their own drives to the velocity the *Gorgon* had already piled atop the gas giant's orbital velocity. Sarnac gave up trying to calculate it all, and merely watched, with a strangely calm fascination, as the first wave of missiles came into range of their laser.

Dots of flame began to appear and disappear in the view-aft screen, and missile blips flickered and vanished in the tank. The little ship's fire-control computer had plenty of time for targeting, given the long flight times of missiles launched at extreme range on a stern chase, and it was making the most of it. But the missiles kept coming.

Then the tiny dots of decoy drones began to move ahead of the onrushing picket ship in the tank. The little dots passed *Norlaev* and plunged toward the oncoming Korvaash missiles, whose relatively primitive homing systems they could easily fool. But a picket could only carry a few of them. More flashes appeared in the view-aft as what was left of the first wave of missiles—and most of the second wave—expended their nuclear fury on the drones.

Sarnac watched, mesmerized, as the blips of *Norlaev* and the picket passed in opposite directions, almost grazing each other in the tank. The picket could now bring its antimissile lasers into play, but it was closing with the Korvaash missiles at a relative velocity which allowed scant time for targeting solutions.

"What's the picket doing?" Rael wondered out loud as the blip accelerated onward. Sarnac was silent, for he suddenly knew.

Then Saefal also grasped it. "He's headed straight for the Korvaash ship!" he blurted. "He's going to try to ram!" Everyone else looked stunned; apparently the *kamikaze* tradition was foreign to the Raehaniv.

"Tell him to veer off," Rael said in a shaken voice. "It's not worth it . . . it's, well, it's somehow . . ." She could find no words. But then it became academic, for one of the missiles homed in on the picket and the largest flash yet lit up the view-aft.

After a moment of awkward silence, Saefal spoke in carefully neutral tones. "Approaching displacement point. Two missiles still closing."

No one could think of anything to say as they watched their fates being played out in the tank. Sarnac discovered that, without a word or a glance, he and Tiraena had clasped hands. With agonizing slowness, the blip that represented their five lives crawled toward the displacement point. Less slowly, the two tiny missile blips closed on them. No one even broke the silence to cheer when one missile flickered into nonexistence, for its mate was nearing them in the tank, and it was almost touching. Tiraena's grip on Sarnac's hand grew painful.

"Stand by for transit!"

Saefal's announcement shattered the silence just before the universe seemed to contract and then reexpand into a new pattern. As Sarnac came out of the familiar feeling of strangeness, he noticed that Saefal was leaning back in his command chair—drenched with sweat. The command pilot must have known how close the missile had really come before flashing through the empty space where *Norlaev* had been and continuing on into the void between the stars.

"What about the Korvaash ship?" Tiraena's voice was steady, and she had let go of Sarnac's hand.

Saefal raised his head wearily and gave it a slow shake. "Can't say. It was trying to line itself up for a transit. As to whether they'll succeed in getting into the right angle of insertion or not . . ." his voice trailed off dully.

So their vigil continued as they drove on into this stellar system toward the region where Sarnac, though no astrogator, knew from memory held the displacement point that led onward into the Capella Chain. With the search thus narrowed, *Norlaev*'s grav scanners sufficed to locate the displacement point with the requisite exactness. For a time they waited in a kind of drained torpor as delayed reaction to their escape set in. Then tension began to mount anew as the time approached when the computer, drawing on its last observations of the *Gorgon*, predicted that their pursuer's displacement transit to this system, if successful, could be expected. A grav scanner was kept trained on the displacement point. They waited, saying little.

When it came, the scanner's audible alarm signal was all too much like the tolling of a bell.

"Well," Saefal said unnecessarily, "they transited." He stared at the holo tank, the red Korvaash blip reflecting off his wet brow in the semidarkness. "At least I don't see any missiles."

"No." Sarnac's voice was low, as if wary of shattering the brittle quiet. "As I said, they shot their wad back in the Lugh system. They'll have to get within beam weapon range of us." He did not add that the instant that happened would be the instant of their deaths.

Saefal's expression became, if possible, even more intense. "This ship is designed for comfort and endurance, not speed. I suppose this . . . *Gorgon* class can overhaul us eventually?"

"Yeah. Remember, that's a *big* brute—they've got a

lot of tonnage to push, but they also have powerful drives and lots of tankage for reaction mass. And they've had plenty of time to tank up, skulking around that gas giant. Oh, it'll take them time to catch us. In fact," he added with a wry smile, "I calculate that they won't do it until the system just before New Laurentia."

"But," —Rael spoke hesitantly as she ventured onto unfamiliar ground— "why can't we simply use our continuous-displacement drive and leave them far behind?"

Saefal gave her a sharp glance, then softened, and carefully explained what was, to him, elementary. "There is a radius around each sun called the mass limit—it varies depending on the strength of the sun's gravity— within which the continuous-displacement drive won't function. And in the case of most stars, including all those on our route, displacement points occur within this limit. So, travelling between displacement points within systems, we're never going to be in a region where we can engage the drive."

"But," she persisted, "couldn't we change course and . . . ?"

"No," Saefal shook his head. "Our reaction mass is sufficient to get us to this New Laurentia system the direct, economical way, but with nothing to spare for unplanned maneuvering or acceleration. And where would we go on continuous-displacement drive? We've no notion of where the stars of the Solar Union are located in realspace."

"Neither do I," Sarnac admitted. "I wouldn't even if I were a trained astrogator. We've never needed to know. For us, interstellar travel simply means following the displacement chains."

"So," Saefal went on remorselessly, "all we can do is continue along our planned course and hope for a stroke of good luck—or, rather, of bad luck for them."

The two blips continued to crawl across the tank.

✧ ✧ ✧

Sarnac stood unsteadily for a moment after his cabin door slid shut behind him, in a twilight state beyond fatigue, before toppling forward into his bunk.

They had managed a little rest while they proceeded toward their second transit. But afterwards, when they lay in yet another new sky, had come the stress-fraught ritual on the bridge—waiting in silence for the Korvaash ship's appearance. When the sensors had announced that their nemesis had transited on schedule, the pervading fog of doom had seemed even thicker than before. At least this time they hadn't had to wait quite as long for his arrival.

That's got to be some kind of new record for putting the best possible face on things. Even thinking was an effort. *One more time and I'm gonna smash that audio signal.* His mind wandered on in a kind of exhausted petulance. Sleep began to enfold him.

The door chimed for admittance. He rolled over with a groan and said, "Enter." The computer, told to obey his voice when it spoke to this door, now slid it aside. Against the lighted corridor beyond, he recognized Tiraena's silhouetted figure. She stepped into the cabin with uncharacteristic stiffness, and the door closed.

"We're not going to get away, are we?"

So much for small talk. Sarnac raised himself on one elbow and tried to sound nonchalant. "Oh, we can't really say that. We've got two more transits before they can catch us. That's two chances for them to blow it and miss a transit—in which case we'd be home free."

"But how likely is that?" Her voice was calm, but her body was still held rigidly.

"Well, you know how crude their instrumentation is. . . ."

"But how sophisticated does it have to be when we're transiting each displacement point ahead of them, showing them the exact coordinates and angle of insertion?" She shook her head, and he thought he saw an odd little smile in the gloom. "No, all they have to do is follow us. And we can't even run away from them!"

This was the true essence of the hell they were in. *Norlaev* could have piled on acceleration, pulled ahead of her pursuer—and run out of reaction mass short of her goal. The same applied to any evasive maneuverings in the systems through which they were passing. They could only proceed on schedule, with death gradually closing the range astern.

She stirred in the semidarkness, and this time he was certain that he could make out a smile. "We Raehaniv used to be masters of self-deception, before the Korvaash occupation. But generations since have swung the other way. Looking the truth squarely in the face has become almost a fetish with us."

"But you're not entirely Raehaniv, you know. What about the part that's Terran?"

"My great-grandfather fled from a world that was throwing rationality to the winds as it slid backward into a new dark age. The Terran exiles' influence had a lot to do with the new outlook."

"So now you don't bullshit yourselves. But you don't seem to be the fatalistic type either."

"No. We'll fight our doom for as long as we can. But we don't, as you say, bullshit ourselves about it. And when it becomes unavoidable, we recognize that our time is limited, and we treasure whatever comfort we can give each other."

She drew a breath, then reached up and touched a spot above her left breast. Her shipsuit fell open along a diagonal seam and hung loosely about her now-relaxed body in the shadows.

Sarnac realized that he wasn't as exhausted as he had thought.

CHAPTER SEVEN

It was depressingly soon after their next transit when the Korvaash battlecruiser appeared behind them at the displacement point, producing a mournful noise from the grav scanner and a crimson blip that was now noticeably closer to their green one in the tank.

Saefal stared fixedly at the tank, and his abstracted expression could only partly be accounted for by his direct neural linkage with the ship. Sarnac understood. *Norlaev* might not exactly be a capital ship, but Saefal was her captain, responsible for the safe arrival of his passengers, and he was failing. His lack of fault for the failure was immaterial, for his was a responsibility that admitted of neither excuse nor mitigation.

He disengaged his linkage cable and turned slowly toward the others. "Well, there's no longer any room for error in the calculations. They won't catch us in this system, but if they manage the next transit on schedule they'll come up to beam-weapons range in the system after this, before we can transit from there to New Laurentia." He stopped, awkward with the silence into which his words had dropped, but unable to continue. What more can you say to people after pronouncing their death sentence?

It hasn't registered yet, Sarnac knew. *It's too unreal. Standing here in the silent, comfort-controlled perfection of this ship's life-support system only a few feet from vacuum, while our doom approaches.*

He tried to speak, then cleared his throat and tried again. "Look, this is normally not my style, but . . . well, maybe when they catch us we could make a show of surrendering and then, assuming that they accept, wait for them to get close, and then blow up this ship, taking them with us." He felt almost embarrassed, for it was *definitely* not his style—it was like something out of bad VR adventure. But it was all he had to offer.

Saefal gave him an annoyed glance. "Don't be ridiculous! The *Taelarn*-class isn't intended to be blown up. It might be possible if this was a warship. But all we've got is the powerplant—and fusion power generators are so designed that it's *impossible* for them to detonate. I can't imagine there's any way to do it. Of course," he continued thoughtfully, "the Korvaasha don't have tractor beams, any more than your people do. Maybe we could try . . ." He trailed to a miserable halt. "Now I'm the one being ridiculous. At our first attempt to make a ramming run, they could obliterate us with their beam weapons. No, we can't hope to hurt them. And our only hope of survival is to surrender."

"Knowing the Korvaasha," Tiraena said stonily, "that offers only short-term survival, probably under conditions to which a quick, clean death would be preferable."

No one had anything to add. Sarnac's eyes strayed from the tank to the viewport and the stars in the familiar configurations he remembered from the trip out, seemingly more than a lifetime ago. He looked ahead at the primary star, still a remote blue flame with its white dwarf companion invisible. Then his gaze swung to the little yellow-white star in Cygnus, and he reflected on the irony. So near and yet so far away. . . .

Hey! Wait a minute!

After a time, he became aware of Tiraena's concerned voice, as if from a great distance. "Bob, what is it? You look as though . . ."

"Jesus H. Christ!" he exploded. "Do you realize where we *are*? What system this is? But no, of course you don't." He forced himself to stop babbling and sprang to the viewport, pointing theatrically at the primary star. "This is *Sirius!*"

"Well, of course, Bob." Tiraena wore the same puzzled look as the others. "We all know this is serious. Desperate, in fact."

"No, no, no! Sirius is the name of this system's star! We identified it on our way out from Sol—which is *there!*" His pointing finger swung toward Cygnus and the yellow-white star.

Saefal sailed out of his command chair. "What . . . I mean . . . are you saying that Sol is within naked-eye distance of this star?"

"Sure. Why do you think we have a name for Sirius? We've been looking at it throughout all our history!" He took a deep breath. "The Capella Chain doubles back on itself in realspace, which you must know occasionally happens. We're still five displacement transits from Sol—but there it sits, eight-point-six Terran light-years away, as the photon flies!"

"But," Rael spluttered, "you've been aware all along that this displacement chain we're following passes through this system. . . ."

" . . So why didn't you tell us?" Taeronn finished for her, glaring at Sarnac.

"Well, to be honest, I just didn't make the connection. I mean, to us of the Solar Union the displacement network defines the only stellar interrelationships that count. The realspace arrangement of the stars is just a matter of pretty lights in the sky! The fact that this displacement chain comes so close to Sol in realspace was interesting but irrelevant. It's been a long time since I've even thought of it. Sol might as well be in the Andromeda Galaxy for all we could reach it from Sirius, not having your continuous-displacement drive."

"But we *do* have it!" Saefal looked like exactly what he was: a man who had been shown a road out of hell. He flung himself back into the command chair, reinserted the linkage cable and became one with the ship. Almost immediately, the stars began to crawl across the viewport as *Norlaev* reoriented herself. Grav generators compensated smoothly but could not prevent a thrumming from running through the soles of their feet as the torch drive began to push them outward, accelerating to reach the mass limit in the minimum possible time with all restraints of reaction-mass conservation removed.

A bit of time passed before the red blip began to change course in the tank.

"They must be shitting in their pants, or whatever Korvaasha do," Sarnac chortled.

"They must think we've lost our minds," Taeronn breathed. "Now that we've changed course, it's no longer a stern chase. Look, they're coming into an intercept course, based on our present vector. They must calculate that they can overhaul us before we'll be able to reach wherever it is we're going."

"Which they must think is another displacement point in the outer reaches of this system," Saefal said in the abstracted way of one linked directly with a very complex computer. "When we pass the mass limit, they'll *really* shit in their pants," he added, getting into the spirit of the thing with the help of the translation program.

"And by then," Tiraena put in, sliding an arm around Sarnac's waist and squeezing, "it will be too late. They'll be stranded in this system, surveying for displacement points."

"With any luck, the *thrufarn's* ships will arrive here while they're doing it," Sarnac added happily, returning Tiraena's hug and watching the yellow-white star in the viewport.

Sol was not visibly brighter when they passed the mass limit, but Sirius was little more than a very bright blue star in the view-aft.

Saefal cut the drive. It must have been final proof to their pursuers that they had lost their sanity. He used gyros to point the free-falling *Norlaev* toward the bright star in Cygnus. Then he gave a command, and the impossible—as defined by Sarnac's civilization—began to happen.

There was no physical sensation, and no apparent change in the outside universe. But in the view-aft, Sirius was receding from them at a rate of many times lightspeed, with no Doppler effects.

Sarnac had been told many times what to expect under continuous-displacement drive. There was no Doppler shift because there was no real velocity beyond what *Norlaev* had already built up. Instead, a series of gravitational pulses—akin to the effect that allowed displacement point transit, but far more intense—caused her to make a succession of effectively instantaneous transpositions of a few hundred meters each, without crossing the intervening distance. Given titanic amounts of power, the process could be repeated millions of times per second, and light could be outpaced. In effect, they existed in normal space at a certain "frequency." Any nearby objects would have been subject to mind-shaking visual distortions—but there were no such objects. There were only the distant stars, still in the same relative positions each time *Norlaev* popped back into the universe.

He had heard it all explained, and he was even fairly sure he understood the explanations. Nevertheless, his flesh tingled as he watched Sirius dwindle at a rate forbidden by the laws of physics and merge into the star-fields as merely another star. He was relieved to note that, as he had been assured, the myriad small transpositions of continuous-displacement travel did not produce the disturbing sense of wrongness that accompanied the single astronomical one between two displacement points.

Saefal swung around to face his passengers. His face was still haggard from lack of sleep, but now there was life behind it.

"Our course is laid in. The computer can handle everything until we reach Sol's mass limit." He looked at Sarnac in an almost shamefaced way that baffled the Terran. "Now, you must realize that while the *Taelarn* class can ordinarily make a respectable pseudovelocity—over fifteen hundred times lightspeed—the powerplant burns up a lot of fuel doing it. On this trip, we didn't anticipate operating under continuous-displacement drive at all, but we did want to make New Laurentia without having to stop and skim reaction mass from some gas giant. So a trade-off was made: more reaction mass for less fuel. So we're going to have to travel at a rate that . . ." He trailed off, looking apologetic, and Sarnac began to feel worried. "Well, the long and short of it is that we're going to be en route for almost six days before arriving at Sol."

Sarnac was momentarily without the power of speech, but quickly returned to form. "Oh well, I suppose it'll have to do," he said airily, "if you're *sure* that's *really* the best you can manage." Everyone laughed with a spontaneity almost unnatural for Raehaniv, and Tiraena punched him in the ribs before he could continue his petulant tourist number.

"Don't get cocky," she warned. "I still haven't forgiven you for waiting until the last minute to tell us we were within easy range of Sol . . . which I'm sure you did deliberately!"

He had given up protesting that he still couldn't adjust to the notion of eight-and-a-half-plus light-years as easy range, after a lifetime of knowing the stars to be, by definition, accessible only via the displacement network. So he changed the subject.

"I wonder what the Korvaasha thought just now? I suppose we simply vanished, as far as they were concerned."

"Well," Taeronn said, "if they had a grav scanner trained on us, they got a very strong reading from the series of rapid-fire grav pulses—which they'll have difficulty interpreting. But as far as visual effects are concerned, you're right. A ship under continuous-displacement drive is effectively invisible to anyone, except an occupant of another ship travelling along with it, with both ships' drives synchronized to jump in and out of normal space in unison. Existing at the same 'frequency,' they can see each other, communicate with each other . . ."

"But . . ." Sarnac hesitated. "Look, I don't know too much about it, but it seems as if it should be impossible for two ships to travel in formation like that. I mean, the drive can't function at all inside a gravity well of any significant strength, right? Well, each of those two ships is generating a very strong artificial gravity field— a zillion times a second. If they're doing it at the same time, shouldn't they interfere with each other's drives?"

"In theory, yes," Saefal acknowledged. "But the grav pulse is a very localized phenomenon, and it doesn't affect the universe outside the drive field. The two ships would have to be very close together for that to happen." He stood up with a long, shuddering stretch. "But that's all academic now. The Korvaasha don't have continuous-displacement drive, and we're free and clear of them."

"Good riddance to bad rubbish," Sarnac said with feeling. "With any luck, they won't have enough reaction mass left to get back to either of the Sirius displacement points. And even if they do, they can only go on toward New Laurentia or back the way they came. So the only question is whether the New Laurentia Defense Command or Murchison gets to reduce them to their component atoms!"

"Precisely." Saefal smiled for the first time in far too long. "And now, by the authority vested in me as captain, I decree a small celebration. This ship can provide quite a little banquet if need be!"

The voyage to Sol went quickly, the days seemingly compressed by the exhilaration of escape—or perhaps it was only the contrast to the tense stretches of distended time they had spent watching their pursuers inch closer. And then, too, Sarnac was kept busy apologizing to Tiraena in the traditional way.

But there came a time when Sol, while still undeniably a mere star, was by far the brightest object in the heavens—a yellow-white flare, for which the ship must polarize the viewport, lest its passengers turn their fragile eyes directly upon it. It began to wax perceptibly if you watched it long enough. And Sarnac found himself doing that more and more.

"How much longer to Sol's mass limit?" Rael asked.

"About an hour and a quarter," Saefal replied, his translator obligingly converting the Raehaniv units for Sarnac, to whom he now turned. "So you have that long before you have to start broadcasting."

"No rush even then," the Terran assured him. "It'll be a while after we cut the drive, before anybody notices us. And there won't be any grav scanners trained on us before that." His computer-assisted holo constructions had confirmed that neither of Sol's displacement points was anywhere near their straight-line course from Sirius. They would appear in a part of the sky where no one had any business being, and he couldn't help sniggering at the thought of the cat they'd put among the beribboned pigeons at Fleet HQ.

But for now he could only gaze at the indescribable beauty of the not-quite-sun ahead. Some tiny blue star beyond Sol was barely visible just to the side of its flame, and Sarnac imagined that he was discerning the blue planet of his birth, orbiting close to Sol's life-giving warmth. . . .

There was no physical sensation, no tumbling about a wildly canting deck. But they all suddenly looked at each other, aware that something had *happened*. An instant later Saefal, in linkage with the ship, stiffened. Before he even spoke, Sarnac returned his gaze to the viewport and knew, with chill certainty, that Sol had stopped growing.

"The continuous-displacement drive has cut off without orders," Saefal said rapidly. "I don't know why. Maybe. . . ."

"Look!" Rael's voice, quavering on the edge of panic, brought all their heads around. She was pointing at the view-aft screen that they had all been ignoring.

Most of it was filled with the brutally massive bulk of what Sarnac recognized at once as a *Gorgon*-class battlecruiser.

For a long moment they were all struck dumb by the image. Not by its overwhelming size, nor by its asymmetrical hideousness, although like all Korvaash engineering it seemed to go beyond mere crude functionality into realms of gratuitous ugliness. Not even by the death they knew it held. No, it was the sheer, mind-numbing impossibility of its presence that left them speechless while the *Gorgon* crept even closer, blotting out even more of the stars. Nobody even mentioned the possibility of activating the fusion drive in an attempt to get away, at this ridiculously short energy-weapon range.

Finally, Saefal gave his head an old man's, slow, unsteady shake.

"It can't be," he whispered. "The Realm of Tarzhgul can't have continuous-displacement drive . . . can they?"

"Of course not." Sarnac spoke a little more loudly. "If they did, the worlds of the Solar Union would be all bones and ashes by now."

"Then how . . . ?" Saefal began—and then something happened that was, in its way, even more startling than the *Gorgon*'s appearance.

Throughout all of the long way from the Lugh system, the ship had provided them with a steady one Raehaniv gravity—0.87 G Terran—and compensated effortlessly for all accelerations and course changes. So the sudden jolt, mild as it was, shocked them. The artificial gravity resumed control over inertia, even as they were steadying themselves with whatever was at hand to grab, and they all looked back to the view-aft, and saw the *Gorgon* growing.

"They can't have tractor beams either," Saefal said quietly.

"But *we* do." They all stared at Tiraena as she hurried on. "Remember what the *thrufarn* said about one of his frigates being missing and unaccounted for after the battle?" She looked at each of their blank faces in turn. "Well, can anybody think of any other explanation?"

"Tiraena, are you saying that the Korvaash survivors captured the frigate and somehow managed to duplicate all of its technology—the continuous-displacement drive, the tractor beam—while hiding in the outer system of Lugh?" Saefal couldn't keep the disbelief out of his voice.

"No, of course not. That would be impossible. They didn't copy it. They *used* it!" She turned to Sarnac. "I imagine a Korvaash ship this big would have a large hold for auxiliary craft."

"Oh, yeah. Cavernous. They like to carry around all sorts of . . ." His voice trailed off as realization came. "Do you mean this Raehaniv frigate is sitting inside the *Gorgon*?"

"I strongly suspect so. They must have tortured the crew into showing them how to operate things. And, since there's no need for the frigate to be kept in operational state, they could cut it open to allow themselves access. Saefal, couldn't the drive field be made to encompass that battlecruiser, and a good deal more besides?"

"Well, yes, but the frigate's drive would be designed for a ship of its small mass, and, as you know, ship mass is a factor in its efficiency. . . ." Saefal seemed to deflate. "But that wouldn't make it impossible, would it? It would just slow them down—which is why it's taken them this long to catch us, as we ambled along!"

"And when they did, the drive fields prevented each other from working, as you were explaining before. But . . ." Sarnac frowned in perplexity. "*How*? How could they gradually close the range from astern, without us even noticing them?"

"Remember what I said about a ship under continuous-displacement drive existing at a certain frequency? Ships at different frequencies are absolutely undetectable to each other. They must have calculated how long it would take to overhaul us and waited till then to switch to our 'frequency.' " Saefal was speaking like an automaton. "So now we've resumed the vector that we possessed at the moment we engaged the drive back at Sirius. . . ."

The communicator squealed for attention, causing them all to jump. Taeronn looked questioningly at Saefal, who nodded slowly and acknowledged it.

All Korvaash translator devices produced the same uninflected Standard English. But Sarnac was trained to distinguish individual Korvaasha, and he knew the face in the comm screen to be that of the Interrogator.

"As you are aware," the Korvaasha began, "you have been tractored. You will be brought inside our ship. There, you will open your hatches and prepare to be boarded. You will be killed at the first sign of resistance."

The screen went blank. They were left looking at each other, and at the view-aft, now completely filled by the *Gorgon's* belly, its hold gaping open to vacuum.

"Could they be bluffing about killing us?" Rael sounded as if she was trying to convince herself. "After all, they could have killed us already if they wanted to."

"Oh, they doubtless would prefer us as prisoners," Saefal said listlessly, eyes fixed on the screen as the hold seemed to come down and swallow them up. "But they won't hesitate to kill us . . . one at a time, to intimidate the survivors." A clang was heard, and felt through the soles of their feet, as *Norlaev* was lowered to the deck formed by the massive doors that had slid shut. Filling most of the vast, dimly lit hold was the ravaged hull of a *Torafv*-class frigate—the source of the tractor beam that had reeled them into the *Gorgon's* bowels.

Saefal's voice firmed. "I am still commanding officer of this ship, and I will not permit any useless gestures. It is our duty to remain alive as long as possible." He stepped to the control board and shut down all the ship's systems except basic life-support. The heavier gravity of the Korvaash homeworld clamped down, somehow setting a seal on their captivity.

Shortly, a squad of Korvaasha emerged into the hold— heavily armed but without vac suits—confirming what instrument readings had already reported concerning the return of atmosphere. Saefal opened the hatch. Chill, vile-smelling air began to invade *Norlaev*.

For a while nothing happened, and they began to fidget. Then clanging, booming sounds began to be audible throughout the hull.

"Guess they're not taking any chances," Sarnac said, even as the intruding air began to take on the odor of capture gas. He and Tiraena had time for the briefest eye contact, but did not quite succeed in falling to the deck facing each other before paralysis overtook them.

When the Korvaasha entered, moving awkwardly through spaces designed on the human scale, it became clear that they were taking even fewer chances than he had thought. Sarnac's sluggishly moving eyes caught sight of one of them aiming a sonic stunner.

When he awoke, his head felt as though it was being split apart by a spike. He was on a kind of long balcony overlooking what must be the *Gorgon*'s bridge—enormous, crowded with instrument consoles, lit with the same burnt-orange gloom as all Korvaash interiors, and half-surrounded by a wide-curving viewport of transparent armorplast. The starlight that flooded the vast chamber, especially that of the bright yellow-white star dead ahead, did nothing to ameliorate its squalid, hideous functionality. Nearby were consoles with screens—one showing *Norlaev* resting in the hold, and another, apparently the view-aft.

But none of that registered until later. He was aware of nothing but the Interrogator, regarding him with that single, disturbing eye. And he knew he had awakened into a nightmare from which there would be no awakening.

CHAPTER EIGHT

At first the Interrogator didn't speak, and Sarnac began to struggle to awareness of things other than the sickening headache, the oppressive gravity, and the air that was only marginally breathable in its thickness and foulness.

He noticed that his arms and legs were strapped to some kind of frame, extending not quite upright from the deck. Then he heard a low moan. He turned his head— at least *it* wasn't secured—and saw Tiraena stretched on another frame beside his.

"I see that you both have recovered consciousness," came the murmur of the Interrogator's translator pendant. "You need not look around for your three fellow inferior beings. They are in cryogenic suspension, where you will join them as soon as I have satisfied myself that you are, indeed, two of those I captured on the planet's surface."

You know damned well we are, Sarnac thought. Humans were more individually variable than Korvaasha, and an intelligence specialist like this could surely have no trouble distinguishing one human from another. But he must go through the motions of seeming to have difficulty doing so, for inferior beings were beneath notice. It was a quintessentially Korvaash form of stupidity, and Sarnac was heartened by this evidence of weakness.

He swallowed to moisten his mouth. "Why cryogenic suspension?" he croaked. "Why not just kill us? Come to think of it, why did you bother to take our ship? You've already got the frigate down there" —he jerked his chin toward the screen monitoring the hold— "with all its technological goodies."

"You may still be useful sources of information when we reach the Realm. You will be frozen because we anticipate a long voyage and cannot spare the food to keep you alive." The Interrogator's silence about the frigate provided confirmation.

"How do you even expect to find the Realm? You don't even know where you are."

"But we do," the mechanical hum said remorselessly. "We have learned from your ship's log that we are approaching the capital system of the Solar Union. Its location is an interesting datum in itself. We knew your destination was the Solar Union because you departed via the displacement point through which you had entered the Lugh system." He must, Sarnac reflected, have added the name to his translator program's Standard English repertoire after learning it from their log. "As for how we will find our way home, our computer has inferred our realspace location from the positions of various identifiable giant stars. By comparing this sky with its records of the skies of our various worlds, it has pinpointed a system of the Realm, close enough to be reachable by continuous-displacement drive."

"But," Tiraena asked unsteadily, "how could you be sure that you'd be able to locate such a system when you started to follow us?"

"We could not. But it was our only hope of escaping from the Lugh system. The displacement point leading directly to the Realm was heavily guarded. Besides, returning home was only one of our objectives. The other was stopping you."

"Why?" Sarnac asked through the haze of pain in his head, even though he thought that he already knew the answer.

"When your ship departed toward the Solar Union, its objective was obvious: to make contact, and to reunite the two separate branches of your noxious species. Such an alliance, with Raehaniv technology, could . . . possibly cause the Realm serious inconvenience."

Sarnac looked him straight in the eye. "Yeah, that's one way to put it," he said softly. "But you haven't prevented it, you know. Another ship has departed for Raehan, carrying officers of the Solar Union. They'll try again to reach Sol, and they'll succeed. You can't stop it from happening." He was fully aware of his recklessness, but didn't care, for he knew that he was already dead— and had accepted it. *Being dead has its advantages*, he thought. *Liberating, somehow.*

An instant passed before the Interrogator made a surprising reply. "You are correct," came the expressionless cybernetic vocalization. "The alliance is inevitable, but your voyage to Sol was clearly intended to expedite it. By stopping you, we have delayed it, giving the Realm more time to prepare by copying the Raehaniv technology we will bring back. More importantly, we will know about that technology's capabilities, and not be caught by surprise. Also, knowing that the alliance *is* an alliance, we can take measures to break it by offering a separate peace to one party or the other."

"That will never work with the Raehaniv," Tiraena said, her voice cold and hard. "We know from experience what the Korvaasha are."

"Then we will target the Solar Union. One of the defining characteristics of humans is their willingness to betray their own kind for the merest hope, however unrealistic, of personal gain."

All at once, Sarnac's headache worsened. *He may actually be right*, he thought sickly. *Probably not about the separate peace ploy—at least I don't think the Solar Union is that naive. And their copied technology will always be one step behind what we'll be able to field. But the unexpectedness of the continuous-displacement drive and the rest is an advantage we've been counting on. Without that element of surprise . . . oh, we'll still win. But how many more humans will die for that victory?* Another jag of pain spiked through his head.

It occurred to him that the Interrogator had been unusually talkative for a Korvaasha. Garrulous, in fact. Then insight came, and he spoke insouciantly.

"Yeah, very clever on your part. So clever that you needed to tell somebody about it. Somebody who could appreciate the cleverness . . . which means somebody besides the members of your own society, who've been overspecialized and cyberneticized into organic robots!" He shook his head slowly. "God, what a hell your life must be! You're probably one of the few genuine individuals you know, because there aren't many others whose jobs require the capability of original thought. And almost all of those must be either above or below you in the caste structure—they might as well be different species!"

"Bob, don't!"

He barely heard Tiraena's frantic whisper, for he was eyeing the Interrogator closely, and he thought he could detect the same signs of emotion that he had once before, on a beach on Danu. And to be even barely perceptible across the chasm of species and worlds, the emotion must be volcanic indeed. But the words from the voder were, of course, as flat and uninflected as ever.

"Enough. I demean myself by talking to inferior

beings—an occupational hazard of my work." He turned and addressed a guard, though the translator continued to translate in default of a contrary command. "Take them to Cryogenics and commence the freezing procedure.'"

The guard pointed an instrument at them, and the clamps securing Sarnac flipped open. Massive hands like mechanical grapples seized both of his arms and hauled him to his feet. Tiraena was also upright, and they sought each other's eyes . . . when Sarnac was distracted by a sudden motion. The Interrogator swung around, incongruously swift for so large a being, to face a Korvaasha at a console.

The console operator's words—his neck-slits were rippling with obvious haste—were of course inaudible. But the voder continued to generate Standard English translations of the Interrogator's replies. *Must be easy for him to forget that the thing is on*, Sarnac reflected, *since he can't hear the sounds it emits*. It was like listening to one end of a phone conversation.

"What do you mean a 'gravitational anomaly, stationary with respect to Sol'? Explain. . . . Very well, order Piloting to secure from free fall and prepare to change course. . . . What? Yes, I am aware that a fusion drive cannot be activated instantly . . . Are you saying that we cannot avoid this thing? How long before we . . . ?'"

The Interrogator must have remembered the translator was on, for he suddenly rounded on the guard. "Remove them!" But Sarnac didn't even hear him, for his universe had narrowed to what he was seeing in the viewport.

At first there was a tiny distortion, dead ahead, that made the bright yellow-white star that was Sol flicker and twinkle, rather than shine with the steady, diamond-hard luminescence that stars displayed in the vacuum of space. Then, as the *Gorgon* plunged on in free fall at a velocity built up through two planetary systems' worth of acceleration, it resolved itself into a torus-shaped distortion in the universe, growing at an ever-increasing rate. Then, faster than thought, almost too fast to register on Sarnac's retina, it rushed up, a hoop of insubstantial unreality flung by a playful god. And they were through it. . . .

Sarnac found himself sagging in the grip of the Korvaash guards, fighting a sensation of wrongness akin to that of a displacement transition, but far worse. It was as if his entire being knew that something truly unnatural had been done, some outrage performed upon the proper order of Creation.

He grew aware that Tiraena was also hanging limp, her expression as disoriented as he knew his own must be. But none of the Korvaasha seemed to be experiencing the sensation. The Interrogator gazed at the viewport, where the stars continued serenely in their accustomed array, and resumed his conversation with the console monitor.

"Good . . . no damage or casualties reported from any station. . . . What was that? Slight discrepancies in Astronomy's observations? Well, order . . ." He suddenly remembered the humans' presence and swung around to face the guard. "Why are they still here?"

The guard's reply was inaudible, but the gesture he made to his underlings transcended language. Sarnac and Tiraena were shoved toward a hatch, but before passing through it they heard one mechanical word from behind them: "Wait." Their captors brought them up short with brutal suddenness and spun them around to face the Interrogator.

"One moment. You appeared to experience some distress following our passage through the . . ." Sarnac wasn't sure whether it was the Korvaasha himself or his translator that seemed to be at a loss for words. "I am curious as to this, since the phenomenon, while admittedly unexplained, is manifestly harmless."

Even as Sarnac opened his mouth to reply, he knew something was bothering him about the scene before him. *Probably something childishly simple—what's wrong with this picture?* Then he knew . . . and his mouth remained open.

"Well," the Interrogator prompted.

At first, Sarnac could not reply—it was a thing so small, and yet so overwhelming. When he did speak, all he could manage was, "Look at the view-aft."

The Interrogator did, and so did Tiraena. And for a time beyond time, none of them moved. They could only stare at the center of the screen, where the bright bluish spark of Sirius had been. The star that had replaced it was even brighter. And it was red.

The Interrogator was the first to recover. He turned to the console operator, who had also been staring at the view-aft, and spoke—again forgetting that his translator was operative.

"Inform Astronomy that their instrumentation is at fault; the visual displayed is inaccurate. Have them go to backup systems. . . . They have? Very well, go to tertiary systems. . . ."

"Tiraena!" Sarnac's whisper was charged with urgency. "You remember the data on Sirius A? It's a fairly massive main-sequence star. According to Raehaniv understanding of stellar evolution, could it have gone into the red-giant phase in the last few minutes, while we were distracted by that . . . thing we passed through?"

"No. Impossible. The process is far less gradual than was once thought, even abrupt—but not *that* abrupt! And there's a lengthy buildup, with unmistakable warning signs, none of which Sirius A displayed. Bob, what's happening?"

"Happened," Sarnac corrected. "Whatever it is, it's already happened." He flashed a rueful smile. "I'm just quibbling, of course. The answer to your question is that I haven't a clue. If there hasn't been time for anything to happen to Sirius A . . ."

He stopped as the Interrogator turned to face them. The translator worked both ways. Their conversation had been comprehensible to him.

"Do you have some insight into the cause of the anomalous astronomical observations?"

Sarnac suppressed his natural impulse to play dumb. "No, I'm just speculating."

The Interrogator gestured to a guard, and Sarnac's left arm was jerked upward behind him with a strength that could splinter bone, but Sarnac managed not to cry out.

"We will hear your speculations," came the computer-generated ersatz speech.

"All right, all right! But I tell you, I don't know anything. The nearest thing I had to a theory has been blown away. That star back there is obviously a red giant, and eventually Sirius A will turn into one, and later, a white dwarf. But there hasn't been time. . . ."

He stopped, for the words "white dwarf" seemed to resonate just beneath the level of consciousness, as though there was a connection he should be making.

The Interrogator gestured again, Sarnac's arm was pulled up another notch, and in a blaze of pain the realization ignited in his brain. *Odd, the focusing effect pain can have*, some remote part of him thought dispassionately.

"Wait, wait," he gasped, and the pressure on his arm relaxed a trifle. "Listen, I know this sounds crazy, but . . . you remember that Sirius has a white-dwarf companion? Well, I just remembered reading—God knows where— that that companion must have collapsed into the white-dwarf stage in historical times. You see, our astronomers, as recently as the Classical era—that's two or three thousand of our years ago—described Sirius as a red star. So Sirius B must have been a red giant then, brighter than Sirius A. It must have evolved into a white dwarf during the Dark Ages that followed, when people weren't recording astronomical observations. We've always had trouble with the idea—it seemed like stellar evolution ought to take longer than that. But Tiraena's people have learned that the transitions between the stages of a star's life span go a lot more quickly than we've believed."

He was gasping for breath by the time he had finished, and he became aware that his arm had been released. The Interrogator gazed at him for a moment before speaking.

"What is the relevance of this to our present situation?"

"I don't know. But . . . look, I overheard you describe whatever that was we passed through as a 'gravitational anomaly.' Could it have somehow, well . . . warped time? Flung us back a few millennia?"

"Preposterous!" In contrast to the flat tone of the voder, the Interrogator looked agitated. "Time travel is fantasy."

"Why?" Sarnac challenged heedlessly. "We routinely distort space in various ways. Why couldn't time be distorted as well?"

"No, Bob," Tiraena said. "He's right. Time travel would allow for too many paradoxes. It would make nonsense of the very concept of causality itself! Maybe there's some chaotic universe in which time machines can be built— but not ours. As one of our scientific philosophers once said, 'Reality protects itself.' "

"Yeah, yeah. We've speculated about these things too, you know. If you went back and shot your grandfather before he met your grandmother, then how could you have been born? And so how could you have shot the old geezer? Well, what about strictly one-way time travel into the future? *That* doesn't violate causality in any way that I can see. Maybe we've jumped ahead into an era when Sirius A has ballooned into a red giant. Of course, the proper motion of the stars would have altered the constellations—although noticeable changes would take a very long time."

"Our astronomy section has reported certain minor discrepancies. . . ." The sounds from the translator pendant stopped abruptly, then resumed. "No. It is absurd. There must be some other explanation."

"All right! Fine! You explain it! Explain those little discrepancies. Explain that one big discrepancy," he cried, pointing at the red star. "Explain. . . ." He stopped short, for the Interrogator was no longer listening; he had turned in response to the uproar—or what must be an uproar in the Korvaash auditory range—from the bridge area below them, and was looking again at the viewport. Sarnac followed his gaze. "Explain . . . *that*," he finished in a hushed voice.

No one paid any attention. A small arrowhead-shaped spacecraft had flashed up to a position just to starboard, without benefit of any visible means of propulsion, and stopped dead with relation to the *Gorgon*.

Sarnac again found himself listening to one end of a conversation as the Korvaasha spoke into an interstation communicator.

"Scanning! From what bearing did that craft approach? . . . Why was I not informed it was incoming? . . . What? . . . Impossible. . . . Well, now we can track it visually. . . . Gunnery, lock in on target with all weapons that can be brought to bear."

"No!" Tiraena tried to struggle forward. A guard gripped her with irresistible strength. She didn't cry out, but when she spoke it was through tightened lips. "You haven't even tried to communicate with them!"

The Interrogator turned ponderously to face her. "Why should I? They are clearly not Korvaasha. Therefore, by definition, they are inferior beings, and hostile."

"Just as clearly, they are *very* goddamned advanced,"

Sarnac said. "Doesn't that suggest that they might be worth talking to?"

"And," Tiraena added with elaborate sarcasm that the translator unfortunately wouldn't convey, "that an unprovoked attack might be ill-advised, as they might be able to make their displeasure felt?"

Nothing came from the pendant, but Sarnac would have sworn that the jerky half-motions of the Interrogator toward the console suggested indecision.

Finally, the tinny sounds arrived. "Silence. Further attempts to interfere will be punished." The Korvaasha turned back to the console. "Gunnery, is the targeting solution complete? . . . Fire!"

Laser beams are naturally invisible in vacuum. But the visual effects of the plasma weapons made them look almost as lethal as they were. Bolts of superheated hydrogen flashed blindingly along laser guide beams to the enigmatic little ship. Sarnac, knowing that such a small vessel could not last more than seconds at the focus of those converging energy beams, silently screamed at it to flit out of harm's way as swiftly as it had appeared.

But the strange ship didn't move relative to the mountainous Korvaash battlecruiser. With apparent indifference, it held its position inside a glowing bubble, dissipating the energy being projected at it into sheets and streamers of light.

Sarnac and Tiraena watched openmouthed as the Interrogator ordered the attack stepped up. "That can't be anything related to our grav deflectors," she whispered, clearly shaken.

Sarnac nodded; he had seen imagery of the device— a Raehaniv application of artificial gravity that lay beyond the Solar Union's horizon—in action. The shield of force it projected was disc-shaped, because the physics of the effect made a bubble-shaped "force field" inherently impossible. It was also an energy hog. The Raehaniv interposed it between a ship and incoming attacks like an ancient swordsman using a buckler.

Yet here sat this impossible little craft, seeming not to even notice an attack that should have volatilized it!

Sarnac dragged his attention from the viewport to the Interrogator, who stood silently looking at the stranger. And even from across the gulf that separated them, it was obvious that he was shaken to the core. Finally, the Korvaasha spoke into the communicator.

"Engineering, bring the drive on-line. I want maximum acceleration. . . . What was that? Did you say we're being held by a tractor beam?"

Through the mechanical blandness of the voder's tones, Sarnac could barely make out a faint bass tone like a distant foghorn. He had heard that, contrary to popular belief, Korvaash vocal apparatus could with great difficulty produce a sound loud and high-pitched enough to reach the lower threshold of human audibility. The Interrogator's voice must have risen to a full scream on his last words. Sarnac could sympathize: a tractor beam that could hold this ship—from a vessel only a tiny bit larger than *Norlaev*—which was rated as too small to hold a tractor beam generator . . . !

"I never felt a jolt," he whispered to Tiraena.

"No reason you should," she whispered back, expressionlessly, "if the tractoring ship has matched vectors *precisely* with the target before activating the beam."

"Oh," he nodded . . . and continued to nod. It was all he could do other than watch the Interrogator and the other Korvaasha sag to the deck—and realize that he was sagging with them.

Before consciousness fled, he had time for one clear thought: *Oh no, not again!*

CHAPTER NINE

Afterwards, Sarnac could never decide which he had noticed first after regaining consciousness with a blessedly clear head: the fact that he was still on the Korvaash bridge, or the incongruous figure that was gazing down at him. The two thoughts probably entered his mind in that order, for he felt an instant of despair at the former, immediately washed away by the latter's obvious concern, sympathy . . . and humanity. For the man seemed to be middle-aged, and, while strikingly exotic, undeniably human.

Details began to register. The man was of medium height and average build, with brown skin that could have come from any of a number of Earth's ethnic groupings, and features that resembled none of them. He wore a one-piece garment of unfamiliar material. Others, similarly garbed, were moving about the bridge, examining instruments and unconscious Korvaasha, of whom the Interrogator was the nearest.

And there was something new on the command balcony. Sarnac thought it was a holographically projected display screen such as the Raehaniv used, roughly two meters high, and one meter wide. But he couldn't tell what was being projected, for he was seeing only the edge of it from the side, where he was sitting with his back against a bulkhead.

He heard a sigh beside him, and turned to see Tiraena open her eyes. A quick succession of emotions chased across her face as she saw him, their surroundings, and then the kind-looking man, who immediately beamed at them.

"Oh, good! You're both awake. We were so concerned, after this dreadful mix-up! We had no reason to think that you *wouldn't* awaken in fine fettle. Still . . ."

"Wha . . . wha . . ." Sarnac struggled to form words. "Who are you? And how do you speak English?"

"Oh, I've had to acquire English, you know. I've been working in your time, after all, and . . ." He stopped when he saw their expressions, and his own face took on a look of gentle befuddlement. "Oh, I *must* be more careful in introducing unfamiliar concepts! But you should understand that this is all most disconcerting. So please excuse me if I'm not at my best." He seemed to gather himself. "Let me begin at the beginning. My name is Tylar. And you are?" They introduced themselves. "Ah. Well. I and my people belong to an era which, from your perspective, lies in the remote future. Until just now I have, to repeat, been in your time period—myself and my colleagues are historical researchers, you see—and . . ."

He got no further, for both of his listeners came out of shock simultaneously.

"So I was right!" Sarnac yelped, just as Tiraena sprang to her feet with an incredulous "So we're in the far future!"

"Well, er . . . no. I'm afraid there are complications. Dear me! This is going to be even harder to explain than I thought!" Sarnac was afraid Tylar was about to start wringing his hands. But then the fellow brightened. "Why don't we go to my ship? We'll be more comfortable in my quarters, and I'm sure you have no desire to remain here. Knowing the Korvaasha from my stay in your era, I imagine your experience here was less than pleasant."

"You could say that." Clearly, there was something about Korvaash constructs that all humans found psychologically oppressive. And Sarnac was more eager than he wanted to admit to see the inside of Tylar's ship. He wondered how comfortable the living quarters could really be, on the little vessel that was still holding position outside the viewport. He had already seen more of the strangers than their ship looked able to accommodate.

"Wait," Tiraena said. "There are three more of us here. The Korvaasha said they were in suspended animation."

"So they are," Tylar affirmed. "We've inspected the medical facilities and found three humans in cryogenic suspension. Using our own medical sensor apparatus, we've determined that they are in no danger—especially now that we are monitoring the equipment. So, for the time being, I suggest we leave them as they are."

"Well," Tiraena said dubiously, "if you're sure they're all right."

"Quite sure. Indeed, if awakened they would represent additional complicating factors in what is already a rather complicated situation, as I'm sure you'll agree after I've explained." He gestured as if ushering them on.

"All right, then." Sarnac stretched and shook his marvelously pain-free head. No doubt about it, Tylar's people had zapped them something a lot more humane than sonic stunners. "Lead on. I suppose your shuttle is in the hold, where our ship is."

"My . . . ? Oh, dear! I keep forgetting that you are . . . ahem! The truth of the matter is, we won't be using that particular method. Just follow me." He walked toward what Sarnac had assumed was a holographically projected display screen.

It had a small, odd-looking device at the lower left corner—presumably the generating machinery. And it was outlined with . . . what? Rods of spatial distortion, it seemed, glowing faintly with refracted light. And within the frame was a corridor of some kind. *Not* an image. It seemed to be the corridor itself, as seen through a doorway.

Sarnac, his sense of reality wavering, stepped around to the other side of the immaterial portal and looked through it. There was Tylar, and Tiraena, and beyond them the vista of the Korvaash bridge. Feeling slightly silly, he stepped back around it and rejoined the others . . . and looked again into that impossible corridor.

"Are we ready?" Tylar stepped through the portal. Standing in the corridor, he beckoned to them. Sarnac and Tiraena looked at each other, then the former stepped forward. *Ugh! Male hunter lead way for squaw into woolly mammoth's cave,* he gibed at himself. There was a barely perceptible resistance to his passage, but then he was standing in the corridor, looking back through the same—or an identical—immaterial door at Tiraena. He became aware that he had been holding his breath. To cover his embarrassment, he gestured peremptorily at Tiraena, who joined them.

Tylar, with a smile whose gentleness was somehow more infuriating than outright condescension would have been, led them forward along the corridor, which looked like it would fit easily into the strangers' ship. Its otherwise featureless walls were lined with door-sized outlines.

" 'Any sufficiently advanced technology is indistinguishable from magic,' " Sarnac mumbled.

"What?" Tiraena looked puzzled, then brightened. "Oh. Narliel's Law."

"No, Clarke's Law."

"Whatever." She addressed Tylar, "Obviously, you couldn't have initially entered the Korvaash ship that way."

"Oh, no. Members of our crew with . . . specialized

abilities effected ingress first, and set up one of the paired portals.

"Ah, here we are." He stopped in front of one of the seemingly useless rectangular outlines in the walls, which were made of an unfamiliar metal.

Whether some device had detected him, or whether he had simply thought a command, was a question that never had a chance to enter their minds. For, all at once, the solid, blank wall held another doorway, not unlike the one through which they had just entered. Tylar led the way into the landscape beyond. They followed, wondering.

A bridge curved over the tinkling stream that flowed among gracefully drooping trees. Beyond it, the exquisite little lakeside pavilion was so appropriate that it was impossible to imagine it not being there, against the backdrop of the wooded hills. The scene would have inspired a landscape painter of Sung Dynasty China beyond endurance.

"Tylar," Sarnac said through a constricted throat, "please tell me this is all a holo projection."

With a grave look, Tylar pulled a leaf from the limb of a tree and handed it to him. The species was unfamiliar, but it crumpled in his fingers exactly like any other leaf.

"It's quite real," the time traveller assured him. "So is everything else. Well, the sky *is* a projection." He glanced at the blue vault overhead, with its fleecy clouds and gentle afternoon sun. "You see, we're in an artificially generated parallel reality, accessible only through a specialized version of the kind of portals we used for intership transit. This universe is only a few kilometers in diameter, and the unconcealed view from within it can be . . . disconcerting."

Tiraena's mouth was hanging open. "You mean . . . ?"

"Yes. All of our living quarters, plus supply storage and fuel tankage and, in fact, everything that doesn't have to interact with the natural universe, are tucked away in these pocket universes. You've probably wondered how our ship can be so small. Well, all it has to carry are the access portals. Speaking of which, I really should deactivate this one." He made no sound or movement, but the hole in the universe vanished.

"And now," he continued, "let me offer you refreshment. I'm sure you're famished." He led the way across the foot bridge, walking like an altogether ordinary human. They followed, looking around in silence.

Sarnac began to understand what had made him think of Chinese landscape painting: it was the seeming lack of vanishing point perspective, as though the "three distances" doctrine that Natalya had once tried to explain to him in the art museum at Tharsis was somehow reflected in the natural laws of the space they were in. He walked on, grimly concentrating on the everyday quality of all the immediate sensations—the air, the warmth, the scrunch of fine gravel under his feet.

They seated themselves in the pavilion, and Tylar busied himself serving refreshments that had appeared they knew not how, but whose presence seemed somehow appropriate and unremarkable. Sarnac sipped herbal tea and nibbled on some kind of seafood and vegetables, gazing at the dreamlike landscape and glancing down at the fishlike life forms that darted about in the lake, close enough to the surface for the sun to bring out their iridescence.

"So, Tylar," he heard Tiraena say, "you and the rest of your people are descended from ours?"

"Precisely. Having been in your era, I can identify you as a Raehaniv, and your companion as a Terran. We are descended from your two peoples. It is entirely possible—indeed, almost a statistical certainty after all these generations—that I am a remote biological descendant of yours!" Tylar seemed delighted by the thought.

Suddenly, Sarnac shook loose from the lassitude that had been stealing over him.

"Hey!" he cried, "If you people are descended from us, then we must have won the war! You must know what happens in our future . . . and our past! My God, you must know the answer to the riddle of how there came to be humans on both Terra and Raehan! You must know . . ."

As he was speaking, Tiraena also seemed to come alive, and began talking rapidly, her words tripping over his. "And how can time travel be possible, however advanced your technology is? The concept involves insoluble philosophical problems! You'd inevitably change the past and generate all kinds of paradoxes. . . ."

They both trailed off, partly because the sheer number of questions was overwhelming, but mostly because they found themselves unable to concentrate on anything except Tylar's eyes, whose dark brown depths seemed to draw them in where they couldn't even see the look on the time traveller's face—a look of compassion with no lack of respect. But they could hear Tylar's voice, and there was nothing at all befuddled about it, and it seemed to fill this strange universe.

"These are reasonable suppositions, Robert and Tiraena. But there are certain things which I may not tell you, and which you may not know."

Then the moment was over, and Tylar was fussing over the tea in the pleasant lakeside pavilion, and what had passed was not even a memory. But no more such questions were asked.

"So," Tylar resumed, "our ancestry explains our presence here. Earth is, of course, the ultimate homeworld of the human race, and we are engaged in the lengthy— even for us—task of reconstructing its past. Naturally, we concentrate on crucial eras like yours, and eras which are poorly documented. As I mentioned, I've been working in your era. This ship had just departed from it when, by sheer bad luck, the Korvaash ship carrying you passed through the temportal we had used, just before it was deactivated."

Tiraena's head jerked up. "So that ring of spatial distortion we passed through was a temportal? The Interrogator—the senior Korvaasha aboard that ship—called it a 'gravitational anomaly.' Does the effect depend on an application of artificial gravity, then?"

"No. Earlier forms of time travel did, indeed, employ a variant of gravitic propulsion. We still use such vehicles, but largely to emplace temportals, which represent an application of the same technology we just used to access this place. But all forms of time travel will only function within, and in relation to, a gravity field. Necessarily so, if one thinks about it; otherwise, one might take a temporal vehicle to another time only to find oneself in vacuum, with the planet somewhere else in its orbit around the sun! The same applies to all forms of portal technology—energy conservation problems, you know. Imagine what would happen if you stepped through a portal from a planet's surface to a satellite moving around that planet at orbital velocity! So for a spacecraft-sized temportal out beyond a sun's gravitational influence we have to generate a stable artificial gravity field, identical in both of the times in question. *That* was what the Korvaash ship's sensors detected, not the temportal itself, which is imperceptible to them."

"But," Tiraena began hesitantly, "if these spatial and temporal portals of yours aren't based on spacetime distortion through gravitics, then how *do* they work?"

"Oh, I couldn't possibly give you a detailed explanation. Quite out of my field, you know. But . . . I believe the Raehaniv of your era have begun to understand the nature of psionic phenomena."

"Yes. Just enough to confirm that it's too weak a force to be useful to humans. But yes, we've determined that it's rooted in the effect neural activity above a certain level of complexity—exceeding the minimum required for self-awareness—has on the possible outcomes of events."

Tylar smiled. "Yes, you are approaching the beginnings of understanding. So perhaps you will understand when I say that portal technology is based on the distortion not of space or time, but of *reality*." He stopped, frowning. "No, that doesn't convey the concept of *nareeshyan* at all. I'm afraid English, or even Raehaniv, lacks the necessary terminology."

Sarnac squirmed in his chair. "Look, I'm not following this at all. But the important thing is that we passed, purely by accident, through this 'temportal' of yours." He paused, and shook his head slowly. "Can you imagine the odds against that happening? I mean, do you have any idea how *big* space is?"

Tylar looked uncomfortable for an instant, but then his poise returned. "I quite agree that it was a very low-probability event. In fact, we've never had such an accident before. But" —he spread his hands apologetically— "even low-probability events do occur."

Sarnac felt unsatisfied by the reply and wanted to pursue the matter, but found it hard to frame the questions he wanted to ask. He was still trying when Tiraena spoke up, derailing his train of thought.

"But," she pursued, "why bother with a spaceship-sized temportal at all? Why not just put a much smaller one on Earth's surface, with its termini in your era, and in the era you want to reach?"

"In many cases, we do precisely that. But Earth in your time frame is a difficult place in which to conceal temportals. You're getting altogether too technologically sophisticated! We are largely reduced to observation from space. Also . . . well, without going into the details, Earth is a somewhat out-of-the-way place in our time. Most of our personnel and equipment have to be brought in from out-system."

"All right," Sarnac resumed, doggedly, "we can provisionally accept all that. The basic fact is that we passed through your temporal. But you said earlier that we're not in your time period. So where—or rather, *when*—are we?"

"Ah. Well." Tylar seemed to gather his forces. "As I mentioned, we are historical researchers. Normally, we have several projects in hand at once. In fact, given the capability of time travel, 'at once' is a somewhat elastic concept. The temporal that you passed through was a temporary one. It enabled us to move on from your period to another area of history that we've been investigating. I've already visited it repeatedly, over a period of several of my own subjective years, and established a solid local identity. We intend to complete our investigation over the next few subjective months. In the meantime, the temporal that we—and, inadvertently, you—used has been shut down."

An awkward moment passed before Sarnac found his tongue. "So you're telling us that we're stuck here until you've completed your research?"

"That is a not inaccurate statement." Tylar looked uncomfortable. "Although the incident occurred quite unintentionally on our part, we are fully sensible of our ethical responsibility, and are prepared to return you to your proper time as soon as possible. In the meantime, we will do our utmost to minimize the tedium of your unintended stay in this period."

"Hmm. . . . What, exactly, is your utmost, Tylar?"

"Well, if you wish, we can place you in a temporal stasis so that when the time comes for you to return to your era, no time will seem to have elapsed—because, in fact, no time *will* have elapsed for you."

"Hmm. . . ." That, Sarnac reflected, would certainly take care of the tedium problem. But it seemed such a waste. . . .

Tiraena seemed to be having parallel thoughts. "Your 'if you wish' seems to imply other alternatives, Tylar. What are they?"

Their host took a sip of tea, then leaned back in his chair and eyed them appraisingly over steepled fingers. "It occurs to me that if you prefer to make some use of your time in this era, you could perhaps assist us in our research."

"What?" Tiraena thrust her head forward. "You mean land on Earth in whatever historical period this is?"

"To be precise, it is the fifth century of the Christian Era—late in the year 469 A.D., in fact," Tylar supplied.

"But Tylar," Sarnac said, "I'm sure you people are very experienced at what you do, and have in-depth knowledge of ancient times in general, plus the specific ins and outs of, uh, 469 A.D. We haven't got any of that. Aren't you afraid we'd screw things up for you and your research team, as well as getting ourselves killed?"

"Not in the least," Tylar assured him. "We would supply you with the tools and information you need—we have the capability to do so in a very short time. And besides, I honestly believe you undervalue yourselves." He suddenly looked abashed. "I'm afraid I haven't been entirely candid with you. Before you awakened, we examined the database of the Raehaniv craft in the Korvaash hold. So we know your background. Both of you, as officers of your Survey services, have been trained and biotechnically enhanced to survive in primitive settings. You should be precisely in your element.

"Furthermore," he continued earnestly, "I would be less than honest if I didn't admit to an ulterior motive in suggesting this. As you surmise, we are very experienced at this sort of work—so much so that I fear we may be in danger of becoming somewhat doctrinaire. We need to bring fresh viewpoints to bear on the human past. Your insights could hardly fail to be of value to us, inasmuch as you are—no offense intended—far closer to this era, culturally and technologically, than we."

Tiraena cocked her head to one side in a gesture Sarnac had come to know. "So you get the benefit of our . . . insights. What do we get, besides the chance to spend our enforced layover in something more interesting than stasis?"

Tylar spread his hands. "Why, I should think that would be obvious. You get something that the people of both your cultures have only dreamed about: the chance to view the past at firsthand. The two of you would not do what you do for a living if you did not hear the call of new frontiers. Well, the Earth we are en route toward is, from your perspective, as much an unexplored frontier as any newly discovered planet—and far more colorful than most!"

Sarnac thought about it. He couldn't deny that Tylar's offer was tempting.

"Uh, tell us a little more about the plan, Tylar," he temporized. "I mean, what part of Earth would we be going to? Not that I know much about this period of history, you understand."

"Our area of operation is Western Europe. Specifically, the region known as Gaul in this era, and as France in yours."

"Hey! That's where my father's family originally came from way back when—the province called Brittany."

"Well, then, this will be almost a homecoming for you!" Tylar beamed, as though it was all settled. "Our exact destination is on the lower Loire, next-door to what is currently in the process of becoming Brittany. You see, it is only in the last generation that immigrants from Britain have been the dominant element there. . . ."

"Tylar," Tiraena interjected, "my knowledge of Earth's history and geography are a little sketchy, so you're losing me. For now, can you just tell us why your people are so interested in this particular time and place?"

"Remember what I said earlier about poorly documented eras? This one is almost uniquely ill-documented—infuriatingly so, given its importance. For this is when the ancient world dies and the Middle Ages are born."

Tiraena brightened. "Oh, yes, the Middle Ages! Knights in shining armor! Aleksandr Nevsky!"

"Ah, I'm afraid you might find *him* something of a disappointment. And we're almost a thousand years too early for the kind of armor I think you're visualizing. Permit me to summarize the situation at the present time.

"The Roman Empire, which conquered and superficially civilized Western Europe, has been split into eastern and western halves for two centuries. And now the Western Empire is in its death agony. Later ages will say it was conquered by barbarians; more accurately, its economically precarious superstructure of urban gentility is collapsing into a ruder social order, of which the barbarians are taking control. Understandably, these events are poorly recorded, leaving a vacuum in which legends will be free to proliferate. We are, you might say, trying to weed out the legends so the facts they've overgrown can be glimpsed."

"If the period is so obscure," Tiraena inquired, "how did you even know where to start?"

"We started with one of the best sources of hard information we have: an individual named Sidonius Apollinaris. He belongs to the last generation of Romanized aristocrats in Gaul, and he is considered one of the leading literary lights of the age—which, I'm afraid, is a comment on the age. He is also an amazingly prolific letter-writer."

Sarnac shook his head. "I can't get used to the way you keep referring to this guy in the present tense."

"Why should I not? He is very much alive, even as we approach Sol. To continue, Sidonius has documented *himself* so thoroughly that he was easy to locate. I approached him last year in Rome, where he was serving as City Prefect. Last year for *him*, that is; it was a number of subjective years ago for me, during which years, I've spent a small part of my time serving as his secretary in the course of a number of brief trips to this era. In fact, my visits haven't all been in chronological order from my own standpoint."

Sarnac's head was starting to spin. "Doesn't it get confusing?"

"Well," Tylar allowed, "it does call for a certain presence of mind."

"And what if you, uh, run into yourself?"

For the first time in their acquaintance, Tylar sounded miffed. "My dear fellow, we like to flatter ourselves that we know what we're doing! And," he added in a milder tone, "it's really not as confusing as it sounds in English, which lacks several of the requisite tenses for discussing time travel. At any rate, we're moving the focus of our operation to this point in time because matters are coming to a head."

"Why? What's happening?"

"The Western Empire's final loss of Gaul to the barbarians has now commenced. A last effort is being made to stop it—an effort which, because it fails, will become a mere footnote to history. But we believe that it represents the last instance when the course of events *might* have been reversed. Afterwards . . . well, the official end of the Western Empire seven years from now will be a mere formality."

"What kind of effort? I mean, if the Western Empire is so far gone . . . ?"

"Two generations ago, the islanders of Britain were abandoned by the Empire. Since then, they've managed to contain their local barbarian invaders and to establish a kingdom which includes Brittany—still officially 'Armorica.' This has necessitated involvement in Gallic

affairs, and now the British High King has allied himself
with the Western Empire and brought an army to Gaul.
Fortuitously, Sidonius has corresponded with the High
King—actually, Sidonius corresponds with *everybody*!
And his term as City Prefect is up, so he's returned to
Gaul. So it was easy to influence him to attach himself
to the Imperial deputation that recently met the arriving
British. The next step, after we arrive on Earth, will be
to persuade him to attach me to the High King's entourage
as a liaison—in which capacity," he addressed Sarnac
briskly, "I will, of course, need a bodyguard! We should
have no trouble manufacturing an appropriate identity
for you. . . ."

"What about me?" Tiraena asked. "This sounds like a
rough era, so you ought to be able to justify a need for
two bodyguards."

"Ah . . . I'm afraid we must find some other role for
you, as that one would not be altogether suitable in the
current milieu."

"Why?" Tiraena inquired with a look of genuine
puzzlement.

Tylar's embarrassment became almost comical. "Oh,
my! This may take a certain amount of explaining. In
fact, I may leave that to specialists. Yes, I believe that's
an excellent idea! For the present, why don't I show you
to your quarters?" He gestured at the elegant villa that
could be glimpsed beyond the trees. "You must be
exhausted after your experiences. After you rest, we can
set to work in earnest." He ushered them from the pavilion
and along the footpath.

"Did we agree?" Tiraena whispered as they walked
through the intricate landscaping. "I suppose we must
have."

"I suppose so," Sarnac agreed dubiously.

CHAPTER TEN

It was Earth's night side that brought home to Sarnac that he was in the distant past.

They had approached his birthworld from the day side, and the cloud-swirling blue loveliness that he had seen (would see?) so many times in his own era had made him homesick. But then the ship had curved around, descending over Europe, and the poignant warmth that he'd felt was blighted by chill.

For it was *dark*. The dazzling illumination that bejewelled the nights of his Earth was nowhere to be seen in this unrelieved blackness. The blazing galaxies of the great conurbations, the stars of lesser metropoli, the strings of light that marked the maglev routes—all had vanished without trace into a Stygian well. And all at once he *knew* that this was an Earth before electricity. Before internal combustion. Before interchangeable parts. Before steam. Before printing. Before gunpowder. Before windmills.

The reality of it finally hit him, leaving him shaken.

Of course, the observation deck—you couldn't call it a "bridge," for all piloting and navigational functions were taken care of by a small part of the ship's complex artificial intelligence—was no place to feel shaken. Sarnac was still having to fight off vertigo in the featureless little chamber that produced, at the touch of Tylar's thoughts, an all-around, holographic exterior view, as if the ship did not exist.

Tylar followed Sarnac's eyes downward, toward the blackness where the nighttime glow of Paris, London and the Rhineland should have been, and seemed to read his thoughts. "You'd find it less strange in the daytime—at least in this part of the world. If we were over China, you wouldn't be able to make out the Great Wall. It was begun by Shih Huang-Ti almost seven centuries ago, but it won't be completed in its final form until the Ming Dynasty. Now, it's just an earthwork."

Sarnac gazed at Tylar, standing in space and silhouetted against the stars, wearing clerkly fifth century garb of a rather coarse fabric, but far from poorly made. It was one of the two or three outfits that were all Sidonius' secretary owned or expected to own, all these centuries before the Textile Revolution and house designs that included closets. He was considerably better-dressed than Sarnac, whose buskins and tunic of what seemed to be quilted cloth were serviceable, and little else. But Sarnac was more than willing to forego a reputation as a fifth century dandy, in exchange for the outfit's other qualities.

Tiraena hadn't been too surprised when Tylar explained the network of tiny sensors that detected any incoming object whose kinetic energy threatened harm. The material would stiffen into a hardness exceeding steel at the instant of impact. The Raehaniv had produced similar armor experimentally—still enormously expensive, and there was no disguising what it was—so it hadn't caused her to quote Narliel's Law. Neither had the minute device that had been painlessly implanted in Sarnac's head. Raehaniv neural-interface implants would accept data storage discs that provided instant access to skills and areas of knowledge. But these were mere built-in reference books, no substitute for practice and experience. Tylar's people had advanced further. Sarnac could now ride a horse and wield a *spatha* with the trained reflexes of an experienced soldier of fortune. He could speak, like a native, the Celtic language that had not yet differentiated into Welsh and Breton, and he had a working knowledge of military Latin.

Thinking of it made him recall the conversation he had had with Tylar after the brief operation, sitting on a couch that had extruded itself from the floor of the little . . . infirmary, he supposed he must call it.

"Tylar, is this permanent?" he had asked, examining the area behind his ear in vain for any trace of the intruder. "I mean, when I get back to my era. . . ."

"Not at all," the time traveller had assured him. "After a certain amount of time, the device will biodegrade tracelessly in your body. And now," he had continued briskly, "as to the details of your synthetic persona. You are the son of a British emigrant to Armorica and a local woman of mixed Gallic and Roman blood. Your personal appearance is not incompatible with such a background. Your parents died in your early adolescence. For the last few years you have been soldiering in the Eastern Empire." Sarnac found that he "remembered" a tavern in Constantinople's harbor district near the Golden Horn . . . blows exchanged with a Hun, whose people were still raiding occasionally though they no longer had the great Attila to lead them . . . a mountain hut and an Illyrian peasant girl. He dragged his mind back to Tylar's discourse. "Now you're working your way home, and have applied, through me, for employment with Sidonius."

"Do I have a name?" Sarnac had inquired dryly.

"Oh, let's make it . . . Bedwyr. It's as good a name as any. Your absence in the East should account for your not being *au courant* with the local gossip. Still, you should try to avoid contact with the Armorican British troops that have now joined Riothamus' army."

"Riothamus?"

"The British High King." Tylar had hesitated for the barest instant. "It's an honorific, by which he's generally known on the Gallic side of the channel. His personal name, which the Britons normally use, is Artorius."

Sarnac had frowned, for the name had a vague familiarity. But Tylar had hurried on. "I'm telling you this instead of having had it incorporated into your implanted knowledge because you're not *supposed* to know it in any depth. Remember, you're just back from the East, and, in any case, you're a simple sword-for-hire, in whom too much knowledge would seem suspicious. And now, let's go over some more details of your personal background. . . ."

Sarnac returned to the present as the ship descended still lower. He wasn't sure how he knew that it was doing so, on this moonless night, for the land below was still an undifferentiated blackness.

"Tylar, what do these people *do* after dark? Uh, besides the obvious, that is."

"Drink too much, for the most part. Of course, really self-destructive drinking won't become widespread until the nineteenth century, with the combination of distilling—a Renaissance invention—and the grain surplus produced by the Agricultural Revolution. But that's neither here nor there. Why don't we take a clearer look?" The holo display included a light-enhancing feature. The landscape below was mostly forest, but scattered farmsteads could be seen in the ghostly illumination.

"Well," Sarnac drawled, "I suppose drinking as much as possible of whatever they've got in this era is appropriate behavior for the simple mercenary I'm playing. . . ."

"Lucky you!" A door in the simulated panorama had appeared behind them, and Tiraena stepped through. Her expression was as thunderous as it had been since one of Tylar's subordinates had succeeded in getting across to her the status of women in this world. "At least you get to wear something that lets you move!" She was still adjusting to the floor-length gown and took an equally dim view of her tubular headdress, though Tylar had assured her it was a stroke of luck for them, concealing hair the shortness of which would have taken some explaining.

"Whine, whine, whine!" Sarnac grinned, rubbing his jaw. The bristly skin—what currently passed for clean-shaven—still itched. "Look on the bright side, Lucasta," he continued, using her cover name. "You'll probably be up to your ears in exciting court intrigue. And you'll be a lot higher on the social scale than a grunt like me."

"Ha! Just because I'm going to be living in some larger-than-average pigsty they call a palace, where I'll be married off like the rest of the sows. . . ."

"Now, now," Tylar chided gently. "The engagement is purely *pro forma*, as Koreel is well aware. And besides, you are getting the benefit of some implanted historical knowledge which was deemed unnecessary and inappropriate in Robert's case."

They had settled on a cover for her that would operate within this era's rigid limits on women's lives and also account for her exotic looks. She was to be a niece of Tylar—or Tertullian, as he called himself in this world—who was going to Britain for an arranged marriage with a distant cousin named Ventidius, a successful merchant with ties to the High King's court. There, she would be a lady-in-waiting to Riothamus' queen, thanks to the good offices of Ventidius—or Koreel, as he was called in his own time and world.

Tiraena also had received one of the minute implants. Tylar had been too tactful to speak of Raehaniv biotechnology's primitivism, and merely cited its incompatibility with his people's data storage media. But the information it endowed her with was quite different from Sarnac's. She now spoke Latin as a first language, but only a few heavily accented phrases of British. She also had acquired various social graces, and an in-depth academic knowledge of the period's history.

"Still . . ." she began, sounding dubious.

"Come on," Sarnac jollied her. "You'll be the toast of Riothamus' city—what did you say the capital is called?"

"Cadbury," Tiraena replied. "And it's more a fortress than a city. The Roman cities in Britain were never much more than glorified towns, and even those have been decaying for a century." To Tylar: "I'm still concerned about the Korvaasha you captured aboard that battlecruiser. Are you certain that they're secured? Their leader—the Interrogator, as he calls himself— is very dangerous."

"Have no fear on that score. They've been imprisoned in a pocket universe, access to which is controlled strictly from our side. Ah, I see we're about to land."

The three of them seemed to drift from the night sky, past the treetops, magically stopping a few meters above ground level.

"And now," Tylar continued, gesturing them toward a portal that had appeared, filled with blackness, "it's time to go." Sarnac cradled a Model 469 helmet under his left arm. The helmet was standard issue, except for the microscopic generator that reinforced the iron's molecular bonds whenever it was in physical contact with him. He and Tiraena hoisted the bags containing their possessions, and they stepped through the portal into Earth's night.

They were in a clearing, noisy with the nocturnal fauna

of Earth's middle northern latitudes. Through the trees a galaxy of campfires could be glimpsed. Sarnac inserted his light-gathering contact lenses, and the distant campfires became ample to see by. He took a deep breath of the warm air. "Smells like home."

"Yes," Tylar nodded. "I suppose it does to you. You come from well beyond the age of hydrocarbon-burning engines. If I could arrange for you to step through a temportal to a busy city street of three centuries before your time, you would imagine yourself on a planet with a toxic atmosphere—and you would not be far wrong. If a person from that time came to this one, he would find the air disconcertingly clean-smelling."

Tylar turned toward the portal, and it vanished. He then picked up the little device that generated it. As usual, he did and said nothing, merely held the metallic object in his hands . . . but it began to writhe and ripple, stretching out into a heavy dagger, or short sword.

Sarnac had seen the instruments of Tylar's people do this before, but he still felt a need to moisten his mouth.

"It seems smaller now," Tiraena said, in a voice whose steadiness did not fool Sarnac for a second.

"Mass remains constant, but not necessarily volume. Density can be varied within limits, you know." Tylar slid what was now a crudely forged blade of low-carbon steel into a scabbard such as Tertullian might carry for self-defense in these perilous times. "Shall we go?"

They proceeded through the trees, toward the campfires, the contact lenses automatically reducing their light-gathering efficiency as the need for it decreased. They finally emerged into the cleared area, entering surreptitiously behind a tent. Tylar then led the way into the camp, and Sarnac got his first look at the people of this era.

They were *small*. He had been barely of average height in his own milieu, but he was clearly going to be counted

as a tall man here. Tylar, who was a little taller than
he, was very tall by contemporary standards. And
Tiraena, who could practically look him straight in the
eye, must be truly towering among this era's women—
none of whom were in evidence among the campfires.
Sarnac's "memory" of his Balkan campaigning told him
that there was an area where camp followers, and the
local talent from nearby Nantes, plied their profession.

Tiraena's presence had to be the cause of the stares
they drew—any obviously respectable woman would have
drawn them, even without Tiraena's stature and exoticism.
But Tylar was obviously a familiar figure, and the troops
went back to sharpening their weapons, their games of
chance, and all the rest of the camp's ordinary activities.

As they walked, Sarnac began to notice a subtle change
in the troops around the campfires. The red and white
tunics were only part of what gave their dress a
uniformity which was lacking elsewhere in the camp—
and, he suspected, in most armies of this place and
time. In some indefinable way, they carried themselves
like members of an elite outfit.

Tylar halted before a large tent. "Wait here. This is
Sidonius' tent. I'll go in and tell him that I've found an
applicant for the bodyguard job, and that my niece has
arrived."

"But," Sarnac said, "I thought you were going to have
to talk him into telling you to stay on with Riothamus
after he goes home."

"Oh, my! It's the problem with tenses again. You see,
at this point, that's already been done. I came into this
time about a year and a half ago in terms of my own
consciousness, and took care of it. Of course, that was
only yesterday here; Sidonius last saw me about twenty-
eight of his hours ago." He stepped forward, exchanged
a greeting with a guard, and entered the tent before
Sarnac's mouth had closed.

They stood for a few minutes, gazing around. Tiraena continued to attract interest, and Sarnac concentrated on looking menacing. He found that the glances slid away when he met them. *Of course. I forgot. Amazing what a difference it makes when you're a big guy and can forestall trouble just by standing around with a no-nonsense expression! It must affect your whole personality—you don't have to be glib. I wonder if Tylar took account of that?*

Oh, well, he keeps telling us he knows what he's doing.

Tylar finally emerged from the tent. "It's settled. He wants to meet you, Lucasta." —they used their cover names at all times once on the ground— "Just be polite and address him as Prefect. People still call him that, even though he's no longer City Prefect of Rome. And he doesn't rate an ecclesiastical title, as he hasn't been elected Bishop of Clermont just yet."

"Elected?"

"Oh, yes. The Catholic Church isn't nearly as hierarchical an organization as it will later become. A bishop is elected by the substantial people of his diocese. He's as much a civic leader as a religious one, stepping into the power vacuum of these times and interceding for his flock. But come, let's not keep the future bishop waiting!"

They stepped through the flaps, and their contact lenses automatically adjusted to the glare of the numerous candles. Sarnac's pseudo-memories told him how much candles cost in this era.

Two men sat on folding camp-stools at a game board that looked to be the ancestor of backgammon. One of them was slightly plump and seemed to be settling well into middle age. Sarnac recalled that Sidonius Apollinaris was thirty-seven.

"Ah, Tertullian, do introduce us to your charming niece." Sarnac had to concentrate to follow the civilian Latin.

Tylar introduced Tiraena, who inclined her head as was appropriate. Sarnac almost wished the curtsey had been invented, if only to relish Tiraena's gritted teeth. Sidonius responded graciously, then turned to Tylar.

"Tertullian, you didn't tell me what a striking young lady Lucasta is! Like an Athena of the East, divinely tall! Don't you agree, Excellency?"

The other man, older-looking than Sarnac suspected he actually was, chuckled and shook his head. "There you go again with your pagan allusions, Sidonius! What will we do with you when you're a bishop?"

"I shall depend on my older and wiser colleagues to correct my errors . . . especially you, Faustus old friend," Sidonius replied with a serene good nature that seemed habitual. "But correct literary form requires that we follow the modes of expression laid down by the ancients. And surely there can be no harm in it, so long as we recognize the fables as mere fables, by which our ancestors lighted, however dimly, the darkness before the coming of the Word. . . ."

Tylar harrumphed softly, interrupting what was evidently a long-standing debate. "Ah, Prefect, you asked to see the bodyguard I interviewed."

"Oh, yes." Sidonius motioned Sarnac forward and greeted him with grave courtesy, clearly rooted in deeply held convictions concerning the obligations he owed his social inferiors. "Bedwyr, isn't it? Well, Bedwyr, guard my secretary with your life! Tertullian, I still don't know why I let you talk me into letting you stay on here, especially when Mars is about to burst the . . . ahem!" He reined himself in before launching into the excesses of the classically educated. "At any rate, it is likely to become quite dangerous in this vicinity soon! Especially in light of the news from Angers." He gestured vaguely toward the southeast. "Tertullian, remember to write faithfully. I want an ongoing account of what I confidently

expect will be Riothamus' triumphs . . . with God's help
of course," he added with a glance at Faustus.

"Yes," the bishop nodded. "A most remarkable man.
My earlier misgivings at the prospect of meeting him
have been quite laid to rest." Sarnac recalled Tylar
mentioning something about Bishop Faustus' British
dynastic connections. He also recalled his jitters at the
thought that the present incumbent might see him as a
potential rival, despite the older man's years. Tiraena
undoubtedly knew the details from her implanted historical
background; he'd have to ask her . . . but no, she was
about to leave for Britain. *Which is probably a better
place for her than here, if Sidonius is right about what
Mars is about to do*, he thought. The archaic protective
impulse surprised him. Were the surroundings getting
to him?

"Well, Tertullian," Sidonius said, "do what you think
best as regards the arrangements. I depart at first light
for home—and Papianilla." A faint sigh? "I'll try not to
let my affairs get into too much of a muddle in your
absence! And, Tertullian," he added as Tylar bowed
himself and his companions out of the tent, "do be careful
and don't cut yourself with that thing!" He gestured at
the short sword that was a device far beyond his capacity
to imagine miracles, and smiled affably as the flaps closed.

"I kind of like Sidonius," Sarnac remarked as they
walked through the camp toward Tylar's tent.

"Yes," the time traveller nodded, and a sad little smile
played around his mouth in the light of the campfires.
"Almost everybody likes Sidonius. He's a snob and a
literary *poseur*, but he's a thoroughly nice fellow, living
in an age that isn't at all nice." The smile departed, leaving
only the sadness. "He's one of the last men to really believe
in the Western Roman Empire, and it is his fate to watch
it die. As Bishop of Clermont he will lead his people's
resistance to repeated Visigothic sieges—not an unusual

role for a Bishop in these times. But he'll fail in the end, and die a broken-spirited old man of forty-eight." A ghost of the smile returned. "At least he'll get posthumous recompense in the form of canonization."

"In the form of *what?*"

"Oh, yes, he becomes a Roman Catholic saint. I didn't mention it before because I knew you'd be unduly impressed. It isn't really all that much of a distinction in these times; sainthood seems to have been a kind of celestial retirement benefit for early churchmen of any note." He suddenly looked alarmed. "Oh dear, I hope I'm not giving offense!"

"Nope," Sarnac reassured him. "Lapsed Catholic."

"Well, perhaps you can nonetheless join me in wishing that Sidonius will find peace, if not beyond the grave, as he himself believes, then perhaps for some little time before it." Tylar's voice dropped to a barely audible whisper. "I hope it may be so."

Sarnac wrapped his cloak a little more tightly around his shoulders against a chill that had nothing to do with the summer night. For he had had a glimpse of the sorrows of those who rode the timestream, buffeted by the waves of fate. What induced them to do it? He was still contemplating this, unable to quite articulate the question, when they reached Tylar's tent.

Once inside, with the flaps securely tied, Tylar laid the sword on the ground, where it shape-shifted into the little device that distorted reality. The insubstantial portal appeared, and a man of Tylar's people waved a greeting from the dimness beyond, before stepping through.

"Lucasta, this is Ventidius, your intended." Tylar smiled, as did Koreel, who gave Tiraena a small bow and shook hands with Sarnac, according the customs of their respective peoples. "He'll keep you concealed," Tylar went on, "until enough time has passed for you to have plausibly made the journey. You can make use of the time by bringing yourself up to date on affairs in Britain."

"Yes," Koreel spoke up, "there have been a few changes. Ambrosius is back earlier than expected."

"Oh, dear, that could be awkward! As regent during Riothamus' absence, he's been making a circuit of the Saxon settlements to keep them properly submissive. We were hoping he'd be at it a little longer. He and the queen . . . well, you'll find out. Right now, you'd better go."

Tiraena hoisted her satchel and squeezed Sarnac's shoulder with her free hand. "Take care of yourself. Don't wear yourself out with high adventure . . . and with the local tavern wenches, or whatever they're called."

"Fat chance! You'll probably see a lot more excitement than I will. With my luck, I'll end up as latrine orderly in this army!"

"Come, come!" Tylar was fidgeting. "Can't keep the portals activated forever, you know." Koreel was already through, and beckoning.

Tiraena gave Sarnac a quick, hard hug, and then turned to the portal and stepped into Britain.

"So long," Sarnac called after her. "Give my regards to Queen, uh . . ." He was groping for the name, and Tiraena was opening her mouth to supply it, when the portal vanished, leaving the tent seeming perfectly normal save for the metal object that was stretching and reshaping itself into a short sword.

"Tertullian, what *is* the name of Riothamus' old lady? I don't think you ever mentioned it while telling me about—"

"Ah, here comes Basilius," Tylar cut in, peering through the crack between the tent-folds. "He's Sidonius' chief clerk, and he'll be here to see about getting you on the payroll. We'd better let him in."

He did so, and in all the bustle, the question fled Sarnac's mind.

CHAPTER ELEVEN

They topped the ridge and looked down at the valley of the Loire.

"I was here on vacation once," Sarnac said wonderingly. "I mean, I will be here . . . or . . . well, you know what I mean!"

"You'll find it quite different now," Tylar smiled. "None of the grand chateaux have even been thought of."

It spread out before them toward the east, with the Loire on their right, flowing toward its confluence with the Maine, beyond the village that was their destination. They could see the Maine in the distance, snaking away to the north where, five or six miles from here, lay the fortress town of Angers—and its besiegers.

Tylar and Sarnac had spent only a short time in the camp outside Nantes, while Riothamus had held court for the benefit of his Armorican subjects and cleaned out the Saxon raiders from south of the Loire who plagued them. Then had come the news that the Saxon chieftain Odovacar had launched a massive offensive across the Loire, fifty miles to the east. He was advancing up the left bank of the Maine, toward Angers, trusting in the Maine and his swarms of flat-bottomed boats to shield his flank from the allies.

So the Britons had set out along the north bank of
the Loire. Delays in getting the cumbersome alliance
forces moving had caused them to grumble, complaining
that they'd be better off going it alone, without the bloody
Gauls. (Tylar had been at a loss to understand Sarnac's
stifled laughter.) But finally the advance had begun—
not a day too soon, in Sarnac's opinion, for they had
already tarried longer than any army of this sanitation-
innocent era was well advised to remain encamped in
one place. He recalled having read that the Second World
War had been the first war in history in which enemy
action had surpassed disease as a cause of death. Now
he could believe it.

They had moved eastward, through the lands of the
Gallic Andecavi, slowed by constant small clashes with
the Saxon raiding parties that infested the area. Now, at
least, the Saxon control of the Loire had been broken;
the Frankish auxiliaries of King Syagrius of Soissons,
in a daring night action, had swum out to one of the
Saxon-controlled islands near the confluence with the
Maine, massacring its drunken defenders and seizing their
boats. Now the allies had paused at this village to plan
their next move, and here Tertullian and his bodyguard
would catch up with the advance.

As they trotted down the slope, they passed a cavalry
patrol—the village had only just been taken, and there
were Saxons still believed to be in the area. They
exchanged greetings with a couple of the men, who wore
the red and white of the Artoriani. Tylar had explained
the origin of the name. It was common late-Roman practice
for a specially favored unit to be named after its
commander, and these were the elite troops of Artorius
Riothamus. But this particular name had other roots as
well, sinking much further into the past. Tylar kept
promising to tell him the full story.

They entered the outskirts of the largely burned-out

village, and Sarnac braced himself. It was well that he did. Travelling in the wake of the advancing army, this was not their first sight of a village that the Saxons had occupied. But it was the worst, for they had now caught up to the main body of the army and fresh remains were still being burned or buried. They entered a central square where soldiers were removing that which the Saxons turned human bodies into.

Hanging from the X-shaped wooden frame to which he had been strapped, over a puddle of blood and worse, what seemed to have been a young man stared lifelessly at them with a face frozen in the horror of transcendent agony. There was something about his back—it couldn't quite be made out from this angle. Then they rode past him, and Sarnac saw. But his mind rejected it. The world spun, and he tasted bile.

A soldier began to cut the remains of another man from the frame. He was one of Syagrius' troop, and he wasn't young—he must have fought Saxons before, must have seen atrocities like these. His face was pale but rock-steady.

Sarnac held himself upright in the saddle and tried to gain control of his rising gorge. *I can't let these men see me vomit.* He nudged his horse forward, but not too fast, and left the scene from Hell behind. Tylar rode next to him, watching him gravely.

"Were they trying to get information out of him?" he asked because he needed to talk, anything to fill the silence.

"Oh, no. Carving the Blood Eagle is for fun." Tylar's face hardened into an expression Sarnac had never seen on it. "We have to accept things as we find them, throughout human history. And because we may not interfere, we make it an inflexible rule never to take sides. But some people make that very difficult. The Saxons, for example. They are . . . animals."

They trotted on, beyond the village, to a field where tents had been raised and a long table set up. Around it, the commanders studied what this era was pleased to call maps, while their subordinates stood around under the trees. Servants moved about replenishing goblets with the local wine, which may have come from the vineyard off to one side—at least *that* was a reminder of the Loire valley Sarnac knew. He and Tylar dismounted and waited diffidently, trying to ignore the charnel smell from the village.

He looked curiously at the group around the table. Syagrius was short, even by current standards, young but stocky and tough-looking. He was wearing a Roman-style field uniform that, in this century, included trousers. His vassal king, Childeric of the Franks, was a striking contrast, a tall man with blondish, greying hair he wore in the distinctive style—drooping mustaches, side braids, and a rather ridiculous-looking topknot, with the back of the head shaved—and sported the garishly striped tunic favored by the Franks. Tylar had mentioned a widespread suspicion that he worked at being a colorful figure who the Romans were apt to underestimate. Sarnac, who had known similar types, was inclined to agree.

And then there was Riothamus. Sarnac had seen him a few times before, but not often, and only at a distance, for the High King had been spending most of his time in Nantes.

"Using the captured boats, we've taken these other islands," Syagrius was saying, pointing at a map. "For now, we control this part of the Loire. We can ferry our troops across the Maine and advance on Angers from the south. We can crush the Saxons between the anvil of Angers and the hammer of our advance!"

"Aye," Riothamus said slowly. "So we can. If, that is, they wait to be crushed. Now, if I were Odovacar I'd have some of my boats beached to the north of Angers, so I could escape with some of my forces in the event of an attack from the south, however successful."

"But that would mean going past the fortress at Angers!"

"That it would. And, to be sure, the defenders could do some damage from where they sit, overlooking the Maine. But most would get away."

"To meet my warriors among the Loire islands! Let them come!" Childeric tossed off a gulp of wine and belched resoundingly. *Yeah*, Sarnac thought, *he really does overdo the Barbarian Bruiser number.* But, he reflected, it might have something to do with the fact that Childeric, shortly after ascending the throne thirteen years ago, had been exiled for reason of overindulgence in distinctively Roman forms of vice. Afterwards, his people had sought the protection of Syagrius' father, Aegidius, beginning the Franks' subordination to the Kingdom of Soissons. Now, restored to the throne, Childeric clearly felt a need to appear more Frankish than the Franks. At least he couldn't try the noble savage number, having never heard of it; it lay far in the future, waiting to be invented by Jean-Jacques Rousseau (who never met real savages) and confirmed by Margaret Mead (who did, but chose to lie about them).

"Ah," Riothamus replied, "but Odovacar doesn't know for certain that the islands have been taken. At least we hope he doesn't. And so he'd sail on down with the fearlessness of ignorance—which, as we all know, can often work wonders in war, because we always assume our enemy will act sensibly." *And that*, Sarnac thought, *is as cogent a critique of games theory as I've ever heard.*

Childeric seemed disposed to further bluster, but Syagrius waved him to silence. "But, Riothamus, what are you proposing? We *must* raise the siege of Angers!"

"Of course. But I don't just want to chase the Saxons away from Angers. I want to *annihilate* them!" Riothamus' dark eyes had taken on a look Sarnac hoped never to see across a battlefield, and responding growls arose from the men around the fringes of the field. Sarnac wondered what had ever given him the arrogance to think these men could have ridden through this village without feeling what he had felt.

"But how . . . ?" Syagrius began.

"I've been talking to some of the local Andecavi. They tell me there's a place up the Maine—about fifteen miles from here, nine or ten past Angers—where the river can be forded at the height of a dry summer like this one. I'll take the Artoriani north, while you cross the Maine down here with your forces and my infantry. We'll strike Angers from the north, when you've begun your attack from the south. The Saxons will be trapped, even if Angers has surrendered to them in the meantime!"

"But the risk!" Syagrius was visibly shaken. "You can't hazard your own person—the person of the High King— in this way! Send the Artoriani under the command of a trusted subordinate, and remain with the main body of your infantry."

Riothamus replied in a perfectly normal tone of voice, but his deep baritone filled the little clearing. "My place is at the head of the Artoriani, Syagrius, as it was the place of my fathers before me. For I was the *Pan-Tarkan* before I was the High King."

The term was not British, but Sarnac had learned it among the Artoriani. It meant "Dragon Leader" in the Iranian tongue of the Sarmatian horsemen, who had lost almost all the rest of the language through the generations in Britain. Even that term survived in a worn-down form—*pan* had originally been *panje*. But its meaning was not worn down at all, for it was the title of the hereditary commander of that unit from which Riothamus' heavy cavalry had grown.

As if in response to his words, a slight breeze picked up, causing the red dragon standard that had been set up on the edge of the clearing to stir and flutter. And the red and white clad men near it seemed to stand a little straighter.

Syagrius also knew its meaning. "Well, if you must . . ."

Riothamus smiled, and Sarnac realized that it had been a while since he had looked at, or for that matter *seen*, anyone other than the High King. "Cheer up, Syagrius! You have my word that I'll meet you before the walls of Angers!"

"Then I know you'll be there. You never broke your word to my father. And now," Syagrius continued, all business, "I need to give the orders for my troops' crossing of the Maine." The meeting broke up, and Tylar made a slight motion that Riothamus noticed.

"Ah, Tertullian! I see you've caught up with us. What news from your master?"

"He is well and sends his regards, Riothamus. His journey home was uneventful, and he has received confirmation of his election as Bishop of Clermont."

"Splendid! They couldn't have made a better choice. Convey my congratulations to His Excellency, and tell him I hope to see him early next year, after we enter the Auvergne."

"His Excellency shares that hope, Riothamus, and in the meantime, he asks a favor of you."

"Anything!"

"He has charged me with sending him a faithful account of this campaign—I believe he plans a new panegyric, of epic proportions. And he asks if I may be permitted to travel in your entourage, to be close to events."

Riothamus looked dubious. "You probably heard us just now, Tertullian. In the morning, I depart at the head of the Artoriani for Angers. It will mean hard riding, and harder fighting at the end. I'd feel responsible to Sidonius for your safety. Do you know how to use that . . . ?" He indicated what looked like a short sword.

"Alas, Riothamus, I fear I'm no fighting man. But I've engaged the services of a bodyguard, so you should not have to concern yourself with my survival." He gestured to Sarnac to step forward. "This is Bedwyr, under whose protection I should be quite safe."

"*Ave*, Riothamus," Sarnac greeted as he had been instructed. The honorific was used as a form of address, like "Augustus" for the Emperors—except by members of the Artoriani. They, and they alone, were entitled to address him as *Pan-Tarkan*. Recruits from the hills of western Britain, as was their way, wore the title down still further; on their lips it sounded something like *Pendragon*.

"Bedwyr, eh?" The High King smiled easily. "A fine British name if ever I heard one! Are you from the island?"

"My father Gerontius was, Riothamus. I was born in Armorica."

"Gerontius! I think I met someone by that name on my last visit to Armorica—I've spent almost as much of my reign there as in Britain, you know."

"My father died when I was a child, Riothamus," Sarnac said hastily. "And I've been away, in the service of the Eastern Emperor."

"Ah!" Riothamus' eyes flashed with interest. "In the Emperor Leo's army you must have seen cavalry that used stirrups. Did you get a chance to try riding with them?"

"I did, Riothamus." He caught a surprised glance from Tylar, but it was a safe statement. His implanted riding skill was with the stirrupless saddles of the Romans, but in his own world, he had done a little riding in his younger days. It should come back to him in no time—it was *so* much easier than clinging to a horse's barrel with your legs for dear life!

"Good! You'll be able to keep up with us. Tertullian, are you willing to try?"

"Your wish is my command, Riothamus. But . . . well, no offense intended, but it seems . . . ah, *innovative*."

"Ha! Barbarous, you mean! So the legions thought at

Adrianople, ninety years ago, when the Gothic heavy cavalry rode over them. And the damned Goths learned about stirrups, and all the rest of it, from my Sarmatian ancestors!" He shook his head ruefully. "Well, then, it's settled. You can come. Good!" His face lit up with a smile whose boyishness was somehow not inappropriate among the grey hairs that were beginning to invade his dark beard. "I admit it: I'm just vain enough to relish the thought of being immortalized by Sidonius Apollinaris! Be sure to send him full accounts of the campaign . . . which of *course* won't be at all exaggerated!"

"Certainly not, Riothamus." Tylar was blandness itself.

"I am reassured." The dark eyes twinkled. "Kai, where are you?"

"Here, *Pan-Tarkan*." The young man's name was of Sarmatian origin but he couldn't have looked more Celtic, with his spun-copper hair and green eyes and the freckles beneath his weather-beaten tan.

"Kai, issue Tertullian and his bodyguard standard horse-gear. Tertullian may need help with it, but I don't think Bedwyr will."

Kai gave the grin that seemed to be his face's natural configuration. "Come on, I'll get you outfitted. It's over here. Bedwyr, you look like you're from the north country, being so dark but with blue eyes." Sarnac trotted out his cover story and kept Kai distracted from specifics until they had gotten their new horse-furniture. It turned out to include, in addition to the stirrups, a saddle deeper and with a ~~higher~~ higher cantle than the Roman ones.

"You know, Tertullian, this is something I've wondered about," Sarnac remarked when Kai was gone and they were alone with their horses. "Since Riothamus and his boys use stirrups, why doesn't *everybody*? I mean, it's such an improvement!"

"You underestimate the conservatism of preindustrial societies. It's not uncommon for a useful invention to be in clear view for centuries and not obtain general acceptance. The Artoriani use the device not because it's demonstrably more efficient, but because it's traditional—for *them*, in their own subculture. By the way, Riothamus is absolutely right about the Goths having acquired the entire panoply of heavy cavalry warfare from the Sarmatians, from whom they conquered the South Russian steppes. But after the events we're going to be witnessing, the stirrup will be forgotten; that, too, often happens in preindustrial societies. It will be reintroduced to Europe a century from now by the Avars, a people from Chinese Turkestan. Many later scholars will mistakenly hold that it was *initially* brought to this continent by them."

But Sarnac had stopped listening after the words, "the events we're going to be witnessing." He had begun to wonder if he really wanted to witness what he knew must happen.

It was just past dawn when they set out for the north, a full *cuneus* of five hundred heavy cavalry with their grooms and other support types, leaving the village and its ghosts behind, and swinging to the east, out of sight of the Maine. The Artoriani kept up as good a pace as they could without wearing out their horses. Those horses were as much a part of Riothamus' striking force as the men, for they were a special breed that could carry heavily armored and equipped men, plus the hardened leather armor that protected their own forequarters. It wasn't really too grueling, although Tylar protested piteously, if only to stay in character.

Kai clucked about the inadequacy of Sarnac's armor and offered to finagle him something better, but Sarnac assured him that he was used to what he had. Then the column rounded a curve in the decaying Roman road, and the Saxons appeared.

Sarnac's first warning was the nerve-tearing series of war cries from the hillock the road curved around, followed immediately by a shower of throwing-axes, most of which clattered off hastily raised shields; only a few found their mark in human or equine flesh. A nearby horse reared and whinnied in pain, throwing their part of the column into confusion as the Saxons began bounding down the slope.

Kai turned his horse away, shouting the nearby men into formation. Sarnac drew his *spatha*, letting his implanted reflexes act for him. Tylar had vetoed any special embellishments for the straight, three and a half foot cavalry sword—blows glancing off a helmet or cloth armor could be attributed to luck, but boulders severed by a micromolecular-edged blade would have taken some explaining. Still, the weapon's balance and heft were good.

"Get back," he yelled at Tylar, who was already taking shelter behind the column, when the first Saxons appeared among the still-disorganized horsemen. They were the first live specimens Sarnac had seen—bareheaded, and clad in heavy cloth tunics and cross-gartered leggings except for a few leaders who had helmets and mail shirts, wielding the short *seax* that had given them their name. To Sarnac, it looked like a large Bowie knife. They rushed in, trying to get in under the riders' weapons and disembowel the horses. The Artoriani responded with practiced efficiency, reining their mounts aside and striking downward with their *spathas*.

A Saxon appeared just below Sarnac, holding aloft his shield. Sarnac got a glimpse of wild blue eyes and contorted ruddy features as he brought his *spatha* down, smashing the shield aside with an impact he could feel up through his right shoulder. Before the Saxon could return his shield to position, Sarnac's *spatha* whirled and bit, sundering the florid face. He looked around through the melee, spotting Riothamus up ahead, just around the bend where the attackers had probably hoped to isolate him. The High King turned his horse on its haunches, swinging his sword in powerful figure-eight sweeps that kept a ring of Saxons at bay.

Sarnac spurred his horse forward, just as a half-naked Saxon leaped down at him off the ridge to his right with a scream. Without thinking, Sarnac stood in his stirrups, grasped the *spatha* with both hands—it wasn't designed for it—and put all of his strength into a vertical slash that caught the Saxon across the abdomen in midair. He fell to the ground, squalling in agony and rolling about in the dust trailing ropes of gut until he vanished beneath the thundering hooves.

Sarnac spurred on toward Riothamus just as a throwing axe struck him in the side. The impact armor rigidified at the split second of impact, without interrupting the tunic's fold pattern. The axe spun away, dented. He caught sight of the Saxon who had hurled it. The man stood stock-still and openmouthed for an instant, until a horseman came up from behind and split his skull. Sarnac rode on, emerging from the press of struggling figures just in time to see a Saxon get in under Riothamus' guard, and deal his horse a vicious hamstringing cut.

Riothamus managed to roll free of the falling horse and was on his feet and fighting. Sarnac spurred his horse into a gallop and was suddenly among the High King's attackers, bowling over two who were coming up behind the High King, then bringing his *spatha* down on the helmet of one of the wealthy armored warriors. It glanced off, but the blow staggered the Saxon backward, exposing his throat. Sarnac brought the *spatha* around and thrust it into the man's head from under the lower jaw. It was primarily a slashing weapon, but it had more of a point than later medieval swords. That point continued inward until it scraped on the inside of the cranium. The Saxon died in the almost bloodless way of those killed instantly.

Sarnac had a moment to see Riothamus—now free of the worry of an attack from the rear—take on another Saxon noble. Their swords and shields met in a clinch. A quick movement by Riothamus sent both spinning around, and the High King, recovering first, brought his *spatha* around in a wide cut that sheared through mail and severed the Saxon's spine. This was nothing like sabre fencing; it was more like a crude *kendo* with shields, aimed at maximizing the force a human body could put behind a sword edge. Whatever you called it, Riothamus was obviously very good at it.

Then a wave front of the Artoriani reached them, riding down the fleeing Saxon survivors. On open ground, it was a slaughter, and as it swirled on past them, he and Riothamus were left among a scatter of Saxon bodies.

Matter-of-factly, Riothamus went to his feebly thrashing horse and administered the mercy stroke. For an instant the High King stood, head lowered, in a silence Sarnac was not about to break. Then he turned, his face as animated as ever. "Bedwyr, I'll thank you to lend me your horse—and I'll be thanking you for more later. I've seldom seen a man fight with greater courage!"

Yeah, and you've seldom seen a man with impact armor and a helmet of power-bonded iron, Sarnac thought as he swung down and passed the bridle to the High King. He felt a strange depression that he recognized as combat reaction. Oddly, though, he felt no need to yield to the shakes. Later, maybe.

Riothamus rode off, leaving Sarnac alone for a moment. Then Tylar cantered up. "Well," the time traveller said briskly, *"that's* over! Strange—there weren't enough Saxons to have hoped to defeat this entire force. The attack was probably aimed at Riothamus personally. Clearly, the plan was to cut him off at the head of the column and kill him before his men could disentangle themselves from the melee and reach him." He shook his head. "Say what you will of the Saxons, they are not without bravery."

"Fine. Give 'em a medal and then kill 'em." Sarnac knew how surly he sounded but couldn't bring himself to care. Tylar gave him a quizzical look.

"You seem rather subdued, for someone who just made quite an impression. You should have seen the looks you were getting from some of the Artoriani."

"That's the problem, Tylar. It wasn't *me!* If they're going to make a hero out of anybody, it should be whoever made the technology that protected me and enabled me to do what I was doing."

"So you feel you were somehow cheating?"

"It just wasn't me," Sarnac repeated mulishly.

"But it was," Tylar replied gravely. "No implant made you ride to Riothamus' aid. I believe you would have done that with just as little hesitation if you'd had no special advantages at all. In fact, I'm quite certain of it."

Sarnac didn't see how he could be so certain, but he felt the sense of dissatisfaction ebb from his soul. Then the Artoriani began to return from their Saxon-killing in a great noisy crowd.

"Bedwyr!" Kai trotted his horse toward him, motioning a knot of his companions to follow. "There he is! Bedwyr, I was just telling the ones who didn't see it how you practically cut that damned Saxon in two as he leaped at you! Ha!" He suddenly looked puzzled. "But what was it you shouted as you fought? I couldn't understand it."

Oh, God, did I forget and say something in English? I can't recall. But, come to think of it, my throat does feel raw; I must have been screaming at the top of my lungs!

"Right," one of Kai's friends said. "I heard it too: *'Oh, shit!'* or something like that. What does it mean?"

"Er, it's the war cry of a tribe called the Vulgarians. I picked it up in the Balkans."

He was saved from further explanations by Riothamus' arrival, in a clatter of hooves and a storm of cheers. "Ah, Tertullian! God be praised, you're all right. I would have had to find another way to supply Sidonius with inspiration!" He gave his disarming smile and swung to the ground. "Bedwyr, here's your horse back. That loan was the least of the favors you've done me this day." He gripped Sarnac's arm and their eyes met.

"Riothamus, it was nothing," Sarnac began, feeling ridiculously inadequate. Not for the first time, he was aware of this man's indefinable vividness that always made whatever setting he was in seem just that—a setting for him.

"I'm thinking it was a deal more than nothing," Riothamus said in the British tongue, suddenly serious. Then he turned to Tylar and the smile was back, as was the Latin. "Tertullian, Bedwyr seems to be doing more guarding of me than of you, so let's make it official. I'll assign someone to you, if you'll let him join my personal guards. I think I want him near me at Angers. What say you, Bedwyr?"

Sarnac looked at Tylar, whose expression said "Well, after all, I can hardly refuse, my dear fellow!" as clearly as his voice could have, then at the circle of Artoriani that had formed around them, and then at Riothamus. And he heard himself speak, in words whose absolute rightness he knew with a certainty beyond mere knowledge.

"Aye . . . *Pan-Tarkan*."

Belatedly he realized what he had said and glanced around at the Artoriani, braced for he-knew-not-what reaction. But none came.

Kai, as usual, was grinning.

CHAPTER TWELVE

They hadn't needed to make cold camps since fording the Maine and coming into position north of Angers. A range of low hillocks shielded them from the Saxon siege lines, and the Saxons were too sloppy to patrol the area's outskirts—at least this was the unvarying experience of the Artoriani. But the ambush they had undergone had shaken their certainty, and they had maintained constant patrols of their own to take out any Saxon scouts.

But there had been no such scouts, and the Artoriani had settled in to await the word of Syagrius' approach. The word had finally come, by way of their own scouts, and their contacts among the local Andecavi, who had suffered at the hands of the Saxons since Odovacar and his brood had fastened their rule onto the lands south of the Loire estuary. So tomorrow morning they would ride to battle—but at least for now they had campfires to warm them against the waning summer's nighttime chill.

Sarnac walked among those campfires with Tylar, who was in full lecture mode. "Yes, the battle tomorrow will be most interesting; in fact, it may settle a vexed question concerning this period. You see, as a last resort the Saxons always fall back on the shield wall. And the lay of the land at Angers suggests that Riothamus will be faced with the task of charging *uphill* against such a shield wall. Shades of Hastings!"

"Hastings?" Sarnac blinked a couple of times. "Oh, yeah. Norman conquest of England. 1066. Who was it who said that was one of the two really memorable dates in history? It must be, if I remembered it!"

"What was the other one?" Tylar asked, interested.

"I don't remember," Sarnac admitted.

"Well, at any rate, you know that Hastings lies six hundred years in the future. And William the Bastard—whom flatterers will later rename William the Conqueror—will need indirect fire support by his archers to break *that* Saxon shield wall with his heavy cavalry. Admittedly, he will face a better shield wall than Riothamus will tomorrow. But Riothamus will have *no* archers, unless he waits for Syagrius to supply them; and attempting a rendezvous in the presence of the enemy is risky in any age. Yes, it will be most interesting to see how Riothamus handles this."

"I'll try to give you all the details—assuming that I don't take one of those Saxon throwing-axes in the face!"

"The probability of that is low enough to make the risk quite acceptable," Tylar said serenely.

I'm so glad you *think it's acceptable!* Aloud: "Just don't joggle my elbow with too many questions via implant communicator. You'll have no way of knowing when I'm in a tight spot where distractions could be fatal."

"Understood." Tylar had an implant that was compatible with Sarnac's subdermal communications equipment. But they had intentionally limited their use of the capability—habitual dependence on it might have put them into hard-to-explain situations.

Their stroll carried them past a campfire surrounded by an exceptionally large number of Artoriani. "Old Hamyc must be holding forth," Tylar remarked.

"So he is. Let's listen; he tells some good stories."

Hamyc, like Kai, had a name of Iranian origin. But unlike Kai, his looks matched his name, with a dark, hawklike face and thick black brows, which grew together above his long, narrow hooked nose. He was in his fifties, and rated respect just for having had the competence, divine favor, or plain good luck to survive so many years of deadly warfare and deadlier medical attention. But his special status among the Artoriani went beyond that, for he was the hereditary storyteller. It was not an official position, but it was nonetheless real. He and his forefathers had preserved, among these almost uniformly illiterate men, an oral tradition that had enabled them to maintain their identity for centuries, on an island far indeed from the steppes.

And yet whenever he opened his mouth, Sarnac was reminded that he, like all of them, was by now more Celtic than anything else.

Hamyc had just wound up a story when a man spoke up who, from the look of him, could scarcely have carried a non-Celtic chromosome. "Hamyc, tell us the tale of how our forefathers came to Britain."

"Well, now, talking of matters so dusty old is infernally thirsty work, especially for one of my years." His scarred face looked crafty in the firelight. Sarnac suspected that he had, around other campfires, bemoaned his age and enfeeblement to some of these men's fathers. Someone passed him a wineskin, from which he partook deeply. Then he waited until there was complete silence for his voice to fill.

"Long ago, so long that no one can remember how many winters it was, the Sarmatians rode out of the land from which the sun rises and drove the Scythians from the sea of grass that stretches from the Caspian waters westward to the rampart of the Carpathians. None could match them in horsemanship—not even the Scythians, who were such riders that the old Greeks, after seeing them, made up a silly fable of creatures half man and half horse.

"Among the Sarmatians, no clan stood higher than the Iazyges, who had led the way west to the Roman frontiers. But there they fell in with German tribes—always bad luck for any people." A collective growl arose from these men who had spent their lives fighting Saxon former *foederatii.* "The Germans beguiled the chieftain Zanticus into an alliance against the Romans. Betrayed by his faithless allies, Zanticus was forced to sue for peace. And the Romans' wise emperor, Marcus Aurelius, set it down in the treaty that the Iazyges must supply him with horsemen. Being wise, he saw that he needed Sarmatians to fill the ranks of his cavalry, for a Roman trying to ride a horse is like a eunuch trying to ride a woman!" A ripple of coarse laughter ran around the campfire. Hamyc smiled in response, but then smoothed his face out into seriousness. "Save for one Roman only," he said quietly, and the laughter ceased. As if on cue, a voice spoke.

"Lucius Artorius Castus."

"Aye." Hamyc nodded. "He was a Roman of noble family, but a real man for all of that. He had fought against the Iazyges, and knew the Sarmatians to be his kindred in all but blood. Afterwards, as Prefect of the Sixth Legion in Britain, he commanded a unit of Sarmatian *cataphractii*—and knew how to use them! They rode the Pictish raiders into the ground for him, and later he led them to this land to put down rebels in Armorica. Aye, he was a man and a leader of men, riding and fighting at their forefront and laughing their fears away! When the first *Pan-Tarkan* of those in Britain fell in battle, they chose Artorius as his successor—and he understood what that meant, even if no other Roman did.

"By the time their term of service was over, many of those men had taken up with British women and sired children. And besides, it was a long and weary way back to the steppes! So most remained in Britain, accepting the Romans' offer of land—a veterans' colony at Ribchester. There they bred sons who married more British women, so that as generations passed the tongue of the steppes was lost while the blood of the steppes spread thinly indeed. But they never forgot who they were. And they continued to supply *cataphractii* for the Emperors of Rome, for they came of a breed who kept their oaths. And they named not a few of their sons Artorius.

"So it was that when our *Pan-Tarkan* became High King, he named us after himself, as was the custom of Roman emperors. But it was also right in a way the Romans could not understand, for we still remembered another Artorius."

Hamyc paused and looked thirsty until the wineskin was passed back to him. "But Hamyc," someone said from the shadows, "tell us of the great march south from Ribchester, and how the *Pan-Tarkan* became High King. You yourself can remember that."

"Aye," Hamyc admitted, coming up for air. "That was sixteen years ago, when some of you young colts were barely weaned! But I was there, in the high summer of my life, before old age overtook me." He sighed with a self-pity that only another pull on the wineskin could assuage. "I was there when we cut our way south through country swarming with Saxons to join Ambrosius Aurelianus. And I was there when the *Pan-Tarkan* claimed the High Kingship by right of his deeds as well as of the blood he had married." Sarnac felt movement by his side, as if Tylar was fidgeting. "But," Hamyc continued, "that is another tale, which will have to wait for another night. We must be up before the dawn, and I for one am not as young as I once was."

The old buzzard plays an audience like a Stradivarius, Sarnac thought as the crowd broke up with moans of disappointment—a disappointment Tylar didn't seem to

share. In fact, Sarnac got the impression that the time
traveller was relieved at Hamyc's choice of a stopping
point. He wondered why.

The sun was breaking over the eastern treetops as
they were thundering along the riverbank toward Angers,
shattering the shallow water into fountains that the
morning light turned into showers of rainbow.

Ahead of them to the southeast rose the plateau on
which, centuries hence, would stand the castle where the
Counts of Anjou would hold court. It rose almost sheer
from the banks of the Maine to their right, but the slope
steadily gentled on the inland side. Here the Romans had
raised a walled town on the old hill-fort of the Andecavi.
Around it spread Odovacar's Saxon host, which knew
no siege technique except blockading into submission.
Beyond it, Syagrius would even now be assaulting the
southern siege lines—if he and Riothamus had succeeded
in coordinating the operation through couriers, who had
to swing wide through the countryside east of Angers.
No one ever thought of command-and-control problems
in connection with ancient warfare, Sarnac reflected. What
people *did* think of was what he and the Artoriani were
doing right now: galloping down the riverbank toward
the Saxon ships, drawn up on shore behind the
northernmost end of the siege lines, with the blood-red
dragon flying above them in the wind of their passage,
charging into the spreading panic of the Saxon camp.

For a while, it was all a blur to Sarnac—he later
remembered striking at running figures among the
collapsing tents, and sometimes feeling the shock as his
blade struck home. Then they reached the line of long,
narrow boats pulled up on the riverbank.

"Flavian! Owain! Take your sections and burn them!"
Riothamus waved his bloody *spatha* at the ships.
"Everyone else gather up your men—I'll have no looting.

We've no time to lose." He had his helmet off and his grey-shot dark hair, which had grown a little shaggy on campaign, whipped in the wind, as did his scarlet cloak. He controlled his horse, which seemed to have absorbed some of its rider's sheer restless vitality.

Sarnac took a moment for a look around. Directly ahead was the steep slope, crowned with the fortress of Angers. To the left, where the slope gentled, scattered Saxons could be seen swarming up to join a mass of their fellows that was forming in front of the walls. From the southwest, beyond the plateau, came the sound of this era's battles—a roaring of voices, and a semi-metallic thunder of iron-bossed wooden shields crashing together.

"No time, indeed!" Kai, who had joined him, looked as grim as Sarnac had ever seen him, as he pointed at the dark mass of Saxons on the slope. "The shield wall—they'll be ready to welcome us by the time we get our heads into the sunlight!"

But it took less time than Sarnac would have thought possible before they were riding away from the impassable rise near the river, toward the foot of the gentler slope that ran up to the walled town. They had just halted when a courier galloped up, whipping his horse in a way that drew frowns from these men, and saluted Riothamus. Sarnac couldn't catch the conversation, but a low growl began to spread from those who could. Kai heard the story first and cursed imaginatively.

"The bastards have fought Syagrius to a standstill over there." He waved toward the battle sounds. "He didn't use our infantry properly—the damned Gauls just had to lead the attack, and their fat guts must have made perfect targets for throwing-axes! By Mithras—by God and His saints, I mean—we'd be better off without those greasy buggers!" As Kai raged on, Sarnac studied the map that seemed to appear in the air in front of his eyes. They were due south of Angers now, and Syagrius was approaching from the southwest. The Saxons were concentrated in a triangular space, one side formed by the walls of Angers, whose defenders must be too worn out to manage a breakout against the barbarians outside the gates, another near the front, where Syagrius was trying unsuccessfully to fight his way uphill, and the third next to the shield wall, which they would try to break—with three hundred cavalry charging uphill.

Commands rang out, and they began to deploy. Sarnac moved to his assigned position, near the center with Kai's squadron, donning his helmet and tightening the cheek-pieces. The rather special helmet he wore made him especially concerned with leaving as little of the face exposed as possible.

He looked around curiously. These were experienced troops and it showed. But it is only in the lying recollections of superannuated veterans that anyone goes into battle with a song in his heart—and without a dryness in the mouth, a tightness in the stomach, and a churning in the bowels. As the Artoriani dressed their lines, curbing horses that could sense the tension, they glanced up the slope at the dense, weapon-bristling line of overlapping shields, and a subdued quiet stretched.

"Hallo!" In a clatter of hooves, Riothamus rode up the line, scarlet cloak billowing behind him, followed by the standard-bearer and the red dragon. He wheeled his horse around and ran his flashing dark eyes over them, frowning with such boyishly obvious fakeness that you had to smile. Sarnac glanced at the sky and saw to his surprise that the overcast that had moved in during the morning was unabated. Hadn't it gotten lighter?

"Hamyc, you old croaker!" The High King greeted the storyteller. "Have you been wasting these men's time complaining about the new lance technique again?"

"Well, *Pan-Tarkan*, it's just that my father and his father before him used their lances the old way." He hefted the eight-foot lance into an overhand grip and made a jabbing motion. "I ask you, what's wrong with the way it's always been done?" Sarnac wondered how much of Hamyc's kvetching was cultural conservatism and how much was overindulgence in the wineskin the previous night.

"Ha! Hamyc, you're a broken-down old warhorse who can't be taught new maneuvers! I'm thinking I'll have to let you out to pasture, now that you're too old for battle!"

As laughter began to burble up from the ranks, Kai's voice rang out. "But, *Pan-Tarkan*, it's too late! He's too old to be put out to stud!"

The laughter was a full eruption now, joined by everyone except Hamyc, who was muttering about the respectlessness of the younger generations and the rest of the general tragic decline from the good old days. *Yep, he's definitely hung over*, Sarnac decided. He glanced up the slope and detected a wavering of uncertainty in that solid formation as the wolfish sound of the laughter reached it. But mostly he was watching Riothamus, laughing with his men and calling out greetings as he rode past.

He's crazy! Absolutely certifiable! And if those Saxons up there had gauss miniguns—and these guys knew what that meant—they'd still ride up this hill for him.

Then the High King drew level with him. "Bedwyr! Hasn't anyone gotten you a lance? Kai, see to it!" He drew closer and spoke in a quieter voice. "You may not have seen this technique before—I thought of it myself." He demonstrated with his own lance.

"I have, *Pan-Tarkan*." In fact, Sarnac *had* seen it—in VR adventures and in the historical reenactments that were popular in his world.

"Good! I'm sorry that we haven't had time to give you some practice, and to get you proper armor." He held

Sarnac's eyes. "If you want to ride in the rear, and use your sword after the initial breakthrough, no one will think the worse of you."

"If you will, *Pan-Tarkan*, I'm thinking I'd as soon stay where I am," Sarnac returned, in British.

Riothamus said nothing—his expression made it unnecessary. He moved on, calling out more greetings. Sarnac shook his head in bewilderment. He could get Tylar's information just as well in the rear, he knew. *Good Lord, am I as crazy as the rest of them?* He shook his head again, in irritation, and activated his implant communicator.

"Tylar, I've got something for you." He described what Riothamus had just shown him.

"So! This is *most* interesting!" The ghostly voice in his head was jittery with academic excitement. "It seems I haven't been giving Riothamus enough credit. He may have received much from the Sarmatian element in his heritage, but he's also an innovator! Of course, it's another innovation that will be lost; William's knights at Hastings will be holding their lances overhand and thrusting with them. In fact—"

"Wait a minute, something's happening." He described the forming-up, ahead of them, of a single line of riders who lacked the long, heavy lances but held a shorter kind of spear.

"Aha! Javelins! I begin to see what Riothamus is up to. . . ."

"Gotta go!" Sarnac accepted the lance Kai handed him. He held it as he had been shown, couched under his arm. The rest of them were doing the same when orders rang out—he glanced down the line and saw that Hamyc was doing it as smartly as any of them. He could make out a muttered " 'Too old,' is it?" from that direction.

Then another command was heard, and they spurred three hundred horses forward as one.

❖   ❖   ❖

Sarnac had read in historical fiction that at moments like this "the earth shook," and had always regarded it as wildly overwritten. Now he knew it wasn't. Not at all.

He also knew that those reenactment hobbyists who tried to do heavy cavalry simply didn't have a clue.

They started up the slope slowly, then gradually built up momentum until the thunder of twelve hundred hooves overpowered the entire being, not just the ears. Dry weather had left the ground solid, but it also caused clouds of dust to rise from the line of javelin men ahead. But Sarnac wasn't aware of it; he was caught up in what had become a race up the slope. In all the shouting around him, he heard some men yell approximations of the "Vulgarian war cry." *Well, why not? It seems to work for ol' Bedwyr.*

Then, up ahead through the dust, he saw the riders of the first line twist in their saddles in an odd way, then reverse the motion, flinging their javelins. Then they wheeled away, peeling off to left and right . . . and there was the shield wall, showing rents and confusion from the javelin shower it had just weathered—and maybe also from the sight of the blood-red dragon. And then, before the Saxons could restore their formation, the charge reached it.

Sarnac, existing in an odd state of distended time, felt his lance head slide along a skewed shield and punch into a Saxon's gut, then tear loose as he rode past the disintegrating Saxon battle-mass. Then he was through, suddenly conscious of the hellish din his mind had shut out, and spared a split second to glance backward at the red ruin where the shield wall had been. Then he was riding with the Artoriani through what was no longer a monolithic formation, just a mob of panic-shrieking individuals, caught up in a battle that had ceased to be a battle, and had become a trampling, hacking slaughter.

All at once, he understood the Middle Ages.

It was very straightforward, really. You could even express it in terms of physics. Take the mass of a man, and a large horse, both armored. Multiply it by the velocity of a good gallop. Then, by bracing your feet in stirrups, and holding a lance couched underarm, concentrate all that kinetic energy behind the point of that lance. It might not seem like much to Sarnac's civilization, which incinerated life wholesale with nukes, whiffed it out of existence with lasers, and shredded it with streams of hypervelocity metal slivers. But here and now, it was enough to change the face of Eurasia from the Loire to China, where the Turkish Toba were lording it over the north, having stopped at the Yangtze only because rice paddies make poor cavalry terrain.

Oh, heavy shock cavalry could be stopped. All it took was an unshakable formation of pikemen—horses, unlike men, have better sense than to crash at full tilt into an apparently solid barrier. But it took generations to create that kind of infantry, who would die in formation before they would break ranks in the sight of their comrades and the regiment's ghosts. The Swiss would do it, a thousand years hence. But until then, the battlefield belonged to the *cataphract*—the knight.

Everything else flowed from that. The feudal system, for instance. The only way the peasantry could survive was by turning themselves into serfs, tying hundreds of near-subsistence farmers to one *cataphract*, whom they supported with their individually paltry surplus, so that he might devote his life to perfecting himself in this very specialized martial art.

But feudalism still lay in the future. How did Riothamus support this kind of outfit?

The answer could only be that he was still living off what was left of Rome's capital. The money economy wasn't quite dead yet in Western Europe. Revenue could still be collected in the form of coinage. A generation from now, they'd be back to barter and nobody in Britain would be able to operate in Riothamus' style. Even now he must live very close to the bone. To survive, he couldn't let his economic base contract an iota. *That's what he's doing here in Gaul. He can't let his Breton holdings go. And he thinks he can use the leverage he's developing with Syagrius & Co., and what's left of the Western Empire, to expand his base—while it's still worth expanding. He's never heard the expression "window of opportunity," but he sure as hell knows what it means.*

All this ran through Sarnac's head in the time it took him to notice that his lance had been broken. He dropped it and pulled out his *spatha*, spurring his horse forward through the thinning melee. He reached the crest of the hill, then paused and looked around.

Ahead of him was Angers, whose defenders had taken advantage of the spreading Saxon rout to sally from the gate. Now a mob of lightly armed citizens was pouring down the slope to his left, catching the Saxons who were beginning to fall back from Syagrius' advance. To left and right the mounted javelin men, having thrown away their missiles, were closing in on the Saxon flanks with drawn swords, herding them inward to the killing ground.

He contacted Tylar and described it all. The latter was close to academic ecstasy. "Yes! Yes! This is absolutely extraordinary! I would never have believed that an army in Dark Ages Western Europe could be capable of this kind of tactical finesse. Most battles in this milieu are nothing but drunken brawls, you know. And . . . are you all right, my dear fellow? You don't sound altogether yourself."

You wouldn't either, if you'd been here, Sarnac didn't say. He had let combat reaction catch up with him as the killing had swirled on past, coming down from a high whose origins he had difficulty defining. He was trying to describe the sensations to Tylar when Kai rode up.

Instead of the euphoria Sarnac expected, the Briton's face wore annoyance. "Well, I'll have words for my squadron after *that*, you can be sure! Of course, you can only expect so much, charging uphill . . . but we might as well have been riding pigs! Bedwyr, I'm overcome with embarrassment!"

By God, he's not faking it! He really thinks what just happened was a pitiful display of ineptitude! You'd think we'd lost! What must it be like when these characters get to charge downhill, or even on level ground?

Then he followed Kai's gaze toward the gates of Angers. Riothamus and a group that included a courier and several of his officers were talking animatedly. "Wait here," Kai said, and trotted off to join the colloquy. Sarnac took advantage of his sudden privacy to report Kai's reaction to Tylar. There was a long pause before the time traveller replied.

"Yes. Yes. I'm very glad we have this opportunity to observe Riothamus' operations at first hand. Clearly, there's more here than we had imagined. Oh, we've always realized that his army isn't the typical European Dark Ages rabble. But we hadn't fully appreciated the degree to which he is in a class by himself." Another long pause. "Yes, this must be thought on."

Sarnac was about to ask him what he meant when Kai returned. If he had looked irritated before, then he looked infuriated now.

"Kai! What is it?"

"God damn all the Gauls who ever lived to eternal hell!" Kai took a deep breath and continued more calmly. "It seems Odovacar was with the force facing the southwest slope. He's surrendered to Syagrius."

"This is bad news?"

"That blowhard Childeric must have been in contact

with Odovacar. He's worked a deal by which he'll take the surviving Saxons into his own service. And Syagrius is going along with it." Kai's habitual good nature was slowly reasserting itself. "Ah, well, at least they'll be moved to the Frankish lands. We won't get to make a clean sweep of them, but our people in Armorica will be free of them."   ·

Well, well, Sarnac mused. *Underneath all of Childeric's noise lies one shrewd son of a bitch. He's probably had a bellyful of being Syagrius' vassal, and he's positioning himself to make a bid for more independence. And Syagrius is trying to mollify him.*

Then Riothamus was riding past, waving to the men who cheered him. But he got close enough for Sarnac to see that his face was clouded.

CHAPTER THIRTEEN

"Are you *sure* I can't ride?" Tiraena looked beseechingly at Koreel. "Maybe if I did it sidesaddle, or whatever they call it . . . ?"

Koreel smiled down at her as he rode along beside the litter. "They haven't started doing that yet. And no, I'm afraid it would be inappropriate for a woman of your background. You'll just have to do it this way."

As if to rub it in, the litter lurched as one of the hired bearers stumbled. Tiraena cursed fervently in Raehaniv—it didn't matter if people occasionally heard the language on the lips of such an exotic-looking lady, they simply assumed it to be some Eastern tongue or other—and resigned herself to watching the scenery as they proceeded west on the old Roman road.

The rolling Somerset countryside was touched with autumn. There had actually been some sun this morning—she had begun to wonder if this country *had* sun—but now the clouds scudding in off the Bristol Channel promised more rain. The "Summer Country" to the northwest had begun to turn back into marsh and water, beyond which she could see Glastonbury Tor rising in the distance. Its seasonal change back into a virtual island left the monks who were its inhabitants isolated for three quarters of the year—which was as they liked it. Her implanted historical knowledge told her that the fully developed monasticism of Europe's Middle Ages still lay in the future. But communities of reclusive holy men did exist. This one dated back at least to the time of Magnus Maximus, and the monks claimed to have a number of notable relics, including some relating to Joseph of Arimathea, who was already reputed to have brought a certain cup to Britain.

Her thoughts were interrupted as they took a left turn, and Cadbury rose ahead of them.

She observed her surroundings in silence until they had passed through the first two lines of earthworks on the lower levels of the hill. "Do these extend all the way around, Ventidius?" she asked, remembering to use Koreel's cover name.

"Oh, yes. So do the other two lines. This was a center of the old Celtic people's resistance after the Romans came. And it had been a hill fort of their tribes long before that. And before *that*, it had been a stronghold of peoples who had spoken earlier forms of Celtic—or, more correctly, Celto-Ligurian. It was close to the Great Temple they raised over yonder on the foundations laid by their own predecessors." He gestured eastward, toward Salisbury Plain and Stonehenge.

She was silent again as they climbed the hill and passed through the next two lines of earthworks, trying to analyze the sense of awe she felt. Ancient sites were nothing novel to her, for the Raehaniv had been civilized long before the Sumerians had built this world's first cities. But she had always been accustomed to thinking of her Terran ancestors as brash newcomers who had burst on the galaxy in the time of Varien hle'Morna, emerging from a darkness illuminated only by the disjointed legends she had heard. She had never even seen an accurate map of this world; all such maps had been destroyed by her Terran ancestors when they had fled the Solar System. Now she was here amid a past that reached back in an unbroken line to the origins, not only of Robert's people, but of the Raehaniv themselves. So in a sense, *nothing* on Raehan could ever seem as ancient as things rooted in the soil from which the human species had sprung.

Then they were through the final earthwork and approaching the citadel at the southwesternmost and highest point of the hill. Koreel trotted his horse forward and called upward to a guard standing behind the timber breastwork that topped the unmortared sixteen-foot stone wall. After a brief colloquy, the guard waved them forward, and they passed through a square gatehouse and emerged into a surprisingly spacious enclosure that held a cruciform church, as well as Riothamus' timber hall.

"Most of this must be new, Ventidius," Tiraena said, a statement rather than a question. "That gatehouse, for example. It's Roman in design, and incorporates secondhand Roman materials."

"You are correct. Riothamus has extensively refortified this old site since making it his headquarters. The decision to base himself here was as much political as military, for this place is a symbol of Celtic resistance to the Romans. So it was a way of reassuring those who felt he was coming too much under Roman influence. 'Roman,' you must understand, is in this place and time the label not of a national or ethnic identity, but of a political orientation—a resolve to keep alive what Rome once represented." Koreel smiled wryly. "Of course, it was just a sop to the Celtic diehards. Riothamus is, in the contemporary sense, a thoroughgoing 'Roman.' And his chief henchman, Ambrosius Aurelianus, is even more so. The Roman influence you noted in the architecture of the refortification is largely his work."

"Oh? I thought he was a general, not an architect."

"He is, primarily. But in a social setting like this one,

roles are not as structured as they are in the kind of society to which you are accustomed."

Tiraena smiled. "No professional credentialism?"

"Precisely. This has good and bad implications. Ambrosius is one of the good ones. He has had to turn himself into something of a polymath in his efforts to preserve or restore as much of what existed before as possible."

Tiraena was silent for a moment, as they approached the great hall. Then she remembered something. "Ventidius, I seem to recall hearing what the stronghold Riothamus has reconstructed here, at the southwest summit of Cadbury, is called. Doesn't it have a particular name?"

Koreel hesitated for the barest instant before stating what was, after all, common knowledge. "Yes," he answered. "Camalat."

"My dear! Your hair!"

Tiraena cursed silently to herself. She had forgotten. Her dark reddish hair had had time to grow beyond its usual length. But as soon as she and the others had followed the Queen into her chambers and they all removed their headdresses, its shortness stood revealed, in contrast to the almost waist-length hair of the other women. That was the fashion of this day, even though all the luxuriant growth was generally kept pinned up in public.

"I suffered from a malady last year, Lady," Tiraena addressed the Queen. "The physician ordered that my head be shaved, as part of his cure. By God's mercy, the treatment succeeded."

"Ah." Gwenhwyvaer nodded, evidently satisfied by the cover story. There were so many schools of "medicine" running around loose that no prescribed cure, however bizarre, surprised anyone very much. The only surprising thing was when the patient survived.

"Well, Lucasta," continued Riothamus' consort, "we

must all join with Ventidius in thanking God for your recovery. Otherwise, you would never have come here. You must have so many stories to tell. After all, you're from Rome itself!"

"Yes!" One of the other ladies-in-waiting broke in, obviously eager to show off her Latin. "Is it like everyone says it is? Are the streets really paved with gold?"

If they were, Tiraena thought, *the Vandals would have stripped it off in 455!* But she looked into the eyes of the women, shining with wonder, and could not be flippant. "Actually, Lady, I'm from Milan, where my family has been settled for generations. I haven't been to Rome since I was a child."

But the ladies-in-waiting were having none of it, and bombarded her with questions until Gwenhwyvaer raised a peremptory hand.

"Enough! Lucasta has only just arrived, and she must be weary enough from her journey without you honking at her like a flock of silly geese! Besides, I need to speak to her in private. All of you, get about your work!" The ladies-in-waiting subsided with no good grace as Gwenhwyvaer led Tiraena into her inner bedchamber. There, she gave the newcomer a grave regard that Tiraena returned.

Gwenhwyvaer was very tall for a woman of this age, but not much shorter than Tiraena herself. She must have inherited it from her great-grandfather Magnus Maximus, whose tallness was still proverbial. Otherwise, there was little about her that could have come from that Spanish usurper. Rather, her reddish-gold locks must have been those of his British wife, or of other Britons who had joined the bloodline since. That hair, obviously once stunning, had begun to fade as she entered the premature old age that overtook all these women in their thirties. But, unlike most, she hadn't thickened out from repeated childbearing.

Finally, the Queen spoke. "I was glad when Ventidius requested that I make a place for you in my household, Lucasta. He said that on your journey from Italy you would meet my husband's army in Gaul. You must have seen him there."

"I was never actually presented to the High King, Lady. It was only from a distance that I glimpsed Riothamus—"

"I say, you *have* been in Gaul! We almost never use that honorific here, except when we're being dreadfully formal and stuffy. He's 'the High King' or, among ourselves, 'Artorius.' Did he look well?"

"Very well, Lady, as far as I could see. But I bear no new tidings. It is only since arriving in Britain that I have learned, like everyone else, of his triumph at Angers." In fact, she knew from Koreel that the Britons, along with Tylar and Robert, had subsequently proceeded westward along the north bank of the Loire, as planned. They had now crossed the Loire into Berry and occupied Bourges, where they would go into winter quarters. But she had to be careful not to reveal more up-to-date knowledge than she could plausibly possess, in this age when Britain and Gaul were like two separate planets.

"Ah, yes!" Gwenhwyvaer's eyes were alight. "What stories we have heard about that battle! Naturally, such stories always gain with the retelling, when every courier from Gaul knows that the free drinks will last as long as his tales do! Besides the tidings of everyone's relatives and sweethearts, we've heard some new names—like a certain Bedwyr, who evidently saved the High King's life, and slew a hundred Saxons. . . . My dear, are you quite well?"

Once Tiraena's coughing spell was under control, she gasped, "Forgive me, Lady, but I met this Bedwyr in the camp outside Nantes. He was a mercenary who had been hired as a bodyguard for my uncle Tertullian, secretary

to the Bishop of Clermont, who is accompanying the
High King." All at once, some imp seemed to take control
of her. "I must say, Lady, I'm surprised to hear that this
wandering rogue has made a name for himself! Frankly,
he impressed me as a braggart and an impudent rascal.
In fact . . ." She gave her best attempt at a demure look.
"I must ask you not to tell Ventidius, for he would be
terribly angry, but before I left the camp this Bedwyr
made highly improper advances to me. Indeed, some of
his suggestions are quite unfit for your ears!"

Gwenhwyvaer had clasped her hands over her mouth
to stifle her splutters. Now she took a breath and spoke
with mock-imperiousness. "In that case, I *command* you
to relate them!"

Tiraena went on, inventing freely, until she and
Gwenhwyvaer were both breathless from laughter. "Well,"
the Queen uttered, "you're right: Bedwyr is a dubious
character indeed! And *certainly* a braggart!" They both
dissolved in mirth again. Finally, Gwenhwyvaer spoke
seriously.

"Ah, Lucasta, I'm glad you've joined the household.
It's so good to have someone new and stimulating—and
who speaks educated Latin! Time hangs heavy for me."

Tiraena looked at her face again, and saw more
clearly the lines, the encroaching gauntness. When
she had laughed, revealing her teeth, it had been
necessary to remember that they were unusually good
ones for a woman in her middle thirties, in this era.
*I'm older than she is, and she thinks I'm in my early
twenties*, Tiraena realized. And she saw, stretching away
behind that face, a long, long line of other worn faces:
women, countless generations of them—throughout
nearly all of history—martyrs to the perpetuation of
the species.

"Surely, Lady," she ventured, "your lord's absence is
made more bearable by the glory he has won. Why, the

Emperor of the West himself has had to seek his aid
to save Gaul from the barbarians!"

"Oh, yes. Artorious is a great warrior, no doubt of it."
Gwenhwyvaer smiled, and for an instant she seemed
almost a girl. "I remember my first sight of him, when
he led the Artoriani south to join Ambrosius. Not at
Thebes, nor at Troy, was there such a hero! I was a young
girl then, and in love. And," she continued, almost
inaudibly, "I believe he loved me."

There was a long silence, while Gwenhwyvaer
wandered, lost in memory, and Tiraena felt uncomfortable
to the point of desperation. Then the Queen looked up
and smiled at her.

"I'm sorry, Lucasta. I shouldn't burden you with these
matters. But you must have heard the gossip since arriving
in Britain."

Tiraena *had* heard, as part of her orientation. "It is
hardly my place, Lady, to . . ."

"Oh, tosh! Everyone knows. Everyone talks. Let them!"
Again, Gwenhwyvaer's voice sank to little more than a
whisper. "I know he loved me then. And I gave him my
love. . . ."

You also gave him the High Kingship, Tiraena thought,
drawing on her implanted knowledge. *The old Celtic
custom of matrilinear succession has never died out.
Vortigern acquired legitimacy for his High Kingship
by marrying Sevira, and Artorius did it by marrying
you. No doubt about it, the female descendants of
Magnus Maximus are prime breeding stock!*

Except, of course, for one little thing. . . .

". . . Then came the years of waiting and praying while
no child came," Gwenhwyvaer was saying. "Oh, Artorius
was never actually unkind. But the distance grew and
grew."

Who knows which side the deficiency lay on, Tiraena
reflected. *In this world, it's automatically the woman's*

"fault," and *"barren"* isn't a nice word. Little by little, Artorius must have lost whatever nonpolitical feelings he may have had.

"Perhaps, Lady," she offered, "it was only the long absences. The High King must have been away on campaign much of the time."

"Indeed he was! Fighting Picts and Saxons while I played the woman's part and wondered if I'd ever see him again. And when I did . . . one thing that never changed was what I felt on my first sight of him whenever he returned from the wars."

Suddenly, a commotion arose in the outer chamber. Gwenhwyvaer nodded to Tiraena, who opened the door to reveal a frightened-looking lady-in-waiting.

"Your pardon, Lady, but the Count of the Saxon Shore has returned, and demands to see you."

" 'Demands!' " Gwenhwyvaer's sky-blue eyes flashed. "How typical! Well, let's get this over with. Come, Lucasta." She rose to her feet in a way for which there was no possible word but "regal," and swept out of the bedchamber and through the outer room. Tiraena hurried to keep up, and the other women followed in a frightened gaggle—all but two, who opened the apartment's outer door to reveal the entrance hall and a small group of travel-dusty soldiers. One of them had his back—covered by an unusually rich cloak—to them. He whirled around and greeted Gwenhwyvaer with the most perfunctory of bows.

"Record," Tiraena mentally commanded an implant, and everything she saw and heard began to go onto an almost microscopic disc for later retrieval. *Tylar's going to love this!*

Ambrosius Aurelianus was a late middle-aged man of average height for these times, his iron-grey hair and beard closely cropped. Everything about him suggested lean, wiry toughness, as though decades of war had

sandblasted him down to the indestructible essentials.
He had been in the forefront of the Britons' initially
disorganized resistance to the Saxon *foederates'* revolt
in the 440s, gradually becoming its leader. In 454 he
had supported Artorius' claim to the High Kingship (left
vacant by the discredited Vortigern), and was rewarded
with the military high command of the ongoing effort
to hem the barbarians into their coastal settlements. It
had been touch-and-go throughout the 450s, but by the
460s, the worst of the devastation was over. Artorius had
turned his attention more and more to his Armorican
possessions, leaving the island to Ambrosius' regency
during his frequent absences.

It was fitting that his title was a revived Roman one,
for his life had become totally consecrated to the ideal
of Rome—the only imaginable alternative to barbarism
from without and squalor from below. His concept of
Rome was his shield, and he loathed anything that he
saw as an impurity in its gleaming alloy—such as the
woman at whom he now glared.

"Welcome, Count," Gwenhwyvaer said with frosty
politeness. "We were told that you requested" —a slight
stress— "to speak to us. We trust that your tour of the
Saxon settlements revealed no disturbances."

"It did, Lady." Ambrosius' voice was as harsh as his
features. "The Saxons are quiet. Artorius has no cause
for worry—from *them*."

His emphasis was too blatant to be overlooked with
dignity. Gwenhwyvaer's voice dropped a few more
degrees. "Whatever do you mean, Count?"

The brittle shell of bogus politeness dropped from
Ambrosius and seemed to shatter on the floor. "I have
been back long enough to hear the rumors, Gwenhwyvaer.
It is being said that even as your lord is striving against
the barbarians in Gaul, you are disgracing his marriage
bed here in Britain!"

The silence was a palpable physical presence, not merely an absence of sound. When Gwenhwyvaer finally spoke, her near-whisper seemed deafening.

"How *dare* you repeat this slander before witnesses? By God, Ambrosius, when Artorius returns—"

"You deny the accusations, then?" Even Ambrosius' officers shuffled nervously at his rudeness in interrupting her.

Gwenhwyvaer's features remained frozen, but her voice gained steadily in volume. "Accusations? What accusations? I have heard nothing but camp gossip, repeated by a prig with the soul of a village busybody! And as for denials, I am not answerable to you in any way, Ambrosius!"

"But you are, Lady. Everyone in Britain is, for I am the High King's regent in his absence. Your personal life is of no concern in itself—you can rut with whomever you please for all of me. But when you cuckold the High King, you diminish the High Kingship, which is all that stands between us and chaos."

Gwenhwyvaer's lips curved slightly upward into a bitter smile. "You never give up, do you, Ambrosius? After your failure to uncover any proof of infidelity two years ago . . ."

"No *proof*, no—but we both know it was true, don't we, Lady? And . . . why shouldn't you? Those old Celtic queens before the coming of Rome, from whom you like to boast of your descent, took lovers freely."

Gwenhwyvaer's smile grew even tighter, and more ironic. "Now we come to it, don't we? You *need* to believe I'm an adulteress, and probably worse besides, because to you I stand for what we were before Rome, what you fear we may become after Rome. Yes, Count, *we—you* are more British than Roman in blood! As for me, it's true that I'm descended from Maximus, but I'm equally descended from the British wife he took." It was clear she was speaking to *all* the audience now. "And after he was shortened by a head, his daughters became wards of the Emperor and were married off to British chieftains who wanted cultivating. So perhaps I understand better than you that the Empire is *dead*, Ambrosius—at least in the West. It was always an imported hothouse plant that never really took root, or smothered the native life beneath. And now, as its dead husk falls away, that life is feeling the sunlight again!"

For an instant, no one could speak—even the terrified whimpering of the ladies-in-waiting was momentarily stilled. Tiraena was amazed to discover that she herself had forgotten to breathe. She was even more amazed when Ambrosius broke the silence—not with a roar of outrage, but in an almost conversational tone.

"You're quite right about the Western Empire, Lady—but not about *Rome*! Rome will exist as long as there's a civilized man alive. It will exist as long as the Latin in which we're now speaking to each other! So your husband has always believed, and he's always striven to keep its light from guttering out."

"Oh, Artorius and I aren't as far apart as you suppose, Ambrosius. He wants to preserve what was good in Rome. But he knows that it can only be preserved in ways that will work for the Britain that now is. Haven't you noticed that while people called Vortigern High King of *Britain*, they call Artorius High King of *the Britons*? Have you considered what that means for the direction our world is going?"

"A mere form of words," Ambrosius said, a little too emphatically.

"You may convince yourself of that, Ambrosius. But the future will take no notice." Gwenhwyvaer drew herself up. "You have every right to communicate your suspicions to the High King. On his return, I will submit willingly to his justice, and we will see which of us is vindicated. And now . . . you have our leave to go!"

Ambrosius gave her a quick nod and turned on his heel. After the last of the soldiers had clanked out, Gwenhwyvaer turned to the ladies-in-waiting.

"All right, everyone, return to your tasks. Julia, stop snuffling and wipe your nose!" As she led the way back into her apartments, she turned to Tiraena. "Lucasta, I'm sorry you had to see that just after your arrival."

"I hardly think it will be the last time, Lady, so I had better get used to it."

"Just so. And you certainly seem to hold up under that sort of unpleasantness far better than these others." She looked quizzically at this tall young woman who, though come of well-to-do merchants, had nothing aristocratic in her background to account for her self-possession amid the temper tantrums of rulers. Of course, if she was really unshockable . . .

"Your must understand," she continued, "that Ambrosius is wrong—this time." She smiled, for she had clearly made an impression. "Oh, yes, I've taken lovers in the past. I think Artorius even knows. But not lately. I'm getting too old, and I *won't* become one of those pathetic hags who end by paying pretty boys to go to bed with them for no better reason than habit! And besides . . . it never meant anything. For I spoke the truth earlier. Even now, my every sight of him is still like the first."

Then she shook herself, and was all business. "Come, let's get some candles lit. The darkness is falling."

It was also growing dark at Clermont, and Bishop Sidonius read the letter by the feeble light of the setting sun. Then he was silent for a long time, as the sun continued to set behind the Puys range to the west and the chamber grew gloomy.

"Excellency . . . ?"

"Leave me." The curtness was so unlike Sidonius that

the secretary was startled. He motioned the scribes out and bowed himself through the door.

Sidonius rose heavily to his feet and walked to the western window, oblivious to the chill. He watched the sun setting and crumpled in his hand the letter he wished he had never seen.

He had asked a friend in Rome to keep him apprised of Arvandus' trial. The friend had obliged, describing the convening of the court—five Senators, presided over by Sidonius' successor as City Prefect. He had also related what everyone in the City now knew: the matter was far more serious than Sidonius had realized. The charge against his old friend was not to be graft and extortion. It was to be treason.

After the earlier charges had been brought, and Arvandus ordered to Rome to face them, a letter had been intercepted en route from him to King Euric of the Visigoths. The friend had included portions of it, and Sidonius had grown soul-sick as he had read. The former Praetorian Prefect had urged Euric to make war on the "Greek Emperor" Anthemius, and to strike immediately at the British troops that were then north of the Loire, defeating them in detail while they were separated from the armies of the Kingdom of Soissons.

The ass even presumed to draw up a foreign policy for Euric, Sidonius thought bitterly. *Advised him to detach the Burgundians from their Roman alliance and partition Gaul with them. We should have let the letter be delivered—Euric might have died laughing!*

Except . . . *except that Arvandus is absolutely right in his central point: Riothamus' army is the key threat to Euric, and this is the time to attack it, catching it in a forward position, unsupported. Yes, it is very fortunate indeed that that letter never reached its destination!*

Sidonius found that he was trembling, but not from the cold—in fact, he had broken a sweat. He wiped his brow and reviewed the rest of the letter in his mind. Arvandus had scandalized everyone with his jocular familiarity with the judges. *They don't know him as I do. He's quite mad—I see that clearly now. I'm sure he'll be genuinely surprised when he's found guilty, even though he's admitted writing the letter. The rest of the world isn't real to him; he owes it no loyalty, and it can do him no harm. He probably turned traitor simply in a fit of pique over being accused of corruption.*

No, there's nothing at all surprising about his conduct at the trial. But some of us are still sane, still conscious of our obligations. I will say nothing of this to anyone. Arvandus has a right to not have his case further prejudiced. And it's bad enough that the details of his advice to Euric have been bruited about as much as they have. The contents of this letter will go no further.

The sun vanished behind the hills, leaving Sidonius standing in chill darkness.

CHAPTER FOURTEEN

The Britons' winter quarters overflowed the walls of Bourges, a spreading growth of wooden huts. But the High King had appropriated the old mansion of the Roman governors. Tertullian had been assigned a nearby house, where Sarnac arrived one bleak afternoon bringing a miserably nervous traveller from the south.

The fellow—he had "small landowner" written all over him—had brought a cover letter from the Bishop of Clermont instructing Tertullian to deliver to Riothamus the enclosed letter of introduction, and then present the bearer to the High King. The three of them made their way to the mansion, where the new arrival waited in an antechamber while Sarnac and Tylar were escorted to the office where Riothamus conducted business before a roaring fire.

"Ah," the High King sighed after breaking the seal and reading the letter, "I'm afraid Sidonius is cross with me. He's back to addressing me as Riothamus! Or maybe not—he's just doing as he's bound to do, now that he's Bishop and representing the interests of his flock."

"What is the letter's subject, Riothamus?" asked Tylar, who already knew the answer from a traceless scan, which used techniques that meant little more to Sarnac than they would have to the High King. "If I may know, that is."

"Oh, it's nothing confidential." Riothamus leaned back in his chair, plunking his feet on the heavy wooden table and waving the letter in the air. "It seems our foraging parties have been straying over into the Auvergne."

"Ah," Tylar smiled. "Poaching from members of His Excellency's congregation?"

"Undoubtedly! But that's not what the letter's about. If it was just a matter of pig stealing, I doubt if Sidonius would involve himself. No, the problem is not pigs, but men."

"Slaves," Sarnac stated from near the door. He wasn't sure he had any business speaking up, but slavery was something that had never stopped bothering him about this world.

"Yes." Riothamus nodded absently. "Just as they've been doing on the estates here in Berry, our men have lured away some of this man's slaves as recruits. He appealed to his Bishop for redress, and Sidonius has sent him to me with a letter intended to influence me in any way possible. I'm afraid Sidonius rather lays it on." He squinted at the letter in the pale winter afternoon light and quoted, " 'I am a direct witness to the conscientiousness which weighs on you so heavily, and which has always been of such delicacy as to make you blush for the wrongdoing of others.' Ha! He's referring to the times he saw me holding court at Nantes, and gently reminding me that I've always done whatever was necessary to maintain discipline in my army. There's more needling on that point further on. 'I fancy that this poor fellow is likely to make good his plaint, that is if amid a crowd of noisy, armed and disorderly men who are emboldened at once by their courage, their number, and their comradeship, there is any possibility for a solitary unarmed man, a humble rustic, a stranger of small means, to gain a fair

and equitable hearing.' " Riothamus chuckled, while
Sarnac tried unsuccessfully to frame a Latin or British
translation of the quaintly old-fashioned expression "laying
on a guilt trip." Then the High King sobered.

"It's a thorny problem. You see, our men haven't been
doing this sort of thing just to hunt for recruits. Most of
them genuinely hate slavery. I think it goes back almost
exactly a century—to 367, if I remember correctly,
although my old history tutor thought that anything after
Julius Caesar was too recent to be worthy of notice. That
was when *all* the barbarians—Saxons, Picts and Irish—
descended on Britain together, from three directions at
once." His eyes took on a faraway look. "God, but I'd
love to have talked to the unknown, illiterate genius who
organized *that*!" Tylar looked mildly scandalized, but
Sarnac remembered what he had heard about the perverse
admiration felt by a good cop for a really smart crook.

"At any rate," Riothamus resumed, "as the hordes of
looters swept across Britain, they were joined by slaves
fleeing from the burning villas. The whole country was
in anarchy. It was all put down in the end by Theodosius,
father of the emperor of the same name. But nothing
was ever the same again; the old villa system couldn't
be restored, the landowners had to adjust to a world
without slave labor. The escaped slaves melted into the
general population, and their attitudes became part of
our British. . . ." He groped unsuccessfully for the term
he was after, and Sarnac restrained himself from
supplying, "national character."

"Sidonius can't understand this, of course," Riothamus
went on. "He comes from a line of aristocrats reaching
back to the Flood! For him, it's simply an issue of property
rights."

"Under Roman law, Riothamus, that's exactly what it
is," Tylar said smoothly. "Did not the blessed Saint
Augustine himself admonish slaves to obey their masters?

And has slavery not always been the basis on which civilized life rests?"

"So we're told. Maybe that's why it seems to rest so uneasily!" The High King shook his dark head, scowling. "What's gotten into me? The problem at the moment is to do justice to what's-his-name without alienating my own troops. And it *is* necessary to do justice to him." He got up and started pacing in a way which suggested not nervousness but restless strength under flexible control. "Partly as a matter of equity—he didn't invent the system, and when he bought the slaves he was just doing what his own laws told him he was entitled to do—but also as a matter of policy. After this campaign is over, if I'm to hold on to my enlarged holdings on the continent, I must allow the people here to live under their own laws."

Aha! Sarnac thought.

"This is the first time I've heard you speak of 'enlarged holdings,' Riothamus," Tylar observed blandly.

"Is it?" The High King's smile was all affability. "Well, it follows inevitably, doesn't it? My original objective was to secure the safety of Armorica, and for that, certain strategic acquisitions are necessary. Otherwise, all this will have been in vain. Sometimes I feel as if my long-range plans are being made for me—one step seems to lead logically to the next.

"Anyway, this isn't getting my business done with Sidonius' landowner. Send him in!"

It had turned dark by the time Sarnac rode back into the encampment, but the night was less chilly than most of late, and a circle of the Artoriani were gathered around a fire, Kai among them. He waved a wineskin at Sarnac, who waved back and dismounted, hitching his horse to a nearby post and joining the men, who were listening to Hamyc.

This, he realized as he took a pull at the wine, was a

night not for history, but for old Sarmatian hero tales. Hamyc was concluding one about somebody named Batradz, the leader of a war band of demigods.

"Ah," Hamyc sighed, after lubricating his throat, "that was long ago, in the days before the Sarmatians ever reached the threshold of Rome. And far away, in the country where the Black Sea laps the feet of the snowcapped Caucasus. There, halfway back to the land where the sun rises, our ancestors dwelt in the days when the gods walked among men and sired children by mortal women!" None of these nominal Christians took exception. But they weren't about to let Hamyc get away with one of his trademark cliff-hanging cutoffs tonight.

"The death of Batradz! Tell about the death of Batradz!"

"Well, if you insist," —Hamyc smiled in the flickering firelight— "although, as you know, nobody ever really *saw* Batradz die! And some say he's merely sleeping, awaiting a time when he is needed again."

Something stirred at the back of Sarnac's mind. It was an annoying sense of having missed something very obvious—something hovering just outside his consciousness like the shadowy figures at the edge of the fire's circle of light. What could it be? Something dimly remembered from long-ago history classes? Or from even further back? He shook his head and listened to Hamyc.

". . . And so his faithful followers, Uryzmag and Sozryko, bore the grievously wounded Batradz from the battlefield. Soon they wearied, and paused near a lake to rest. Then Batradz spoke to Uryzmag. 'Take my sword and throw it into the lake, returning it to the magic from which it came. Only thus may I come to the end of my suffering.'

"Uryzmag and Sozryko looked at each other, reluctant to throw away the wondrous sword with which Batradz

had slain so many foes throughout the years he had
led them. So they took the sword and hid it, then
returned and told Batradz that they had done as he
commanded."

Kai, spellbound as always by the tale, didn't notice
that Bedwyr had suddenly stiffened convulsively beside
him. He did hear a mutter in some strange tongue—
probably one of those Balkan languages Bedwyr had
picked up, although Kai could have sworn that it resembled
some of the sounds the Saxons made. He went back to
listening to Hamyc's narration.

" 'And what did you see when you threw the sword
in the lake?' Batradz asked them. Again they looked at
each other, not understanding.

" 'Why, nothing, Lord,' Uryzmag replied. 'Only the
ripples as the sword struck the water.' "

" 'Ah, faithless dogs!' Batradz cried. 'Return to the
lake, I command you, and . . .' "

Kai became aware that no one was there at his side.
He looked over his shoulder, just in time to see Bedwyr
riding away toward the town, faster than was prudent at
night. What had gotten into him? Kai shrugged and
returned his attention to the grand old story.

Tylar was studying a data-retrieval device that was yet
another of the manifestations that his "short sword" could
assume, when Sarnac stalked unceremoniously into the
room.

"Tylar . . ."

" 'Tertullian,' " the time traveller corrected him, raising
a cautionary finger. "Remember, cover names at all times
while we're . . ."

"Tylar, we need to talk! And I want Tiraena in on it!"

"I'm afraid I haven't been entirely candid with you."

"Has anyone ever told you that you say that a lot?"

Tiraena glared at him. Her mood had started at rock-bottom upon being awakened and bundled off to Bourges, and had gone downhill from there. The revelation that Koreel could—contrary to what she had been told—get her out of Camalat and send her to Gaul via the portals, and could have done so at any time, didn't help. "You'd better start talking straight, because I'll be missed if I don't get back to Camalat before—"

"Back to *where*?" Sarnac cut in, his voice rising to a yelp.

"Why, Camalat. It's the name of the residence Artorius has built, or reconstructed, at Cadbury. That's where I've been, as part of Queen Gwenhwyvaer's household."

"Queen . . . ! Alright, that's it!" Sarnac rounded furiously on Tylar. "Why the hell didn't you tell us?"

"Tell us *what*, Bob?" Tiraena was growing even more exasperated. "What's this all about?"

"Tell her, Tylar! Tell her just what we've stepped into, and just who we're talking about—this Artorius Riothamus, whose career we seem to have become part of."

Tylar sighed, seeming to resign the game. "King Arthur," he said simply. "The real one."

Even though Sarnac had known it beyond any real possibility of doubt, actually hearing it took the wind out of him. As if from a distance, he heard Tiraena's bewildered voice.

"But . . . but I remember hearing stories about him and his knights when I was little. Those stories were fantasies! They took place in a kind of never-never land, with dragons and giants and . . ."

"Yes," Tylar smiled. "The legends that will grow up around Artorius during the Middle Ages will naturally take on an even more vague and unhistorical quality among your Terran ancestors. For them, Earth itself will have become a 'kind of never-never land,' without even a clearly defined geography. Of course it never occurred to you to look for traces of such fairy tales amid the mundane realities among which you've been living."

Sarnac shook himself into mental gear. "Yeah . . . now I see why you've kept Tiraena and me separate. I got the legends in a form that at least had some connection with Britain in this general period—but I don't know squat about history. She has the historical knowledge, via brain implant. Together, we could have figured it out in a minute! But, damn it, I should have seen some of the clues on my own—starting with the name 'Artorius,' especially the way the backwoods Britons pronounce it." He slowed down. "But . . . I guess I haven't heard it all that much. I haven't exactly been moving in social circles that are on a first-name basis with him. And the Gauls all call him 'Riothamus.' "

"Precisely." Tylar nodded. "That's why his identity will eventually be lost sight of. In all the scraps of authentic history from this side of the Channel in which he's mentioned, he's referred to by the honorific. Meanwhile, in Britain, he will pass into legend under his given name."

"But Tylar," Tiraena protested, frowning with concentration. "I'm reviewing the history through my implant, and this doesn't seem *right*. Isn't the man at the root of the Arthurian legend supposed to come later than this? Isn't he supposed to lead the Britons at the Battle of Badon, around 500? And isn't he supposed to die in another battle, at Camlann, even later?"

"Yeah," Sarnac pounced. "Killed by Mordred, the bad guy of the story! Where is *he*? And," he hurried on as the old tales began to come back to him in a flood, "where are lots of other people, like Lancelot? And what about the Round Table? And—"

Tylar raised a hand. "If I may answer your questions in order," he said, turning first to Tiraena, "I must confess that the historical data you were given were slightly edited.

No, not so much edited as extremely old-fashioned. The surviving references to the two battles you've mentioned will long be regarded as the bedrock proof of Arthur's historical existence. But it's a fallacy. You see, this society is about to sink into a period of profound illiteracy—Sidonius belongs to the last generation of classically educated people in Western Europe. Those who come after will mangle the surviving records, and they'll have no recollection of the Roman custom of naming elite military units after their commanders. They'll read references to the Artoriani—some of whom will get back to Britain and function on a freelance basis for a few more generations, gradually descending into brigandage—and think Artorius himself is being referred to. The Artoriani will form the backbone of the British collection of war bands that temporarily stops the Saxons at Badon, a generation from now when there's no longer a High Kingship, nor any economic basis for it. And at Camlann the unit will finally tear itself apart in internal strife—stirred up, our researches suggest, by someone named Medraut."

"And as for the other elements that seem to be missing," he continued, turning to Sarnac, "they are mostly embellishments, added on by troubadours during the later Middle Ages. Lancelot, for instance; they'll be performing for an aristocratic audience of Norman French-speakers, so . . ."

". . . So they'll have to bring in a Frog hero," Sarnac finished for him, nodding slowly.

"Yes, and work him into the already well-established tradition of Guinevere's infidelity. In earlier versions of the story, Mordred is her lover."

"So," Tiraena put in expressionlessly, "some of the mud will stick."

"Indeed. Medieval moralism will require that her 'wantonness' be the cause of Camelot's downfall.

Actually," Tylar went on, warming to his theme, "a number of these apparently missing elements have some kind of basis in what you have seen. Merlin, for example: a sixth-century bard named Myrddin will go bonkers and start spouting prophecies, and, like so many others from various centuries, will end up in King Arthur's legendary court. But the form he takes in the legend will also owe something to Ambrosius Aurelianus, whose Roman learning will make him seem almost wizardly to the coming generations. In fact, in Geoffrey of Monmouth's retelling of an early form of the legend, 'Ambrosius' is an alternate name for Merlin."

"Yeah," Sarnac said bitterly. "Clues strewn all over the landscape, and it took the folk tale Hamyc was telling tonight to make it all click for me. It sounded so much like . . ." He blinked. "Wait a minute! Do these old Sarmatian yarns also enter into the legend?"

"Quite possibly," Tylar allowed. "Yes, I *knew* this would happen eventually. I couldn't keep you from hearing Hamyc's stories, so there was no preventing it."

"But why did you *want* to prevent it?" Tiraena's voice was almost plaintive in its incomprehension.

"Yeah," Sarnac challenged. "To get back to my original question, why didn't you tell us in the beginning?"

Tylar regarded them levelly. "Because it would have meant the end of your usefulness as unbiased observers. It would have filled you both—especially you, Robert—with too many preconceptions and expectations from your cultural heritage."

"Ah," Tiraena breathed. "So *that's* what you meant about our 'fresh insights.'"

"Just so. We needed observers who weren't burdened with the knowledge of what Artorius will come to mean to posterity, who would be able to see these people as people, not as symbols and archetypes. And who would be able to view with detachment what is going to happen."

Sarnac felt a chill, although the small room was really very warm. "You mean . . ."

"Yes. You know how this story ends. The legend is quite clear on that, and history leaves no question about how it *has* to end—how it must be *allowed* to end." He paused, then resumed with a sad little smile.

"Remember what I said a moment ago, about the echoes of history that can be heard, however faintly, in the legends that will attach themselves to Artorius? Well, one such echo is that King Arthur dies a victim of treason. But the traitor isn't Mordred, who, as I pointed out, belongs to a later generation. No, the real traitor is named Arvandus. . . ."

It was a mild winter day even for these southern lands, and it was quite comfortable at the open window that overlooked the roofs and walls of Toulouse, the flowing Garonne, and the countryside beyond.

King Euric took a deep breath and wondered, not for the first time, what his remote Gothic ancestors in their frigid Baltic *urheim* would have thought of this smiling, snowless land, where the western branch of the *volk* had found its home. But they couldn't have imagined it, any more than they could have foreseen the epic wanderings that would bring their descendants southeastward from the forests, into the steppes that they would seize from the Sarmatians, then into the lands of Rome, recoiling from the Hunnish hordes that galloped out of the rising sun, then onward through those Roman lands, as they first fought back against the Empire's arrogant oppression, and then became that same Empire's saviors from the Huns, when those horrid semi-human creatures had finally arrived in Gaul.

Yes, it had been like something out of saga . . . but no, it dwarfed anything in those naive old hero-tales from the days before his people had attained Christianity—

in its true, Arian form, fortunately for the good of their
souls! And it was by no means over. Under his reign the
Visigoths would reach pinnacles of glory of which he
did not dare to speak aloud—even to his closest associates.
Someday the bards would place the name of Euric above
those of the old heroes—perhaps even above that of Odin.

He scowled inwardly and chided himself for thoughts
that wandered into the borderlands of paganism. *I am
but the servant of God*, he reminded himself as he so
often did, *and everything I do is in furtherance of His
plan.* Of course, God sometimes worked in ways not
readily understood by petty, short-sighted mortals—like
three years ago, when Euric had ascended the throne by
murdering his brother Theodoric. *Theodoric was an
ineffectual weakling,* he thought dismissively, *and it was
not God's will that he rule over the volk at this crucial
time in our history. Besides, only hypocrites raised their
eyebrows; hadn't Theodoric himself murdered our oldest
brother Thorismund fifteen years earlier?*

*No, Theodoric had to go—in this, as in all things, I
was but the instrument of God's will. He had no vision.
Not even a glimpse of God's plan for His Arian Visigothic
people.* Theodoric was content to remain a Roman
foederate. *The highest ambition he could conceive was
to make himself Master of Soldiers at Rome—as Stilicho
was in his day, and Ricimer is now.* Euric seethed with
the anger he always experienced when he thought of
Ricimer. *But*, he reminded himself, *what could one expect
of a renegade mongrel like that? Half Visigothic and
half Suevic, and a damned Catholic to boot!*

No, Gaiseric the Vandal was right. There was no future
in ruling this decomposing corpse of an empire as
generalissimo for some puppet emperor or other. *But
Gaiseric's just a brigand, content with his little North
African pirate kingdom. It was to me that God granted
the revelation that it isn't enough to break free of Rome.*

No, we must replace *Rome with something nobler: an Arian Empire, ruled by the Visigoths, as God clearly intends.*

He had made a good start, he told himself. Over the last two years he had brought practically all of Spain under his rule, crushing the Romans and penning the Suevi into the northwest corner. Next would come the incorporation of the rest of Gaul. Gaiseric could be bullied into an alliance, and would be allowed part of the spoils— for now. Then would come Italy. Then . . .

Euric shook himself. Dwelling too long on his grand design was like drinking too much of this land's wine. It was too intoxicating, it rendered one incapable of attending to practicalities—like listening to this Italian merchant that Namatius had just brought in. He turned from the window and faced the fellow, who waited in respectful silence for a response.

"So," he said, "you say Arvandus has been found guilty?"

"Indeed, sire. And sentenced to death. At the time I left Rome, his relatives and friends were trying to get the sentence commuted to exile."

"They'll probably succeed," Euric mused. "It would be typical. A nation that knows in its bones that it's no longer worthy of loyalty can't feel any real indignation about treason." He considered the document that the merchant had prepared. It lay on the table where Namatius had set it after reading it aloud.

It was absolutely incredible. After having intercepted the letter this Arvandus creature had written to him, the Romans had proceeded with a *public* trial, shouting that letter's contents out upon the winds of Rome, to be heard by anyone—including this itinerant trader who had for years supplemented his income by selling Namatius the latest Italian news.

"Namatius, does this information ring true?"

"It does, sire," his spymaster replied. "We learned of Anthemius' British alliance last year. It was clearly directed at us, even though the initial campaign was against the Saxons of the lower Loire. As for the Britons' subsequent deployment and future plans . . . yes, it is consistent with our other sources."

Euric nodded. "All right. You have done well," he told the merchant. "Namatius, pay him a suitable bonus." The informant blubbered his gratitude as Namatius ushered him out and turned him over to a clerk before returning to the room and facing his master.

Euric gazed for a moment at the Gallo-Roman. Clever fellow, like so many of them. Catholic, of course . . . But that didn't matter. Euric had always made use of the best talents among his subjects, without regard to their religion. This surprised some people.

Fools, he thought scornfully. *Like those Visigoths who think we should go beyond merely breaking the authority of the higher Catholic clergy, and forcibly convert the Gauls to Arianism.* That would have defeated Euric's master plan for the future Empire, ruled by a Visigothic elite which was preserved by religious barriers from assimilation into the native multitudes of Gaul and Spain and eventually Italy, and all the rest. He knew full well that, since settling here in southwest Gaul, the men of the *volk* had lost no time in acquiring a taste for the dark, fine-boned local women. *Let the lads have their fun,* he thought indulgently. *It does no harm, and everyone knows that all women really want to be raped. But as long as a religious difference makes actual marriage out of the question, the purity of the* volk *will remain inviolate and the clever Romans will perform their cleverness under the direction of a ruling class whose Visigothic soul-strength is illuminated by the true Arian faith. This is God's design, which I am commanded to implement by any means necessary. It is all so clear!*

He turned his attention to the spymaster. "So, Namatius, what do you suppose was Arvandus' motive in attempting to contact us? Has he been a target of yours?"

"No, sire. This is purely a gift from God. As to the motive, Arvandus was under indictment for graft. Perhaps he was simply seeking an employer who would better appreciate his talents. Or perhaps he was acting out of sheer embitterment."

"Either way, there's no reason we shouldn't make use of the information he wanted to give us, now that the Romans have seen fit to give it to us for him!" Euric bellowed with laughter, while watching Namatius for a reaction and seeing only blandness. *Do you resent being reminded of what contemptible human scum you come from? Or do you already know it so well that you're no longer capable of resentment?* He quieted down, and stroked his full, dark gold beard reflectively.

"This worm Arvandus has a point. If we act quickly, we can smash the Britons while they are still the alliance's only force south of the Loire. After that . . . Syagrius won't interfere without support. And maybe we can detach his Frankish vassals from him—I know you've already been cultivating contacts with Childeric!" Namatius inclined his head in acknowledgment.

"Very well, Namatius," Euric continued. "Send me the captains of the war-host! I know that all the men have gone home for the winter after this last Spanish campaign, but we can recall them early. And we can have the plans ready before they're assembled." He strode to the map that hung on one wall, hitching up his belt over his gut— no doubt about it, he was becoming heavyset in middle age, and grey hairs were appearing in his beard. *But God will grant me the time I need!* "Yes," he muttered, staring at the map. "According to Arvandus' version of the plan, the Britons will advance from Bourges *this* way, and then halt, to await the arrival of Syagrius' forces—probably around *here*." He stabbed his finger at the map, for all the world as though it were an accurate representation, and not a vague approximation of the landscape through which they would wend their way, with the help of local guides. "This is where we will catch them." His finger continued to rest on the map, near the symbol for a little place called Bourg-de-Déols.

"Indeed, sire," Namatius murmured. "We'll have them at every conceivable disadvantage. Only . . . I have contacts in Armorica, and everything I have heard about their High King, this Artorius Riothamus, indicates that . . ."

"Yes, yes," Euric said impatiently. "I know his reputation, and that of his army, especially the cavalry. Naturally—against Saxon yokels and Pictish primitives *any* competent cavalry would seem fearsome! It will work to our advantage. The more impressed people are by him, the more impressed they'll be when we crush him! That's why I want the entire war-host mobilized early. I want to come against these Britons in such numbers that we'll overwhelm them, not just defeat them. That is part of my objective—creating a sense of the futility and hopelessness of opposing us. Now go!"

Namatius hurried out, and Euric went back to the window and gazed out over his lands.

Yes, he thought, *forget the old sagas*. The great Gothic adventure was only just beginning.

CHAPTER FIFTEEN

"Ho, Bedwyr!"

Sarnac turned from checking his saddle girth and saluted Artorius—he never thought of him as "Riothamus" any more. The High King acknowledged and leaned down from his saddle.

"Well, Bedwyr, are you as anxious to get moving as everyone else?" His gesture took in the camp outside Bourges, now a beehive of activity as the army prepared to advance into Berry. The scene embodied the excitement of imminent change, without the apprehension of immediate danger. They were simply deploying into an advanced position, to be joined later by the Roman and Frankish forces from Soissons. Only then could fighting be expected, for the Visigothic farmer-warriors were only just beginning to return to arms for their fixed campaigning season.

Or so it was entirely reasonable for Artorius to suppose. . . .

"Aye, *Pan-Tarkan*," Sarnac replied slowly, trying to make himself remember Tylar's admonitions against interference. "Of course you know best about how soon we should advance, or whether we should wait for Syagrius. . . ." He clamped his mouth shut.

Artorius cocked his head. "What ails you, Bedwyr? This isn't like you at all."

"Oh, nothing, *Pan-Tarkan*. It's just . . . well, call it a feeling, from some of the campaigns I remember in the East." He could not allow himself to say more. He had already said too much.

Artorius' eyes narrowed, and for a heartbeat or two they locked with Sarnac's. Then the moment was past; Artorius was straightening up in his saddle with an offhand "Cheer up, Bedwyr!" and riding off to exchange greetings with other men.

They left Bourges in early spring, riding southwestward into a world of sun and blossoms, in which Sarnac was almost able to escape from his foreknowledge.

"Don't let this countryside fool you," Kai was saying earnestly. "Berry is a land noted for witches and sorcerers. I was talking to this amulet seller in Bourges, and he told me about the time when . . ." Sarnac let him rattle on, listening with half an ear and watching the advancing army.

Artorius wasn't taking his entire force into the field, for he had left Bourges strongly held. But what he was taking was his elite: armored heavy infantry, with the sun glinting off their ring-mail *loricae* and the tips of their spears, picked units of archers and javelin men, and the main body of the Artoriani. He and Kai rode with the Artoriani past the advancing columns of infantry, exchanging shouted greetings and ribaldries. Further back were the baggage train and various noncombatants, including Tylar. Sarnac now wore the scarlet cloak of the Artoriani but continued to stubbornly decline the usual scale hauberk, clinging to his accustomed quilted-cloth armor. He claimed to be superstitious about it; it was an explanation these men could accept.

"Tylar," he subvocalized, unnoticed by Kai, "I still don't

entirely get it. It seems like this campaign in Gaul should be remembered in the legends."

"But it is," came the pseudo-voice vibrating through his mastoid. "Of course, the facts will be misplaced—as is the way of legends. As always, one of the first things lost sight of will be the identity of the enemy. In the early versions, Arthur will be portrayed fighting the Romans, rather than allied with them. Later, when the romantic aspects become predominant, the campaign will turn into an expedition to capture Lancelot and the faithless Guinevere. In both versions, he'll be called back to fight his last battle against the traitor. . . ."

"Look, Bedwyr!" Kai pointed ahead, where the blood-red dragon floated lazily over the head of the column in the spring warmth.

"Signing off," Sarnac told Tylar. Then, aloud to Kai: "Yes, I see! We're halting. Over there must be where we'll make camp." His pointing finger followed the distant dragon standard as it moved off toward the right, onto a rise. He gave a silent command and studied the map that seemed to appear in front of his eyes. It showed their present position—near a village called Bourg-de-Déols, he noted—and the surrounding country, with the River Indres to the south and the town of Chateâuroux beyond that. It was a gently rolling landscape, and the rise—toward which the line of march was now curving—was unexceptional. Nothing more was needed in the way of a defensive position; it wasn't as though Berry was enemy territory.

The advance guard of unarmored light horsemen trotted off toward the low hills on the horizon, scouting ahead, as the army piled into the campsite with a composite din of shouted commands, neighing horses, clanking armor, and a thousand other sounds. Sarnac, trotting through the organized chaos, recalled Tylar's remark about the shadowy quality of this wretchedly documented era,

a sense of ghostly armies and dim battles glimpsed only
by occasional flashes of lightning. It was hard to think
in such terms amid the sweaty, dusty, profane, and entirely
prosaic reality that surrounded him. Even the technological
primitivism seemed less exotic than he had expected.
He'd had to adjust to the lack of various amenities, and
then had simply adapted to what was available. Much
of the uniqueness of his world's technology lay in realms
of the impalpable and the submicroscopic. As far the
human senses were concerned . . . well, a handle was a
handle, whether it was on a sword or a tacscanner.

He realized that the gap that separated him and even
Tiraena from these people was nothing compared to the
gulf that yawned between all of them and Tylar. He still
didn't know just how far in the future the time traveller's
native era lay, and he wasn't certain that he wanted to
know.

Nevertheless, he decided to ask, as he and Tylar stood
gazing out over the encamping army. But Tylar had
warmed to the subject Sarnac had raised earlier.

"Yes," he was saying, "like most English-speakers, you
identify the Arthurian legend with Britain alone. But the
continental tradition will be, in some ways, closer to the
truth. Medieval poets, like Wolfram von Eschenbach,
will have Arthur holding court at Nantes, and send him
to Britain only as an afterthought."

Sarnac nodded absently, looking around. The Indres
flowed past on their left. It wasn't much of a river, but
spring rains had made it unfordable. Ahead was an open
plain, long ago cleared of trees, with the low hills beyond
it. And . . . what was that? Several of the light horsemen
were coming back from those hills at a gallop. He squinted
toward the early afternoon sun and saw the riders lashing
their horses. What . . . ?

"Tylar. See those scouts coming back?"

"Why, yes, and in some haste!" He brushed an

insect away and seemed to consider. "What do you suppose . . . ?"

Then the first of the riders came into voice range of the sentries and began shouting. The sentries shouted in turn, and in a ripple of sound, a cry spread through camp.

By the time Sarnac and Tylar caught the words "the Visigoths" amid the roar, they had already seen the masses of soldiery begin to debouch onto the plain from the hills. For an instant their eyes locked—Sarnac's almost wild with the sudden knowledge of what he was about to watch happen on this drowsy spring afternoon, and Tylar's oddly serene. Then the time traveller nodded.

He knows, Sarnac thought with a calmness that surprised him. *He's known all along.*

"I can't understand it," Kai was saying again, simply to be saying something. "They must have hauled their warriors off their farmsteads much earlier than usual—before the winter was over—to get organized and into Berry so soon. But *why*? It's as if they knew where we were going to be."

"It's the damned Gauls!"

The speaker, a few places away in the ranks, spat feelingly. "We were betrayed. What else can you expect? One of their swells who knew the plan must have sold it to Euric."

"Probably for a promise to keep him supplied with boys," Kai snarled. He was in an uncharacteristically jittery mood as he stood waiting. All of them were, and Sarnac knew why: it was the very fact that they *were* standing, dismounted by Artorius' order. He had placed the Artoriani alongside the heavy infantry, in front of the archers and javelin throwers, in the hedgehog formation he had hastily fashioned. Sarnac had kept expecting the Visigoths to plunge ahead with the headlong ferocity that supposedly characterized barbarians and catch the British off balance as they were forming up. But the huge, unwieldy enemy host was incapable of any such lightning maneuvers. Instead, it had flowed like spreading syrup around the low hill on which the Britons stood, surrounding them on three sides—the Indres secured the fourth. Now they were close enough for Sarnac to get a good look at them.

The infantry were generally helmetless and protected only by shields—wooden and iron-bossed like his own—and a double tunic, the outer one of fur-trimmed leather. In contrast to their drabness, the heavy cavalry massed in the background were spectacular, seemingly armored in gold, although he'd been assured that the mail corslets were really gilded iron. Also gilded, and adorned with flowing horsehair plumes, were their helmets, which otherwise were standard Roman cavalry issue. They were armed like the Artoriani, with long lances and swords which, like the Roman *spatha*, were descended from a Sarmatian original. But they lacked mounted javelin men. All their missile-armed troops were afoot. And they had a lot of them—archers and spear-throwers both, now waiting in formations that seemed to sway impatiently, in time with the growl that rumbled from them.

Suddenly, there came an atonal blare of horns from behind those enemy formations. The rumble rose to a roar as the Visigoths surged forward, into what seemed to Sarnac to be an insanely short range for a duel of missile weapons.

"Well," Kai said, jitters gone as they grounded their lances, "now we just have to take it for a while." They raised their large round shields to shelter the archers, as was their function at this stage.

Sarnac had examined those bows. The late Roman compound bow was actually not that poor a weapon. The problem was the way they used it, drawing it back to the chest like boys playing Robin Hood. They hadn't discovered the advantage of drawing it to the cheek. *Hell,* he thought, *if Tylar would hop ahead to the fourteenth century and bring back some English longbowmen, it would change the whole picture. Better yet, a platoon of twenty-third century Fleet Marines in powered combat armor.* He decided he really must mention it to the time traveller, who now waited with the other noncombatants in the hedgehog's hollow center.

A hail of missiles began to glance off his shield, and Sarnac heard screams all around him as arrows found exposed flesh. Surely, he thought, the Visigoths in their thousands would overwhelm them with sheer volume of fire. But the response from the British bowmen was effective enough to keep the Visigothic archery disorganized. The Visigoths' technique was no better than the Britons', and their wooden self-bows weren't quite as good. The only advantage that bows had over javelins in this era was that an archer could carry more arrows than a javelin man could carry javelins. As these half-assed arrows rattled off his shield, Sarnac decided it was just as well that serious archery wasn't being practiced at this range—it would have been a mutual slaughter, with the good guys on the short end.

Then the guttural Visigothic roaring rose in pitch and beat on the Britons from all sides in waves of noise. The thinned ranks of enemy archers parted as massive columns of infantry charged forward, crashing against the British hedgehog.

Sarnac braced as the charge impacted on his part of the perimeter. Barbarian bodies were thrust onto bristling spearheads, as much by the pressure of their massed comrades as by the battle frenzy for which they were renowned. Standing in the front rank, he just held his ground. He would have preferred to be in the rank behind; they could at least use their lances for stabbing. Then, after a timeless interval of hell, the enemy hosts drew sullenly back like an ebbing tide, leaving a wrack of bodies. The Britons hadn't given an inch.

"Well," said Kai, removing his helmet and mopping his brow, "that was just a test. Next they'll try a cavalry charge. The important thing will be to hold formation." He replaced his helmet, laced the cheekpieces together under his chin, regrounded his lance, and . . . waited. Looking around, Sarnac saw nothing but steadiness.

Then shouting spread along the ranks from their left. Artorius was approaching, as he rode the circuit of the British hedgehog, calling out to men by name, and laughing.

"Kai! That's a rare fine pile of dead Visigoths out there! I see you're managing to hold this section, even though you've got old Hamyc here! Are you sure he's not too decrepit to remain standing without being propped up?"

Laughter began, growing louder in response to Hamyc's grousing about cocksure young innovators who lacked the respect for one's elders that had characterized his own generation in the days of his youth. Then it came to Sarnac. *It's an act! The men have gotten so used to it that when they hear it they assume everything must be S.O.P. I'll bet Artorius and Hamyc rehearse it. But no, they've been doing it so long they don't need rehearsals. They could do it in their sleep!*

Artorius joined in the laughter, beaming. Then he spotted Sarnac. "Bedwyr," he called out, then leaned down from his saddle and spoke more quietly. "I know you don't like standing in ranks any more than the rest of them. But we'll be riding out against the bastards soon, I promise."

Sarnac had never understood the readiness of the High King of the Britons to confide in him, a newcomer. Now he realized that the question answered itself. He *was* a newcomer to the tangled web of interrelationships that permeated any long-established organization, but a newcomer who had won respect. Artorius could talk to him with an openness that was not possible with men who had followed him for years. So he played a role that filled a very real need for the High King—and he suddenly felt a need of his own, to play that role to the hilt.

"Ah, this formation isn't so bad, *Pan-Tarkan*," he drawled. "At least you've got us facing outwards in all directions so the Visigoths can't get *behind* us. I've heard they've been in this land so long they've picked up some of the Gauls' habits, if you take my meaning!"

Artorius laughed with pure pleasure. "I'm glad to know, Bedwyr, that you've been listening to everything I've been telling the men about the Visigoths," he said after catching his breath. Then he leaned lower and spoke for the two of them alone. "Of course, there are a few things I haven't chosen to emphasize. Like the fact that those" —he pointed at the serried ranks of armored horsemen beyond the Visigothic archers— "are the men who just conquered Spain in two campaigns, and whose grandsires trampled the Legions into the mud at Adrianople!" A quick, dazzling smile, and he was gone, riding along the lines and acknowledging cheers. Sarnac was left gaping after him, with barely enough time to settle back into his position in line before the shrill, barbaric horns sounded again and the Visigothic cavalry broke into a charge.

Spreading his feet wider apart and waiting to receive heavy shock cavalry, Sarnac subvocalized—sheer habit, in this rising thunder of hooves—into his implant communicator.

"Tylar, I'm sure you've got the situation well in hand. But whatever you're planning, now's the time!"

There was no reply. He made the motion that activated the comm link, confirming that it was already activated.

"Tylar, this isn't funny! Talk to me!"

Dead silence inside his skull.

"Tylar? *Tylar!*"

Then the Visigoths were on them.

It wasn't as bad as he had expected—the worst never is. It *would* have been, had the Visigoths come at them with couched lances. Instead, they used the traditional overhand lance technique, which of course blunted the impact. But it was bad enough.

Sarnac staggered backward as a Visigoth was impaled on his lance by sheer momentum. The falling rider dragged the lance downward, and Sarnac, unable to keep it upright, sank to one knee, lowering his shield. At the same time, another Visigoth reared his horse, and flying hooves lashed out over the British shields. One of them caught a man's head with what Sarnac imagined would have been a sickening sound if it could have been heard in this universe of hideous noise. The Visigoth regained control of his horse and forced the animal into the small gap that had been torn open.

Like lightning, Kai stooped, and then came up, too close for the enemy rider to use his lance, and jabbed upward with his *spatha*. With an ear-tearing shriek, the horribly wounded horse reared, throwing his rider, then toppled over, continuing to bellow in agony.

"Fall back!" Kai roared. They did so, reforming their shield wall. Sarnac had to watch the horse die in front of him. But then the attack resumed, and he could think of nothing except fending off the stabbing lances and flailing hooves as the armored horsemen beat on the British formation like the hammers of some giant, demonic blacksmith. He didn't know how many times his impact armor had saved him; he couldn't stop to think about it—or anything else.

Then, with disorienting suddenness, there was no more pounding or stabbing, and the Visigoths were drawing back. The British ring of steel had contracted a little, and altered its shape, but it hadn't broken. *If the Visigoths had any notion of how to use their infantry and cavalry in conjunction*, Sarnac thought, *we'd be dead meat*.

He sank to one knee, using his shield and lance to prop himself up, and took stock. He was wearier than he had ever imagined possible; every muscle in his body seemed to scream at him in protest. He wondered dispassionately if sheer exhaustion was what was keeping his throat-stinging thirst from driving him mad.

A boy from the baggage train came around with water and he took a drink, grateful for it and for the artificially bestowed immunities, without which he wouldn't have dared to drink water that didn't come straight from the source of a stream. Then he looked out across the field, where Visigothic riders were swarming about in disturbed anger, as their leaders harangued them. *They've never been stopped before*, he realized. *And they've decided they don't like it much*.

He felt a hand grip his shoulder. "Come on, Bedwyr," Kai said. "We've been recalled—we're going to mount up and launch a counterattack."

Sarnac knew his jaw was hanging loosely open, and couldn't help it, or even care. A counterattack? In his current state of exhaustion? But Kai was already headed toward the center of the shrunken formation, and he saw the other Artoriani moving in the same direction. He could only lever himself to his feet with his lance and follow.

As he mounted his horse alongside Kai, he saw that the idiot was actually grinning. "This'll be different— we've never fought other heavy cavalry before. The *Pan-Tarkan* wants to catch 'em off balance as they're beginning their next charge. And *this* time we have a little bit of a slope in our favor, so I'm glad you're here to see it!"

That makes one of us, Sarnac thought with a kind of groggy incredulity. Then he remembered that Tylar ought to be around here somewhere, inside the perimeter. He looked around frantically and called silently via his implant communicator. No contact.

Then Artorius rode slowly forward to the head of their formation, alone save for the standard-bearer, and an odd hush fell. Sarnac, standing in his stirrups and gazing over the heads of the infantry ranks, saw that the thousands of Visigothic horsemen had stopped their bee-like swarming and were starting to move, as though with one purpose. At that instant, Artorius lifted his lance high, then brought it slowly down until it was pointed forward. Commands rang out, the perimeter parted, and in a thunder of hooves and voices the Artoriani charged.

The Vulgarian war cry on his lips, Sarnac charged with them.

The Visigothic cavalry, caught completely by surprise, were unable to alter the direction of their advance in response. The Artoriani thundered down the slope in a tight wedge-shaped formation, with the blood-red dragon arrowing overhead like some supernatural bird of prey. They struck the enemy masses at an angle, bowling over horses, and spitting men in a deafening chaos of blood and agony.

Sarnac managed to stay in his saddle as he smashed a horse and rider to the ground, letting go of his lance as he felt it snap and pulling out his *spatha*. Then they were in the midst of a disorganized crowd of Visigothic cavalry, whose formation had disintegrated under the impact of heavy lancers who used lances the way they were supposed to be used. Most of the Artoriani were wielding swords now, and they hewed their way steadily through the Visigothic battle-mass.

Sarnac exchanged a couple of blows with an enemy rider before battering the man's shield aside, and slashing the throat beneath a blond beard, severing trachea and muscles. Blood fountained past the head that flopped loosely, now attached to the body by little more than the spinal column. Sarnac spurred his horse on, not waiting to watch the man fall, and all at once they were past the Visigothic horse and among infantry that fled from the trampling hooves and whetted steel. He fought his way on, and the universe narrowed to a kind of tunnel of horror down which he moved, striking muscle-shocking blows whose effect he usually couldn't see, then drawing a gasping, whistling breath and striking again.

Finally, he was in the clear, and saw Artorius ahead of him. He also saw that they were alone, except for the standard-bearer, who appeared to be wounded, but was keeping the saddle. Ahead of them, a fresh formation of Visigothic infantry advanced toward them.

He heard renewed shouting from behind. Turning in his saddle, he saw columns of enemy cavalry arrive from elsewhere on the field, cutting them off from the rest of the Artoriani, who they were pressing hard.

"Back," Artorius roared. "Fall back!"

The Artoriani obeyed, fighting all the way. But now additional infantry were moving in to complete the High King's isolation. And Visigothic archers were nocking their arrows at a range from which even *they* couldn't miss.

A richly accoutered Visigothic noble rode up alongside the archers and barked a guttural command. Bows were raised, and Sarnac, wheeling his horse around, saw no way out. *Well, the impact armor will stop the arrows, but then they'll overwhelm me, and I don't think I want to be taken alive by these guys.* So he removed his helmet to give them a clear shot at his head—the heat of the damned thing was killing him anyway—and closed his eyes. *Farewell, Tiraena.*

But no arrows came . . . and he became aware that it had grown oddly quiet. He opened his eyes, and saw that Artorius was calmly facing the Visigothic noble and holding his *spatha* up in a kind of stately sword salute. For a long moment, the Visigoth—a huge man, almost a giant in this era—gazed back. Then, without a word, he motioned his men's bows down, raised his sword in a gesture that mirrored the High King's, and applied his spurs, sending his horse plunging forward.

They met with a clanging impact of swords, then were past each other, reining their horses around and clashing again. Suddenly, as though recoiling from the fury of their meeting, they separated, circling each other warily. Then, with the same deliberation with which he had issued his wordless challenge, Artorius hung his shield from his saddle bow, gripped his three and a half foot *spatha* with both hands, and raised it over his head. The Visigoth stared for an instant, and plunged forward again with a roar.

Too quickly for the mind to grasp, he was level with the High King, and Artorius brought the *spatha* down on his enemy's right shoulder with a force that sheared through mail, leather, flesh and bone, continuing halfway down to the left hip. For a split second the tableau held. Then, with a convulsive jerk, Artorius wrenched the sword free—and, following it out, came a jet of blood from the severed heart. Sarnac had seen an old-fashioned fire plug knocked open; this was like that, only in dark scarlet. Artorius was drenched with it, and a collective gasp arose from the masses of men around them. As if in slow motion, the almost bifurcated Visigoth slid grotesquely to the ground.

A screamed command in the Visigothic tongue from a group of richly dressed men on a hill behind the enemy's ranks brought Sarnac out of shock. The archers, moving slowly and fumbling, raised their bows. Sarnac composed himself for death again . . . but Artorius nudged his horse forward and began to move at an unhurried walk along the line of archers, running his eyes over them, as though in an inspection—and, as he passed, bows lowered in silence. Then the High King looked up at the group on the hill and, for what had to be several heartbeats, locked eyes with the most richly dressed of them all, a rather paunchy, full-bearded man who stood frozen.

Finally, Artorius turned with his affable smile. "Come, Bedwyr." And he started back toward the British army, followed by Sarnac and the standard-bearer. The Visigoths opened ranks to let him pass. The signs they made with their hands were not Christian.

It wasn't until they had reached the cheering British perimeter that Sarnac saw that not all of the blood that covered Artorius belonged to others. He had taken a wound in the left thigh.

King Euric was like a man possessed. The highest nobles of the Visigothic nation shrank from his fury.

"Dogs! Sons of Spanish whores and their African pimps! You still have at least five men to their one, yet there they stand, laughing at you for the puking cowards you are! By God, all it takes is one real man to make you wet yourselves with fear! But this Artorius Riothamus is only a man, I tell you—he's *just a man!*" Euric paused for breath, wiped flecks of spittle from his beard, and calmed down. "I command you to finish this before the *volk* and the true Arian faith suffer any further disgrace and humiliation. Attack at once, from all sides. And. . . ." He paused. It was as though his rage had burned away some kind of barrier, for he had a new idea. "Have our bowmen loose their arrows while the horsemen are charging. And keep doing it when the charge reaches the British formation."

"But," gasped one of his listeners, "then our own cavalry—men of noble blood—will be in danger of being killed by our own archers!"

Euric rounded on him and smashed him across the face, a backhanded blow that sent him spinning to the ground. "The Devil take them and their 'noble blood'! If they can't break the British line unaided, they're useless anyway!" He glared at them, eyes half-wild again. "Who else dares to question my command?"

A couple of them had seemed on the verge of saying the unsayable to their king. But the moment passed, and they hurried off to implement his orders. He watched them go, gradually bringing himself under control.

We'll win, of course. I am God's unworthy instrument, so He will grant me victory as He always has before. All the world knows the Visigothic war-host is invincible—we've beaten the Romans, the Suevi, the Vandals, and the Huns! This pathetic little band of Britons can't stop us.

Besides, what I told them is true. He's just a man. Isn't he?

"Tylar! Where the hell have you been?"

The time traveller had appeared, looking none the worse for wear, while Sarnac and the rest of the Artoriani were catching a moment's rest inside the perimeter. It was all Sarnac could do to keep his expression restrained, and remember to subvocalize.

"Oh, I *do* apologize, my dear fellow! But I had to take advantage of everyone's preoccupation with the first Visigothic cavalry charge to activate a portal and go to consult with Koreel."

"That's what I wanted to talk to you about. This situation is unravelling fast. How do you plan to get Tiraena out of Britain? I assume you've got some brilliant scheme for getting *us* out of this!"

"Oh, don't worry about Tiraena. That situation is under control. As for us . . . well, the fact of the matter is, it will probably be necessary for us to eschew any technologically advanced techniques in extricating ourselves from this battlefield."

"Wait a minute, Tylar," Sarnac began, forcing himself to concentrate. He felt like his brain was sinking into a bottomless pool of fatigue toxins. "Are you telling me we can't get out of here?"

"Not in the least! I'm merely saying that you will have to escape in a normal—by contemporary definition—way, along with Artorius and his men."

"What? You mean they're going to escape from this debacle?"

"Some of them will. That much is clear from the known historical facts. Of course, just how they manage it is unknown—and, at the moment, far from apparent! But I'm sure the details will become clear as the situation develops. The important thing is that you get back to Bourges, and from there to Dijon, in the Burgundian lands."

"Dijon? Why there?"

"I haven't time to explain. But I think you'll find that the Britons' escape route will take you in that direction. It will be a matter of . . . 'going with the flow' is, I believe, the expression."

"Now hold on, Tylar," Sarnac began frantically. But then Kai interrupted.

"Come on, Bedwyr. We're all mounting up. The Visigoths are forming up for another attack, and the *Pan-Tarkan* wants the Artoriani facing east. If necessary, we're to break out in that direction and fight our way back to Bourges." He was clearly delighted at the prospect of further action. Sarnac would have throttled him to death, but it was too much like work.

Mounted, they could see over the heads of the infantry perimeter. The Visigoths were moving around in sullen masses of men, their leaders shouting them into a growing rage. The roaring from thousands of throats beat in on the Britons from all sides, like surf.

"Will you listen to them, Bedwyr! Noisy buggers, aren't they?"

Sarnac had to chuckle, albeit weakly, at Kai's insouciant tone. Then the Briton began to hum a tune. After a couple of bars, he began softly singing it. The men nearest him laughed and began to join in. Kai laughed in return and let his voice out in a full-throated tenor. More of the Artoriani added volume, and the song began to spread along the infantry ranks, whole units coming in with seamless harmony, as if in response to some invisible director. The Visigoths grew louder in reply, but the Britons were now one great chorus, belting out a song into which the roaring of their enemies drowned tracelessly.

Sarnac tried to identify the song, but the lyrics were unfamiliar and seemed completely inappropriate—something about a girl—but he was certain he'd heard the tune in his own world. Then it came to him, and he joined in with what little he could remember of the words to "Men of Harlech," in an English that no one could hear in that overpowering storm of sound.

By the time they had reached the final note, the angry swarming-about of the Visigothic horde had acquired a single direction, and with a blood-chilling collective scream they advanced.

First the enemy archers came within range, and the duel of missile weapons began again. But this time the Visigothic cavalry charged past the archers . . . who kept on releasing even as they went down in windrows, and even as the mailed lancers neared the British lines.

"Look, Bedwyr!" Kai leaned forward in his saddle and stared at what was happening. "They'll shoot their own men and horses! They must have gone crazy!"

No, Sarnac thought, feeling a chill lump in the pit of his stomach. *They're just getting smart. They've grasped something that's escaped a lot of people throughout history: that victory often depends on willingness to*

*accept losses from friendly fire. At least one Visigoth
has managed to grow a brain.*

He watched the British line crumple here and there
under the impact of the arrow storm. The messy gaps
closed back up before the Visigothic cavalry charge struck
home, in almost all cases . . . but not quite all. Where
they did not, the barbarian riders fought their way in,
and it became a melee. The losses to the Visigothic cavalry
were devastating, from their own side's archery as well
as from the Britons', even before the hand to hand butchery
began. But the British perimeter was forced inexorably
inward. And, with a deep-throated roar, thousands of
Visigothic infantry came on in a massive second wave,
pressing the Britons even further back by sheer weight.

Then Sarnac's attention was drawn from the battle,
for Artorius was trotting up slowly, riding without any
blatant sign of his wound. But Sarnac, who knew, thought
he detected a certain pallor. He gave orders to runners,
then faced the westering afternoon sun and raised his
lance aloft.

A reserve of heavy infantry had been positioned in
front of the Artoriani, just behind the western front of
the hedgehog—a front that had been pushed back almost
to the position where they waited. Now they advanced,
throwing their weight into the struggle. In a supreme effort,
they punched through the Visigothic front and then
advanced to right and left, rolling the enemy back. At
that moment, Artorius levelled his lance and spurred
forward, and the Artoriani followed him.

They rode through the gap opened by the infantry
Ambrosius had trained—the last real heirs of Rome's
legions—and smashed through the Visigothic rear
elements. Enemy cavalry frantically closed in from both
sides to cut off their escape, and Sarnac became too busy
to wonder where Tylar had gotten to now.

He saw the Artoriani break through in groups and vanish

in the dust to the west. He saw old Hamyc go down, his voice stilled forever by a lance thrust. And he saw Artorius smash one Visigothic horseman, and then another, finally becoming entangled with a knot of infantry, one of whom slipped under his guard and thrust upward with a short single-edged sword that entered the High King's abdomen under his scale-armor hauberk.

With a cry that welled up from he knew not where, Sarnac spurred his horse forward, and he saw that Kai was with him. Together they charged into the Visigoths crowding around the High King, striking left and right in a delirium of slaughter until the survivors had fled, howling their terror. Kai grasped the reins of the horse to which Artorius clung, and they rode off toward the west. Behind them, the sounds of battle died away.

CHAPTER SIXTEEN

King Euric looked out over the carpet of dead on the field of Bourg-de-Déols, and was sick to the core of his being.

Oh, he had won. He held the field, and his forces were harrying the British remnants westward toward Bourges, which could not hope to hold out. Yes, he had won. . . . He recalled a tale the Romans told, of a king named Pyrrhus of Epirus, who had fought Rome before the City's rise to empire. Pyrrhus, too, had won—and afterwards had written: "One more such victory and we are undone."

It wasn't just the wholesale slaughter of the flower of the war-host that made this victory too costly. Something had gone out of the Visigoths besides the torrent of blood saturating this field. They had lost that sublime certainty of victory that had carried them forward on a tide of fearlessness since Adrianople, and the loss was as irrevocable as the loss of virginity. For now they felt fear—he could see it in their faces, and it was a fear he could do nothing to exorcise.

He had tried, of course. He had had the head cut off a British corpse of about the right looks. He had set that head, its face mutilated beyond recognition, on a lance and proclaimed it to be the head of Artorius Riothamus.

Not even his own men believed it. He had heard the whispers, that the terrible Briton could not die. Some of his brainless wonders of nobles had wanted to make examples of those who repeated such talk. But Euric knew he could not kill a whisper, any more than he could smite with his sword the disease-bearing vapors of a swamp.

He forced himself to look to the future. The elimination of the Britons as a factor would make it possible for him to annex the Auvergne, although an unwelcome voice told him it would take years, not the one lightning campaign that the world would expect from the conqueror of Spain. And the Romans of Soissons would hold out, with the help of their Frankish vassals—who, he suspected, would not remain vassals for many more years. *Yes, the Franks will give us much trouble in Gaul,* he foresaw, taking refuge in practicalities from the realization that his great dream was dead. The Rhone and the Loire would be the limits to Visigothic rule, and the Arian Empire would be stillborn.

The blood-red sun sank, shuddering, leaving King Euric staring unseeing into a darkness that mirrored the inside of his soul.

"*Now* can you tell me what's happening?"

Tiraena put the question to Koreel as he followed her through the portal into the moonlit enclosure of the ruined villa. She had restrained herself when he had awakened her in her bedchamber at Camalat, ordering her to dress and follow him through the portal, whose glow she had hoped no one would notice in the crack under her door. But now she planted her feet and looked at him with a stubbornness he had come to know even in the course of a limited acquaintance.

At first he didn't reply, but busied himself with the device that projected this terminus of the portal connection. After the portal vanished, he turned to her and spoke rapidly.

"I talked to Tylar earlier. Matters in Gaul are coming to a head, and it's imperative that we get you over there to join him and Robert."

"Is Robert . . . ?"

"He's all right. But the British army has been broken, and now they're evacuating Bourges. In fact, the leading Visigothic elements will have reached the city. You'll emerge from a portal there."

"And be picked up by Tylar?"

"Not immediately. Tylar is unavoidably occupied with certain other matters."

"Now wait a minute, Koreel! You're saying you want me to step through a portal alone, into the middle of a routed army and a city being sacked by barbarians . . . ?"

"Oh, don't worry! Tylar has positioned a device which will activate at the exact moment Robert is nearby. You'll have no difficulty making contact with him. And Tylar will pick up the two of you as soon as possible. So you see," he beamed, "you have absolutely nothing to worry about. The situation is under control." Suddenly, his eyes went unfocused and he blinked. "Aha! It seems the time is now." He set the device on the ground, and a portal appeared, framing a darkness which was faintly illuminated by distant flames. She looked dubiously through at Bourges, but could see little of it. The energy field that caused the slight resistance one felt stepping through the thing also had a sound-muffling effect, but she could hear a background roaring with undercurrents she didn't like.

"Quickly, now! We can't keep this portal open forever, you know." Koreel gestured impatiently. "Oh, and be sure to pick up the portal device Tylar left; it will reconfigure itself into a dagger after you have passed through."

Tiraena took a deep breath and stepped through the portal. As soon as she did so, it blinked out of existence. She saw the little device changing shape on the ground, but her attention was monopolized by the scene which had replaced the moonlit peacefulness of the deserted British villa.

She was in an alley between two buildings of obscure function. The firelight she had seen came from what her implanted sense of direction told her was the west. The roaring was a composite of many distant voices, and it suffused the very air with the stench of panic. *And, speaking of panic, I don't see any sign of Robert.*

She started toward the end of the alley, then cursed as she remembered the ridiculously impractical outfit she had on. Gripping the fabric of her gown, she tore a long vertical rent in the skirt, then ran. Emerging in an east-west street—if you could call such an aboveground sewer a "street"—she looked to the west and saw nothing. Then to the east . . . and, in the distance, was a group of men on horseback and afoot, moving away from her and around a corner. Bringing up the rear was a trio of riders. She recognized the one on the left.

"Bedwyr!" she called, remembering just in time to use the cover name. He didn't hear her, and he was approaching the corner.

Frantically, she sprinted after him, yelling his name.

Sarnac kept himself upright in the saddle by sheer willpower and even managed to lean over and hold Artorius steady as they moved along the dark street, following the last of the bands of fugitives that could no longer be called a retreating army. Tylar's advice to "go with the flow" had been easy to follow, for his options had ranged from limited to nonexistent.

He and Kai had managed to get themselves and the High King to Bourges, riding through an eternity of nightmare after the battle. Artorius had amazed him: he had to be in agony, but he had stayed on his horse, and had even managed to say a few words to the refugees as the evacuation had begun. Their retreat to the northwest—toward Soissons and Armorica—was cut off; they could only continue eastward, into the lands of the Roman-allied Burgundians. From there, some of them might be able to find their way back to Britain.

But Artorius was finally fading. Whatever incredible store of vitality had kept him going was depleted at last, and he could only sit his horse with assistance.

Sarnac and Kai exchanged glances from opposite sides of the High King's horse. "We'll have to find some other way of transporting him if we expect to get him to the Burgundian lands alive," the redheaded Briton stated calmly.

"Right," Sarnac agreed. "But there's no time to think about it now." No time at all, as the retreat collapsed into rout. The Visigoths had begun to arrive at the western gates of Bourges at twilight, while the withdrawal was still in progress, and panic had descended. There had been no real resistance; the barbarians were already in the city, delayed only by the collapse of their own organization in the presence of plunder. Sarnac had been too busy even to wonder what had become of Tylar. "Let's just get out of Bourges right now," he continued. "We'll think about rigging something afterwards."

Kai nodded, and they started off after the column of survivors they had managed to collect. As they were about to turn a corner of the street, Sarnac turned in his saddle for a last look to see if they had missed any stragglers. No . . . just some woman. Maybe they could bring her along—the Visigoths were getting closer.

The running female figure stopped, drew a deep gasping breath and yelled, "Bedwyr!" with all the volume she could muster. He recognized that voice.

"Kai! I've got to go back."

"Go back?" Kai turned and saw the figure in the otherwise empty street. "Leave her, Bedwyr! I know— it's a damned shame what's going to happen to her. But we can't bring all the women and girls in Bourges with us."

But Sarnac was already turning away. "I've got to, Kai! Go on ahead—I'll catch up with you." Then he applied his spurs and headed back up the street. He had almost reached a gallop before he reined the horse in and swung himself out of the saddle and into Tiraena's arms.

"How did you get here?" he asked after a while.

"Koreel sent me through the portals from Britain. He said I'd have no trouble contacting you, and that Tylar would pick us up. By the way . . . where *is* Tylar?"

"I wish to God I knew! I lost track of him during the battle. But he told me I'd have to escape with the British survivors—which is exactly what I've been doing—and get to Dijon, east of here. And," he continued grimly, "that's what the two of us will have to keep on doing, for now. Whether or not Tylar and Co. have the situation as well in hand as they claim, we sure as hell can't stay here in Bourges!" He grabbed his horse's bridle. "Let's go. I told my buddy Kai that I'd catch up with him and the others."

She smiled gamely. "Well, I complained about not getting to take part in the action! Of course, a low tech escape isn't exactly what I had in mind. Right now, I wouldn't mind going via the same portal I came through. Wait a minute . . . !" She slapped her forehead with her fingertips in a gesture which was pure Raehaniv, but which wasn't out of place in this part of Earth. "I forgot! Koreel told me to retrieve the portal device Tylar left here in Bourges. Maybe it doubles as a homing device or something."

"Yeah, maybe that's how he's going to find us in this chaos! Where is it?"

"Between these two buildings back here." She started back toward the alley. Sarnac looped the horse's reins around a post and followed.

"In here," she said. Sarnac turned the corner . . . and the world exploded into pain and whirling darkness, and then disappeared.

Fresh pain brought him around—the pain of his arm being pulled back and upwards by some very strong individual behind him, outside the range of his vision but not, unfortunately, of his smell. He couldn't have lost consciousness for more than a moment, because he was still in the alley, dimly lit by the flames to the west, and Tiraena was backed up against a wall with three Visigothic infantrymen standing around her in a half circle, grinning and making comments in their own tongue, as they put away the weapons they clearly regarded as superfluous. They looked slightly unsteady, probably from the same wine Sarnac could smell on his captor's breath.

He wondered why they hadn't simply killed him. Then he decided it was because of the cloak he wore; they must be under instructions to take prisoners, and weren't drunk enough yet to have forgotten those orders. Why they hadn't killed Tiraena was self-evident. . . .

One of the trio around Tiraena, a stout man with a nose like a pig's snout, prodded his horse-faced comrade in the ribs and made a remark that drew a bark of laughter from Sarnac's captor, as well as from Horse-Face. The fourth Visigoth, a beady-eyed type who was obviously the intellectual of the group, took a step forward and, with what he probably thought was a smile, spoke in what he probably thought was Latin.

"No worry, tall foreign lady! Us not kill you! Not even hurt you much! Just have good time, yes?" Pig-Nose and Horse-Face giggled drunkenly and made comments to each other. Sarnac couldn't understand a word, but he imagined they were discussing what an awesomely smooth operator Beady-Eyes was.

Tiraena, keeping her hands in fighting position and measuring distances with her eyes, spoke levelly. "If I understand your offer correctly, I decline it. My companion and I have no valuables." —she omitted mention of the horse— "Please let us go."

Beady-Eyes considered this and farted thoughtfully. "But, tall foreign lady, you only think you won't like because you've never had real man before—only Roman boy-buggers! You'll like—in fact, you'll beg for more!" Evidently feeling his reputation as a sophisticate was on the line, he clutched his crotch for emphasis. This occasioned renewed hilarity from Pig-Nose and Horse-Face, and also from Sarnac's captor, who evidently felt that such scintillating wit deserved another upward tug on his captive's arm.

Tiraena fell into an apparently relaxed posture that the Visigoths misinterpreted, but concerning which Sarnac saw no reason to enlighten them. Unfortunately, the shift in position moved her torn skirt so as to reveal an expanse of coppery leg that did nothing to moderate the barbarians' mood.

"To repeat, I decline your . . . invitation. I advise you to let us pass!"

Beady-Eyes' smile twisted into an altogether different expression. He spat out something that Sarnac roughly translated as a protest against Tiraena's appalling insensitivity. Then, with an animal-like noise, he lunged forward, arms spread wide—which was a mistake.

What Tiraena had trained in was not Tae Kwon Do, although it had absorbed influences from it. But what she delivered to Beady-Eyes's solar plexus was the functional equivalent—at least—of a flying side-kick. He doubled over with a kind of whistling sound, unable to produce a scream, as Tiraena landed, sprang past him, and hit the ground rolling. She came up grasping something Sarnac had missed: an undistinguished-looking dagger that had been lying in the alley.

Pig-Nose and Horse-Face came out of shock and charged, roaring. In a smooth motion, Tiraena hurled the dagger. Pig-Nose fell to the ground choking on the blade that transfixed his throat and took no further interest in the proceedings. Then Horse-Face was on top of her with a momentum that she herself continued, grasping his arms and rolling them over, with her on top. At the same instant, she drew her right arm back and then thrust it forward, using the heel of her hand to drive the bridge of Horse-Face's nose up and inward, where it achieved the difficult feat of finding his brain.

Sarnac's captor had gone slack at the sight of the manifestly impossible and unnatural, which allowed Sarnac to free his right arm and drive the elbow sharply backward. The Visigoth doubled over, and Sarnac spun around and brought his clenched hands down on the back of the man's head and his knee up into his face. A quick punch with his two leading knuckles to the Visigoth's temple finished it.

He stood up in time to see Tiraena walking toward him, past the remains of Pig-Nose and Horse-Face. Beady-Eyes, still emitting weak shrieking noises as he tried to breathe, was equally ignored. She wore an expression of genuine puzzlement. "I don't understand it! I *told* them I wasn't interested—you heard me, didn't you? So why did they persist?"

"Er, never mind—I'll explain later." She was, he decided, a lot further removed from this era than he was, after all. "I suppose that dagger is Tylar's portal gizmo."

"Yes." She stooped and retrieved it from the late Pig-Nose, who gave a spasmodic twitch as it left his throat. "Pity that we don't know how to make it reconfigure," she reflected as she wiped off the blood.

"Wouldn't do us any good if we did," Sarnac said, as he went back to the street and unhitched his horse, "unless we knew where there was another portal it was linked to, and how to signal that portal to activate. Tylar and his people obviously interface with these things mentally—we haven't a prayer. No, we'll just have to continue with this 'low tech escape.' " He swung into the saddle and offered her a hand. "Climb aboard behind me, and let's get out of here before we meet any more Visigothic good-humor men. I expect we've got a long way to travel."

As it turned out, they were on the road for two days and nights. They didn't catch up with Kai, but they saw no more Visigoths, and Sarnac relaxed after they passed the ill-defined Burgundian frontier. As they got closer to what would one day be Switzerland, the land became more and more rolling, then downright rugged. He had hoped to find, beg or steal another horse for Tiraena, but no such opportunities had presented themselves. They didn't dare push the one overloaded horse beyond endurance; they could only proceed slowly into the highlands, encountering occasional peasants. From these, Sarnac used the few coins he had to buy food—he soon found himself hoping never to see an onion again—and information as to where the Britons had gone. The trail of Kai and the other fugitives soon led them slightly to the northeast of the direct route to Dijon.

On the third day they passed through a low range of hills, beyond which the afternoon sun glittered on a lake, and gazed down upon a pretty valley, with a little town perched atop a rocky promontory at its far end. But Sarnac had eyes only for the group stopped in the middle distance under an elm tree beside a stream.

"It's them!" He nudged the horse forward into a trot that was the most the exhausted animal could manage. "Kai!"

"Bedwyr?" The Briton stood up from the supine figure beside which he had been kneeling. He was haggard and disheveled, but his grin woke to unconquerable life when they approached. "Bedwyr, it *is* you! I thought we'd seen the last of you!"

Sarnac dismounted and clasped arms with Kai, feeling a happiness he didn't bother to analyze. "I told you I'd catch up, didn't I? I had to get Lucasta here" —he offered a hand to Tiraena, whose implanted riding skills were relatively limited— "out of Bourges. She's a kinswoman of Tertullian, who's still sort of my employer."

"Ah." Kai nodded. "Yes . . . Tertullian. I haven't seen him since the battle. He must have been . . ." He gulped to a halt, flushing, and avoiding Tiraena's eyes. "He'll probably catch up with us, too," he resumed with forced heartiness. It would have been funny save for its clumsy kindness.

Sarnac's eyes ran over the other Artoriani, finally coming to rest on the figure on the ground. "How is he?"

"Dying," Kai said in a tone that was itself dead. "He's lost too much blood—he can't continue." He knelt again beside the improvised bedding.

Tiraena put her lips close to Sarnac's ear. "Is that . . . ?"

"Yes." Sarnac left her staring and knelt beside Kai, bending over the High King and thinking how very wrong that face looked, drained of almost all the life force that those around him had drawn from to become, for a little while, more than they could otherwise be.

"He's been conscious off and on," Kai continued, "but he's delirious—his mind is starting to wander."

As if in response, the High King's eyes opened. He stared at Sarnac and Kai, and at something beyond them. When he spoke, his voice was weak, but distinct.

"Uryzmag! Sozryko! Are you still here? Go, I command you, and return my sword to the lake, that its magic may cease to keep me imprisoned in this suffering flesh!"

Yes, Sarnac thought, *his mind is starting to wander. It's wandering into the old Sarmatian hero-tales he grew up on.* All the men had heard them, and now they stood gaping.

With a weak, fumbling motion, Artorius sought the sword that lay on the ground beside him. When he found it, his hand closed around it firmly, all trembling gone. And, with what must be his last reserves of strength, he grasped the front of Sarnac's tunic with his free hand, and drew him down so their faces were inches apart.

"Uryzmag, as you love me, obey my command!" he gasped. Then his eyes went strangely clear, and he actually smiled. "Bedwyr," he whispered, "I know you're not what you claim to be, though I know not what you really are— nor do I wish to know, for I believe that knowledge lies beyond the proper ken of mortals. But whoever you may be, grant me this one last favor!" And he pressed the sword against Sarnac's chest.

For a long, stunned moment, Sarnac was held immobile by the High King's eyes, and he found he had taken hold of the sword. Artorius smiled again and released him, and then the wild light was back in his eyes. "Go, Uryzmag! Go! Release me from the magic that prolongs my suffering!"

So he knows, Sarnac thought. *What did he see or hear? I don't suppose it matters now. All that matters is that he wants me to do this thing for him. Why? Does he somehow know that this is how he will become one with legend? That doesn't matter either.*

"Aye, *Pan-Tarkan,*" he said. He stood up, holding the sword. "There's a lake to the west," he told Kai.

The Briton stood up. "I'm coming too."

Sarnac nodded and turned to Tiraena. "Stay here with him. This won't take long."

❖   ❖   ❖

It was late afternoon when they emerged from the woods at the shore of the lake that stretched away to the west.

Sarnac looked around at the calm waters and the surrounding wooded hillsides. There was no visible sign that Man had ever set foot on Earth. But there was no sense of ancientness, as there was on the Breton coast, where a forgotten people had raised the standing stones to their forgotten gods. No, they had ridden into a realm of suspended time.

They exchanged a look, and by unspoken consent Kai held his horse motionless while Sarnac walked his forward to the lake's edge.

He hefted the sword—as good quality a *spatha* as was currently obtainable, but with absolutely no ornamentation to distinguish it. And it was filthy with dried gore and mud. Sarnac looked at it for a moment that stretched, and felt a strange reluctance. . . . *No! I won't put us through* that *part of the story!*

Without risking further delay, he reached back and, with all his strength, threw the sword toward the middle of the lake. As it arched out over the glassy water in a high trajectory, tumbling end over end, it flashed blindingly in the afternoon sun as if somehow cleansed of the encrustation of filth, leaving only a gleaming purity that was foreign to this world and must perforce leave it. When Sarnac could see again, there were only ripples spreading in concentric circles before vanishing.

He turned to Kai. "Could you see it hit the water?"

"No. The sun got in my eyes." The voice was dull, and when Sarnac drew alongside him he saw that the redheaded Briton wore a lost, hurt expression that was shocking on that face.

"Bedwyr, what will we do? He's gone, or will be soon! As gone as Batradz—what you just did brought that home to me. I can't imagine the world without him in it. And we've failed, and . . . Bedwyr, was it all worth it? Did it all *mean* anything? Will anyone remember that we even tried?"

Something flared coldly inside Sarnac. *To hell with Tylar!* He leaned over and grasped his friend by the shoulders, hard. "Kai, listen to me! Because he, and all of you, tried to hold back the darkness, he will be remembered as long as men love the light. And not just by Britons—all the peoples who will live on the island in ages to come will pretend that their own heroes rode with his *cataphractii*! He will be remembered when all the other men of this sad time are forgotten. He will be remembered when men have left this world behind and gone to dwell among the stars!"

Kai drew back from his grip, and his face wore another expression that Sarnac never thought he would see there: one of fear. "I don't understand these words, Bedwyr!"

Sarnac's head slumped, and the icy fire inside him—which, unknown to him, had been visible through his eyes—flickered out. "Never mind, Kai. Just remember that his name will live longer than you can possibly imagine. He can never be forgotten—so, in a way, he can never die."

Kai's mouth fell open. "You say he can . . . never die? Are you sure, Bedwyr?"

Oh, God, what have I done? Clearly, his last words were the ones that had registered. *Better quit while I'm ahead. I don't really know what I'm playing with here.*

"Come on," he said. "We'd better go if we want to get back before dark."

They departed, leaving the lake to its timelessness.

The sun was low in the sky when they returned to the valley. The Britons and a few locals were where they had left them. But the High King was not.

"Where is he?" Kai demanded as they dismounted.

"Three women came while you were gone, with

bearers," Tiraena said. "They said they'd take him to the town."

"To the House of Holy Ladies there," one of the Artoriani amplified. "They said they'd ease his suffering."

"It's as well," Kai said, gazing at the town on the crag. "By the way, what town is that? What's it called?"

"Avallon," one of the Gallic rustics told him. And Sarnac found himself nodding slowly. *It's complete. He's passed through into legend.*

"I suppose we ought to go there," Kai began, when a rider wearing the uniform of the Artoriani appeared to the west, lashing his horse frantically.

"Visigoths!" the man gasped. "A strong force of cavalry, only an hour's ride behind me!"

Sarnac and Kai exchanged glances. "So they've entered Burgundian territory," the latter said.

"Yes." Sarnac thought aloud, not noticing the looks he got as he went into matters beyond the usual horizons of a simple hiresword. "Surprising, considering that King Euric wants to detach the Burgundians from their Roman alliance, leaving the Auvergne strategically indefensible. He must want something badly to risk offending them by violating their frontiers. . . . Kai, it must be the *Pan-Tarkan*! They've been sent to capture him, or else bring back his body to prove he's dead! We've got to draw them away from here."

"But won't they search the town?"

"He'll be well hidden there," Sarnac stated confidently. A bunch of Catholic nuns would have no reason to love the Visigothic heretics. "And while they may ask questions, they won't go so far as to ransack a Burgundian town. I'm sure they're under orders to avoid provocations. And they won't stay long if we give them a trail to follow away from here."

"Right." Kai nodded. "Well, we were going anyway. We've heard there are other British survivors at Auxerre, to the northwest. We'll join them—together we can maybe fight our way to Soissons, and get home from there."

Sarnac and Tiraena exchanged glances. "Kai, I'm afraid I must leave you. Lucasta and I have to continue east to Dijon."

"Dijon? Why there? It's deeper into Burgundian territory, which we now know is no guarantee of safety. And it's even further from Britain."

"I know. But Tertullian made me promise to take Lucasta there if anything happened—she has kinsmen there. I made a promise, Kai!"

"Ah, well, if you must. At least it'll confuse the Visigoths if they have two trails to follow!" He bawled at the Artoriani to mount up, then faced Sarnac and clasped arms with him. "Farewell, Bedwyr! Follow us later if you can."

"I will, Kai," Sarnac said, hating the lie as he told it.

As Kai mounted up, he gave the town a long look. "I don't suppose we can stop . . ."

"No, Kai, there's no time. We all have to get away as quickly as possible. And, Kai . . . remember what I said earlier. And when you get home, and people ask, you can tell them truly that you never saw him die!"

Kai gave him a long look. Then, with a final wave, he went to the head of the little column, and they rode off along the road to the north of Avallon. Sarnac watched them until they were out of sight. He saw that Tiraena was looking at him strangely. And he realized that, for the first time since early adolescence, he had without thinking made the sign of the cross.

God, if you exist, don't hold my unbelief against Kai, who does not share it. Let him find his way home. Then his familiar imp reawoke. *Remember, it's in Your best interests to demonstrate that the good guys don't always lose. Otherwise, people may begin to wonder about You.*

"Let's go," he said aloud to Tiraena. "We'd better put as much distance between us and the Visigoths as we can before nightfall."

CHAPTER SEVENTEEN

They awoke the next morning to an unseasonable damp chill. They had bought some food from the local peasants before heading east, so they were free from the belly-twisting hunger that had sometimes accompanied their flight from Angers. However, for the cold of the uplands night there had been no answer but shared body warmth.

They finished off the heel of bread they had saved, washing it down with the rough local wine—Burgundy, Sarnac decided glumly, had a long way to go. Then they mounted up and resumed their weary eastward trek.

"Did Tylar give you any details about how he's going to pick us up at Dijon?" Tiraena asked after a time.

"Not a word. Come to think of it, he never even said he was going to make the pickup there. He only said to proceed in that direction. So, as usual, he didn't tell us diddly! I'm going to have a few words for him when we meet!"

"If we meet," Tiraena corrected. "We have to consider the possibility that things have gotten so badly balled up that we're stranded in this time permanently."

"Don't talk dirty!" Sarnac shuddered. "Tylar'll find us. You know what kind of resources he's got."

"He's not a god. And he has his own agenda. We'd

better decide on a course of action in case we have to make do in the here and now."

"Come on! Everything will work out okay. . . ."

It was then that they heard the rumble of hooves and the clink of harness behind them on the forest trail.

Without a word, Sarnac spurred the weary, overloaded horse, knowing as he did that they could never outrun properly mounted pursuers. Then he saw, off to the right, what looked like a break in the forest, in terrain their horse might be able to manage.

"I'm going to try and lose them," he said, and guided the horse off the trail and over a low ridge. They found themselves in a clearing, facing a semicircle of Visigothic archers.

A guttural command rang out, bows twanged, and their horse reared and went over with a scream. They managed to throw themselves free before the animal collapsed, and got to their feet just in time to see the Visigothic riders enter the clearing.

Sarnac hauled out his *spatha*, Tiraena drew her dagger, and they stood back to back as the barbarians edged inward. There were no more arrows. *So my shit-hot armor is no help,* Sarnac thought. *And even if it was, it wouldn't do Tiraena any good. . . .*

"Tiraena," he spoke levelly, turning his head around, toward her, "if you wish it, I'll . . . make sure they don't take you alive."

Her head snapped around, and he could see her eyes widen. They had talked about what had happened in Bourges, and he had tried to explain what the relationship between the sexes could mean in this milieu when taken to its ugly extreme. He wasn't sure it had really registered—it ran too counter to the social assumptions she had grown up with. Now she swallowed, drew an unsteady breath, and opened her mouth to speak.

Then, with a wild cry, a Visigothic cavalryman started toward them, and the rest of the barbarians followed. Sarnac turned to face the advancing rider, raising his *spatha* in a two-handed grip. The Visigoth applied his spurs, the horse plunged forward . . .

And stopped.

The Visigoth didn't rein in his mount. They simply froze, in a gravity-defying tableau of charging man and horse, two hooves in midair.

At the same time, Sarnac became aware of how quiet it had become. There was no more sighing of wind in the trees . . . every leaf was fixed in place. No more chirping of birds . . . he looked up and saw an unmoving thrush suspended in flight. And all the Visigoths were paralyzed in mid-charge, part of the still photo the world had become.

He and Tiraena stared at each other, the only two moving things in the universe, fearful to shatter the unnatural silence by speaking.

"I think it's time we were going."

The quiet voice was, at that moment, the most startling of all possible sounds. They whirled around to see Tylar walking toward them, stepping carefully between two living statues of Visigoths. He was holding something that was sometimes a short sword, but now was wearing a shape they hadn't seen before.

"Tylar," Tiraena said in a choked voice, "are you a . . . a god?"

"Good heavens, no! I'm as mortal as yourselves, if rather long-lived by your standards. I merely belong to a society that has had a bit longer than yours to accumulate knowledge. Well, actually *quite* a bit longer."

"But, Tylar," Sarnac managed to croak, "what have you done? What's happened to them?" He gestured at the grotesquely frozen Visigoths. "What's happened to the *world*?"

"Oh, nothing at all, my dear fellow. You see, it's not them—it's *us*." He slipped into his accustomed pedagogic mode. "Remember I mentioned that we know how to induce a state of temporal stasis? That involves generating a field within which time is slowed to almost nothing— a second for every few hundred million years of the outside universe, say. Well, in its present configuration this device places its bearer in a kind of reverse stasis. For me, time is vastly accelerated."

"But what about me and Tiraena?"

"Ah, yes, I never quite got around to telling you about that, did I? Well, along with the devices you already know about, I took the liberty of having very small temporal-distortion generators implanted in you. When my own field is activated within a very short range, these automatically place you in the same state of accelerated time." He looked sheepish. "I really should have mentioned it, but it quite slipped my mind. At any rate, the outside universe seems frozen because, from our standpoint, everything in it is taking place at an infinitesimal fraction of its normal speed, too slowly for us to see the motion, even if we stayed here for the rest of your lifetimes—or even *my* lifetime. By the same token, it will seem to the Visigoths that you have simply vanished into thin air. I daresay they will decide among themselves that the better part of valor is to tell King Euric they never found any British survivors."

Sarnac tried to speak, succeeding on the third attempt. " 'Slipped your mind' my left one!" he exploded. "Tylar, you've got a lot of explaining to do!"

The time traveller sighed. "Yes, I suppose I do owe you an explanation. But we really must be going. Your temporal-distortion implants have only a limited operating time—something had to be sacrificed in exchange for such miniaturization, you know. If I may . . ." He extended his hand to Tiraena, who wordlessly handed over her dagger. It took on the shape of a pocket-sized portal generator. Tylar laid it on the ground, standing close to it so it would be enclosed in the bubble of accelerated time that surrounded him, and the portal appeared. They stepped through to the clearing outside Nantes, where their ship had landed in what seemed like a previous life, leaving the Visigoths to find nothing but the strange woman's dagger.

The Visigoths left it lying untouched on the ground, for fear of contamination with witchcraft.

"I'm afraid I haven't . . ."

"Tylar," Sarnac said from his slumped posture in the chair in the little lakeside pavilion in Tylar's private universe, "if you tell us one more time that you're afraid you haven't been entirely candid with us, I'm going to take that thing" —he indicated the mutable device that now lay on the table— "and shove it up your ass, and we'll see what it turns into *then!*"

"Ahem! Well, your annoyance is understandable. As I've admitted, you deserve an explanation. But before I begin . . . think back a moment. In all your time in this era, you haven't asked me—or even yourselves—any of the philosophical questions implicit in the concept of time travel. Yet you're both intelligent people. Haven't you ever wondered about things like the Grandfather Paradox, as I believe it's called?" He leaned back and waited for an answer, smiling.

"Well, of course," Tiraena began.

"Sure," Sarnac chimed in, straightening up a little. "In fact, we were talking about questions like that aboard the Korvaash ship, just before you showed up. Come to think of it, didn't the subject come up right here, when we were here the first time . . . ?" His voice died, and it was as though a gauzy veil, through which he had been seeing the world, slipped away. He turned to Tiraena, mirroring her wide-eyed, open-mouthed stare.

Tylar smiled again. "Yes, I see that you remember now. When we were having our first discussion here, it was necessary to place a restraint—or perhaps 'damper' would be a better term—on your natural curiosity about these matters. It was a necessity which I genuinely regretted, for it involved a violation of the ethical restrictions we place on the use of certain . . . capabilities. I solemnly assure you that in all other respects your personalities have been left inviolate."

Sarnac barely heard him, for all the questions he had been prevented from asking, or even wondering about, now flooded in. "Yeah," he finally breathed. "All this time I've been blundering around the past like a bull in a china shop, never even wondering whether I was changing my own past, maybe killing one of my own ancestors in battle! Never even considering the question of how time travel could be possible in a universe of cause and effect! Tiraena, how did you phrase it when we were talking to the Interrogator?"

" 'Reality protects itself.' It's been a basic tenet of Raehaniv thinking on the subject for a long time."

"Well," Tylar said, "it's absolutely correct. The answer to all your questions lies in just *how* reality protects itself.

"Long before I was born, my people learned how to travel in time. Or, rather, they *will* learn." He shook his head in annoyance. "The lack of certain essential tenses in English poses a very real problem in discussions of . . ."

"Tylar," Tiraena began in a tone of awful warning.

"Well, I'll use the past tense for clarity. Those first time travellers knew that 'branches of time' and 'alternate realities' are fantasy. There is but one reality, and they believed that it could not be altered, for the past was fixed. The 'grandfather paradox' was, in their view, a chimera; one *couldn't* go back in time and shoot one's

grandfather, simply because one self-evidently *hadn't*.
This belief may have held an element of wishful thinking,
or even self-justification, for it assured them that their
temporal travels could do no harm. But the earliest
experimental findings tended to confirm it, causing a
philosophical crisis by calling the concept of free will
into question.

"But then certain obscure hints began to pile up, leading
to a growing realization that history could, indeed, be
changed—and that the time travellers had, in fact, been
doing it in a multitude of very small ways ever since
they had first begun time travelling. Where there had
been a philosophical crisis before, this discovery caused
a philosophical panic—the majestic structure of reality
seemed to be built on sand. But on further reflection it
appeared that nothing essential had been changed. So a
new theory arose, holding that history has a very tough
'fabric'; if you try to tear it you may break a few threads,
but the fabric won't part.

"Then, in a famous incident involving . . . Well, the
details wouldn't mean anything to you, it lies too far in
your future. Suffice it to say that a certain time traveller
impulsively intervened in history in a very important
way—not to change it, but to *preserve* it—when faced
with a situation in which things could not come out as
they were supposed to, without his intervention. The
intellectual impact dwarfed all that had gone before. It
was realized that while the 'tough fabric' model of history
is, in general, correct, there are certain periods when the
fabric is weak, even frayed. During such periods, changes
that would normally be inconsequential can have vast
and far-reaching effects."

"So," Tiraena interrupted, "you're saying that both sides
of the inevitable-course-of-history controversy are right,
but for different eras?"

"You might say that. I've never much liked the 'fabric'

analogy that has become an inescapable part of the jargon. I prefer to think of history as possessing tremendous inertia—but sometimes its course requires it to turn a corner. And as it is doing so, a minimal amount of force, correctly applied, could deflect that course.

"But, to continue, the incident to which I refer had a second, even more momentous intellectual consequence, which set our civilization on the road it has travelled ever since. Or, more correctly, it made us realize that on the day of our first time-travel experiment we had unwittingly set our own feet on that road, and that there was no turning back. For that history-preserving intervention forced our thinkers to recognize that the time travellers had become a *part* of the history they had thought they were merely observing. But with a very special quality: the knowledge of what had transpired— what *must* have transpired—in the history of which they were themselves the culmination. Out of sheer self-preservation, we had to not merely observe the past, but *police* it. We had to determine which were the unstable periods of history—the areas where the fabric was weak— and monitor them in case intervention was necessary to keep history on course.

"So you see, Tiraena, you're quite right: reality protects itself. I and my people are the instrument it has fashioned with which to do so."

Sarnac forced his brain, staggering under a kind of conceptual overload, to function. "But, Tylar, what does this have to do with what *we've* been put through?"

Tylar spread his hands. "Isn't that obvious? This era is one of the weakest parts of the historical fabric, which is troublesome for us because it's so poorly documented. Investigating it, we quickly determined that intervention was required to preserve certain extremely important resonances in later Western culture—specifically, the fact that Sarmatian legendry will give shape to the Arthurian story. For it became apparent that a key figure in this development was a temporally displaced person from the twenty-third century."

"You mean . . . ?"

"Yes." Tylar nodded. "You. There seemed no other possible way you could be in this time, so we had to make certain that you were. History required it." He paused reflectively. "Most of the elements of the story will be assimilated naturally. The Grail legend, for example: the Sarmatian legends of the magical cup called the *Amonga* will blend into the Christian tradition that is already present in Britain" —Tiraena nodded slowly— "and give it mythic form. But certain other elements are your doing. Oh, yes," he smiled, "Kai will get back to Britain. The story will be passed on."

"But, but Tylar, anybody could have done what I did!"

"Ah, but 'anybody' *didn't* do it. *You* did. Knowing this, we had to make certain you were there to do it."

Sarnac shook his head slowly like a punch-drunk boxer. " 'Beyond the proper ken of mortals,' " he quoted softly. "Artorius was right, Tylar. You people have taken too much upon yourselves. Haven't you ever wondered what would happen if you simply stopped policing history? Maybe reality would take care of itself."

"Perhaps—but we don't dare find out. There's an old saying that the only thing more dangerous than riding a tiger is trying to dismount."

"But you don't really know, do you? You stood by, and let Artorius fail for the sake of a theory!"

"Let him fail? If necessary I was prepared to intervene to *ensure* his failure!" He met their shocked looks with a gaze that had nothing of the absentminded professor about it.

"But why?" Sarnac groped for words. "In a world run by barbarians and fanatics, he was the only man with the inclination and the ability to do something worthwhile! Do you *want* the Dark Ages that are coming in Europe?"

"Oh, I'm quite aware of his extraordinary qualities. In fact, he's one of the few legendary personages—Charlemagne is another—who was actually greater in life than in legend. This, even though he will come through the legend mill looking better than most similar figures; Charlemagne, for example, appears in the Carolingian Cycle as a silly old fool. It was precisely his capacity for greatness that made it *necessary* that he fail." Tylar took a breath. "Recall what I said earlier about the instability of history's course in certain eras. Later ages will persuade themselves that the breakup of the Roman Empire was inevitable. And yet the Chinese Empire, which has also collapsed as a consequence of the Cavalry Revolution, will be reunited in the next century by Yang Chien. It would be harder to reunify the Roman world, which lacks China's inherent unity. But it could be done. Some later historians will speculate that Charlemagne could have played Yang Chien's role in the West by conquering Byzantium. Our projections indicate otherwise; by his lifetime, the opportunity will be gone. The 'fabric' of that era's history will be too strong to tear. But in this era, when matters are still in a state of flux . . ." He looked at them solemnly. "Those same projections—using methodology which I won't try to describe, for it would mean nothing to you—indicate that Artorius was the right man in the right place at the right time. He never really had imperial ambitions, but each of his moves led him inevitably to the next—we heard him on that subject. If his Gallic campaign had succeeded, there is a strong possibility that he would have gone on to restore the Western Empire!"

"That's bad?" Tiraena asked hesitantly.

"Catastrophic!" Tylar's vehemence wasn't like him at

all. "Don't you realize . . . ? Well, perhaps you don't.
But carry the analogy with China one step further. It will
be reunified—but the price of unity will be stasis. The
same fate would overtake a restored Western Empire.
The late Roman educated class, people like Sidonius and"
—a wry smile— "Tertullian, are as hostile to innovation,
to any departure from an idealized Classical past, as any
Neo-Confucian mandarin. But that class will now cease
to exist as Europe devolves into a chaos, upon which no
single pattern can be imposed. It will be ugly. But out
of it will emerge that Western civilization which, for all
its endemic war, its political stupidity, its regrettable
tendencies toward religious and racial bigotry, will
nevertheless give birth to the Scientific and Industrial
Revolutions, the first fundamentally new departure in
human history since Neolithic man thought of growing
his food instead of gathering it.

"The irony is that the West will do so using Chinese
inventions which China itself could not permit to be used
because they would have upset its Confucian equilibrium!
You see, inventiveness is not enough. There must also
be a society which rewards innovation—and you have
no idea how rare such societies are. One is about to arise
here in Europe. If it did not, the odds are overwhelming
that Varien hle'Morna would find no advanced civilization
here with which to break the Korvaasha, only a world
lying defenseless in its stagnant Medievalism!"

"All because the good guys won," Sarnac breathed.

"It's a not uncommon form of irony. Think back before
the Battle of Angers. Given the power to do so, you would
have unhesitatingly wiped out every Saxon in the world.
But in future centuries the descendants of this era's Saxons
are going to invent parliamentary government, trial by
jury, and the language of Shakespeare!" He shook his
head. "No, the only safe course for us is to preserve the
history we know—the history which will produce us,

far in your future, from a fusion of Terrans and
Raehaniv." He smiled at their expressions. "Yes; I really
am telling all, you see. Your alliance will win the war . . .
thanks to you. For of all the crucial periods of history—
the 'weak fabric' areas—your own age is by far the most
crucial of all. We've had to be especially careful in
policing that era. Never has there been, nor will there
be, a time when individuals acting in their own small
ways can produce such cosmic consequences. The
slightest failure of anyone involved" —he met their eyes
gravely— "to perform up to his or her ultimate potential
would have incalculable results. In fact, I simply don't
know what the outcome would be, for we would be
faced with the grandfather paradox on a stupendous
scale. If your two peoples failed to come together as
history requires, then we could not exist . . . and
therefore our Raehaniv ancestors could never have
existed in the first place. After all, we created them."

Deep within a whirling vortex of shock, Sarnac heard
Tylar's voice continue, and he could hear the gentleness
in it. "It was our single greatest act of policing history.
We knew our own ancestry, and we knew that it involved
a patent impossibility, for the human species—or any
species—could not possibly have evolved independently
on two worlds. So we travelled back thirty thousand years,
confirmed that humanity had indeed evolved on Earth,
and . . ."

"Tylar," Tiraena broke in, amazing Sarnac with her
calmness, "are you about to say that *you* transported the
ancestral Raehaniv from Earth to Raehan?"

"Nothing so crude. We obtained genetic material of
various humans of that period, and of other Earth life
forms necessary to establish an ecology that would sustain
the humans, and then duplicated them on Raehan. So,
you see, your races are even more closely related than
you think."

"So," Tiraena breathed, "you—our own remote descendants—were the mysterious prehistoric spacefarers who have haunted Raehan's imagination for two centuries! But why did you leave behind the deserted bases in the Tareil and Terranova systems to tantalize us?"

"Surely, Tiraena, you know the answer to that. Think about it."

After a moment, she nodded slowly. "You had to. Your own history said we had found them there."

"Yes, and that the one at Terranova had provided Varien with certain technological hints, instrumental in liberating Raehan from the Korvaasha."

Sarnac struggled to shake loose from intellectual vertigo, but could not find a steady point to focus on, in what seemed an infinity of wheels within wheels. He started to speak, but then Tylar held up a forestalling finger.

"Excuse me," the time traveller said, and his eyes momentarily lost focus, as he gave his attention to a voice only he could hear. Then he nodded, and faced the other two with a smile.

"Your pardon, but I was receiving a report concerning the Korvaash officer who calls himself the Interrogator, and his most recent movements since his escape."

"*What?*" Sarnac sprang up out of his chair, head suddenly clear, with Tiraena close behind. "Tylar, you've got to do something! That is one very dangerous being! If he gets loose on Earth in this era . . ."

"Compose yourselves! He has, in fact, already done so, using a stolen gravitic raft . . . as he was intended to do."

"Intended? Damn it Tylar, if this is another of your little games . . . !"

"No games. Just another bit of the past that required policing. He was pursued—or, in reality, shepherded—just far enough to the west to make sure that his vehicle crashed in western Ireland, leaving him stranded among a proto-Celtic people known to later tradition as the Fomorians. His translator pendant incorporates a language analysis function which will enable it to produce the Fomorian tongue, after a time. He will earn his keep by terrifying the tribe's enemies and providing advice on strategy."

"You don't seem too concerned about all this," Tiraena observed darkly as Tylar settled even further back in his chair and took a sip of tea.

"Not in the least. You see, we had become aware that a Korvaasha, inexplicably present in this milieu, was the basis of the Irish legend of Balor, the one-eyed giant who was the Fomorians' champion. It was just one more thing we had to make certain of, albeit a relatively unimportant one."

They settled slowly back into their chairs. "Well," Sarnac said dubiously, "I don't suppose he can do any real harm."

"It seems unjust, though." Tiraena was clearly not mollified. "He's getting off too easily."

"Easily?" Tylar raised one eyebrow. "I would hardly say so. The only member of his species on this world, marooned under primitive conditions among a race he despises . . . and remember, his translator can't continue to function forever. Sooner or later it's going to give out, leaving him unable to communicate at all. I imagine he'll have gone quite mad by the time some local hero manages to kill him, as the legend requires.

"And one of the things driving him mad will be the knowledge that he failed, that the Solar Union and the Raehaniv will form an alliance against which the Realm of Tarzhgul cannot hope to stand. You, on the other hand, can take satisfaction in knowing you have made that alliance possible." He looked at them with an unreadable expression. "Whatever you may have felt in the presence of the technological trickery at my command, is nothing compared to what I feel in the presence of you yourselves.

For I exist because of you. When you are once again in your own time, you will be able to look forward into a future made possible by what you did."

"Tylar," Sarnac said after a long moment, "there's still one thing I don't understand about that. You talk about preserving history as you know it. But aren't you going to change history by returning us to our own time? I mean, when we get back there knowing what we know now, knowing all you've just told us . . ."

He let the sentence die, when he noticed an expression on Tylar's face that he had never seen there before. It was complex and mostly unreadable, but one thing was unmistakable: an odd sadness.

"Ah," the time traveller said, "but *do* you?"

Sarnac scarcely heard him, for reality began to waver and swirl, leaving nothing for consciousness to focus on, save the dark pools of Tylar's eyes and his suddenly all-pervading voice.

"Farewell, Bedwyr. You were a true and gallant knight, *sans peur et sans reproche*."

"What . . . what . . . ?" Sarnac tried to speak, but the spinning of reality was a whirlpool that sucked him down into oblivion.

CHAPTER EIGHTEEN

Taeronn turned from the communications console and smiled at the others.

"The escort squadron is matching orbits with us. It won't be long now."

"It sure won't," Sarnac agreed, giving Tiraena's hand a squeeze and grinning in the sunlight that flooded *Norlaev's* bridge. Then he glanced at the holo tank. "That's a fair-sized squadron—they've even got a Sword-class battlecruiser for a flagship. Yeah, we'll be in Earth orbit before you know it." His grin flashed again. "And not a minute too soon. I mean, you're all great company and all that, but . . . !"

"Easy for you to say," Rael put in when the chuckles had died down. "I'm the only one who'll have any work to do, negotiating with the Solar Union. The rest of you can just sit back and be lionized!" Nevertheless, years seemed to have fallen from her age.

"With all the modesty we can muster," Saefal added from the command chair.

Their uneventful voyage under continuous-displacement drive from Sirius had ended shortly after they had come within Sol's mass limit and Sarnac had begun broadcasting. He had been picked up more quickly than he'd expected—maybe the butt-warmers in Surveillance did something for their salaries after all—and it hadn't taken long for him to convince Fleet that he really was who he claimed to be. Now they were coasting on a sunward course that would intersect Earth's orbit. But before reaching the mother planet they would rendezvous with the squadron that Fleet had dispatched to serve as an honor guard for the little ship that carried an end to years of war and centuries of bafflement.

Tiraena pointed at the tiny blue point of light in the viewport, not yet close enough to show a planetary disc. "Earth," she breathed. "I always knew intellectually that it was a real place, but the idea of actually seeing it is still hard to accept."

"You're going to love it," Sarnac promised. "So many things I want to show you. . . ."

"Robert," Taeronn spoke again from the comm station. "I've got another hail from the flagship. This one's personal, for you!"

"What? I didn't know there was anybody aboard that ship I knew. Put 'em on visual."

The screen awoke, revealing SUS *Excalibur*'s communications officer. She was smiling—a lot of people had seemed to be doing that since their arrival.

"Lieutenant Sarnac, I've gotten a request— repeatedly!—to contact you. Now that we're close enough to eliminate any significant time lag, the individual in question has gotten positively insufferable, and the skipper has decided to put me out of my misery by letting me grant the request. I'm going to patch you into the wardroom pickup."

Excalibur's wardroom appeared. In the background was the bulkhead with the traditional mural illustrating the legend of the sword for which the battlecruiser was named. But in the foreground, in front of a small crowd

of ship's officers, was a woman whose face was a dark
sun of joy.

"Winnie!"

"Bob! I'd just been assigned to *Excalibur* for an
expedition out along the Achernar Chain when the
news of your arrival hit. You wouldn't believe what
it's like on Earth—everybody's going nuts down there!
Some of the rumors we've heard . . . well! Bob, what's
happened?"

"Winnie, it's a long story." As he paused and tried to
decide where to begin, his eye strayed to the mural on
the bulkhead behind Winnie Rogers. And as his mouth
opened to speak, his words died aborning. He could only
stare at that mural, in which Sir Bedivere, clad in fifteenth
century armor, *a la* Thomas Malory, gazed out over the
water at the samite-clad arm of the Lady of the Lake,
rising from the waves and grasping the bejeweled
broadsword he had just thrown.

Dimly, he heard a voice that he recognized as his own
speak in bewildered tones. "No . . . that's not right . . .
it wasn't . . ."

"*What* isn't right, Bob?" He didn't hear Winnie's
question. In fact, he didn't hear anything at all, until he
became aware that he was slumped in Tiraena's arms.
She was kneeling on the deck, and the others were looking
down at him anxiously.

"Bob, are you all right? What happened?"

He looked up into Tiraena's concerned face, and
reflected that that was a damned good question. What
had caused him to momentarily blank out? What had
he thought he'd seen? He clutched vainly at tantalizing
scraps of memory, like those of an old dream, but they
fluttered off into darkness and were gone.

"Yeah, sure, I'm fine," he assured them as he struggled
to get up. "Was I out long?"

"Only a couple of seconds," Saefal said. "Just long

enough to say something about not being able to see because the sun blinded you. What did that mean?"

"No idea," he answered honestly as he rose to his feet. "Sorry, everybody. Winnie, I'm okay now," he said, turning to the anxious face on the screen. "But there's too much to tell right now. When we're all dirtside, we'll get together and I'll tell you all about it. And . . . there's someone I want you to meet."

"That was inexcusably sloppy," Tylar said in a voice of flint. "You were responsible for editing their memories, and your instructions were clear. Everything since the moment before the Korvaash ship overhauled them was to be wiped, and replaced with synthetic recollections of the short time that they would have spent en route to the point to which we returned them, just outside Sol's mass limit. Do you have any idea of what the consequences would have been if he had gotten a firm grasp on the vignette you left just below the surface of his consciousness, and gone on to recall everything?"

Actually, not even Tylar had any conception of the full potential of those consequences, and he had been badly frightened by the close call they'd had—which, he admitted to himself, was why he was being such a prick, to use the vernacular of this early Solar Union era in which they were temporally located.

The chief neural technician stood her ground. "Memory erasure is not, and never can be, an exact science, especially when it's being done selectively. Anyone not an ignoramus in the field knows that—and that there was no real danger of the kind of mnemonic chain-reaction you're imagining. And how could anyone have foreseen that they'd be met by that particular battlecruiser, before the press of present-sense impressions had had time to push all of the unavoidable subliminal residue into

oblivion?" She visibly dug her heels in. "If you impose
any disciplinary sanctions, I shall appeal! The facts will
bear me out. And," she added sulkily, "you're in no
position to be criticizing!"

"I beg your pardon?"

"You know precisely what I mean! The *really* dangerous
memories were the ones you yourself created by telling
them things they had no business knowing!" Her
indignation gave way to mystification. "I can't understand
why you did it. Aside from being a major breach of
protocol, it was all so pointless. After all . . ."

Tylar suddenly smiled and gestured acquiescence.
"You're right, of course. I apologize for overreacting,
but as you know, we've all been under a strain. There'll
be no disciplinary proceedings. It was a near thing, but
it wasn't your fault. And . . . all's well that ends well,"
he finished, quoting the title of what he had always
regarded as its author's most underrated play. He had
once pulled rank to catch the world premiere.

"But," the other persisted, "I still don't understand why
you . . ."

"Because they had earned it," Tylar stated simply. "They
deserved to know the truth, if only for a few moments.
And, to be perfectly honest, after all my prevarications
I felt a need to 'get it off my chest' as Robert would say.
It was a profound relief, and I don't regret it in the least."

"But the pointlessness! Why give them knowledge that
you knew they couldn't be allowed to keep?"

"Why," Tylar said blandly, "that's the whole point. I
was able to assuage my conscience *harmlessly*." He waited
for the gasps and splutters to subside, then continued.
"And I didn't quite tell all, you know. Oh, everything I
said was true as far as it went. But I never conveyed to
them the real criticality of what was happening in both
eras, especially this one."

Critical indeed—so many factors to juggle. There had

never been even a momentary lull in the tension, as they had interposed the unwieldy temporal in the path of the Korvaash ship, as though catching a butterfly in a net. The problem had been unique, for nowhere else in the timestream was there a case in which the same individuals were at the focus of events in two different eras.

It had all been so fragile! They had had to return them to their home era, but not until Robert had done what posterity required, what was necessary for the completion of a myth basic to the emerging Western culture which carried the future in its ignorant, unsteady hands. Their researches had left no room for doubt, however incredible the conclusion had seemed: he, born in 2234, had played that key role in 470. It was just one of the facts that kept turning up, self-evidently impossible, and therefore requiring intervention to assure that they happened as reality demanded.

What if we hadn't learned of his role? What would have happened then? It was the thousandth time Tylar had asked himself that question, and he gave himself the same answer he always did. *But of course we learned of it. Or, if we hadn't, our descendants would, and travel back—a little further than we had to—and take care of it. Otherwise, it could never have happened! Robert asked me what would happen if we simply stopped policing the past. The really terrifying questions concern what would happen if we stopped researching the past.*

Yet that line of thought led around in the same circle. *But clearly we don't, at least not until we've arranged everything that has to be arranged in history. And how can we know when that point is reached?*

Ah, Robert and Tiraena, be happy in your time, when problems were so very simple!

The thought of those two awoke an odd impulse in him, and he activated one of the many capabilities he had never revealed to them. And he gazed at a man and woman, young in this day when humankind was young, standing arm in arm in the sunlight flooding through a viewport and looking out at the mind-numbing blue loveliness of Earth, as their ship entered low orbit.

Yes, it had all somehow worked. The humans of Earth and Raehan would reunite, as his own existence required. The future was secure.

"Now it begins," he whispered.

HISTORICAL NOTE

With the obvious exception of Tertullian, all the people introduced or mentioned in the Prologue are historical, and my fleshing-out of their personalities and motivations is consistent with what we know of the words and deeds of these dwellers in the shadows. It is unlikely that all the men I've included in the welcoming committee were actually on hand—Jordanes merely states that Riothamus "was received as he disembarked from his ships"—but I've found it useful to have them there. There is no conclusive proof that Sidonius Apollinaris ever met Riothamus, but his one surviving letter to the High King, as quoted in Chapter Fourteen ("I am a direct witness . . .") couldn't hint at it much more strongly; and they unquestionably corresponded, so I haven't invented a relationship that didn't exist.

There are, naturally, some areas where I've engaged in informed speculation. One is the parentage of Bishop Faustus of Riez—a reasonable inference from the known facts. Another is the details of the battles of Angers and Bourg-de-Déols, and the rest of Riothamus' Gallic campaign. Yet another, of course, is the question of just who Riothamus really was.

The quest for the factual basis of the Arthurian

legend makes for an intriguing historical detective story. To the interested reader, I recommend *The Discovery of King Arthur* by Geoffrey Ashe, and "The Sarmatian Connection" by C. Scott Littleton and Ann C. Thomas in *Journal of American Folklore*, no. 91. Coming at the problem from different directions, these offer theories which in no way contradict each other and, in fact, dovetail neatly—a point in favor of both, to my mind. I've attempted a synthesis of the two, and I take this opportunity to acknowledge the debt.

Judging clarity to be more important than antiquarian atmospherics, I've used modern place names. (The major exception is "France," which seems so inappropriate a name for a country in which the Franks were not yet dominant, that I've opted for "Gaul.") In the same spirit, dates are given according to the modern calendar.

A PREVIEW OF

S.M. STIRLING

DAVID DRAKE

**COMING IN MARCH 1995
FROM BAEN BOOKS**

CHAPTER ONE

"Raj?" Thom Poplanich muttered.

Then, slowly: "Raj, how old are you?"

Raj Whitehall managed a smile. "Thirty," he said.

The perfect mirrored sphere of Sector Command and Control Unit AZ12-b14-c000 Mk. XIV's central . . . being . . . showed an image which seemed to give the lie to that. Raj was tall, 190 centimeters, broad-shouldered and long-limbed, with wrists that would have been thick on a much larger man. His eyes were grey; there were wrinkles beside them now, and deep grooves running from beak nose to the corners of his mouth; grey frosted the bowl-cut black hair at the temples. It wasn't the grey hairs or the scars on the backs of his hands that made him seem at least forty, or ageless.

It was the eyes.

Thom looked at his own image. Nothing at all had changed since that moment when he'd frozen into immobility, five years ago. Not the unhealed shaving nick on his thin olive cheek, or the tear in his floppy tweed trousers from a revolver bullet. Raj had tried to shoot their way out when they'd been trapped here, far below the Governor's Palace, in labyrinths unvisited since the fall of galactic civilization. It hadn't worked. There was no escaping from some things.

life is change, Center said. The voice of the ancient computer was like their own thoughts, but with a vibrato overtone that somehow carried a sense of immense weight

1

like a pressure against the film of consciousness. **even i change.**

Raj and Thom looked up, startled. "Center? You're alive?" Thom asked.

No words whispered in their skull. Thom looked at his friend. *Raj looks like an old man.* For five years he'd fought the battles of the Civil Government, under the orders of Barholm Clerett, current occupant of the Chair . . . and with the ancient battle-computer whispering at the back of his mind. Five years of that could change a man.

I haven't changed a hair, outwardly . . . but that's the least of it. Five years of mental communion with the machine that held all Mankind's accumulated knowledge. Five years, or eternity. He thought of his life before that day, and it was . . . unimaginable. Less real than the scenarios Center could spin from webs of data and stochastic analysis. He'd been as carefree as a young man could be, whose grandfather had been Governor until the Cleretts usurped the Chair. Free enough to strike up an unlikely friendship with a young professional soldier, to share an interest in the relics of pre-Fall Federation civilization hidden down here.

The two men gripped forearms, then exchanged the *embrahzo* of close friends. Thom could smell coal-smoke and gun-oil on the wool of his friend's uniform jacket, that and dogsweat and Suzette Whitehall's sambuca jasmine perfume.

The scents cut through the icy certainties Center's teaching had implanted in his mind. Unshed tears prickled at his eyes as he held the bigger man at arm's length.

"It's good to see you again, my friend," he said quietly. "Back from another campaign?"

"Back from the Western Territories, nearly a year," Raj said. "It went . . . successfully. On the whole."

observe. The cool voice of the unliving mind spoke in their brains:

✧ ✧ ✧

A trumpet sounded, flat blatting notes under the lowering rainclouds, echoing back from the narrow shoulders of the cutting heading down to the river. The platoon columns of Civil Government troops halted and the giant riding dogs crouched. Men stepped free and double-timed forward, spreading out like the wings of a stooping hawk. Thom could see the advancing enemy columns halt; they were barbarians in the black-and-grey uniforms of the Brigade, the rulers of the Western Territories for the past five centuries. Their banners held the double-lightning flash, white on red and black.

Before the enemy a few hundred meters ahead had time to do more than begin to recoil and mill, the order rang out:

"Company—"

"Platoon—"

"Front rank, volley fire, *fwego.*"

BAM. Two hundred men in a single shot, the red muzzle-flashes spearing out into the rain like a horizontal comb.

The rear rank walked through the first. Before the echoes of the initial shout of *fire* had died, the next rank fired—by half-platoons, eighteen men at a time, in a rapid stuttering crash.

BAM. BAM. BAM. BAM.

Center's viewpoint was Raj, looking out through his eyes. The field-guns came up between the units.

"If they break—" the officer beside Raj said. Thom recognized him as Ehwardo Poplanich, his cousin.

The troopers advanced and fired, advanced and fired. The commanders followed them, leading their own dogs.

"If," Raj replied.

The guns fired case-shot, the loads spreading to

maximum effect in the confined space. Merciful smoke hid the result for an instant, and then the rain drummed it out of the air. For fifty meters back from the head of the column the Brigaderos and their dogs were a carpet of flesh that heaved and screamed. A man with no face staggered toward the Civil Government line, ululating in a wordless trill of agony. The next volley smashed him backward to rest in the tangled pink-grey intestines of a dog. The animal still whimpered and twitched.

Only the smell was missing. Thom swallowed dryly, past a tight throat.

The advancing force had gotten far enough downslope that the reserve platoon and the second battery of guns could fire over their heads. Shock-waves from the shells passing overhead slapped at the back of their helmets like pillows of displaced air. Most of the head of the Brigaderos column was *trying* to run away, but the railroad right-of-way was too narrow and the press behind them too massive. Men spilled upslope toward the forested hills where the Civil Government's nomad auxiliaries waited.

Just then the mercenaries themselves—Skinners from the northeastern steppes—opened up with their two-meter sauroid-killing rifles. Driving downhill on a level slope, their 15mm bullets went through three or four men at a time. A huge sound came from the locked crowd of enemy troops, half wail and half roar. Some were getting out their rifles and trying to return fire, standing or taking cover behind mounds of dead. Lead slugs went by overhead, and not two paces from him a trooper went *unh!* as if belly-punched, then to his knees and then flat.

The rest of his unit walked past, reloading. Spent brass tinkled down around the body lying on the railroad tracks, bouncing from the black iron strapping on the wooden rails.

"Fwego!"

❖   ❖   ❖

Raj shook his head slightly; his hands were making unconscious grasping motions.

"Yes, that's . . . well, I came to say goodbye."

"Goodbye?" Thom asked sharply.

"That's right," Raj said, turning slightly away. His eyes moved across the perfect mirrored surface of the sphere, that impossibly reflected without distorting. "Things . . . well, Cabot Clerett, the Governor's nephew" —and heir, they both knew— "was along on the campaign. There were a number of difficulties, and he, ah, was killed."

observe:

❖   ❖   ❖

Cabot's snarl turned to a smile of triumph as he leveled the revolver at Raj; he was a stocky dark young man, much like his uncle. His finger tightened on the trigger—

—and the carbine barked. The bullet was fired from less than a meter away, close enough that the muzzle-blast pocked the skin behind his right ear with grains of black powder. The entry-wound was a small round hole, but the bullet was hollowpoint and it blasted a fist-sized opening in his forehead, the fid of hot brain and bone-splinters missing Raj to spatter across his desk. Clerett's eyes bulged with the hydrostatic shock transmitted through his brain tissue, and his lips parted in a single rubbery grimace. Then he fell face down, to lie in a spreading pool of blood.

Strong shoulders crashed into the door. Raj moved with blurring speed, snatching the carbine out of his wife Suzette's hands so swiftly that the friction-burns brought an involuntary cry of pain. He pivoted back towards the outer doorway.

Raj's officers crowded through. Among them was a short plump man in the knee-breeches and long coat and lace sabot that were civilian dress in East Residence.

His eyes bulged too, as they settled on Cabot Clerett.

Raj spoke, his voice loud and careful. "There's been a terrible accident," he said. "Colonel Clerett was examining the weapon, and he was unfamiliar with the mechanism. I accept full responsibility for this tragic mishap."

. Silence fell in the room, amid the smell of powdersmoke and the stink of blood and wastes voided at death. Everyone stared at the back of the dead man's head, and the neat puncture behind his ear.

"Fetch a priest," Raj went on. "Greetings, Illustrious Chivrez. My deepest apologies that you come among us at such an unhappy time."

Chivrez's shock was short-lived; he hadn't survived a generation of politics in the Civil Government by cowardice, or squeamishness. Now he had to fight to restrain his smile. Raj Whitehall was standing over the body of the Governor's heir and literally holding a smoking gun.

❖   ❖   ❖

"Spirit of Man of the *Stars*," Thom blurted. "You came back to East Residence after *that*? Barholm was suspicious of you anyway."

Raj gave a small crooked smile and shrugged. "I didn't reconquer the Southern and Western Territories for the Civil Government just to set myself up as a warlord," he said. "Center said that would be worse for civilization than if I'd never lived at all."

an oversimplification but accurate to within 93%, ±2, Center added remorselessly. Over the years their minds had learned subtlety in interpreting that voice; there was a tinge of . . . not pity, but perhaps compassion to it now. **the long-term prospects for restoration of the federation, here on bellevue and eventually elsewhere in the human-settled galaxy, required raj whitehall's submission to the civil authorities.**

too many generals have seized the chair by force.

Thom nodded. The process had started long before Bellevue was isolated by the destruction of its Tanaki Spatial Displacement net. The Federation had been slagging down in civil wars for a generation before that, biting out its own guts like a brain-shot sauroid. The process had continued here in the thousand-odd years since, and according to Center everywhere else in the human-settled galaxy as well.

"Couldn't Lady Anne do something?" he asked. Barholm's consort was a close friend of Raj's wife Suzette, had been since Anne was merely the . . . entertainer was the polite phrase . . . that young Barholm had unaccountably married despite being the Governor's nephew. The other court ladies had turned a cold shoulder back before Barholm assumed the Chair; Suzette hadn't.

"She died four months ago," Raj said. "Cancer."

A brief flash of vision: a canopied bed, with the incense of the Star priests around it and the drone of their prayers. A woman lying motionless, flesh fallen in on the strong handsome bones of her face, hair a white cloud on the pillow with only a few streaks of its mahogany red left. Suzette Whitehall sat at the bedside, one hand gripping the ivory colored claw-hand of her dying friend. Her face was an expressionless mask, but slow tears ran from the slanted green eyes and dripped down on the priceless snowy torofib of the sheets.

"Damn," Thom said. "I know she wanted every Poplanich dead, but . . . well, Anne had twice Barholm's guts, and she was loyal to her friends, at least."

Raj nodded. "It was right after that that I was suspended from my last posting—Inspector-General—and my properties confiscated. Chancellor Tzetzas handled it personally."

"That . . . that . . . he gives graft a bad name," Thom spat.

Raj smiled wanly. "Yes, if the Chancellor didn't hate me, I'd wonder what I was doing wrong."

A flash from Center; a tall thin man in a bureaucrat's court robe sitting at a desk. The room was quietly elegant, dark, silent; a cigarette in a holder of carved sauroid ivory rested in one slim-fingered hand. He signed a heavy parchment, dusted the ink with fine sand, and smiled. A secretary sprang forward to melt wax for the seal . . .

Raj nodded. "I expect to be arrested at the levee this afternoon. Barholm's worried—"

worried at the probability of events which *would* occur were raj whitehall any other man. observe:

❖   ❖   ❖

—and troops in the blue-and-maroon uniforms of the Civil Government's army cantered across the brick-paved plaza before the Governor's Palace. It was late, the gaslights flaring along the streets of East Residence, but the hurrying throngs of civilians crowded aside to the sound of the bugle and the iron clamor of field-guns on the cobblestones. Light sheened on metal, the dull enamel of helmets, brass saber-hilts, the wet fangs of the giant riding dogs.

The troops reined in before the gates and deployed in line, stepping off the saddles of their crouching dogs and working the actions of their rifles, click-*clack* a thousand times repeated. The field guns swung about, teams unhitched, trails falling to the ground with heavy thumps as the gunners lifted them off the limbers. The breechblocks clanged as 75mm rounds were pushed home.

An officer strode up to the gates. "Open!" he barked.

"In whose name?" the watchstander replied, turning grey about the lips. Only a platoon was deployed across the gilded ironwork of the main gate. "By what authority?"

"Fix—" the first officer said.

"*Fix*—" a hundred voices repeated it.

"*—bayonets*."

A long repeated rattle and clank as the long blades snicked onto the rifles. A uniform flash of gaslight on steel as they came to present.

"In the name of the Sovereign Mighty Lord, Governor Raj Whitehall," the officer went on, grinning. He waved back to the riflemen and guns. "And there's my authority."

The watchstander nodded stiffly. "Open the gates."

—and Raj walked through congealing pools of blood in the Audience Hall. The bodies of the Life Guards sprawled across it, where they'd tried to make a stand behind barricades of ornate gilded furniture. Barholm Clerett sagged on the Chair itself, the pistol that had blown out the top of his skull still clenched in one hand.

Raj hooked the body out of the high seat with his toe and turned. A howl arose from the soldiers who crowded the great chamber, a howl that died into a steady chant: "*Raj! Raj! Raj!*"

◇   ◇   ◇

Thom laid a hand on Raj's shoulder. The muscle under the wool jacket was like india rubber. It quivered with tension.

"You *should* make yourself Governor, Raj," he said quietly. "Spirit knows, you couldn't be *worse* than Barholm and his cronies."

Raj smiled, but he shook his head. "Thanks, Thom— but if I have a gift for command, it's *only* for soldiers. Civilians . . . I couldn't get three of them to follow me into a whorehouse with an offer of free drinks and pussy. Not unless I had a squad behind them with bayonets; and you *can't* govern that way, not for long. I'd smash the machinery trying to make it work. Barholm is a son-of-a-bitch, but he's a *smart* one. He knows how to stroke the bureaucracy and keep the nobility satisfied, and he really is binding the Civil Government together with his railroads and law reforms . . . granted a lot of his hangers-on are getting rich in the process, but it's working. I couldn't do it. Not so's it'd last past my lifetime."

observe:

❖   ❖   ❖

—and they saw Raj Whitehall on a throne of gold and diamond, and men of races they'd never heard of knelt before him with tribute and gifts . . .

. . . and he lay ancient and white-haired in a vast silken bed. Muffled chanting came from outside the window, and a priest prayed quietly. A few elderly officers wept, but the younger ones eyed each other with undisguised hunger, waiting for the old king to die.

One bent and spoke in his ear. "Who?" he said. "Who do you leave the keyboard and the power to?"

The ancient Raj's lips moved. The officer turned and spoke loudly, drowning out the whisper: "He says, *to the strongest.*"

Armies clashed, in identical green uniforms and carrying Raj Whitehall's banner. Cities burned. At last there was a peaceful green mound that only the outline of the land showed had once been the Gubernatorial Palace in East Residence. Two men worked in companionable silence by a campfire, clad only in loincloths of tanned hide. One was chipping a spearpoint from a piece of an ancient window, the shaft and binding thongs ready to hand. His fingers moved with sure skill, using a bone anvil and striker to spall long flakes from the green glass. His comrade worked with equal artistry, butchering a carcass with a heavy hammerstone and slivers of flint. It took a moment to realize that the body had once been human.

❖   ❖   ❖

Raj shivered. *That* was the logical endpoint of the cycle of collapse here on Bellevue, and throughout what had once been the Federation; if it wasn't prevented, there would be savagery for fifteen thousand years before a new civilization arose. The image had haunted him since Center first showed it. It felt *true*.

"Spirit knows, I don't *want* Barholm's job," he went on. "I like to do what I do well, and that isn't my area of expertise. The problem is getting Barholm to understand that."

barholm's data gives him substantial reason for apprehension, Center pointed out. **not only does raj whitehall have the prestige of constant victory, but more than sixteen battalions of the civil government's cavalry are now comprised of ex-prisoners from the former military governments.**

Squadrones and Brigaderos; Namerique-speaking barbarians, descendants of Federation troops gone savage up in the desolate Base Area of the far northwest. They'd swept down and taken over huge chunks of the Civil Government, imposing their rule and their heretical Spirit of Man of This Earth cult on the population. Nobody had been able to do anything about it . . . until Barholm sent Raj Whitehall to reconquer the barbarian realms of the Military Governments.

Governor Barholm had officially proclaimed Raj the Sword of the Spirit of Man. The prisoners who'd volunteered to serve the Civil Government had seen him in operation from both sides. They *believed* that title.

"Then stay here!" Thom said. "Center can hold you in stasis, like me—hold you until Barholm's dust and bones. You've done all you can, you've done your duty, now you *deserve* something for yourself. It won't further the reunification of Bellevue for you to commit suicide!"

probability of furthering the restoration of the federation is slightly increased if raj whitehall attends the levee, Center said.

"I must go. I *must*. I—"

Raj turned back, and Thom recoiled a half step. The

other man's teeth were showing, and a muscle twitched on one cheek. "I . . . there's been so much dying . . . I *can't* . . . so many dead, so many, how can I save myself?"

"They were enemies," Thom said softly.

"No! Not *them*. My own men! I used men like bullets! There aren't one in three of the 5th Descott Guards remaining, of the ones who rode out with me against the Colony five years ago. Poplanich's Own—raised from your family estates, Thom—had a hundred and fifty casualties in one battle, and *I* was leading them."

Thom opened his mouth, then closed it again. Center cut in on them, an iron impatience in its non-voice:

leading is the operative word, raj whitehall. you were leading them. observe:

❖   ❖   ❖

"Back one step and volley!" Raj shouted, hoarse with smoke and dust.

Around him the shattered ranks firmed. Colonial dragoons in crimson djellabas rode forward, reins in their teeth as they worked the levers of their repeating carbines. The muzzles of their dogs snaked forward, then recoiled from the line of bayonets.

BAM. Ragged, but the men were firing in unison.

"Back one step and volley!" Raj shouted again.

He fired his revolver between two of the troopers, into the face of a Colonial officer who yipped and waved his yataghan behind the line of dragoons. The carbines snapped, and the man beside Raj stumbled back, moaning and pawing at the shattered jaw that dangled on his breast.

"Hold hard, 5th Descott! *Back one step and volley.*"

❖   ❖   ❖

observe:

❖   ❖   ❖

The men's hobnailed boots clattered on the surface of the pipe; the sound was dulled, as if they were walking on soft wood, but the iron left no scratches on the plastic

of the Ancients. The surface beneath the fingers of his
left hand might have been polished marble, except for
the slight trace of greasy slickness. There was old dirt
and silt in the very bottom of the circular tube, and it
stank of decay; floodwater must run down from the
gutters of Lion City and through this pipe when the floods
were very high.

Behind him the rustle and clank of equipment sounded,
panting breath, an occasional low-voiced curse in
Namerique. Earth Spirit cultists didn't have the same
myth of a plastic-lined tube to Hell; the center of the
earth—This Earth—was their paradise. This particular
tunnel was intimidating as Hell to *anyone*, though.
Particularly to men reared in the open air—there was
a touch of the claustrophobe in most dog-and-gun men.
There certainly was in *him*, because every breath seemed
more difficult than the last, an iron hoop tightening
around his chest.

this is not an illusion, Center said helpfully. **the
oxygen content of the air is dropping because
airflow is inadequate in the presence of over six
hundred men. this will not be a serious problem
unless the force is halted for a prolonged period.**

Oh, thank *you*, Raj thought.

Even then, he felt a grim satisfaction at what Army
discipline had made of last year's barbarian horde. *Vicious
children*, he thought. Vicious grown-up children whose
ancestors had shattered civilization over half a continent—
not so much in malice as out of simple inability to imagine
doing anything different. Throwing the pretty baubles
into the air and clapping their hands to see them smash,
heedless of the generations of labor and effort that went
into their making. *Thirteen-year-olds with adults'
bodies . . . but they can learn. They can learn.*

The roof knocked on the top of his helmet. "*Halto*,"
he called quietly. The column rustled to a halt behind

him.

A quick flick of the lens-lid on his bull's-eye lantern showed the first change in the perfect regularity of the tunnel. Ahead of him the roof bent down and the sides out, precisely like a drinking straw pinched between a man's fingers.

you are under the outer edge of the town wall on the north side, Center said. **.63 of a kilometer from the entrance.**

M'lewis had come this far on his scout; he'd checked that the tunnel opened out again beyond this point, and then returned. Raj had made the decision to proceed, since maximum priority was to avoid giving the entrance away. And the little Scout had been right, air *was* flowing toward him; he could feel the slightly cooler touch on his sweating face.

Of course, the air might be coming through a hole the size of a man's fist.

"Crawl through," he said to the man behind him, clicking off the light. "Turn on your backs and crawl through. There's another pinch in the tunnel beyond. Pass it down."

He dropped to the slimy mud in the bottom of the tunnel and began working his way farther in. The plastic dipped down toward his face, touched the brim of his helmet. Still smooth, still untorn. The weight of the city wall was on it here, had been for five hundred years. Mud squished beneath his shoulder blades, running easily on the low-friction surface of the pipe. The weight of a wall fifteen meters high and ten thick at the base, two courses of three-by-three meter stones on either side, flanking a rubble-concrete core.

Do not *tell me how much it weighs*, he thought/said to Center.

Now he was past the lowest point, and suddenly conscious of his own panting. Something bumped his

boots: the head of the man behind him. One man
following, at least. Two or three more, from the noise
behind. No way of telling what was farther back, how
many were still coming, whether the last five hundred
or five hundred fifty had turned and trampled Ludwig
in a terror-filled rush out of this deathtrap, this anteroom
to hell. The plastic drank sound, leaving even his breath
muffled. Sweat dripped down his forehead, running into
his eyes as he came to hands and knees. He clicked the
bull's-eye open for a look when the surface began to
twist beneath his feet. Another ten meters of normal
pipe, and then—

Spirit, he thought. What could have produced *this?*

**the pipe crosses under the wall at an angle of
forty degrees from the perpendicular. this section
is under the edge of a tower,** Center said with
dispassionate accuracy.

The towers were much heavier than the walls. The
sideways thrust of one tower's foundations had shoved
the pipe a little sideways . . . and squeezed it down so
that only a triangular hole in the lower right-hand corner
remained. This time the fabric *had* ruptured, a long
narrow split to the upper left. Dirt had come through,
hard lumpy yellow clay, and someone recent had dug it
out with hands and knife and spread it backwards.

Raj waited until the man following him came up
behind. "No problem," he said, while the eyes in the
bearded face were still blinking at the *impossible* hole.
"Come through one at a time; take off your rifle, helmet
and webbing belt, then have the man behind you hand
them through. Pass it on."

He kept moving, because if he didn't, he might not
start again. One man panicking here and the whole
column would be stalled all night.

He took off the helmet and his sword belt, snapped
the strap down over the butt of his revolver, and dropped

the bundle to the floor.

"Keep the lantern on," he said to the soldier behind him.

Right arm forward. Turn sideways. Down and forward, the sides gripping him like the clamps of a grab used to lift heavy shells. Light vanishing beyond his feet; they kicked without purchase, and then the broad hands of the trooper were under them, giving him something to push against. Bronze jacket buttons digging into his ribs hard enough to leave bruises. Breathe in, *push*. Buried in hell, buried in hell . . .

His right hand came free. It groped about, finding little leverage on the smooth, flaring sides of the pipe, but his shoulders came out, and that was the broadest part of him.

For an instant he lay panting, then turned. "Through," he called softly. "Pass my gear, soldier." A fading echo down the pipe, as the man turned and murmured the news to the one behind *him*.

It had only been a little more than his body length. Difficult, but not as difficult as concrete would have been, or cast iron, anything that gripped at skin and clothing. The light cast a glow around the slightly curved path of the narrow passage.

Again he waited until the first man had followed, grabbing his jacket between the shoulder blades and hauling him free.

"Second birth," he said.

The Squadrone trooper shook his head. "The first was tighter, lord," he said. His face was corpse-pallid in the faint light, but he managed a grin. Then he turned and called softly down the narrow way:

"*Min gonne, Herman.*"

Not much further, Raj thought, looking ahead. Darkness lay on his eyes like thick velvet.

.21 kilometers.

✧   ✧   ✧

observe:

✧   ✧   ✧

"Quick," Raj said to the man with the charges.

The door opening right into the rooms above the arch of the gateway was barred. Raj thrust his pistol into the eyeslot and pulled the trigger; there was a scream, and somebody slammed an iron plate across it. The cloth bundles of gunpowder tumbled at his feet.

"Good man," Raj said. "Now, pack them along the foot of the door, in between the stone sill and the door. Cut them with your knife and stick the matchcord— right." He raised his voice; more men were crowding up the stairs, some to take the ladder and others filling the space about him. *"Everyone down the corridor, around the corner here. Now!"*

The quick-witted trooper and Raj and a lieutenant— Wate Samzon, a Squadrone himself—paid out the cord and plastered themselves to the wall just around from the door. The matchcord sputtered as it took the flame. Raj put his hand before his eyes.

White noise, too loud for sound. He tensed to drive back around to the door—

—and strong arms seized him, body and legs and arms.

"Ni, ni," a deep rumbling voice said in his ear. "You are our lord, by steel and salt. Our blood for yours."

Lieutenant Samzon led the charge. A second later he was flung back, hands clapped to the bleeding ruin of his face; he stumbled into the wall, and fell flat. The men who followed him fired into the ruins of the door and thrust after the bullets, bayonets against swords, as their comrades reloaded and fired past their bodies close enough for the blasts to scorch their uniforms. When they forced through the shattered planks, the men holding Raj released him and followed them, with only their broad backs to hold him behind them.

✧   ✧   ✧

Raj blinked back to an awareness of the polished sphere that was Center's physical being. That had been too vivid: not just the holographic image that the ancient computer projected on his retina; he could still *smell* the gunpowder and blood.

if you had not struck swiftly and hard, the wars would have dragged on for years. deaths would have been a whole order of magnitude greater, among soldiers of both sides and among the civilians. as well, entire provinces would be so devastated as to be unable to sustain civilized life.

Images flitted through their minds: bones resting in a ditch, hair still fluttering from the skulls of a mother and child; skeletal corpses slithering over each other as men threw them on a plague-cart and dragged it away down the empty streets of a besieged city; a room of hollow-eyed soldiers resting on straw pallets slimed with the liquid feces of cholera.

"That's true enough for a computer," Raj said.

Even then, Thom noted the irony. He was East Residence born, a city patrician, and back when they both believed *computer* meant *angel* he'd doubted their very existence. That had shocked Raj's pious country-squire soul; Raj never doubted the Personal Computer that watched over every faithful soul, and the great Mainframes that sat in glory around the Spirit of Man of the Stars. Now they were both agents of such a being.

Raj's voice grew loud for a moment. "That's true enough for the Spirit of Man of the Stars made manifest, true enough for *God*. I'm not God, I'm just a man—and I've done the Spirit's work without flinching. But I'd be *less* than a man if I didn't think I deserve death for it." Silence fell.

"They ought to hate me," he whispered, his eyes still seeing visions without need of Center's holographs. "I've left the bones of my men all the way from the Drangosh to Carson Barracks, across half a world . . . they ought to hate my *guts*."

they do not, Center said. **instead—**

✧   ✧   ✧

A group of men swaggered into an East Residence bar, down the stairs from the street and under the iron brackets of the lights, into air thick with tobacco and sweat and the fumes of cheap wine and *tekkila*. Like most of those inside, they wore cavalry-trooper uniforms—it was not a dive where a civilian would have had a long life expectancy—but most of theirs carried the shoulder-flashes of the 5th Descott Guards, and they wore the red-and-white checked neckerchiefs that were an unofficial blazon in that unit. They were dark close-coupled stocky-muscular men, like most Descotters; with them were troopers from half a dozen other units, some of them blond giants with long hair knotted on the sides of their heads.

There was a general slither of chairs on floors as the newcomers took over the best seats. One Life Guard trooper who was slow about vacating his chair was dumped unceremoniously on the sanded floor; half a dozen sets of eyes tracked him like gun turrets turning as he came up cursing and reaching for the knife in his boot. The Life Guardsman looked over his shoulder, calculated odds, and pushed out of the room. The hard-eyed girl who'd been with him hung over the shoulder of the chair's new occupant. The men hung their sword belts on the backs of their chairs and called for service.

"T'Messer Raj," one said, raising a glass. "While 'e's been a-leadin' us, nivver a one's been shot runnin' away!"

✧   ✧   ✧

— they do not hate you. they *fear* you, for they know you will expend them without hesitation if necessary. but they know raj whitehall will lead

from the front, and that with him they have
conquered the world.

"Then they're fools," Raj said flatly.

"They're men," Thom said. "All men die, whether they
go for soldiers or not. But maybe you've given them
something that makes the life worth it, just as you have
Center's Plan to rebuild civilization throughout the
universe."

They exchanged the *embrahzo* again. Thom stepped
back and froze, his body once again in Center's timeless
stasis.

Raj turned and took a deep breath. "Can't die deader
than dead," he murmured to himself.

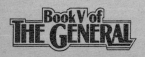

COMING IN MARCH 1995
FROM BAEN BOOKS